HIS HAND SLID OVER HER SHOULDERS . . .

down to the curve of her waist and hips, and he thought of how long he had waited to make her his own.

She lifted her head and gazed at him, her eyes still damp from tears, a pretty smile on her lips. He smiled in turn, slightly, and then lowered his mouth. She was the only woman he'd ever wanted to kiss, and kissing her was nothing short of an epiphany. He and Pamela never touched lips if they could avoid doing so, and he'd never engaged in kissing with the many women he'd taken in past years. It was an intimacy he wasn't willing to share lightly.

But with Clara, it was different. Everything was different. She lay relaxed in his arms, following his lead, clearly enjoying the embrace as fully as he. Her lips were moist and warm, and they parted beneath his tongue's gentle coaxing to allow him entrance beyond. He had kissed her this way before in anger, meaning to punish. Now he stroked and teased, pleasuring her until, with a little moan, she began to return the caresses, tentatively at first, and then with a growing boldness that seduced him almost beyond sense. It was a beautiful dance, and they were perfectly matched. He felt as if he could stand there forever, loving her, joined with her. But his body began to have other, far less noble ideas.

Mary
Spencer

❈

Dark
Wager

A Dell Book

Published by
Dell Publishing
a division of
Bantam Doubleday Dell Publishing Group, Inc.
1540 Broadway
New York, New York 10036

ISBN: 0-440-22491-8

Printed in the United States of America

Published simultaneously in Canada

December 1997

10 9 8 7 6 5 4 3 2 1

OPM

To my friend Vickie Denney, who wouldn't let me put this book aside until I'd finished it; also to my agent, Nancy Yost, whose faith in me and my writing gave me the confidence to pursue this particular dream; and to my editor, Laura Cifelli, who made the way for the dream to become a reality. With all my thanks, ladies.

Chapter One

❦

"It's only marriage, Lucky, not eternal confinement in Newgate. Certainly not anything worth being so maudlin about. Plenty of men before you have come through the thing well enough, and some rather happily. Only look at St. Genevieve." Jack Sommerton, fifth Earl of Rexley, lifted his glass a little higher, making a physical punctuation to his point. "Indeed, that's your example, right there. Only model yourself after St. Genevieve and you're certain to be content with his daughter."

Lucien Bryland, Viscount Callan, pulled his gaze from the wineglass in his hand and looked at his companion. "This, from the man who's sworn he'll never wed? You amaze me, Jack."

The earl proffered a benign smile. "I don't have anything against marriage. Where would most of us be without it, after all?" He gave an imperious sniff. "I haven't got any desire to see the world peopled with naught but bastards. There'd be no way of knowing what class of person one was mixing with, would there? It's dreadful even to contemplate."

"Snob," Lucien muttered.

"True," Jack agreed congenially, tossing back the last of his wine. "And," he continued, setting his glass on the table, "if I ever do get leg-shackled, may God forbid it, I shall make certain to do so with a female of proper breeding. In that regard, at least, your Peahen is an incomparable.''

"Oh, indeed, she is," Lucien agreed quietly, twisting the stem of his glass slowly between two fingers. Clara's image, calm and perfect, formed in his mind's eye. She was always there at the edge of his thoughts, despite his every effort over the past many years to eradicate her memory. "Clara Harkhams is undeniably wellborn. I could search all of England and never find a more suitable female." He lifted his head, his dark eyes glittering. "In that regard, at least."

Jack made a *tsk*ing sound. "Since I've known you, you've made Lady Clara sound like a horse-faced harridan, but I won't be fooled by that a moment longer. Robby assured me only the other day that she's a delightful, quite lovely young lady. Isn't that so, Wulf?" He turned his gaze on the third man who shared their table. "You were with me at the time."

"What?" At the sound of his name, Viscount Severn lifted his dark, rather shaggy head. "Sorry, did you say something?"

"God save us." Jack leaned across the table, plucking away the pencil Lord Severn clutched. "Must you scribble while Lucky's trying to impress us with the great depths of his misery? Have some pity, man."

Wulf glanced at Lucien and said, "Are you still maundering on about your impending marriage to the Peahen, Lucky? Not setting much of an example for the rest of us, are you? Straighten your spine and take it like a man, I say."

"Indeed? Like you're taking your impending marriage to Bella?" Lucien asked dryly.

Frowning, Wulf snatched his pencil back. "What's Bella got to do with it? We're engaged, ain't we? I don't complain about it. Never have. Never will."

"Engaged, yes," Lucien said with a laugh. "For three years now. Or is it four? If anyone's setting a bad example for our fellow men, it's you. And Bella won't wait forever, you know."

"A four-year engagement don't compare to being betrothed from the cradle, as you and the Peahen have been," Wulf informed him, bending to his paper again. "You've had twenty-seven years to get used to the idea, which is more than fair. I can't think of another man who's had that much warning." A familiar look of concentration possessed his craggy features as he scribbled out an equation. "And Bella don't mind waiting to get married. She's a good girl. Never gives me any grief. Wouldn't have asked her to marry me if she did."

Lucien contemplated his friend's lowered head. "You take her far too much for granted, Wulf, and a nice, pleasant creature is Bella. Perhaps we should make a swap."

Still scribbling, Wulf didn't look up. "Swap? What?"

Jack leaned forward, speaking directly into Wulf's ear. "Swap Bella for the Peahen, old boy. Lucky wants your fiancée."

"Wants Bella?" Wulf vigorously crossed out everything he'd just written. "Not six point five at a ratio of twelve," he muttered. "God's feet. It would blow up the entire laboratory." He began to write again. "What's he want her for?"

With a nod at a passing waiter, who stopped to refill their glasses from a bottle set on the table, Lucien replied, "Why, to warm my bed, Wulf. What else? Bella's got the figure to do it nicely, too. She's not thin and brittle, like the Peahen, or short, either. I wouldn't have to worry about crushing her, or—"

Wulf suddenly bolted out of his chair, nearly knocking the table aside. Leaning down from his great height and sticking his face in Lucien's, he roared, "What are you saying about Bella? She ain't that kind of female!"

Laughing, Lucien pushed him away. "Sit down, you oversized brute. I merely wished to get your attention. I meant no disrespect to your good lady, and you know it. Bella's like a sister to me."

Letting out a breath that sounded vaguely like the snorting of an angry bull, Viscount Severn settled his large, muscular person back into his chair. "Damn it, Lucky, don't tease about Bella. I almost saw red for a moment there, and I don't want to kill you, you know."

"Certainly not," said Jack. "And we wouldn't want something like that to happen in White's, of all places." He stared pointedly at a pair of interested onlookers until they turned away. "The last time you lost your temper here you almost got the three of us exiled."

"That was the American's fault," Wulf stated, still glaring at Lucien. "He talked about Bella, too, but I won't have it."

"Indeed," Lucien agreed. "Fine female, is Bella. She even made you forget your beloved chemistry, which is the next best thing to a miracle."

With a huff, Wulf tugged at the lapels of his tight-fitting coat. "If you've got to talk about women, then talk about your own. You've never had any trouble finding something to say about the Peahen."

"Gad, Wulf, don't get him started again," Jack admonished. "Poor chit doesn't know what she's getting into, marrying Lucky. I haven't heard him talk about her this much since we were all down at Oxford together. Beginning to think the fellow's got an obsession with the gel, despite everything he says."

"S'truth," Wulf agreed solemnly, and both men stared at Lucien, who shifted uncomfortably in his chair. "You don't have to marry her, you know. Robby could find a way to get the betrothal broken. It wouldn't be such a difficult matter, and Lady Clara wouldn't suffer any gossip. The betrothal's never been made public, has it?''

''No. It's an agreement between the two families, nothing more.''

''There you go, then,'' Jack declared. ''Nothing could be simpler. Break the betrothal and you're free to wed whomever you wish. Pamela, even, if you could stand her better as a wife than a mistress, which I doubt.''

Lucien looked at him sharply. ''Leave Pamela out of this. She's already given me enough grief about my upcoming marriage.''

''Not enough to push you away, I'd wager,'' Jack said. ''She'd be a fool if she did. The woman's got you properly trained, and she's too lazy to spend the time and effort breaking in another man.''

Lucien's toying fingers fell still on the stem of his glass, and he said in a low voice, ''Don't try me, Jack. I don't tolerate Pamela speaking ill of my friends, and I won't tolerate you speaking ill of her, either.''

Unruffled, Jack lazily drank his wine. ''I but speak the truth, Lucky, and there's no offense in that. She's your mistress. You know the kind of woman she is better than anyone else, I dare say.''

Lucien gave a slight nod, his black hair gleaming in the elegant club's lamplight. ''Indeed. I also know that she suits me and pleases me. More than that, you shouldn't care about. As to the betrothal, it was my father's dearest wish that Clara and I wed. The agreement made between himself and the Marquess of St. Genevieve cannot be broken without some amount of discord, even if I wished it to be, which I don't. I admit that I haven't been in any rush to put an end to my solitary state, but I've always known that when I did marry, it would be to Clara Harkhams. In truth, she'll make the ideal wife. She's well-bred and polite and knows her place. She'd probably break a bone before she'd do anything to publicly embarrass her husband. I won't keep her in London, of course.''

Wulf's eyebrows rose. ''You won't? Then where . . . ?''

''I'll put her away in Pearwood.'' Lucien made a dismissive gesture. ''She should be happy enough there, especially if I keep her breeding. Clara's a country girl, like the rest of St. Genevieve's brood. A gaggle of children and a garden and plenty of rustic swains to admire her and she won't complain, certainly not about being away from London. After six months here, she'll be more than ready to retire to the country.''

''You sound very certain of yourself,'' Jack said. ''What if the Peahen gets a taste of fashionable city life and decides she likes it? She may not go quite so easily.''

''She'll go,'' Lucien replied. ''It would be disastrous for us to try to live together for any longer than necessary. And I'm fairly certain Clara wouldn't even wish to make an attempt. We would only make each other miserable. I'll get her pregnant and pack her off and that will be the end of it. A month or two each additional year to get her with child again will probably be all the more we'll see of each other.''

''You're heartless,'' said Wulf, shaking his head. ''I feel sorry for the Peahen, poor girl. Why do you hate her so?''

A grim smile formed on Lucien's lips. ''Have I given you the impression that I hate her?''

Jack sat forward, gazing at him intently. ''Well, you certainly don't love the chit. After all the years we've spent listening to you complain about Lady Clara, it would be impossible.''

''Would it?'' Lucien closed his eyes and wearily rested his head on the back of his chair. ''Impossible as it may seem, I did love her once. And trusted her.''

''Lucky,'' Wulf said with disbelief. ''All these years

. . . you never even hinted at such a thing. Indeed, I thought you disliked the girl from the moment you met her.''

He opened his eyes and stared at the ceiling. "It's not the sort of thing one tells one's fellows, is it? Being lovestruck by the unexceptional bride one's parents chose? And then being rejected by her. No"—his lips curled into a tight, self-mocking smile—"not the sort of thing one admits to readily. Do you know, I always swore I'd never be such a fool as my father, crawling like a dog after the little crumbs of affection a woman might be so kind as to gift me with. But I nearly did with Clara. So very nearly. It was just before I started university. We hadn't seen each other for some time and I wanted to make certain that my darling betrothed knew how I felt before we endured another separation, so I went to her and threw myself at her feet, heart, body, and soul. It was a rather touching scene, I believe, although the effect was ruined by the arrival of her beau, who made the facts of their mutually affectionate relationship quite clear.''

"Gad, Lucky," Wulf murmured.

"My own mother couldn't have pulled it off more perfectly," he continued softly. "In truth, it reminded me forcibly of the last time I saw my parents alive, on the day of their wedding anniversary, when one of Mother's admirers arrived at Barrington to take her on a drive in the park. Father spent the rest of the day alone in his study, waiting for her to come back so that they might celebrate the happy occasion together, as he had planned. Waiting and waiting, pacing and glancing at the clock every other minute. Sick with worry, as he ever was. Equally sick with love." Lucien gave a solemn shake of his head. "She didn't return until early the next morning. I felt badly for my father, of course, but I don't think I ever really understood how he must have felt until that moment when I stood before Clara and her ardent lover, knowing myself utterly exiled from the affections of her heart.''

"It isn't any wonder that you arrived at Oxford hating women so," Jack said with open sympathy, "and especially the Peahen. I've often wondered at it these past many years."

"It was by far the most idiotic thing I have ever done," Lucien admitted. "You'd think I'd have known better. An affianced husband isn't of much use to an appealing young girl, certainly not when she has every man in her village, both young and old, fawning over her."

His friends regarded him with surprise.

"The plain Peahen?" Jack asked.

Lucien's eyes narrowed as he contemplated the tabletop. "Clara is quite plain, but not ugly. She somehow manages to be alluring despite her lack of beauty. Everyone loves her." He frowned. "She enslaves hearts at every turn, although I suppose she can't help herself. It's the nature of women to be loved at all costs."

His tone was thoroughly chilled, and his friends exchanged glances.

"Lucky," Jack said carefully, "not all women are as your mother was. You can't go into marriage believing that, despite what may have happened with Lady Clara."

"Can't I?" Lucien looked at him inquiringly. "I'll admit that all women aren't what she was. Pamela, for example, is as different a woman from my mother as the Sahara is different from the North Pole. But other women, most, indeed, are as she was. Vain, clinging, obliging creatures who worm their way into your heart until they've taken firm root, and then"—he made a visible effort to control his angry tone—"then, only the heartiest soil can withstand the destruction."

"You should at least give the girl a chance," Wulf argued.

"She wouldn't want it. Not from me, anywise. But I'll give her something better in exchange for her wedding vows. Freedom. Clara will have as much of it as she desires, as many children as she wants, and more money than she could spend in five lifetimes."

"I still don't understand why you even want to wed the girl," Jack told him. "It seems unlikely that your father would have agreed to the match if he'd known how you and the Peahen would feel about each other."

Lucien gave him an enigmatic smile. "You don't understand, Jack. Clara is mine. She was promised to me since she was but a babe in a cradle. I've told myself a thousand times and more to release her from the betrothal, but it's impossible. She is *mine,* and will be for the rest of our lives. I'll not force my presence upon her, but it will be there, all the same. Ever there in the back of her mind, no matter how often or seldom she sees me. She'll always know who has the keeping of her."

"It's revenge," Wulf stated with open distaste. "That's all, plain and simple. She didn't want you and now you're going to make her pay." He gave Lucien the sort of disgusted look he usually reserved for people who didn't understand the mathematical principles of Pythagoreanism. "I never thought I'd see you do such a thing, Lucky. I can scarce believe Robby's actually going along with it."

"Oh, he's all for it," Lucien assured him. "He's certain that marriage is going to reform me, make me into an entirely new man. I doubt it will even make much of a dent." He pressed his hand flat upon the tabletop. "Six months and I'll have her pregnant and on her way to Pearwood. She'll have her life the way she wishes it to be, and I'll have mine. That will be all."

"Would you care to make a wager on that, Callan?"

The three men turned to gaze at the newcomer who was approaching their table in a lazy, smiling manner.

The Earl of Rexley cursed softly at the tall, golden-haired man, Viscount Callan gave a loud groan, and Viscount Severn began growling.

"Go away, Kerlain," Lucien said. "I won't stop Wulf from killing you this time if he feels the need to do so."

P. Lad Walker, Earl of Kerlain, turned his handsome countenance toward Wulf. "He won't feel the need today, I guarantee it. I may be an American, but I'm not such a fool as to repeat an unsuccessful experiment twice. My teeth are still rattling from our last go to. And the bruises only just faded. Whoever said that brains and brawn aren't found together clearly never met him." He pointed stiffly at Wulf, who glared at him. "I give you my word of honor, I'll not even mention Miss Howell's name today." He lifted the hand he'd pointed with up into the air, as if taking an oath. "Swear it on my grandmother's grave, I won't."

Wulf's brow lowered and his expression darkened, but he said nothing. With one last growl he pointedly ignored the newcomer and returned his attention to the paper before him.

"Americans," Jack said with gentle, yet thorough, disdain. "Such manners."

"Go away, Kerlain," Lucien repeated. "I want you to live long enough for me to win back the money I lost from you last night."

"It may not be for the best reason," Kerlain said, "but it's good to know I'm worth something to somebody." Flashing his most charming grin, he pulled up a chair and sat down.

Lucien groaned again. "Are you mad?"

"Not at all," Kerlain replied easily. "Just looking for fair game, as usual."

Jack's eyes narrowed. "I don't speak with Americans if I can keep from doing so, let alone share a table with them. Go now before I have you thrown out."

Kerlain's smile widened. "We have a name for men like you in the States, Rexley, but I'm too polite to tell you what it is. You might be pleased to know that I had a hell of a time getting back into White's, thanks to the behemoth here." He glanced at Wulf, who continued to ignore him. "Couldn't even beg my way in after the little disagreement we had."

"Small wonder, since the club had to replace nearly half its stock of glassware." Jack's blue eyes were chilled. "Exactly how did you manage it, then?"

"The same way I manage everything," Kerlain replied guilelessly, smiling with easy humor.

"Gambled your way in, did you?" Lucien asked, motioning to a waiter to bring another glass to the table. "Who'd you get to sponsor you? Seasely again? He's just foolish enough to keep wagering with you and just influential enough to get the rules here bent. Calm down, Jack," he added, setting a hand on that man's arm when he began to rise. "Kerlain doesn't bite, after all."

"It's a pity you haven't better sense in the picking of your friends, Lucky," Jack said.

"Yes, so I've often thought," Lucien teased, chuckling. "Especially since the day I met you and Wulf. Now sit down and be still. I don't want another scene in here. We've already got everyone in the place watching us."

"Very well," Jack said, sitting and releasing a taut breath.

Lucien gave Kerlain his attention. "I hope you didn't work so hard at getting in here to speak with me. I'll be leaving shortly."

"Yes, to collect your future bride," Kerlain said. "You spoke of Lady Clara at length last night, which is partly what brings me here."

"And?" Lucien asked patiently.

Setting his glass aside, Kerlain said, "I'll just be blunt, as we Americans are given to being.'' He ignored the exaggerated way Jack rolled his eyes. ''I'm barren of wagers at the moment, looking for some fresh sport against which I can earn a tidy sum.''

''Or lose one,'' Jack noted dryly.

''I never lose,'' Kerlain replied, noting with satisfaction that this remark caused Viscount Severn to lift his head and give his attention to the conversation.

Jack leaned forward, pinning him with a sharklike gaze. ''Then what's the sport in it?''

Kerlain grinned. ''Why, in watching the other fellow attempt to be the first to topple me. I don't suppose you'd care to take up the challenge, would you, Rexley? But, no. You're much too cautious a fellow. Now, Callan, on the other hand, has a perfectly good chance of success.'' He turned his harmless gaze on Lucien. ''You spoke freely last night of your coming marriage, and I overheard much the same from you just now. You're to wed Lady Clara Harkhams, the Marquess of St. Genevieve's eldest, are you not?''

Silent, Lucien nodded.

''And you plan to get her with child and send her away— within six months of your marriage? Isn't that what you said a few minutes ago?''

''You have sharp ears, Kerlain,'' Lucien said. ''I shall have to be more careful about what I say, and where. But it is true that those are my intentions.''

Kerlain set his elbows on the table, tenting his fingers beneath his chin in a relaxed pose. ''You sound confident, Callan, but I'll wager ten thousand pounds that at the end of six months of marriage your wife will still be at your side. You'll not wish to be separated from her.''

Lucien looked at him with a measure of surprise. ''You doubt my ability to get her with child in that amount of time?''

"I don't doubt that you will," Kerlain replied, "but that's not of any real importance. Regardless of Lady Clara's state, you'll not wish to be parted from her. You'll not send her to Pearwood unless you intend to remain with her there."

"This is in poorer taste than I had expected even from you, Kerlain," Jack said with unveiled disgust. "To make a wager involving a gently bred female is far beyond the pale. Bid him to the devil, Lucky."

Lucien regarded Lord Kerlain from beneath lazy, half-lowered lids. "You don't mean to suggest that I'll have fallen in love with my wife, do you, Kerlain? You won't wager away ten thousand pounds for something so foolish as that? It would be almost too easy."

"If it is, Callan, then you'll come away the winner."

"Lucky, you can't mean to actually put Lady Clara's name in the betting books," Wulf protested. "Here, at White's? Where every patron coming through the doors could see it? That would be . . ."

"Quite ignoble," Jack finished. "Don't do it, Lucien. It's beneath you, and Robby will have your head on a platter."

The Earl of Kerlain smiled and shrugged. "On the other hand, if you win I'm sure he'd be more than ready to forgive your little lapse. Of course, if you don't think you really will send Lady Clara away, then perhaps we'd better forget the entire idea."

Lucien's gaze darkened. "I'll win. There's no doubt of that."

"And I say you'll lose. Do you really think yourself capable of sending your wife away?"

"It's almost a foregone fact," Lucien said, "for Clara will certainly be residing at Pearwood six months from the day of our wedding."

"Wherever your future wife may be at the end of that

time, Callan, she'll not be there alone. You'll be with her, of your own free will.''

"I never realized you for a fool, Kerlain.'' Lucien lifted a hand to motion a waiter to the table. ''You'd better tell your man of business to set the funds aside, for I'll expect payment in full the day after Clara leaves London.'' He glanced at the server who stood silently awaiting his command, and said, "Bring us the betting book.''

Chapter Two

❧

"Love *suffers* long and *is* kind, it does *not* envy, *nor* parade itself, *nor* is it puffed up."

The day, for mid-March, was sunny and glorious and unseasonably warm. Sitting in the grand stone church in St. Genevieve, Clara Harkhams knew that she, like the other churchgoers, should be anything but chilled. Of course, the other churchgoers weren't sitting beside Lucien Bryland, pressed arm, leg, and hip against him due to the overcrowding in the family pew that was normally, even without his large and imposing presence, a tight fit for the sizable family of the Marquess of St. Genevieve.

"This is what the word of God says about love," Mr. Webster said loudly, staring, it seemed to Clara, straight at her, "and this is what perfect love, created by God, is meant to be."

Shifting slightly to ease her discomfort, trying not to draw the viscount's notice and knowing that she had failed when his hand, resting upon his knee, curled into a fist, Clara wondered if perhaps she should take it as a sign of impending doom that the man she was shortly to wed was as stiff and cold as a mountain of ice.

But that was unfair. She knew better than anyone how mercurial Lucien was, and had been since the time when the Earl of Manning had first brought his orphaned nephew to St. Genevieve. Lucien hadn't done more than stare at her when they were introduced, though she, being only thirteen, hadn't expected anything more. But as the first week of the two that he and the earl spent at St. Genevieve passed, he had kept staring, sometimes following her during the days, so that she would think herself alone and suddenly turn to find him there, silent, watching her. During mealtimes at the table, he would watch her from beneath lowered lashes until Clara became painfully aware of his pointed regard. He had frightened her a little, so dark and silent as he was, so stark. Her parents had warned all of them, Clara and her brothers and the entire household staff, that the young viscount was troubled, and had been since the death of his parents three years before. He was not a dangerous boy, certainly, but he was not to be badgered if he wished to be left alone, or teased for any reason. Clara hadn't known then that she was to marry the viscount someday, else she would have been fully afraid. At least for that first week, while the Earl of Manning courted Aunt Anna and while Lucien, left to himself, prowled silently about St. Genevieve like some half-tame animal.

"It is an abomination to take the name of love in vain!" Mr. Webster struck a fist against his podium, causing it, and all of his parishioners, to jump. "An abomination to the heavens and to God!"

Beside her, Clara saw Lucien's fist unclench and clench, and her heart sank. It was intolerable that he should be treated to such as this. She would speak with Mr. Webster after the service, and make him understand that what was going to happen could not be stopped. Nor would she wish it to be. Her heart had been irrevocably compromised long ago and nothing that he, or anyone else, did could change that.

She never should have gone fishing on the Monday of that second week after Lucien and the Earl of Manning had come. Thirteen years old and as childish as one of her father's overly indulged, country-bred children were all destined to be, she had only been on the brink of knowing what it meant to be female. Yet that day, Lucien had set the course for her life, had imprisoned her so fully that even he had probably never guessed at how strongly she was bound.

She had been used to running free on her father's vast estate; her parents had not believed in keeping their children confined in either houses or fashionable clothes. Rising early, she had donned her oldest dress, a worn pair of boy's shoes, and, without so much as waiting for her maid to brush her hair, had gone down to the kitchen to bribe food out of Cook. Half an hour later, munching a sweet bun and carrying her fishing pole and a small basket containing her lunch, Clara was on her way to the lake where she most loved to spend her days.

Two very pleasant hours passed before Clara, lying lazily upon the bank with her skirts hiked all the way up to her thighs and her bare feet dangling in the water, realized that she wasn't alone. She sat up so quickly that she accidentally knocked her fishing pole into the water. By the time she'd retrieved it, and gotten thoroughly soaked in the doing, Lucien had come out of the forest where he'd been hidden.

He didn't say a word as he reached out a hand and pulled her from the water. He took her fishing pole and set it aside, then bent on the damp, muddy ground to take up fistfuls of her skirt and squeeze water out.

Clara often looked back on the moment and thought of how strange it was that she had stood there, utterly still, staring down at his dark head, letting him wring out her dress. It was only after he had finished and led her by the hand to a grassier area to sit that she found her voice, and asked, "Why were you hiding there?"

Sitting beside her, he replied, "I wasn't hiding."

"Were you there a long time? You should have let me know. It's rude to watch people when they don't know."

He gave a shrug and set his chin upon his indrawn knees, gazing out at the sparkling lake.

Lucien was comfortable with silence, as Clara was to learn during the next several days, but she, coming from a noisy, chattering family, felt obliged to make conversation.

"I came to fish," she said, thinking at once how foolish a thing it was to say when he must have already known it.

But he said, "Yes," and looked at her. "You haven't caught any, though."

"No, not yet." She had never been so close to him before, so that she could look directly into his dark eyes and see how beautiful they were. "Do you fish?"

"No." His chin went back on his knees again.

"It's great fun," Clara went on doggedly, determined to be polite even if he meant to ignore her. "Would you like to try? You may use my pole, if you wish."

"Later, perhaps."

The answer relaxed her somewhat. Fingering the slender blades of grass near her knee, she said, "Have you been enjoying your time at St. Genevieve? My Aunt Anna very much looked forward to you and your uncle coming. She was terribly excited."

He was quiet, and she didn't think he'd reply until at last he said, softly, "Robby was excited, too."

"They look lovely together, don't they? The earl is so handsome, and Aunt Anna's so beautiful. Do you think they'll be happy when they're married?"

Lifting his head, he gave a sigh. "I don't know. I never knew anyone before who was."

The sentiment shocked Clara to her very depths, for she had never known any married people who weren't happy.

"Not even your own mother and father?"

He gave a bitter laugh. "Especially not them."

"Oh." She didn't know what to say. Her heart felt as if a

heavy lead weight were suddenly pressed upon it. "Mine are. Happy, I mean."

He nodded silently.

"And I will be, too, when I've married," she declared.

He looked at her sharply then. "Will you? How do you know?"

She smiled and replied, with the confidence of youth, "I'll make my husband so happy that we will never quarrel, and I shall love him, too, just as my mama loves my papa."

"And what if you stop loving him? What if you find another man you like better after you've married? Won't you go away with him?"

The questions bewildered Clara. She'd never considered such things before.

"That would be very bad, wouldn't it?"

"Yes," he answered solemnly. "Very bad."

"I'd never do such a thing. I shall love my husband, and he'll love me. And we'll have lots of children, too. A dozen, at least. We'll have wonderful times together and always be happy."

A brief smile, the first she'd ever seen on him, crossed his lips. "Will you?"

"Oh, yes," she replied happily. "We'll live in the country, but he'll take me to London once a year, so that we can dance in all the grand ballrooms. My papa has a grand ballroom at his house in London. Did you know that?"

"Yes. I met you there once, but you were very young. Do you remember it?"

"Me?" she repeated, surprised.

"You had just turned seven," he said. "It was the occasion of your birthday, and my parents and I attended the celebration." He smiled again, more fully this time. "You were dressed all in pink and white, with satin bows in your hair." He lifted a hand to gently stroke one of her curls. "Your shiny hair—you looked just like a tiny doll."

She stared at him. "You danced with me," she murmured. "I remember that. You didn't want to, but your mama made you do it."

He dropped his hand. "It was the most stupid thing. We must have looked ridiculous."

She laughed at the memory. "You were so tall! I remember thinking that you were as tall as Papa, but so much more handsome. I made you kiss me, didn't I?"

"You did, at the threat of screaming down the house. You were horribly spoiled."

Her smile died away. "Was I? Really? Did you hate having to kiss me?"

He made a face of impatience. "Of course I did. I was ten. The last thing I wished to do was kiss a seven-year-old girl. You were practically a baby, still."

"Oh." Clara felt foolishly downcast. "I suppose that's true."

He touched her hand with his fingertips. "Don't look like that," he said softly. "It isn't the same now. You're not a baby, and I would kiss you without being made to, if I were asked."

She could feel herself turning red and, looking into his handsome face, felt suddenly afraid.

"Wou-would you like to fish now?" she asked, scrambling up to fetch her pole without waiting for an answer.

He followed her to the water's edge and let her show him how to prepare the hook and line, and they spent the rest of the afternoon companionably. He didn't mention kisses again, much to Clara's relief, though he did reach out and hold her hand as they sat side by side. She didn't mind that so much; she'd held hands with Andrew Blakesley before, secretly, under the table in the nursery when he and his brothers visited at St. Genevieve.

When they grew hungry Clara shared her basket of food with him, and afterward they lay down on the bank, leaving the fishing pole stuck in the damp earth, and gazed at the clouds above.

"Why don't you go to school?" she asked after they had commented at length on how nice the weather was.

His hand, loosely clasping hers, jerked once before he relaxed again. "I used to go to Eton before my parents died."

Hearing the pain in his voice, Clara turned her head toward him and squeezed his hand. "I'm sorry about your parents."

"Robby took me away from school after that," he went on, as if she hadn't spoken. "He's been my tutor ever since. I'll go to Oxford in three years."

"Lord Manning teaches you?" she asked with surprise. "He can do that?"

"He's a wonderful teacher. Much better than any I had at Eton. We've traveled all over Europe, to Austria and Spain and Italy."

"Lovely!" she exclaimed, enchanted by the idea of such far-away countries. "It must have been wonderful! I wish I could see those places."

"Do you?" He propped himself up on an elbow. "Perhaps I'll take you someday."

Her eyes widened. "Would you?"

Solemnly, he nodded, and put his fingertips against her cheek. "If you marry me one day, I will."

"Marry?" she repeated, thinking, in her girlishness, that this must be the most romantic thing that could happen to anyone, much more romantic than playing at being married to Andrew Blakesley.

"If you promise you'll love me and stay with me, I'll take you anywhere in the world that you wish to go." He stroked her cheek. "And I'll give you anything you want, too. But you must love only me. Forever."

Her youth made it easy to promise him that she would

and to believe that she spoke the truth when she said, "Oh, yes. Of course I will, if you're to be my husband."

He nodded with solemn satisfaction, and said, "I'll kiss you then. It's all right for an engaged couple to kiss."

"Yes," she chattered even as he lowered his head. "I've often seen Lord Manning kissing Aunt Anna out in the—"

It was a brief, light kiss, just the barest touch of his mouth upon hers. When he lifted his head he smiled down at her.

"You talk a lot," he said, "but I like to listen to you. When we're married, I hope you'll fill our home with the sound of your voice. Then I'll always be able to find you, just by listening, no matter what room I'm in."

She giggled. "You must have very good ears, then."

He smiled. "I do. Oh, yes, I do."

For the next week she'd lived in a haze, painfully aware of Lucien, whom she spent every waking moment with, and even more painfully aware of the strange and confusing feelings he created in her. Neither her parents nor Lord Manning seemed to realize that Lucien and she were together each day, unchaperoned, though Lucien was ever respectfully aware of her youth. He kissed her occasionally, but briefly and chastely, except for once, when he touched her mouth with his tongue, causing her to shriek with revulsion, after which he laughed and hugged her and apologized, promising he'd not do it again.

It was clear to Clara that Lucien knew a great deal more about life than she did. They would sit together beside the lake, or somewhere dark and quiet in the forest, and he would speak softly, telling her about his childhood and his travels with his uncle. He answered honestly any question she asked, sometimes with pain and sorrow, sometimes with shame, but never with hesitation. When she asked about his parents he told her the truth, that their death hadn't been a carriage accident, as was commonly said. It hadn't been an accident at all, but a cold-blooded murder and suicide that had ended the life of not only Lucien's father and mother, but also of his mother's lover, with whom she'd been running away before Lucien's father caught up with them. Clara was the only person other than his uncle that he'd spoken of the matter with, and she instinctively understood how much he trusted her not to tell anyone else.

"We mustn't have secrets, Clara," he told her one day as they walked beside the lake. "Married people should never have secrets from each other. I will always speak the truth to you, if you will always do the same to me."

And so he had told her, when she had asked, that he had lain with women on five different occasions—his uncle had arranged the meetings for him shortly after his fifteenth birthday, first in Italy with a much older woman who hadn't spoken a word of English but whose patience and skill had filled him with gratitude and admiration, and later in other countries they'd visited—and that he knew exactly how children were brought about. In years to come the truth of this saddened Clara, but at the time, at the age of thirteen, she had merely been fascinated, and had pressed him for every wicked detail. He'd complied willingly enough, shocking her with his factual recountings, but afterward he had pulled her down to the grass to sit beside him and had set his arm about her waist, saying, "I don't want you to think that I shall ever be unfaithful to you, Clara. Uncle Robby says that once a man has found the woman he intends to wed, he must put all other females aside and enter into his marriage in good faith, else he's not an honorable man. I can't go back and change what's done, but I'll not think of another woman, or touch one, until we're wed."

At the end of the week, on the last night before he returned to London with his uncle, Lucien sneaked into Clara's chamber in the middle of the night.

"I only wished to tell you good-bye in private," he said, sitting on her bed, tightly holding both her hands.

"I wish you wouldn't go," she said fervently, weeping. "I'll miss you."

"And I you," he replied, leaning to kiss one wet cheek. "You're young, yet, Clara, and I must strive to remember that. But I love you with my full heart, and will not love another."

"I love you, too, Lucien."

"I will pray that it is so," he whispered. "Clara, you're so young . . . but I beg you, don't forget me or the promises you've made. I'll not forget those I've made you, and one day, I vow it, I shall repay you for all your constancy. I'll spend my life making you the happiest lady on God's earth."

How strange the memory of his words was now, Clara thought as she sat beside him in the church at St. Genevieve, a woman full grown. The gentle, loving Lucien of those days was gone, as if he'd never existed. She had clung to his promises when he and his uncle and her Aunt Anna had boarded the Earl of Manning's elegant coach to head for London, where Lord Manning and Aunt Anna's betrothal was to become official. She had thought that she would see Lucien in a month's time, when her mama and papa would take their family to London to first prepare for and then attend Aunt Anna's wedding. After that, Lucien would arrange for them to write and see each other as often as possible, which would be an easy matter once his uncle and her aunt were man and wife.

But four years were to pass before she saw Lucien again. Aunt Anna returned from London after a month, having broken her engagement to the earl, and had almost immediately afterward married their neighbor, Colonel Huntington, in a small, private ceremony in the very church where Clara presently sat. Clara hadn't understood what had happened to cause Aunt Anna to do such a thing; she had only felt the despair that dampened her parents' household for the months to follow, after Aunt Anna left with Colonel Huntington to follow the army. Papa had grieved deeply, and Mama, for Papa's sake, had worried incessantly. For her part, Clara had longed for Lucien, had waited for word from him, a letter, something. But nothing came, and as the years passed she began to think that perhaps he'd merely been amusing himself with her during that summer, that he'd forgotten not only the promises they'd made, but her, as well. As she grew older her own memories dimmed, especially in the face of the ever-increasing numbers of admirers who began, as she matured, to flatter her with their attentions. Andrew Blakesley was the most ardent among these, making it clear that he intended to one day have her as his wife. Clara, however, and despite the great affection she felt for him, had difficulty thinking of her childhood friend as anything more than a brother.

On her seventeenth birthday Lucien arrived unannounced at St. Genevieve, looking far older and more mature than his twenty years would belie. Tall, muscular, and unfashionably tanned, Viscount Callan was already a man, and so handsome that Clara, looking up from where Andrew Blakesley had been leaning over her, stealing a birthday kiss, set sight upon him and felt her heart drop right into her feet. Stunned and surprised, she'd been uncertain of what to do, and had been unable to make herself go to greet him. Instead, she'd looked away as if he wasn't there, as if his sudden presence hadn't thrust her into complete turmoil, and laughed and smiled at Andrew, behaving so foolishly that the memory never failed to make her groan. When her father finally bade her to greet Lucien she had done so with a horrible giggling nervousness that she'd not been able to contain. He had gazed at her with frowning confusion and asked if he might have the honor of partnering her in the next dance. She might have forgotten that she had already promised it and said yes if Andrew hadn't shown up at once to claim her hand. An hour or more passed before Lucien finally spoke to her again, asking her to accompany him to the garden, where he had already obtained her father's permission to take her.

Sitting beside her on a bench near the fountain, he'd taken her hands in his and spoken in such an earnest rush that she wondered if he was as nervous as she was.

"I don't have any real excuse for not writing all this time, Clara, although I pray you'll believe that I thought often enough of doing so. Robby was in a bad way after your aunt broke their engagement and we started up traveling again, only this time he managed to get us so far away from civilization that we almost never got back."

"Far from civilization?" she repeated numbly, lost as to why he was even telling her this.

"Far from British civilization, I should say, or as far as Robby could get from it." He uttered an embarrassed laugh. "We started out in Italy and ended up traversing the Andes before I could finally convince him to at least bring me back to England so that I could start university."

"The *Andes*?"

"Yes." He squeezed her hands and she felt the calluses that hardened his fingers. "It was quite a journey. I shall enjoy telling you about it someday. We only just arrived back in London a month ago, and there was some trouble to take care of in getting me into Oxford, as I'm already a year late in starting."

"You've been gone," Clara murmured, shaking her head, feeling horribly stupid and self-conscious and utterly unable to behave the way she wished. "All this time, I thought . . . I assumed that you just . . ."

"Clara, please believe me, I meant to write, to explain what had happened, but I had my hands full taking care of

Robby. He was in bad shape for a long while, and by the time I could have written, we were so far away that I don't know if a letter ever would have arrived.''

Bewildered, Clara stared at him. What was this handsome, stunning man saying? That he cared for her? That he had meant everything he'd said to her four years before? That he meant for them to *marry*?

''My lord,'' she began shakily, striving to be polite and thinking, in all truth, that he was really a stranger to her. ''I don't know what to say. I would have greatly enjoyed receiving your letters and carrying on a mutual correspondence. How interesting your experiences must have been these last few years.''

An open expression of worry crossed his features, so reminiscent of the vulnerable boy she'd fallen in love with that her heart felt a sudden ache of longing.

''Clara, you haven't forgotten me, have you? I know how young you were. How young we both were. If your feelings have changed, you must let me know.''

She felt like weeping. ''My lord, you jest, surely. I hold no illusions about my charms. I have not grown beautiful since you saw me last. Indeed, I fear it is quite the opposite. It is your own feelings that must have changed.''

''Ah, no, Clara.'' Lifting a hand, he stroked her cold cheek with the backs of his fingers. ''You're the most beautiful woman in the world to me. You're the girl whom I could trust my heart with. I ask for nothing else. Only that, and I shall be content and shall ever strive to make you the same, I promise. You didn't forget me, did you?''

''No, Lucien,'' she whispered truthfully.

He relaxed visibly, smiling. ''I didn't forget you for even a single moment. Thoughts of you kept me sane at times, especially on freezing nights, when I had nothing but your memory to keep me warm. You'll never know how I longed to see you, to hear your voice.'' He chuckled lightly. ''I would have given a fortune just to hear you chattering the way you did that summer. Clara,'' he said her name as if he still couldn't believe she was there, ''I can't begin to tell you how much I—''

He hadn't been able to speak another word, for that was the unfortunate moment when Andrew chose to interrupt. He and Lucien were the same age, yet Andrew suddenly seemed little more than a youth compared to the other man.

''Clara, I've been looking for you everywhere,'' Andrew said, taking her wrist and pulling her up off the bench. To Lucien, he said, ''Lord Callan, isn't it? We met four years ago when you were visiting St. Genevieve with your uncle, the Earl of Manning.''

Lucien underwent a dramatic change in only a matter of moments. Gone was the gentle, open man who'd held Clara's hands and pleaded with her so tenderly. In his place stood a solemn, rigid, blank-faced peer of the realm, intimidating right down to the soles of his feet.

''Blakesley,'' Lucien said with a nod.

''You've been out here reminiscing, have you?'' Andrew asked good-naturedly. ''Clara's told me what happened that summer when you were here. Calf love and all. I suppose you two will always be able to look back and have a good laugh about it, eh?'' He laughed as if to prove his point, ignoring Clara, who shook her head in a vain effort to make him be quiet. ''You mustn't feel badly, though, Callan. You're not her only victim. Everyone falls in love with Clara eventually. Just being around her is as fatal as catching the plague. A man's fate is sealed before he has the notion to try to save himself. She's a terrible flirt, I'm afraid.''

''Andrew!'' Clara protested weakly, knowing his teasing for what it was and realizing just what it would sound like to Lucien. ''That's not true.''

''It certainly is, you little fake!'' Setting his hands possessively on her shoulders, he mockingly jostled her, grinning all the while. "Even Mr. Webster's in love with her, my lord. You should see the old boy on Sundays, trying to give his sermon while he's gazing at Clara and tripping up every other word." He laughed again and Clara set a hand over her mouth as she saw Lucien's eyes narrowing.

"Oh, there's no harm in it," Andrew went on, oblivious to the tension in the air. "Clara's always been the worst sort of tease, even when she was a girl. Making every man in sight fall in love with her and then dashing their hopes. It doesn't bother me, of course." He gave her another playful shake, then squeezed her in a tight hug that spoke of long familiarity. "I know she doesn't mean any of it, except for what she tells me. Has she told you about our engagement?"

"Andrew," Clara murmured, horrified. "We're not engaged!"

"Not officially," he admitted affably. "But that's only a matter of time." He looked at Lucien. "We're only waiting for the right time to tell her parents."

"Lucien," Clara began, entreating him with one outstretched hand, meaning to reassure him that she had never agreed to any of Andrew's infatuated ideas, but he curtly cut her off.

"That time will never come, I'm afraid," Lucien stated, rigid as a statue. "Lady Clara may not have seen fit to inform you of the fact, but she and I have been betrothed since she was an infant. She is to be my wife."

That, more than anything else she'd experienced that night, shocked Clara to her very depths.

"*Lucien!* Is it true?"

He looked at her so coldly that she actually shivered.

"Yes. My father and yours arranged the matter shortly after you were born. Do you expect me to believe that your parents never told you?"

Dazed, she shook her head.

"Then I regret to be the one to inform you of the fact and to call your happy plans to an end." He seemed a different man than the one who'd sat beside her on the bench. Even his voice was changed, becoming hard and devoid of feeling. "I'm afraid I was laboring under a misconception when we spoke earlier, Lady Clara, and I pray that you'll forgive my presumption. I shall not visit such maudlin sentiments on you again. You have my promise on that."

He walked away without looking back, without seeming to hear her calling after him, and an hour later he had packed his things and left St. Genevieve altogether.

He'd come every year after that, and each time only seemed worse. When she was eighteen he'd arrived and searched her out and found her near the lake, kissing Andrew Blakesley good-bye before he left St. Genevieve to serve in the king's army. When she was twenty he rode into her father's stables and found her laughing with some of the grooms—but that memory was too unsettling to think about; Clara always pushed it away. At twenty-one he'd suddenly appeared in her father's gardens at the inopportune moment when Jeffrey Webster had unfortunately decided to declare his undying love for her. Lucien had furiously knocked the man unconscious, despite the fact that Clara had been attempting to remove herself from his passionate embrace in a more seemly manner, and it was only after Dr. Wardlow had revived the minister that she and Lucien had spoken to each other in what had turned out to be the usual disastrous encounter. Two years had passed since that time; two years in which Clara had to wait and wonder whether Lucien Bryland meant to honor his commitment to their betrothal. At last, when she had made her father write and formally ask him to break the bond between them, Lucien had written that he would not, that the betrothal stood and that he would contest any effort to deny it.

To that end, he had finally arrived two days ago in all his splendor, in his grandest coach and finest dress and most elegant manner, so cold and hard and formal that Clara had nearly wanted to strike him just to make certain he was made of flesh and blood. Even her brothers, who had always liked him, had been frightened into keeping their distance, and her parents, whose warmth and kindness never failed to allay the fears and nerves of the most reticent visitors to St. Genevieve, had gazed at the dark, distant viscount with bewilderment. Clara could only imagine how stiffly Lucien had made his addresses to his future in-laws, for her mother and father had come out of the library after their private meeting with him bearing thoroughly distressed expressions. Her father had assured Clara most insistently, while patting her hand, that she needn't accept Viscount Callan's offer if she didn't wish to do so, despite the fact that it had been his and Edward Bryland's dream to see their children united.

Today, after church services, Lucien would at last ask her to become his wife, and Clara wasn't at all certain how she would answer. She had loved the Lucien she had once known but hated the man he'd become. The love, no matter how often or how hard she had tried to push it aside, refused to die, while the hatred—the hatred had been tempered by every tiny spark of hope Lucien had given her even in his cruelest moments, when she had seen, if only briefly, the Lucien she loved. He existed still, somewhere behind the dark mask that the icy man beside her now wore. The lonely, needy, gentle person who had once sworn his love for her was still there, and it was he whom Clara longed to wed and be wife to.

When the viscount made his offer, she would search his

face and see what she found. If she could still see the Lucien she loved even slightly in that cold countenance, she would agree to the pact. For the hope of finding him again, Clara knew that she would agree to anything at all.

Chapter Three

❧

"Webster," Lucien muttered, shoving the ancient volume of Erasmus back into its place and clasping his hands stiffly behind his back. "The man's a damned vulture. And Clara—typical Clara, wanting to speak with one of her admirers even while she's got a marriage proposal waiting. Especially while she does. Probably a very curst romantic notion, I suppose." Scowling, he paced toward the fire. "As if she hasn't already got every man in this quaint burg falling at her feet, she's got to string him along, make him feel like some noble martyr. Damned fool. He deserves her pity. Or another punch in the nose. That would probably do him more good."

Shutting his eyes and clamping his mouth shut, Lucien thought of the wisdom of silence. *Never give anyone such an advantage as overhearing private thoughts.* It was only those things, the secret, fast-held thoughts of one's soul, that could bring pain if they were brought to light.

He opened his eyes and stared at the fire. "Not that I blame her for wanting to put this farce off as long as she can," he murmured softly.

I should have let her go. I should have been kind enough to let her have some happiness.

He shook his head against the thoughts, unable to argue with the truth of them, unable to give life to those truths. The clock on the other side of the room chimed twelve o'clock. Time for the noon repast, more than enough time for Clara to have dealt with her ardent, pious admirer. Recalling the minister's zealous sermon on the merits of love made him scowl.

He wondered impatiently if she would ever return, longing to have the thing done with and be on his way to London again. The first thing he would do once he arrived home was visit his favorite gaming hell, Mawdrey's, get hideously drunk, and then find his way to Pamela's door, where he would sleep himself sober and wake to find his mistress infuriated with him. The idea made him smile; a good argument with the sharp-tongued Pamela was just what he wanted. That lovely, wicked mouth of hers, matched only by her lovely, wicked mind, was the surest thing to set him on balance again.

She was already angry enough with him for marrying Clara. Not that Pamela had harbored dreams of becoming the Viscountess Callan herself: she simply disliked having the easy routine of her life disrupted. They were lovers and adversaries, as much foe as they were friend, but the cunning battle they carried out during and between the couplings they shared was what made them both feel most alive. Now, because he would have a wife to consider, Pamela believed he would no longer be such capable sport. She had threatened to leave him, but Lucien had quickly put an end to that foolishness. She would go when he said she would, and not before. If there was one thing Pamela had learned about him, it was never to mistake his mere irritation for his anger. There were some lines she wouldn't cross unless she wished to pay the price, and she knew it very well.

His last meeting with his uncle was less cheering to think upon. Robby had been furious—rightfully so—about the gossip that had already sprung loose from White's following what now seemed to Lucien like the most idiotic thing he'd ever done. Just thinking about that absurd wager with Kerlain made him want to groan. What in God's name had possessed him to do anything so foolish? Worse, what had made him actually involve Clara's name in it? And not just her name, but the angry, hurtful name he'd called her by since that hellish night when she'd shattered him into pieces—Peahen—had somehow been overheard and taken up by all those in the club, who'd excitedly become involved in the betting.

"God's mercy." Lucien rubbed at his eyes. *"Idiot!"*

It was just what Robby had called him when he'd cornered him in the library at Manning House with the news that both Clara's name and nickname were being murmured all over town, that Robby himself had heard of the bet in— of all places—the House of Lords.

"And just how will you make your fine offer to that respectable lady, my boy?" Robby had clasped his hands, wringing them dramatically. " 'Please marry me, Lady Clara. Oh, and, by the by, I've already got all of London whispering behind your back and calling you Peahen!' " Robby had rounded on him, glaring. "I'm ashamed of you, Lucky. As ashamed as your father would be now if he were alive to see his son do such a cowardly thing to the daughter of his dearest friend. If you think that's what he wanted you to wed Lady Clara for, to treat her with all the respect of a *whore,* then you are far, far wrong."

His uncle's contempt had left him speechless, and Lucien had felt rather like some lowly form of cockroach. He hadn't blamed Robby for not speaking to him again before he left the home they shared. If anything, Lucien was grateful for the dose of sensibility he'd been given. It was his own madness that drove him to bind Clara to him forever, to make her his whether she wished it or no. Revenge, Wulf had called it, and Lucien was beginning to wonder if that, more than anything else, didn't come closest to the truth.

Not that he would ever know with certainty. Where Clara was concerned Lucien's mind was little more than a roiling muddle of emotions, so hot and confused that he doubted he'd ever sort the mess out.

The library door opened suddenly and Lucien turned as Clara sailed in, merrily smiling at him and removing her bonnet. He felt, as he always did when he set sight on her, a brief, sharp ache, an indefinable longing for the foolish, childish dreams he'd once cherished.

"Forgive me, my lord. I never thought I would be so long." She set her hat upon a chair and moved toward him, still smiling. "My father said that you wished to see me?"

"Yes," he replied, motioning for her to sit on a nearby settee. "There is a matter to settle between us, Lady Clara, and I think you know what it is."

"Thank you," she said, waving at the settee as if to dismiss it. "I'm quite comfortable standing, my lord. Please say what you wish."

She was the most elegantly, beautifully dressed woman he had ever known, but what good did it serve such an unremarkable female to dress herself as if she were a diamond of the first water? Gray eyes, hair the color of a muddy pond, skin that was browned and freckled from the sun—Clara was surely one of the plainest women he'd ever seen. She reminded him of the mannequins used in ladies' modiste shops, faceless, lifeless figures that served only to display beautiful clothes. Clara was a mannequin come to life. She would never humiliate him by wearing the kinds of fashions country girls usually wore when they first came to town, indeed, Clara would never humiliate him at all. Her training had been complete.

She had moved near him and stood quietly, gazing up into his face searchingly. Returning the gaze, Lucien thought that she looked rather sad and solemn for a female who was about to be made an offer of marriage by one of the most sought-after prizes of the *ton*'s marriage market. She must hate him for what he was about to do, for putting her irrevocably beneath his hand. She had wanted to be free of him—he remembered word for word the missive her father, the marquess, had written—but it was the one thing Lucien would never be able to give her.

His gaze dropped to her mouth, which was perhaps her prettiest feature, and he felt a sudden urge to kiss her, to show her what he would give her during the few months they lived together after their marriage. Pleasure, as much as she could take and more, an ocean he'd drown her in so that she'd never be able to look at another man without remembering what it was that he alone could give her. But she knew already, he thought. She'd learned it at the age of twenty in her father's stable, after Lucien caught her there flirting with some of the stable hands. It was impossible that she could have forgotten what they'd shared, despite the fact that he'd not completed the act as fully as he'd wished. He'd left her a maiden on that day, and wondered now if she yet retained such purity. He was more than a little tempted to reenact what they'd done in the stables and find out.

But this was her father's library, in her father's house, which was filled with hungry and expectant people, all of whom were anxiously waiting for Clara and him to emerge and make their announcement, and he had a proposal to make so that he could get on his way to London.

"I'm sure you will agree that there is no need for any manner of pretense between us, Lady Clara," he said evenly, fixing his eyes directly on hers again. "There has been an agreement of long standing between our families, and the time has come for us to embrace it."

She took a step closer, so that he felt the heat of her body and smelled her clean, feminine scent. "If it is what you wish, my lord." Her large gray eyes searched his face.

His smile grew fully meaningful, and he very nearly told her exactly what it was that he did wish, but said, instead, quite correctly, "Surely you are aware of the regard in which I hold you, my lady."

She frowned. "Am I?"

"If not, then I must strive to convince you of my deepest esteem and affection. It is my hope, ma'am, my prayer, that you will give me a great many years in which to prove it to you. Indeed, the rest of my life. Will you do me the honor, Lady Clara, of becoming my wife?"

There. He'd done it with such civil correctness that no member of the *ton* could have argued with the perfection of the thing.

Clara's gaze never wavered, but her brow lowered slightly and her frown deepened.

"Why?" she asked.

He uttered a laugh.

"Why?" he repeated. "You know very well why. Don't try my patience, Clara. If you think you'll get more from me than that manner of proposal then you'd better think again, my dear. Save your romantic notions for Mr. Webster and that Blakesley fellow who was always mooning over you like a daft fool."

Soft color darkened her face. "At least if one of them asked me to wed him, I should know the reason why. There is no need for you to persist in honoring the agreement that my father and yours made so many years ago, Lucien. I release you of it, just as my father will do."

His amusement died away. "I do not wish to be released, and I will not release you." Setting two fingers beneath her chin, he held her face further up toward his. "I perceive that you do not appreciate my efforts to conduct this business in the acceptable fashion. I meant to be kind to you, Clara, to give you the memory of being offered for in the time-honored manner, which I assume every lady craves. If you do not wish to play out such a game, then let us have done with it, for that is exactly what would please me best.''

She jerked away from him, glaring. ''I am very sorry, then, my lord . . .''

But he wouldn't let her finish. Grasping her by an arm, he dragged her close. ''I'll make the arrangements for our wedding to be held at St. George's in exactly two months' time. You may come to London when it pleases you to make yourself ready, to buy whatever finery you desire, to do whatever it is that mothers and daughters and families do when a marriage is at hand. I'll make myself available to fulfill the part of your devoted fiancé.''

''You'll not,'' she stated furiously, struggling to be free. ''I will not wed you, Lucien.''

''Oh, yes, Clara, you will.'' He took hold of her other arm and pulled her hard against him. ''I'll drag you all the way to Gretna Green and bribe a witness to marry us if I must, but whether you say 'yea' of your own will or shout 'no' to the skies the whole while, you will be my wife. Never doubt it.''

''Why?'' she demanded again, stamping on his large booted foot with her tiny slippered one to no effect. ''You hate me, and have done since I was seventeen. You do not want me for a wife, nor do you need me. I will not wed you!''

''Lower your voice!'' he demanded sternly, giving her a shake. ''I meant what I said about dragging you off if I must, but I'd rather not have to do it over your father's flattened body, which is exactly what will happen if he comes in here to find out why you're making such a damned lot of noise.''

''You wouldn't dare strike my father!''

He smiled grimly into her furious, upturned face. ''Do what you will, Clara, but the outcome will be the same. You were promised to me years ago and I demand payment in full. But I'd not worry over a lack of love in our union, my dear. Love and hate are very nearly the same thing in my vocabulary, and I've never known a marriage to survive or fail on either.''

"My parents' marriage—"

"Damn you, Clara. Be quiet!"

He made her be quiet with his mouth on hers, with his hands holding her body against his own, and when she whimpered and struggled he wrapped an arm about her waist so tightly that she squeaked just before she subsided. With his other hand he fondled her breast, ignoring her gasp of surprise, flattening the soft mound with his palm, insolently stroking the hardening nipple with his fingers while his tongue explored her mouth with thorough care, gently ravishing, taking at his leisure as much pleasure as he offered.

"You see," he said when he at last lifted his head, his heightened breathing making the words breathless and harsh, "there's nothing you can do to stop me. I'll have what I want of you, Clara, when I want it. If you try to fight me you'll only make matters worse." He released her, watching as she stepped several steps away, running her hands over her hair and dress and striving to control her fury. Her eyes were clearly bright, he saw, but she mastered her features into an admirably blank expression instead of bursting into the tears another woman might have given way to. And Lucien did admire her. Very much, indeed. And he wanted her so badly that even the idea of taking her here, in her father's library, in her father's house, on the settee where he'd asked her to sit and where he could suddenly envision, quite clearly, laying her down and tossing up her skirts, seemed like the most sensible idea imaginable. He knew what he'd find beneath those skirts, beneath the beautiful clothes she wore, the slender legs and soft skin and delicate breasts. In the years that had passed since she was twenty, her feminine body hadn't changed overmuch, save that her breasts were fuller now, rounder, more womanly.

"We understand each other, then," he said, willing his aching body into submission. "If you're ready, we'll go and make our announcement to your family. I'm sure they've been suffering an agony of anticipation while awaiting the happy couple."

He offered her his arm, but she only stood looking at him.

"Tell me why," she said in a shaking voice. "I'll do what you wish, Lucien. I'll wed you, and I'll be the kind of wife you desire. But at least tell me why."

Still holding his arm out, he looked at her for a long, silent moment before replying, "Because I trusted you once, when there was still something left in me to feel such an emotion. Because I foolishly left what little there was of my heart in your keeping, thinking it safe. It was as nothing to you, Clara. You've proved that time and again. Yet you hold it, and if I am ever to have it back, then I must necessarily have you."

She couldn't have looked more stunned if he had struck her with his fist, he thought, and he felt, suddenly, horribly, as if he were a boy all over again, as if he might weep his heart out for the one thing he wanted more than he even wanted life.

She took a step toward him, lifting one hand beseechingly. "Lucien—"

"Spare me your feminine pity, Lady Clara," he said tightly, insistently offering his arm. "It sickens me thoroughly. Take my arm and play your part while we go to speak with your family. They're expecting a loving, happy couple, and that is exactly what we shall give them."

Chapter Four

May 1816

It had been thirteen years since Clara had been to London, and in her opinion it hadn't changed for the better. The smells and noises and dirty streets made her long for the beauty and quiet of St. Genevieve. She could certainly understand why her parents had become content to remain in the country rather than seek out the social activities in Town enjoyed by their peers. She, herself, had been rather dismayed when Lucien had announced that they were to live in London after their marriage, rather than at his country estate, at least for the first six months. In October they would journey to Pearwood, he'd said, but not before. Clara had the feeling that she'd be counting the days.

Almack's was an especial disappointment. She supposed she'd dreamed of attending the privileged assembly as much as any other girl, but the reality was far different from her imaginings. Considering that an invitation to Almack's was one of the most sought-after social requirements for a young lady's success, it was rather a let-down to find that the assembly's rooms were small and plain, the food and drink unremarkable, and the conversation comprised of little more than gossip. But her dance partners were pleasant enough, if somewhat stiff and proper, and the stares and whispers that had followed her since she'd arrived in Town were less noticeable than usual. Or perhaps she was simply becoming used to them.

It still surprised Clara to be the object of so much discreet interest, although she'd attempted to prepare herself for it as best she could. After all, it was to be expected that people would talk when a peer of the realm who was as handsome as Lucien married such a plain woman, despite that woman's high birth and respectable dowry. The fact of it seemed ludicrous, even to Clara, and if she hadn't known firsthand how determined Lucien was to make her his wife, she never would have believed it. But she'd given him several opportunities to change his mind since she'd arrived in London, and each time he'd only grown angry and insistently repeated that they would wed. She'd finally given up speaking of the matter and had begun, instead, to try to make some kind of peace with her future husband. It had been, thus far, a futile attempt.

True to his word, Lucien played the part of dutiful fiancé very well, at least when he was with Clara in public. If he didn't actually behave in the sort of happy manner one might expect of a man about to be married, he certainly seemed satisfied enough to be in her company at the numerous parties and balls they'd attended. All in all, there was little to fault in his manner. But despite his outward, public attentiveness, Lucien was still, privately, as bewilderingly distant as ever. In truth, he was simply bewildering. When they were alone he was generally silent and brooding, speaking in terse, succinct sentences as if the effort to do more wearied him, constantly watching but never touching her. When they were in public he was sharp-eyed and hovering, introducing her to friends and acquaintances but seldom letting her converse with any of them for more than a few minutes at a time. Even when she danced he watched her, and she hadn't missed the fact that he not only claimed as many dances as he could for himself, but also arranged for her to be partnered in most of her additional dances by either his uncle, Robby, or his closest friends, Lord Rexley and Lord Severn. Was it any wonder that London was talking? She was almost relieved that he'd decided not to attend tonight's assembly after all, despite the fact that he'd said he would.

She tried not to think of what had kept him away, even as her gaze lingered on the entryway, where she somehow expected him to appear. The doors would be closed soon, and then no one would be allowed admittance, not even the Prince Regent himself, if he should suddenly decide that he wished to attend a function so dull.

"He's not going to come, dear," Aunt Anna stated beside her, tapping Clara's shoulder with the tip of her fan. "Don't fret on it. We'll manage well enough."

The words were meant to be encouraging, Clara knew, but there was no mistaking the harsh censure in her aunt's tone. Aunt Anna had made her dislike of Lucien more than clear in the past, and her opposition to the coming marriage had been the cause of no little strife between herself and Clara's father.

"I'm certain there's a good reason for his absence," Clara murmured, careful to keep her tone low and cheerful. The last thing she wished to do was draw the attention of the several women surrounding them by appearing to be distressed.

"Yes, I'm certain there is," Aunt Anna replied smoothly as she smiled and nodded at a passing acquaintance. "If he's anything like his uncle he'll have no end of reasonable excuses for anything he does or doesn't do."

Clara briefly closed her eyes and prayed for divine guidance. It had been a wretched time for the influenza to make its way through so many members of her family. Her parents had been obliged to return to St. Genevieve to nurse Clara's three eldest brothers, and Aunt Anna had necessarily had to travel to London to take her mother's place as Clara's chaperone. As much as Clara loved her aunt, all she could foresee in the arrangement was disaster. Aunt Anna had never spoken of what had happened between herself and the Earl of Manning eleven years ago, or of why their engagement had been so suddenly broken, but every time the earl's name was mentioned a certain look crossed her lovely features that said more than words ever could. It seemed impossible that, with Aunt Anna and the Earl of Manning jointly managing the coming wedding, matters weren't going to become unpleasant.

"Lucien's been more than attentive these past several weeks," Clara said. "I can hardly blame him for wanting to spend one evening in the company of his friends, rather than at this delightful gathering."

Aunt Anna's expression softened slightly, and she smiled. "I suppose there's some truth in that. I've never seen so many people work so hard to gain invitation to an event so dull. Don't laugh, dear, or they'll throw us out, and your mother would never forgive us. Here comes that delightfully handsome American. Kerlain, isn't it? You mustn't waltz with him again, Clara, or you'll shock every matron in the place. Your father told me what happened at Lady Berrydale's ball, and I'm sure the gossips haven't stopped talking of it yet."

Clara knew very well that they hadn't, despite the fact that nothing of real importance had occurred. The Earl of Kerlain had merely kissed her hand at the end of a waltz, and Lucien had suddenly materialized in the middle of the dance floor to snatch her hand away and drag her out to the gardens, where he'd promptly lapsed into his usual taut silence. The *ton* had found it to be a very romantic gesture on Lucien's part, so much so that Clara had already heard several different variations of the incident, each more embellished than the one before. She wouldn't be surprised if the next version had Lucien riding through Lord Berrydale's front doors on a white destrier and bearing her away. A love match, society matrons whispered, with Viscount Callan so besotted by his future bride that he couldn't contain such endearing fits of jealousy. The only trouble, Clara thought, was that it wasn't jealousy at all. It was nothing more than distrust. He was so certain that she meant to be unfaithful to him, as his mother had been to his father, as he must believe Aunt Anna had been to Lord Manning, that he couldn't even trust her to share a charming but meaningless gesture with one of his closest acquaintances.

"Lady Anna," said Lord Kerlain, coming to a smiling halt before them. "Lady Clara." His slight bow included them both. "You're enjoying the evening, I hope? It appears to have become quite crowded."

"I believe you're confused by the number of admirers following you about, my lord," Aunt Anna replied teasingly. "Any more of them and you'd not be able to move about at all."

Lord Kerlain laughed in an open, unaffected manner that Clara found perfectly charming. He was too good-natured to dislike, or even to be wary of, despite the rumors being circulated about him. It was said that Kerlain was looking for a rich, titled wife to rescue him from financial troubles, but if that was true, it certainly hadn't scared off any of the wealthier young ladies who were making their come outs this Season. Rather than avoiding such a disreputable fortune hunter, especially an American, they instead sought him out in droves. The Earl of Kerlain was by far the most popular man in London, as was evidenced at every social event he attended. His unknown financial status and unfortunate nationality were apparently overwhelmed by his charm, good manners, and excessively handsome looks. Clara had found him to be wonderful company since her arrival in London, despite Lucien's clear displeasure over her friendship with the man.

"Another waltz is about to be played," Kerlain said, turning his attention to Clara. "I realize you've been worn down to a nubbin with so much dancing, my lady, but I had hoped you would do me the honor?"

"You're very kind, my lord," Clara began, "but I think perhaps—"

A stirring in the room distracted all of them. Clara glanced toward the entryway and saw the Earl of Manning standing there, resplendent in sapphire knee breeches and coat and a white waistcoat. She never ceased to be amazed, each time she saw him, at how little he had aged in the past eleven years. His blond hair was untouched by gray, his dark blue eyes were just as vivid, and his handsome face just as youthful and unlined as when he'd been thirty-six years of age.

Clara felt her aunt stiffen beside her, heard her murmur, softly, "Robert," in a tone filled with as much sadness as wistfulness. She was staring at the earl, Clara saw, almost as if he were a phantom, and the earl, when his searching gaze at last found Clara and the woman standing beside her, began to stare, too. He looked so utterly shocked and disarmed that Clara instinctively moved to go to him. Lord Kerlain's hand on her arm stopped her.

"The music is about to begin," he said. "My lady?" Releasing her, he held his hand out, palm up, in invitation. Clara looked from the Earl of Manning to her aunt Anna, and after a moment's indecision set her hand in Lord Kerlain's, letting him lead her to the dance floor.

"Whatever that was about," he said after the music had begun and he'd set her into motion, "it looks to be rather complicated."

"They were betrothed many years ago," Clara said, glancing back to where Lord Manning had at last approached Aunt Anna. They appeared to be exchanging polite civilities, albeit rather stiffly. "No one knows quite what happened to bring the engagement to an end."

"Indeed?" Kerlain said with interest. "It sounds a wonderful mystery. Something I should love to unravel. What a handsome couple they would have made. Lady Anna's been in Town for less than two days and she's already caused a stir among any number of single gentlemen."

"Has she?" Clara asked with a smile. "I'm not surprised, of course. She's the beauty in our family."

"Ah. Now I know where you got it from."

Clara laughed. "I think it only fair to warn you, my lord, that I'm not immune to flattery, no matter however false it may be. If you're not careful you'll have me falling at your feet along with the rest of your legion of admirers."

He grinned at her. "You're a wicked tease, Lady Clara. I should truly enjoy such a thing a great deal, save that I'd most likely find myself meeting your fiancé over pistols in short order. I've been meaning to tell you, by the by, that I was sorry to hear that your parents have had to return to St. Genevieve with several of your brothers. I hope the recent spate of illnesses won't keep them from attending the wedding?"

"As do I, my lord," Clara said fervently. "My father will certainly attend, unless he, too, becomes ill, but I don't know if it will be possible for my mother. She vowed to return before week's end, but I fear my brothers will still be too ill for her to do so. This influenza has proven to be quite tenacious, and I shouldn't wish her to abandon them, even for the sake of my own wedding."

"I shall pray, then, that they recover quickly, for both your sake and your mother's. She certainly wouldn't want to miss the marriage of her only daughter."

"No, I know she does not."

"Where is Lord Callan tonight?" he asked, looking

about as if to find that man. "He can't have deserted you to the wiles of such dangerous men like myself, can he?"

"If you're capable of being dangerous in *Almack's*," Clara said teasingly, "then you're even more talented than I perceived, my lord."

His green eyes sparkled with amusement. "My dear, you almost tempt me to prove it. Callan's a fool to let such a treasure go out on her own, although I suppose you must be somewhat relieved to be rid of him for a short while. The man's been constantly at your side, as if he's afraid you'll disappear."

"Hardly that," Clara said lightly. "And as to being on my own, my lord, I pray you'll remember my aunt. She's a tenacious foe in any battle, I warn you. If you so much as step on one of my toes while we dance you'll have her slapping a glove in your face and asking to choose your weapons."

Kerlain's eyebrows rose. "In that case, I shall behave as the perfect gentleman."

"As you always do," she replied with a smile.

"Never say so," he mockingly begged. "My reputation would never survive." He turned her about in a neat spin. "Tell me about Barrington. I hear you've performed a small miracle in resurrecting Lord Callan's ancestral home these past two months. It was unoccupied for fifteen years, or so I've heard?"

"Fourteen."

"Lord Callan's never lived there?"

She shook her head. "Not since he was a boy. He's stayed with his uncle at Manning House whenever he was in Town, and at his estate in the country for part of the year."

"And now he's to live at grand Barrington with his lovely new bride. What a fortunate man. Does he approve of the changes you've made?"

"I hope he will. Tomorrow morning will be the first time he's seen the house completed. I'm rather nervous to discover what he thinks."

"He'll be more than pleased, I imagine. The on-dit about Town is that Barrington will be this Season's showplace."

"It is a beautiful home," she admitted. "I imagine the *ton* is merely interested to see the inside of it again after so many years. It came to Lucien through his mother's line."

"As did his title and fortune," Kerlain said with a nod. "I understand that's partly why his acquaintances call him 'Lucky.' The Barringtons have long been one of England's wealthiest families, is that not so?"

She gave him a curious look. "Yes, although it's not usually spoken of. I can't think Lucien cares for it so much."

"No, he wouldn't. In truth, he doesn't seem to care much for being a nobleman at all. He would have made a good American."

She laughed. "Indeed, he would. I'll ask you not to put such a notion in his thoughts, if you please, or he'll head off for the colonies at the first chance."

"Not without you, he won't," Kerlain told her. "I've only known one other man in my life who was so besotted with the woman he wished to take to wife. Now, why should that make you frown?"

Clara forced a smile back on her lips and tried to think of a light, flirtatious remark to make. She enjoyed the teasing and flirting that was acceptable in *ton*nish society. She was more than a little proficient at the art, and recognized Kerlain as a master of it. His words were meaningless, harmless, intended only to compliment and charm. She strove to remember that as she spoke in an airy tone, "Only because I dislike the competition. Who is the other gentleman you speak of, my lord? Perhaps I should make him one of my conquests and steal him away from his lady."

"He only wishes that you could, Lady Clara. Indeed, he does. But it's impossible, I think. And you'll have your hands full with your husband, once you wed Lord Callan. He's a fine fellow," he said, twirling her about, "and I like him very well, but for all that I believe your life with him may prove to be rather . . . challenging."

Mawdrey's was an elegant club, dark, discreet, and very amenable. The proprietor, Harold Mawdrey, had lived most of his life as a privateer, sailing the seas and plundering foreign ships on Britain's behalf, and was, without a doubt, a rich man. He was also a man who'd learned a thing or two about pleasing the wealthy, both male and female, and about the price such persons were willing to pay in order to obtain those pleasures without remark or scandal. Even the most respectable members of the *ton* could spend an evening at Mawdrey's, pursuing his or her particular path to ruin, and be assured that the news wouldn't be found on the lips of gossips the following day. During those unfortunate moments when the local officers of the law became involved, one could be assured that Mawdrey would take care of smoothing matters over. Once enough money changed hands, no names would be named and no peers of the realm would be involved, for which those who'd been spared would readily show their gratitude. All in all, and given the usually precarious state of such chancy enterprises, Harold Mawdrey made a killing.

Lucien had long been one of Mawdrey's regular customers, partly because he enjoyed the club's dark and somewhat menacing allure, and partly because it was one of the few gaming establishments where he could take Pamela without comment. Unlike the proprietors of other similar gaming hells where the only women allowed were the kind to be had for a few coins, Harold Mawdrey had clearly observed that ladies of the *ton* could just as readily be parted from their money as could the gentlemen.

Pamela was seated beside Lucien, just as she had been for most of the late afternoon and evening, placing her bet as the dealer laid out the cards for the game of *rouge et noir.* Wulf was seated on his other side, calculating the totals almost faster than the dealer could lay the cards down. His little French mistress, Yvette, was sitting in Wulf's lap, looking impossibly tiny compared to her huge, muscular lover. Lucien had never been able to envision the pair of them together without inwardly wincing at the thought of Yvette being simultaneously squashed and smothered by Wulf's amorous attentions. It was a miracle the girl was still in one piece, but perhaps he had it all wrong. Yvette was a dainty bit of muslin, but she certainly knew how to lead Wulf about by the nose. Bella could have benefited from a few lessons by her.

Sitting at the far end of the table, Jack and the woman he'd brought with him were tangled in an ardent embrace that could have made the most hardened madam in the city blush. At Mawdrey's no one so much as turned a head.

"If that goes on much longer," Pamela murmured in Lucien's ear, nodding toward the entwined couple, "we'll have to clear the table off and let them have it. Where does he manage to find these women?"

Lucien gave her a sideways glance. "Where do you think, my dear?"

She smiled. "The so-grand Lord Rexley, with all his maunderings about the superiority of the *ton,* picks all his women out of the gutter. It would make a wonderful topic for *Le Chat,* don't you think?"

"No," Lucien replied dryly. "I don't."

She laughed lightly. "Never fear, darling. I won't touch the dear earl. I have too much respect for life and limb, especially my own. God almighty. The slut's fallen right off his lap and onto the floor. What a spectacle. Which of them is drunker, do you suppose?''

Lucien looked to where a laughing Jack was picking his also laughing companion up off the floor. Where *did* he find such women? he wondered, watching as his friend settled the giddy female back on his lap. She was worse than his usual sort, with her garishly dyed red hair falling untidily out of its arrangement and her face smeared with an unattractive mixture of powder and rouge. She looked more like a comic actress than a woman trying to make a living luring men. Still, Jack appeared to be perfectly pleased with the girl. Tomorrow he would replace her with a new one, and would be just as content with her. It was the one great oddity about his normally exacting friend that Lucien had never been able to understand, but had long since learned to accept. Jack liked women, all types of women, and the more numerous the better. The fairer sex was his downfall, he'd once confided, as well as his greatest weakness, one that was unlikely ever to change. The day would probably never come when he'd settle down with a single mistress, not even when he'd finally gotten married.

''Jack's not drunk,'' he told Pamela quietly. ''I've told you before about that.''

''Ah, yes,'' she said. ''The perfect Lord Rexley, who never drinks to excess and who only acts a fool when he's out and about. I don't know why I keep forgetting, save perhaps because I seldom ever see the man when he isn't in his worst element.''

Lucien sighed and turned away, watching disinterestedly as the dealer laid out fresh rows of cards while beside him Wulf loudly counted out the growing score. It never did any good to get between Pamela and Jack. They hated each other and had done so since the day they'd first met. He'd long since learned to stay out of the path of their fire, and had confined his efforts at peacemaking to keeping Pamela as quiet and inoffensive as possible.

"Aren't you going to play this round?" she asked.

He shook his head and finished off the last of the brandy in his glass, then pushed his chair back.

"I believe I'll stretch my legs."

She looked at him sharply. "You're not thinking of leaving?"

He only wished he were. But it was the last night they'd be seeing each other until after his marriage, and he at least owed Pamela a few hours of his time. He'd been too busy in the last two months to keep up their customary schedule, and she'd made her displeasure well known.

"No, but I will in another hour or two. I promised Robby I'd be home in time for breakfast. Monsieur Dellard has announced that he'll be making his famous crepes, for which dish Robby lured him away from the Duke of Davenport, and the fellow will have a fit of temper if he doesn't have a full audience to appreciate his creation."

Even in the darkness, Lucien could see a dull red flush creep across Pamela's cheeks. She was a flawless and stunningly beautiful woman, blond and blue-eyed, as classical in her features as a Greek statue, but there was something about her anger that sharpened her almost to the point of pinchedness.

"I assumed you would come home with me tonight," she said tightly. "It's been three weeks, Lucien—"

He took her chin between two fingers and tilted her face abruptly upward. "And it will be a good deal longer if you don't keep your wits about you, my dear. I hope you're not forgetting that I don't listen to your demands." Releasing her, he gave her a level warning look. "Enjoy your play. I'll return shortly."

Jack stopped him as he walked past.

"Driven you away at last, has she?" he asked over the

sound of Wulf's counting. "The divine Pamela's not in her best mood tonight, evidently. But, then, when is she ever?" He skillfully juggled the female on his lap, whose loosened bodice gave an open view to anyone passing by, until she was settled on his other knee. "You're not leaving yet, are you? I promise to get you home to Robby on time. You needn't worry about that."

"I'm just heading out for a bit of air," Lucien told him. "There's enough smoke in here to choke an entire regiment."

Jack gave him a curious look. "Same as it always is," he remarked, looking about at the room's thick haze. "Never bothered you before."

A surge of irritation made Lucien's tone sharper than he would have wished. "It does tonight," he said. Ignoring his friend's raised eyebrows, he turned and stalked away.

Mawdrey himself opened the secret door that led to the alleyway, not stopping to ask why Viscount Callan should wish to stand in the cold night air. He offered Lucien a glass of his own private brandy before he disappeared back into the noise and smoke, an offer Lucien gladly accepted. Glass in hand, he stepped into the dark alley and slowly let out a breath.

It was quiet, with no fear of footpads. The alley was often the preferred exit of many of Mawdrey's more discreet customers, and it was well guarded to make certain it was safe. There was no fog tonight, and he could see the stars. The air was cold, despite the warmth of the afternoon, and felt good against his skin. He closed his eyes and felt some of the tension leave him, wishing part of his sorrow would go with it.

He should be at Almack's. Of course, he hated Almack's, but at least a body could breathe there without filling his nostrils with stench. And he could move about. And dance with Clara. Touch her with his hands, and hold her in his arms as they waltzed, taking in her clean, delicate scent. She would smile up at him as she always did, even when he never smiled back. She would madden him, as she always did, too, and make him rigid with want. He would lie awake all night after leaving her, seeing her again in his mind, remembering every word she'd said, every smile, her inebriating scent, and he would call himself a hopeless idiot and know that all the same he'd be up early the next morning, planning some excuse upon which he could see her again.

In two short months Clara had turned him into a lovesickened boy again, desperate for her affection and terrified of losing her, or of never even having her. It had been that way almost from the beginning. He remembered clearly how shocked he'd been when his parents had told him, at the age of ten, that the beribboned child he'd just danced with—and been made to kiss—would one day be his wife. He'd been annoyed at first, perhaps even angry, but as time passed he'd begun to think of Clara Harkhams in an entirely different manner. She had become his secret, and his dream. He'd clung to the idea of her whenever his parents fought, and in his mind's eye he envisioned just how differently things would be between himself and the little beribboned girl. She was going to love him, as he'd always craved to be loved. She was going to save him from his loneliness and misery.

The obsession only grew stronger with age. He'd become so sure of it, of her, that when he'd finally seen her again at the age of sixteen Clara had seemed like more of a demigoddess than a mortal being. He'd been too much in awe to speak to her during those first few days at St. Genevieve, and had instead contented himself with simply following and watching her. The fact that she hadn't grown into a beauty had been a tremendous comfort to him, although he supposed he would have loved her as passionately even if she'd looked like Helen of Troy. But the beautiful women he'd known in his life had proven to be false and hard-hearted, especially his mother. Clara's open, simple features made her seem even more perfect, and Lucien remembered how his heart ached with what he'd believed was love every time he saw her.

But whatever it was that had possessed him before he actually spoke with her on that day by the lake was like some pale pretender in comparison to what struck him then. Love, real love, had fallen down on him like a tremendous, stunning thunderclap. The feeling had overwhelmed him with its intensity, and he had known, even at that youthful age, that his heart would never again be his own. Perhaps there had been an unseen magic behind it, or some kind of inflexible fate, but it couldn't be changed. He was in love with a woman who didn't love him, and no matter what he or she did, he couldn't make it stop.

Lucien took a long swallow of brandy and then gave a silent shake of his head. He was far more pathetic than his father had ever been. Far more. And the worst part was that Clara made him feel it so deeply, made him feel all of his shortcomings to his very bone. She made him want her love until he was ready to go down on his knees and beg for it, and made him know, in almost the same moment, how hopeless such a cause was. There was only darkness in him, an ugly darkness that could have nothing to do with what Clara was. Everyone loved her. She was sweet and good and kind. Men flocked about her as if she were the answer to all their prayers. She made them smile and laugh, even the worst of them. God, he'd *seen* her do it. All so effortlessly. She would have done it to him if he'd given her half the chance. But that low he wouldn't let himself descend. She would never know how utterly she held him captive. Indeed, the past months had only served to enforce his determination to put some distance between them at the end of six months of marriage. It was the only way he would be able to survive with some measure of pride intact, and the only way she could possibly be happy as his wife. He would be unkind to her if she stayed, just as he had been; it was the single defense he had against all that he felt. And her pain and bewilderment at his small cruelties were a torment for them both.

He drained the rest of his brandy, wincing briefly at the burn in his throat. No, it was better this way. Better that he hadn't gone to Almack's. She was probably having a wonderful time without his unpleasant company. He could envision the men she was dancing with, all of them charming and smiling and good. All of them making her happy, as he had once believed he would do. He doubted she missed him at all, or thought of him, except perhaps with some measure of relief at his absence.

With a sudden curse he threw the glass across the alleyway, listening with grim satisfaction to the shattering force with which it hit the opposing wall. His familiar darkness welled up within and he gladly let it come. He wasn't going to be Clara Harkham's slavering dog. He wasn't going to be *anyone's* dog.

"Add the cost of a glass to my bill," he told Mawdrey as he made his way back into the club. Mawdrey merely nodded.

Pamela looked up as he approached. He could tell by the look on her face that she read his mood perfectly.

"Get up," he said curtly. "I'm taking you home."

"Gladly." She stood and began collecting her things. "I don't care to lose more, anyhow. You'll have to start paying me to be your mistress if I keep gaming at Mawdrey's."

Wulf's monotonous counting stopped, and, bleary-eyed from drink and smoke, he blinked up at Lucien. "You're s'pposed to go home to Manning House. Told us so. Remember it distinctly."

"Very good, Wulf," Lucien said, patting his friend's rocklike shoulder. "Don't fret over the matter. I'll take care to get there in the morning. Come along, Pam." He took hold of her arm just as the entryway to Mawdrey's was flung open and a loud whistle sounded out. "Now what?" he muttered.

"It appears the authorities have decided to ruin a pleasant evening once again," Jack said, standing and helping his companion to her feet. "Are you going to stay for the fighting?" He looked pointedly at Lucien.

"I'm taking Pam home."

Jack gave him a long, level look, seemingly unaware of the mad scramble the other patrons made to retreat out the back alleyway door. Lucien gave him no chance to say anything, but with a slight nod turned away, taking Pamela with him.

Chapter Five

❧

The early morning light falling across her bed was nearly perfect, and Pamela knew she'd have to work quickly to capture her subject as she wished before either the light altered the shadows or the naked man on the bed awoke. Lucien disliked being the object of her sketching, yet he remained her favorite, and certainly her most challenging, study. Inching carefully out of the bed, she pulled on her wrapper, took up her sketchbook and pencil, sat quietly in a chair opposite the bed, and began to draw.

She worked for several minutes, drawing quickly, frowning, altering lines, looking back and forth between the bed and her paper. She had never been able to get his face right, though she'd spent hours alone trying to recapture, from memory, the sensitive curve of his lips, his dark, intriguing eyes, the Gallic quality of his high cheekbones and aquiline nose. The features themselves were easy enough; it was the way his emotions molded them, changed them so rapidly, that she wasn't able to capture. Not that Lucien himself helped the matter. He was as unruly as a wind in a storm, calm and delightful one moment, furious and stinging the next, sultry and caressing the moment after that. She'd done several good drawings of him in his various moods, but none had done him justice. The fact gnawed at Pamela's sense of perfection. Even now she felt a growing frustration, though catching Lucien in slumber was a fortunate occurrence. Only covered by a twist of sheet around his hips, he provided a perfect image of the masculine human form, lean and muscular and well proportioned—every serious art studio in London would do anything to have such a model for their students to learn from. But he was hers alone to practice with, Pamela thought with a lazy smile. All hers. Not that she would ever think of using him in one of her public drawings, as she had done with other men she'd kept as lovers. Lucien wouldn't find the compliment to his taste, nor even slightly amusing. The thought made her pause a moment and consider her present drawing. It was undoubtedly the best of him that she'd done yet, but if he knew of it . . .

"Mmmm. What time is it?"

A long half yawn, half groan followed the words, and then Lucien made a great fuss and a good deal of noise about stretching. Pamela quickly flipped the pages of her sketchbook, coming upon a fresh sheet and making a fast, coarse reproduction of the drawing she'd just done.

"What are you doing?" He was blinking at her from his pillow, scratching his chest and scowling, and as Pamela graced him with a slight smile he propped up on his elbows and said, furiously, "For God's sake, Pam! While I was *sleeping*?"

She kept sketching, replying calmly, "You'd rather I tried to murder you?"

"I'd rather you kept your bloody sketches for flowers and trees or some helpless nobody. Now stop what you're doing and help me get dressed. Damn!" He sat up, rubbing his eyes. "What time is it? Robby's going to roast me over Hell's own fires."

Tossing the sketchbook aside, Pamela rose from her chair.

"It's a good thing I have Sibby iron your belongings so early in the mornings," she said as she approached the dresser where her silent, efficient maid had put Lucien's clothes. "Shall I ring for coffee, or will you be able to stay that long?"

"No, just help me to get decent so that I can hire a cab without being arrested."

Eyeing him from head to toe, she gave a husky chuckle. "It won't matter. You'll still look like you've been dragged through the streets behind a hackney." Lifting the lid off a covered bowl, she dipped one finger inside. "Mmm. Water's still warm. I'll be able to shave you, at least. Steady, darling." She laughed again as he tried to pull his drawers on. "You'll fall and hit your head and your dear little bride will have to hear the news that her fiancé died in his mistress's arms."

Trying to make his fingers work on the buttons of his trousers, Lucien flashed a look at her, grinning. "You'd actually hold me, would you?"

"Only when the constable arrived, love. Before that I'd be too busy having my breakfast. I'm sure Sibby wouldn't mind patting your lifeless hand and weeping, if you wanted something that maudlin."

"Shirt," was his reply, as he held out his hand for that article of clothing.

"Let me take one last good look at you, Lucien," Pamela said after she'd passed it to him. "The next time I see you, you'll be a married man. Thoroughly shackled and too tired for pleasure."

Uttering a short laugh, he held his arms up and turned about for her inspection. "Not *thoroughly* shackled, my dear, but most certainly too weary for pleasure . . . from you, at least."

"Bastard." She threw his waistcoat at him.

"Give it up, Pam," he advised, "and put that fertile mind of yours to better use. I gave you fair warning that I mean to use my wife as often as I can. How," he added with mock innocence, "am I to get the chit pregnant, otherwise?"

Tossing his coat and starched cravat on the bed, she strolled away from him. "Plenty of men manage it without a fuss. Why you have to make such a scene about it, I'll never know. You've always been an intelligent man before this."

"A scene?" he repeated, amused, as he generally was by his mistress. "Why, my dear Lady Halling, if it means that much to you, I'll give my solemn vow never to tup my wife in Hyde Park in the afternoons. Or at least not while traffic's busy."

"Bastard," she repeated, yanking on her bellpull to inform her maid that she wanted her breakfast. "You don't give a damn about what I think, or how I feel. I've got a heart, though that fact might surprise you."

"Not at all," he said more softly, sitting to draw on his boots. "I know you've got a heart. A very small heart, but it's there, intact, nonetheless. Why do you think I mean to send Clara away once she's with child? Other than for her own benefit, I mean."

Her eyes narrowed. "It's certainly not for my sake, Lucien. For hers, yes. For yours, yes. For mine . . . don't insult me in such an idiotic manner or I'll get out my pistol and shoot you."

"You don't believe me? I'm wounded," he said, sitting upright to tie his cravat in a rough knot.

"That's because you're a man," she told him sweetly, "and also a fool. You can't bear to face the truth, so you avoid it. Or change the facts to suit your ego, more like."

"Really, darling? Why don't you tell me, then?"

"Oh, no, love. Come in, Sibby." She smiled at Lucien as her maid opened the door and carried a large silver tray into the room. "You're clever enough to figure that out on your own. Though I daresay if you look at your sorry self you'll see reason enough. Why should poor little Clara Harkhams have to endure your wicked person for the rest of her life, after all?''

Standing, Lucien strolled over to where Sibby was setting a coffeepot and plates of biscuits on a table. ''Why shouldn't she? You do, and quite well, too. Good morning, Sibby, love.'' He gave the pretty maid a pat on her bottom and was rewarded with a delighted squeal before she scurried out the door.

''Don't encourage her,'' Pamela warned with a dark frown. ''She's in love with you, you know.''

Lucien bit into one of the biscuits. ''Is she?'' he asked in a muffled tone.

''You know very well she is. I'll cut your heart out if you ever play your little games with her.''

''Goodness, such violence in the morning,'' he said with feigned amazement. ''Sibby's a sweet, charming child. I don't play games on such innocents. I save that sort of thing for people like you, love.''

She felt too weary to continue their verbal sparring, and told him to go away. ''You'd better not take your chances with letting me shave you, after all. My fingers suddenly feel quite unsteady, and you wouldn't want to go to your bride with a slit throat. Go and have your scold from Lord Manning,'' she suggested tartly, ''and then take care of your innocent country virgin. Make her happy and please her parents and when you're tired of all that come back to me. Have a nice wedding, love. Don't choke while you're making your sacred vows.'' She poured herself a cup of coffee.

Lucien made her a half bow. ''Thank you kindly, Lady Halling.'' Then he reached over, took up her sketching pad, and tore the top sheet off. He ripped the sketch of himself into small pieces, which he tossed up into the air. As they settled about his mistress, who eyed him with cold contempt, he added, "Don't make me one of your subjects again, Pamela. You know how it displeases me." At the door he took up his hat. "Good day, my dear. Expect me a week or two after the wedding. I'm sure to be in just the kind of bad mood you like best."

She pushed her breakfast away as soon as he'd gone and grabbed her sketchbook, flipping the pages until she came to the drawing she'd hidden.

"Perfect," she murmured with a sigh of relief, and took up her pencil once more to finish what Lucien had interrupted while her mind was still filled with the image of him sleeping contentedly on her bed.

Hemmet opened the door before Lucien could put his hand on the knob and stood staring down at the viscount as if he were the most unimaginably horrible spectacle on earth.

"Good morning, Hemmet," Lucien greeted, shoving his hat into the butler's outstretched hand and peering around the older man and into the hall. "Yes, I know what I look like, so stop making that face at me. Is Lord Manning awake yet?"

"For more than three hours now, my lord," Hemmet replied evenly, stepping back to let Viscount Callan enter the elegant dwelling.

Lucien controlled the urge to groan aloud. "I see. I'll just go upstairs then and make myself fit."

Shutting the door with care, Hemmet gave a loud sniff. "The earl expressly requested that you be sent to him as soon as you arrived, my lord."

Control dissolving, Lucien groaned.

"Yes," Hemmet observed dryly. "Monsieur Dellard was most unhappy—*again*—when you were not present this morning to appreciate his crepes."

"Gad."

"Quite," said Hemmet, walking in the direction of the breakfast room while Lucien meekly followed behind. "It's the third cleaver he's ruined this week. Threw it right into the kitchen's east wall, where a lovely gash now points the way to the ovens. Mrs. Parks gave notice and has already packed her bags. Half the staff was inclined to do the same. You'll have to apologize on your knees this time, I think."

"Damnation." Lucien ran his hands over his shirt and wished that Pamela had shaved him. A clean face with a slit throat might be a more welcome sight to his uncle than the way he presently looked.

The doors to the breakfast room swung wide and Hemmet announced, in his most thoroughly bored tone, "Viscount Callan, my lord."

The Earl of Manning, sitting at the head of the table, didn't turn. "Ah, at last. Come in, Lucien. We've been waiting for you."

Lucien. It never failed to bode ill when his uncle used his full name.

"Good morning, Robby," he began in a light tone, striding forward as Hemmet left the room and shut the doors. "It's a beautiful morning——" He stopped when he caught sight of a very dapper—certainly in comparison to him— Earl of Rexley smiling up at him from a plate filled with crepes. "Jack," Lucien said with some surprise. "Good morning. I'm sorry about leaving Mawdrey's so quickly last night. How did you and Wulf fare? Didn't mean to leave you in a fix."

"Don't worry over the matter," Jack said reassuringly. "We came out well enough. That little mistress of Wulf's has the most amazing right hook, and quite a ferocious temper. One of the constables made the mistake of calling her a whore and she promptly informed him that she was French, that he was a swine, and then she broke his nose. Good thing Wulf's got her to protect him. Poor fellow stood there like a punching bag, loudly calculating the mounting damages as if that'd make anyone stop throwing things.''

At this, Jack and Lucien chuckled in a forced, overly cheerful manner while the Earl of Manning sat looking patient.

''I don't see any bruises, at any rate. It's good of you to visit.'' Lucien attempted a look of complete innocence at his uncle. ''Did you wish to see me, sir? I really should go and change my dress before we leave to collect Lady Clara and the marchioness.''

Holding his coffee cup in both hands, leaning back in his comfortable chair, the Earl of Manning regarded his nephew with a calm expression. ''Lucky, my dear, if you don't cease this blameless behavior at once, I shall hire pirates to steal you away in the middle of the night, as I probably should have done when you were a boy, you misbehaved, ungrateful whelp, and sell you into slavery on the most remote island in the Pacific, where you will languish for years before I even begin to consider redeeming you. *Sit down.*'' He nodded at the chair on his left, pointedly ignoring the Earl of Rexley's efforts to control laughter in the chair on his right. ''You might as well eat,'' he said once Lucien was seated, and glanced at the stone-faced server who stood beside the buffet. ''Strebbit, you may serve the viscount and then attend to other duties.''

Strebbit did as he was told, and when he had gone, leaving the three men alone, the earl commented, ''I'm amazed at the lengths to which your friends go to keep you well and happy, Lucien. Whatever have you done to deserve such loyalty?'' The gentle words struck Lucien sharply and he glanced at Jack. Setting down his cup, Lord Manning took up his napkin to pat his mouth. ''Rexley's been patiently waiting for over a half hour now,'' he said, folding the linen square with precision, ''only to make certain that I didn't murder you the moment you walked in the door. I'm sure you'll appreciate his efforts.''

Lucien drew in a slow breath, reaching out a hand to take up his own coffee-hot cup. Over the rim he gazed at his uncle and his friend, so similar that the resemblance never failed to shock him. They were like portraits of the same man, one younger and one older, both blond, blue-eyed, hard as stone. They even shared the same expressions, so that when he was drunk Lucien had a hard time telling them apart. If he hadn't known Jack Sommerton's parents for many years, Lucien would have believed the Earl of Rexley to be the Earl of Manning's by-blow. Indeed, it was an idea that had taken plenty of time to fade sufficiently before Lucien was able to fall asleep nights without wondering about it. In broad daylight, in moments such as this, it still haunted him.

In the ensuing silence, as Lord Manning glared at his nephew, the Earl of Rexley commented, helpfully, ''Boys will be boys.''

''Yes,'' Manning drawled. ''Just as fools will be fools. It might interest you children to know that while you were throwing your fortunes away at''—he briefly turned his stark blue gaze on Jack—''*Mawdrey's*''—and gave an elegant shudder which Lucien was glad to see made the otherwise impenetrable Jack Sommerton flush—''the Earl of Kerlain was dancing attendance on Lady Clara. Not that he was entirely successful in the endeavor, of course. Every woman at Almack's was ready to throw her out a window just to have a chance at gaining the man's attention.''

Lucien set the delicate china cup into its saucer with rattling force. ''It's nothing to worry about. He's just doing what he can to win that ludicrous bet. That's all.''

''Really?'' Manning asked with mock astonishment, sitting forward to perch his elbows on the table. ''Do tell.''

Lucien felt himself growing hot. ''Robby . . .''

"Do you know, Lucky, I've never felt quite so close to throttling you as I do at this moment. Not because of that idiotic bet, though that's certainly enough cause, but because you left a complete innocent to fend for herself in the muck that you've birthed. If you can't imagine how all of London is whispering this morning because of your absence last night, because you left your fiancée to dance in the Earl of Kerlain's arms—*twice*—at Almack's, then your wits have gone utterly begging. And *you,*" he said to Jack before that man could open his mouth, "being such a good friend, encourage him!"

"Not really," Jack said meekly. "It's not actual encouragement, my lord. It's more like . . . lending support." He smiled his most charming smile, which only made the Earl of Manning scowl.

"Do you deny that you and Severn betted with him against Kerlain?"

Jack cleared his throat. "Ah, yes, I believe we did. It seemed like the supportive thing to do at the moment."

"Kerlain's a dog," Lucien stated, saying once more, "It's nothing to worry about. I'll make Clara stay away from him."

"God spare me," Manning uttered with savage control. "I vow you tempt me to get my horsewhip and give you what you damned well deserve. Now you listen to me, my boy. Both of you listen." He included Jack in his scorn as he set his palms flat on the table and leaned forward to embrace them with the heat of his anger. "I can't save you from that wager with Kerlain. You've made your own beds there and must take what comes—like men, I pray. But I can keep you from hurting any others, and I will. Understand me, gentlemen, and conduct yourselves accordingly. This is the only warning you get." A moment of heavy silence passed as he looked from one to the other.

"Ahem," said Jack, tugging at his cravat. "Good heavens, look at the time. I must be going or I'll miss an appointment with my man of business. Thank you for the convivial morning, sir.'' He stood. ''Can't think when I've enjoyed myself more or eaten such marvelous crepes.''

The doors to the room opened once more and Hemmet entered, clearing his throat loudly. ''Pardon me, m'lords. Viscount Severn is wearing out the carpet in the green salon and wanting to know whether he should be fitted for mourning clothes, which, considering his size, require no small amount of time and effort for his tailor to produce. He doesn't wish to attend the funeral improperly attired and is certain your lordship will understand.''

''Of course,'' the Earl of Manning replied coolly. ''Please assure Viscount Severn that Viscount Callan is still counted among the living. For the time being. Better yet,'' he added, looking at Jack, ''you go and have a word with him, Rexley. Give him my regards, won't you?'' His meaning was perfectly clear.

Jack made a half bow. ''Certainly, sir. I'll pass them along exactly as you expressed only a moment ago.''

''Thank you.'' The earl gave a sigh, his solemn gaze coming to rest on Lucien, who was methodically eating his crepes. ''Oh, dear. He's got that stubborn look on his face, may God have mercy on me. You children are making me old before my time. You might as well come for dinner, Rexley. I promised Monsieur Dellard he could put on one of his grand events in order to make up for this morning's unfortunate debacle. Bring Severn along.''

''Thank you, sir. I shall look forward to it.''

''Go on with you then,'' the earl said with a chuckle. ''And stop making me feel so ancient with those polite manners. You could drive a Quaker to sin with that meek, convincing face.''

With a laugh, the Earl of Rexley departed the room, and

as Hemmet shut the doors his calm voice could be heard over the sound of Viscount Severn's more anxious one.

"You're rich in friends," the earl commented once the sound of their voices died away, "if not in brains."

Lucien pushed his plate away, his food half-uneaten. "I apologize for the fuss. I apologize for not being home early enough to keep the gossips from talking. I apologize for not attending at Almack's last night." He lifted his chin slightly. "I suppose you'll want to discuss Pamela now."

The smile that curled the earl's lips didn't reach his eyes. "Not at all."

"I'll not be seeing her again until after the wedding, if that's what you're worried about. I shall be the most devoted bridegroom London has ever known. Not that I've failed in that regard yet, despite last night's error. I should think Clara's grown more than weary of my company. And after that debacle at Lord and Lady Berrydale's I've been given to understand that Clara and I are considered a shockingly romantic pair. *Despite* the wager."

"Lucien," the earl said gently, "I don't ask you to go against your inclinations where Clara Harkhams is concerned. It's clear that you can't love the girl, and if you must put her away at Pearwood eventually, so be it. I imagine any woman would be happier living away from an unloving husband than with one. I ask only one thing of you. Don't make Clara pay for the sins your parents committed. She is not your mother and you are not your father. And I can see by the look on your face that you're becoming angry. You really can be tiresome, my boy. It's only morning and already I begin to feel exhausted. Very well." The earl pushed his chair back and stood. "I know you'll do the best you can, and that's all I can hope for. Go and make yourself ready and we'll be on our way. And make certain to scrub yourself thoroughly, please. You stink of Lady Halling's unfortunate choice in perfume, which isn't at all the thing when one is going to visit one's future wife. By the by,'' he added as he stopped at the breakfast room doors, ''Clara's parents made an unexpected return to St. Genevieve yesterday, as several members of their unruly brood—the three older boys, I believe—somehow managed to contract the influenza.''

''They'll return in time for the wedding, won't they?''

''Goodness, I certainly hope so,'' said the earl. ''I don't want to be left in charge of the affair, after all.''

Lucien twisted in his chair as his uncle opened the doors. ''Who's with Clara, then, as chaperone?''

Robert Bryland gave his nephew an even look. ''Her aunt arrived yesterday to take up the reins in St. Genevieve's stead. I'm sure you know who I mean.''

Lucien stared at him with disbelief. ''Robby,'' was all he said, in a voice that never failed to soften the Earl of Manning's heart, as he knew very well that he was the only person alive whom his complicated nephew spoke to with such compassion.

''Yes,'' the earl replied gently. ''Anna Huntington. Heed me and beware, Lucky, for if I can't make you behave in a suitable fashion, Lady Anna certainly will.''

Chapter Six

"Late, of course." Anna Huntington fastened the brooch above her left breast and checked her appearance with quick finality. "He always was. Always will be. Probably late from the start, coming out of the womb, I'd wager. It's supposed to be fashionable to keep people waiting, or so he used to say, and that man is nothing if not fashionable."

Standing behind the chair in which her aunt was sitting, Clara gazed at the other woman's reflection with worry. "I'm sure there's a reasonable explanation for the delay. He did send a note."

"Of course he did." Anna tucked several loose strands of her rich blond hair back into their places. "He's the most well-mannered man on God's earth. If Death walked into the Earl of Manning's sitting room, he'd be given a chair and a cup of tea before Robert got around to asking him to what did he owe the pleasure of the visit."

"The earl has been wonderful since we arrived in London," Clara said. "I don't know how we would have gotten along without him. He's arranged everything for our comfort, and so easily."

"I'm sure he has," Anna agreed dryly.

"He's been very kind," Clara insisted. "What a mess there would be if he hadn't. You know how hopeless Papa is about such matters."

Anna Huntington met her niece's gaze in the mirror and

said, frankly, "I know exactly how your papa is, but even so, I can scarce believe he's let this horrific marriage go through."

"Oh, no, Auntie . . ."

Anna turned in her chair and took hold of Clara's slender hands. "I'm sorry, Clara, but I do not approve of Viscount Callan any more than I approve of his uncle. He'll give you nothing but misery in the years to come, and I could wring my brother's neck for being so naive as to think otherwise. All he remembers is how gentle and kind Edward was, which is natural, I suppose, since they were the dearest of friends. But a dead man's memory is far from reason enough to make a sacrifice of you to his dreadful son."

"It's not a sacrifice." Clara squeezed Anna's hands. "Please understand. I want to marry Lucien, although I'll admit to having had some qualms about it in the past. And Papa never would have made me do so if I hadn't willingly agreed. In all truth, I think he and Mama have been worried, too."

With a sigh, Anna stood and moved toward one of the room's long windows, where she looked down to the street.

"Late," she said with a shake of her head. "Robert, you exasperating man." A moment of silence, then, "They're mad, you know. The whole lot of them. The Brylands cause little more than trouble, whatever they're about. Clara," she said slowly, carefully, "you've got one week left to think about what you're doing. It's still not too late to call it off. I can take you back to St. Genevieve with less than a moment's notice if you change your mind. Right up to the day of the wedding. But if you go through with it, if you marry Lucien Bryland, you may never have another such chance to be free of him."

Clara, joining her aunt by the window, smiled reassuringly. "No, I won't. I don't think I should be free of Lucien even if we abided on opposite ends of the earth. I've tried to change that, but it's no use. I know the kind of man he is, Auntie, and I'd be a liar to say that I'm not a little afraid, but what else can I do?"

"Oh, my dear," Anna murmured. "Is that how it is?" She touched her niece's cheek with her fingertips. "I'm sorry, then. So very sorry."

"Please tell me what happened between you and the earl all those years ago," Clara asked softly, biting her lower lip when she saw pain cross her aunt's lovely features. "Forgive me for asking. I know you don't wish to speak of it. It's just that, last night, when you saw each other at Almack's, I couldn't help but wonder what happened to break things between you. You loved him once. I know you did, for although I was young at the time, I remember it clearly. Last night, when you saw him, you looked at him just the way you used to do. And he looked at you in the same way. As if he were starving, half mad with it, and you were the only food that could cure his hunger."

"Clara!"

"It's true," she insisted, flushing more hotly than her aunt did. "I wasn't the only one who saw it. You stood there like two statues staring at each other for more than half a minute. Everyone in the room was watching by the time he finally came up to speak to you."

"Oh, Clara." Anna made a sound like a weary groan and went to sit on her bed. "It's very difficult to explain. The world looks fully different when one is young and in love. I—he and I both—made mistakes. It's why I don't want you to make one now by marrying Viscount Callan. Mistakes like that aren't simple things, love. They take over your entire life, change the course of it. And when you're older and can see more clearly, then it's too late to go back. The course is set, and you can't return to where you started from."

"You wish you'd married him then?" Clara asked, sitting beside her on the bed. "The earl?"

"It doesn't really matter now," Anna replied gently. "I didn't marry him, and now I have Sarah and a life that Robert Bryland hasn't any part in. But what you really mean to ask is whether I regret the decision I made in breaking my engagement to the earl, although I suppose that's stating the matter too simply. I regret my youth and inexperience and my foolish, girlish notions about what love should be. I can look back and realize with clarity that if I had only known then what I know now, I never would have behaved so rashly in breaking the engagement. Understand me, Clara. Your Uncle Philip was a fine man and a wonderful husband, and I've missed him every day since he died."

"Of course," Clara said quickly. "I loved Uncle Philip dearly."

"As did I," Anna agreed. "And even if I hadn't, he gave me Sarah, who is the most precious joy in my life."

"But you loved the earl so much."

"I did," Anna admitted. "I loved him so much that I thought my heart would burst from the feeling. I used to lie awake nights in my bed and feel a complete sense of awe simply because the man existed. It's difficult to explain," she said with some chagrin. "Looking back, I can see that even the enormity of feeling, the way I fed it and let it grow wild, was immature. Something akin to swimming in an ocean and letting oneself drown because the water gives such a pleasant sensation. And I thought he shared my feelings. But perhaps love isn't fashionable enough for someone like Robert." Her voice took on a hint of bitterness. "Oh, I don't doubt that he had feelings for me. He made that clear enough on a number of occasions. Again, looking back, I can see that for what it was." She gave her niece a half smile. "Physical desire. Little more than that, I'm afraid."

Clara's somber expression held fast. "What happened?"

"I made the colossal mistake of asking him for fidelity. That, my dear, was most definitely unfashionable. A man who doesn't keep a mistress or two on the side will be a shocking disappointment to his fellows. Good heavens, don't look at me that way. I'm not speaking of men like your father." She chuckled. "I should have been more clear. A fashionable man, like Robert, who cares about how he's perceived in the eyes of the *ton*—that's the sort of man we're talking about.

"I knew Robert had a mistress. A very beautiful actress named Diana whom he'd kept for two years before he met me. So, thinking that his love for me matched mine for him, I asked him to be quit of her, and he agreed. In fact, he told me that he'd already decided to put an end to the arrangement before he asked me to marry him."

Clara hadn't expected that. "He did? But, then—"

"They were only words, love," Anna said. "Not the truth. I found Diana and him together in London after Robert brought me here to make arrangements for the wedding. Found them twice, actually. The first time was at Vauxhall, after Robert had excused himself from our party and been gone long enough for me to begin to worry. One of his friends escorted me on my search, and we came across the Earl of Manning and his beautiful mistress in the midst of what I think I should only describe for your tender ears as a very affectionate embrace."

"Oh, dear," said Clara.

"Indeed," Anna said with a faint smile. "That's just what I thought, too. He managed to explain it away as being their final parting, during which he'd necessarily felt obliged to reassure his mistress that he wasn't putting her aside because she'd done anything to displease him. Then, of course, after he'd told her what he was giving her in the way of a settlement, she wished to express her gratitude, which is the touching moment that his friend and I came upon. I must say, I have long since admired the woman's acting abilities. She managed to look both horrified and pleased all at once upon being discovered.''

"Oh, no, Aunt Anna," Clara said with clear distress. "How awful. Did the earl apologize?"

"Apologize?" Anna repeated with a laugh. "My dear, he was positively purple with regret. He went so far as to get down on his knees the next morning when your Great-Aunt Eunice finally let him in through the doors. That didn't matter so much, of course. All the man had to do was kiss me and I was ready to fall at his feet. It was, as I have said, a rather foolish love on my part.''

"You forgave him?"

"Completely," Anna assured her. "I believed every word he told me about what had happened, as well as his promise that he would never have anything to do with the beautiful Diana again. I *wanted* to believe him, and in him, and that he was at least a man of honor. As much as anything else, it was the fact that his promises were really lies that led me to break the engagement. I suppose I could have eventually learned to bear the knowledge of his indiscretions, if he'd chosen not to speak of them, but knowing that he had lied, on his knees, yet, looking right into my eyes . . .'' She shook her head. "I couldn't marry a man whom I couldn't trust. It was impossible.''

"But the earl seems to be a man of honor," Clara countered. "I cannot merit him doing such a thing, not without some reasonable explanation.''

Anna's expression grew solemn, pained. "I caught him leaving his mistress's house in broad daylight only a few days after he'd made all his grand promises and protestations of innocence. It was morning. Your great-aunt and I had gone out early to keep an appointment for the final fitting of my wedding gown. The traffic was heavy, and progress necessarily slow. I have often wondered at how different life would be today if our coachman hadn't decided to take a different route than the one we normally would have followed. I never would have seen Robert leaving her house, otherwise. But there he was, standing in her doorway, his clothing rumpled after what must have been a very long night, his face unshaven. It was clear that he'd spent the night there, with her.''

"You're certain it was her house?" Clara asked. "Diana's? You didn't actually see her, did you?"

"No, I didn't, but I did see Robert, and he saw me. I have never beheld an expression before or since that could match his in that moment. His mouth even fell open. But,'' she said with a sigh, "the Earl of Manning is nothing if not correct. He shut his mouth and put his hat on his head and walked away before there was a chance of anyone else catching us gaping at each other like half-wits. Needless to say, I didn't keep my appointment for the fitting. He arrived in Aunt Eunice's drawing room an hour later and admitted that he had spent the night in Diana's house. He'd been celebrating our upcoming marriage with several of his friends and had gotten drunk enough to be confused about what was what. He took himself off to Diana's out of old habit, he said, because she always took such good care of him.''

"Good heavens," Clara murmured. "I suppose . . . I suppose that makes some sense.''

"I suppose it does," Anna agreed, standing and returning to the window, where she stood in silence for a full minute before saying, "He apologized in a heartfelt manner and promised, again, that the situation would never repeat itself. I asked him why I should trust him a second time, and he said, simply, that I must, otherwise there was no

sense in us being wed. A man and wife should have that
much in common, at least. He had given me his word and
felt that I should take it as offered. He didn't mean to have
to keep trying to earn my faith in him. If I couldn't give it
freely, if I couldn't believe him when he had given his word
of honor, then he wasn't going to beg.''

More silence passed as she gazed down into the street,
her face a mask of impassivity. ''It was almost as if I were
the one at fault, not he, and it was in that moment that I
realized he didn't love me at all. He simply wanted me
physically and as a proper, well-bred countess. He would
marry me and be a good, kind, considerate husband, but he
would never love me. And so,'' she murmured, ''I took his
ring from my finger and gave it back to him. He spoke only
once after that, in the flattest tone I've ever heard any human speak, asking me not to break the engagement.'' Anna
lifted a hand and pressed it flat against the pane of glass she
was gazing at. ''He even said please. But I wouldn't give
way. I was stubborn and angry. And foolish. My heart was
shattered, but not my pride. I told him to leave, and he
did.'' She closed her eyes and pressed her forehead to the
window. ''He did. That was nearly eleven years ago. Last
night in Almack's is the first time I've seen him since.''

''Oh, Aunt Anna, I'm sorry.''

The tears in her niece's voice brought Anna's head up,
eyes open and smiling.

''Don't be foolish, love. It was all a long time ago. Life
must be taken as it comes, and with as little regret as possible.''

''But you loved him!'' Clara cried. ''How could you have
married Uncle Philip, knowing that?''

''I don't regret marrying Colonel Huntington. But I have
admitted to myself that it was a mistake to marry so quickly
without giving Robert, and myself, enough time to make
things right. It wasn't particularly fair to Philip, either. I did

to him exactly what I felt Robert meant to do to me. I married him without love, and only because I knew we could be comfortable together. If I was going to be such a hypocrite, I might as well have been one with Robert, whom I did love. But I had made my choice, you see, and could not turn back.''

''You still love the Earl of Manning,'' Clara stated, wiping away the lone tear that had fallen on her cheek.

''It doesn't matter whether I do or not. I made my bed and have learned to lie there happily and with contentment. The question you should be asking, my dear, is whether the choice you're making in wedding Viscount Callan is the right one for you. I lost Robert Bryland because I wasn't able to make myself think clearly, because I made a decision in the heat of strong emotions and was too proud to change it. Don't make yourself marry that coldhearted man for the same reasons, love. Think a moment before you give yourself into his keeping for the rest of your life. Do you really believe that Lucien Bryland loves you, or even cares for you?''

Silent, Clara shook her head slowly.

''He was a dark, sullen boy,'' Anna said, ''and he's become a dark, sullen man. You've always been as bright and clear as sunshine. If you can manage to bring some light into his life it will be a miracle. I'm very afraid it's going to be the other way around.''

''I love him,'' Clara said, lowering her gaze to the hands in her lap. ''Even if he drags me down into darkness, I shall at least have that.''

With an unhappy frown, Anna Huntington contemplated the top of her niece's lowered head until a movement in the street below drew her attention.

''They've arrived,'' she said. ''And here is Robert, coming out of the carriage with all the slow elegance of a cat. Such a nimble man. I might have known he'd only become more handsome as he aged.'' Leaving the window, she went to collect her hat. ''Other men have the grace to get old, but Robert Bryland must necessarily do better. Come along, Clara. Go and fetch your bonnet. I want to get this over with.''

Chapter Seven

The day was a disaster, complete and total. Leaning with a silent sigh against a sturdy bookcase, the Earl of Manning watched as Lady Anna, Lady Clara, and his nephew made their circumference of the library at Barrington Place. The ladies, although Lady Clara more so, were pointing out all of the changes that had been made to the place in the past month, and Lucien was dutifully, if with questionable interest, nodding and muttering what the earl prayed were some manner of decent responses.

The expedition had been doomed from the start, he decided. His nephew's late arrival had necessarily caused their arrival at the Marquess of St. Genevieve's London house to be equally late, which event would normally have passed as an understandable and minor breech of etiquette if Anna Huntington hadn't greeted them looking like an avenging angel come out of God's heaven and declaring in the kind of polite tone that made one grit one's teeth that some things *never* changed. Lucien, already angry and unforgiving, had set the pace after that, behaving so coldly and sarcastically to Lady Anna that the earl had wanted to pull him off to the privacy of the nearest hallway and throttle him. As it was, he'd set his hand on the back of his nephew's neck in a familiar gesture, one that looked affectionate enough to onlookers but was sufficiently painful to make Lucien aware of his uncle's displeasure. The boy had

behaved a little better after that, although his acid reply of
"You should be an authority on that, my lady," to Lady
Anna's remark about the numerous elderly dragons she'd
had to face down at Almack's had got the war going again.
Gad, they were worse than two alley cats having a quarrel
over a leftover scrap, with Clara playing the part of the
scrap. After an hour of striving to keep the situation peaceful, the young woman looked exhausted, and if Robert
could have managed it, he would have whisked her away to
some quiet, comfortable spot and left the other two to fight
to their hearts' content.

The little girl had been a surprise. A shocking, sweet
little surprise, a tiny duplicate of her mother whose sudden
appearance and obvious identity had sent splinters of shock
all the way from the top of Robert's head right down into
his toes.

She'd been hiding behind the curtains in the drawing
room where they'd been sent to await Lady Anna and Lady
Clara. A few moments after the doors closed he and Lucien
had heard a sniffling sound and exchanged glances, but the
next moment she'd come out, wiping her wet red cheeks
and facing them with admirable boldness.

"I'm Sarah Huntington," she declared with tremendous
pride. Then she thrust her doll forward, using both hands,
one gripping the body and the other the detached head with
all its red curls dangling. "And this is Margaret."

He'd been spellbound, first thinking, *This is what Anna
looked like as a child,* for she truly was a mirror of her
mother, from her gold hair to her dark blue eyes to her
shocking beauty, and next thinking, *Anna had a child and I
never knew.* It was Lucien who'd gone to her first, bending
down and saying, kindly, "My goodness, she's had a fall,
has she? Poor little Margaret. Let's have a look and see if
we can't put her on the mend."

The child had nodded dolefully and Robert had regained

his senses. By the time Anna and Clara arrived they'd all three been kneeling on the floor with Robert suggesting a visit to a very special sort of doctor who'd surely be able to put Margaret to rights.

It had been obvious by her foreboding expression that Anna was displeased for him to have met her daughter, and the child's nurse had been called at once to take Sarah away to the nursery. The nurse, a thin, solemn creature whom Robert was certain gave small children nightmares, scolded the little girl for being so careless as to ruin her toys. Shocked that Anna would allow a servant to publicly speak to her child in such a manner, Robert had opened his mouth to deliver a scold of his own, only to be beaten by Sarah, who lifted her chin, speared the nurse with a frigid gaze, and said in an imperious tone, "Margaret is not *ruined*." She drew the word out as if it applied only to ignorant country girls who became dockside whores. "She only fell off her horse and broke her neck and now she's going to the doctor." With that, the child marched to Robert, placed the doll's head and body in his hands, turned on her heel, and strolled calmly from the room, leaving the frowning, head-shaking nurse to follow.

Anna had tried to get the doll back, but Robert had politely declined on the grounds that he'd given his word to a lady, which as much as constituted a debt of honor. Margaret, both parts of her, now resided in the earl's elegant carriage, waiting in front of Barrington Place for them to finish their inspection. Robert almost wished he were out there with her.

From the time that his parents died, Lucien had hated Barrington, which was his mother's ancestral home and where he had not only been born but had lived until he'd gotten old enough to attend school. Robert had taken him there only once, right after he'd collected him from Eton, two days after his parents' death, to give him an opportunity to take anything he might want to remember them by. The boy had stared hauntedly about the place, so pained by whatever memories he held that Robert had taken him away again almost at once. Over the years he'd made attempts, gentle hints and outright commands, to get Lucien back into the house that was his by inheritance, but had been unable to make him return for any reason. Now he had a gently bred wife to think of and, as Robert had expressly told him during the numerous times they'd argued the matter, it was his duty to provide her with the kind of home she deserved.

Both sober and drunk, Lucien had made every possible attempt to keep from opening Barrington and making it livable. He first suggested that he and Clara would simply live at Manning House. The earl, with polite regret, had declined this pleasure. Then Lucien had come up with the idea of selling Barrington and buying another dwelling. The earl had expressed distaste for this, as the selling of a beautiful, fine, and ancestral home disgusted every noble feeling. The *ton* would gossip wholeheartedly, which always gave Robert a splitting headache. He also pointed out that if Lucien attempted to do such a foolish thing, he'd find that every potential buyer would shortly experience a change of heart after receiving a visit from the earl himself. Defeated only temporarily, Lucien had returned two days later with the threat that he'd burn Barrington to the ground and thereafter rebuild a house so much bigger and better that all of London would reel from its excellence. This, Robert had taken pains to point out, would certainly be entertaining, but Lucien would scarce be able to enjoy it while ensconced in Newgate for the crime of committing arson. The boy had only given in on the day after Clara had arrived in London, when Lucien, having duly paid his fiancée a visit to welcome her to town, had returned to Manning House bearing a dazed expression and saying, with equally dazed amazement, "I took her out for a drive, just for some air. We got through the park and then—gad, I must've been dreaming like a lackwit the whole while. Somehow we ended up at Barrington and I told her I'd have the place opened up so she could make it livable."

It had been an encouraging sign, Robert thought. More encouraging when, as the days passed, Lucien occasionally accompanied Clara and her mother to Barrington to oversee the work being done there by the army of decorators, painters, and carpenters Lucien had hired to do his future bride's bidding. The money and effort had certainly been well spent, for Clara had turned Barrington into an entirely new dwelling, so different from what it had once been when Lucien had lived there as a boy that Robert could only admire her clever, intuitive nature at knowing what would best please his difficult nephew.

She was a thorough delight, he thought as he surveyed Clara's slender form from across the room, where she stood between Anna and Lucien pointing out the ancient tapestry she'd discovered hiding away in the attic and which she had subsequently had cleaned and repaired and hung. Lucien wouldn't realize it for a while yet, but he was a very fortunate man. Clara Harkhams wasn't a beauty by any stretch of the imagination, but she was possessed of qualities far more valuable than mere beauty. And she certainly dressed well, enhancing every feature with the sort of reserved skill that Robert admired in a female. Of course, any female standing beside Anna Huntington would look rather pale by comparison, regardless how well dressed.

Anna was more stunning now than when she'd been twenty and the most acclaimed beauty of the *ton*. She had been a budding flower, then. Now she was a rose in full bloom, so blindingly beautiful that he ached just looking at her. He'd known eleven years ago that his fortune in obtaining her hand had been too good to be true, and in the end it had been. With every unmarried man in England throwing himself at her feet, she'd stubbornly waited three seasons before finally accepting a proposal—*his* proposal— and he still hadn't been able to meet the impossibly high standards she'd set for a mate. He wondered, as he lazily contemplated the curves of her wonderful figure, if that ideal man she'd always maddeningly compared him to, Colonel Huntington, had managed to do it.

"What do you think, my lord?"

Clara's strained voice broke through his reverie, calling him back to attention and to the fact that Lady Anna was clutching her reticule as if she was about to use it as a weapon and that Lucien was so far gone in anger that his lips had pulled back into a snarl, which he was directing, not surprisingly, at Lady Anna. Clara, moving toward him with both hands held out, looked as if she was about to burst into tears.

Taking her hands and squeezing them reassuringly, the Earl of Manning replied, "I think you've done a magnificent job, my dear." He set an arm about her waist and felt, with some unease, just how taut she was. "And that these two don't know anything about the matter. I'm quite worn out from listening to them, fussy as they are, like two old grannies. Aren't you?" He smiled as he led her back toward the others and was pleased to see her smile in turn, although the effort was accompanied by a woeful, watery laugh. "I don't think they could either one be pleased, no matter how hard one might try to do so."

"Maybe not," she admitted, glancing worriedly at both her aunt and Lucien as they neared them.

"You mean to say you *like* this monstrosity?" Lucien demanded, waving a hand at the tapestry.

"Of course I like it," Robert said, glaring at him pointedly. "What's more, I appreciate it, as well as the fact that it was created from the considerate and considerable labor of our ancestors. If one gazes at it long enough, one might be fortunate enough to realize just how invaluable a work it is.''

A stony look came over Lucien's features at that, the same set, stubborn expression Robert had grown used to over the years, which always signaled impending doom. He'd tried every manner of persuasion since he'd had the care of his nephew to make him behave with some sort of polish, from coaxing to bribing to outright punishment, but to no avail. If Lucien was going to lose his temper, then Lucien was going to lose his temper. The best thing that could be done was to get the innocent out of the way of harm, or rather, anyone whom Lucien might consider venting his wrath upon. To that end, Robert gently pushed Clara in his nephew's direction, watching with satisfaction as Lucien's arm circled possessively about the girl's waist, and then turned his attention to Lady Anna. ''Would you do me the great pleasure, my lady, of accompanying me through the gardens? I understand the renovations there are quite stunning.''

She gave him a look that could've frozen a polar bear. ''I will *not* leave my niece alone with this arrogant, ill-mannered—''

''Thank you, my lady.'' Robert's hand closed over her wrist, pulling her forcibly away from the younger couple. ''I can't tell you how grateful I am at having the honor of your company. You children continue on with the tour, if you please. Lady Anna and I will return shortly.''

Anna valiantly resisted the force that dragged her away. ''Clara,'' she said as Robert tugged her through the library doors, ''you needn't stay and suffer that mannerless bore's company—Robert Bryland! I am not a horse to be led about!''

''Certainly not, my lady,'' Robert's gentle voice drifted

into the room before he shut the doors behind them, and then Lucien and Clara were alone.

Silent, Clara pulled free of Lucien's hold and went to stand in front of the ancient tapestry. Presently, she said, ''I should have asked for your opinion before I had the workmen hang this. I'll have it removed at once.''

Behind her, she could hear him releasing a tense breath. ''No, leave it. Robby's right. It's a valuable tapestry, probably something my father admired a great deal but which my mother wouldn't allow to be displayed. Leave it as it is. Please.'' She heard him moving up behind her and stiffened. ''Clara.'' With a tentative touch on her arm, he turned her around to face him. ''My behavior this morning has been inexcusably rude, and I apologize. The circumstances of our marriage aren't what either of us would prefer, but I don't wish to make the matter markedly unpleasant for you.''

Clara found it impossible to believe that he meant the words. She had thought it would be a simple matter to prove herself to him after she'd first arrived in London, but now, after two months of trying, she was inclined to think that Aunt Anna was right. Rather than bringing to life the love Clara knew Lucien had once felt for her, she wondered if he wouldn't, instead, manage to kill all of what she felt for him.

''It's your home, Lucien,'' she said slowly, keeping the emotions she felt out of her tone. ''You should feel comfortable here. If there's something I've done, some change I've made, that displeases you, you must tell me so that I can put it to rights.''

The faint vulnerability that had possessed his handsome features as he'd made his apology vanished, to be replaced by wariness.

''It's going to be your home as well, Clara.'' His fingers

tightened on her arm. "Everything of yours will be here. Every possession you value."

There it was again, that distrust, rearing its ugly head. It never seemed to fade, regardless of how many promises she gave him. Feeling suddenly quite weary, she replied, "Yes, Lucien, I realize that. I've left nothing at St. Genevieve with the intention of returning there. Everything I value most dearly is here at Barrington." *Including you,* she nearly added, stopping herself when she realized that he would only mock the words. She'd tried several times in the past weeks to tell him that she loved him, had loved him since that long-ago summer they'd spent together, that she had never given her heart to another, but he didn't seem to want to hear such things. She doubted he'd believe her, were she able to speak the words.

His expression changed once more with the rapidity Clara was becoming increasingly used to, softening his features again even as his grip softened, until his fingers rubbed gently over the tender flesh on her arm where Lucien probably realized he'd hurt her.

"I'm sorry," he apologized again. "I think seeing your aunt after all these years—remembering what Robby went through after she left him for that Colonel Huntington fellow—I think maybe it's made me a little . . ." He left the thought unfinished, gave a single shake of his head, then smiled at her in an embarrassed, self-conscious manner that made Clara's heart thump painfully in her chest. "The house is beautiful, Clara. I never believed I'd bring myself to live in it again, but you've made it all over into something new. I hardly recognize the place."

Praise from Lucien was as rare as his smiles, so that Clara couldn't hold back the smile that formed on her own lips. "I'm glad, if you like it. You won't remember, perhaps, but you told me once about what had happened between your parents, about some of your memories of

Barrington.'' At the sight of his skin darkening, she hurried
on. ''I don't mean to make you think of all that, Lucien, but
that's why I made so many changes. If we're to live happily
here, then we must put the past behind us and make a fresh
start. We'll replace all of your old memories with ones
we'll make. Good ones, Lucien,'' she added, wanting him
to understand. ''If you want that as much as I do.''

He was staring at her so intently that she gave a start
when she felt the backs of his fingers stroking lightly down
her cheek.

''I remember every word we said to each other that summer,'' he murmured. ''I remember every single moment.
But I never thought you would.''

The warmth of his hand against her skin, this first touching after so many weeks, seemed to make her entire body
tingle. She felt suddenly short of breath and parted her lips
to draw in more air. Lucien's eyes followed the movement,
his gaze lingered, and then he lowered his head slowly and
kissed her with all the gentleness and care that he'd used
when he was sixteen years old. Clara held herself very still,
afraid that any movement might dispel the wonder of the
moment. When he lifted his head and gazed down at her,
her heart soared with hope. He was himself again, the Lucien she had fallen in love with so long ago. In another
moment, quick as the blink of an eye, he was gone again,
retreating behind a mask of indifference, yet the hope in
Clara's heart remained, even as Lucien dropped his hand
and stepped away and said, ''We'd better see the rest of it
before Robby and your aunt return. Have you been pleased
with the servants I hired?''

''Yes,'' she replied, following as he moved to the library
doors. He sounded just as bored as he had all morning, but
Clara didn't care. She was so giddy with delight that she
felt as if she would be walking on clouds for the remainder
of the day, no matter what Lucien either said or did. At the

doors he stopped and turned and, almost hesitantly it seemed to Clara, held out his arm.

"My lady?" he said, making it sound very much like a dare, as if she wouldn't accept his arm otherwise.

The chivalrous gesture surprised her almost more than his gentle kiss had. He had never before offered her his arm when they were alone, but only when there were onlookers to make a public display for.

"Thank you," she murmured, curling her fingers under his arm, feeling the strength of the muscles beneath the fabric of his clothes. "My lord," she added.

They stood thus, looking at each other in silence before Lucien drew in a long, steady breath, straightened resolutely, and opened the doors.

It was the first time in years that they'd spent any amount of time together companionably. Walking with her now through Barrington, feeling the heat of her small hand on his arm, listening to the pleasant chatter that had always seemed to him more beautiful than music, he experienced such a tumble of conflicting emotions that he could barely make sense of anything she was saying about chairs and drapes and floor coverings.

He was a fool, he told himself. She didn't love him, had never loved him, and if she smiled and flirted and gazed at him with desire it didn't mean a thing. She would do the same to any other man who showed an interest in her, just as his mother had done. Hadn't Clara already charmed her way through half of London's male population? Even Jack and Wulf had fallen for her, he thought grimly, glancing into her animated face as she pointed at a large Grecian urn that was set near the house's grand stairway.

Oh, yes, his dearest friends had quickly fallen victim to the Peahen's estimable charms. Jack had elbowed him in the ribs on the night he'd met Clara at the Ramsey ball, after he'd finished partnering her in a waltz, and declared,

''Whatever can you mean to go about calling that delightful girl a peahen? She's not a beauty, certainly, but what a marvelous figure. Slender and sleek as a cat. Makes a man wonder what it might be like to pet her. And such charming manners. It's not surprising she's got so many admirers back in St. Genevieve. Can't you just imagine what that shining hair will look like when it's loose? Gad, I envy you, Lucky.''

Wulf had been more restrained, remarking, ''She's just as nice as Bella. If anybody talked about Bella the way you talk about Lady Clara I'd be rather put out.'' Which was, Lucien knew, Wulf's typically meek way of saying that he'd probably do the offending person mortal harm.

Lucien had promised himself that first year in Oxford, after Clara had shattered him into so many pieces, after he'd finally managed to crawl past the bitterness and anger and misery, that he'd never let himself be so vulnerable again. To anyone. But perhaps it was impossible. Last night, with Pam, he'd determinedly done everything he could to push Clara's image from his mind, but even as he'd bedded his mistress in one of their usual tempestuous encounters he'd found no peace. It was almost as if Clara had been standing by the bed watching them, chiding, making him feel, of all strange things, guilty.

But it didn't matter. He had trusted Clara once and she had carelessly riven him, heart and soul. He wouldn't trust her again. Want her, yes. Have her, yes. Trust her? He'd be an idiot if he did.

And yet, he thought as they went into the study, she had done all of this, changed Barrington so completely be-cause—he could scarce believe he'd heard her right—because she'd remembered what he'd told her of his painful memories. She had remembered, when he had believed, all these years, that the summer that had been so precious to him had meant less than nothing to her.

"Look, Lucien." She was pulling him excitedly across the room. "Do you see?"

He saw, and said, "It's a chess set."

"With wooden soldiers!" She grinned at him. "Just like the ones you used to have. Even the regiments are the same. Do you remember?"

"Yes, of course." They'd been lying near the lake on one of their magical summer afternoons, making pictures out of the clouds that drifted by, and he'd told her of the collection of wooden soldiers he'd cherished when he'd been a boy. His mother had given them to a charity home during the first year that he'd been away at Eton and he'd actually cried over the loss. It was something he'd never admitted to anyone else, not even to Robby. But he'd told Clara.

"Thank you." He heard the words coming out of his mouth despite the fact that he wasn't conscious of saying them. "Thank you, Clara."

"You're welcome." She smiled up at him with the easy charm that he'd always envied, and set a hand upon his coat. "I'm so glad if you're pleased, Lucien."

Lifting her hand, he kissed her palm. "Yes, I am. Very much." Turning to look out across the large, inviting room, he said, "Everything is so changed. Clara, what is that? Never tell me—"

"It's a bagatelle board," she admitted sheepishly. "I thought you might find it amusing."

Laughing, dragging her over to admire the small, finely crafted table with its silver pins and rolling balls, he said, "I can tell that you think I'm a frivolous fellow, to waste his days laboring over such a device."

"Oh, no!" she assured him. "Not at all, Lucien. But I do want this to be the place that you'll always feel is yours. Where you can come to be alone, if you wish, or to bring your friends. It must be your own private refuge. I shall never intrude, or let the servants bother you here."

He dropped into the nearest chair, setting his hands about her waist and pulling her close, between his legs. "I won't mind if you intrude," he said, ignoring all the warning bells that his logical mind threw at him. He loved her. Had unceasingly loved her. She'd done this for him. He would finally grasp the peace and happiness that had eluded him for so many years. "It's perfect."

She resisted as he pulled her closer, saying, with red cheeks, "You haven't seen the upstairs, yet. Or the kitchen and servants' quarters."

"It doesn't matter. If they're half as well done as what I've seen thus far, they'll be more than suitable." He kissed her lingeringly, squeezing her waist lightly with his hands, breaking the contact only when she tried to slip her arms about his neck. "Will we be happy, Clara? Is it what you want?"

She searched his face, his eyes. "Is it what *you* want, Lucien?"

A brief thought that he was about to lose his wager with Kerlain passed through his thoughts, but he pushed it firmly away in the face of everything he was feeling. These were things too rare and hoped for to be denied by the logic he'd lived by for so long.

"What I want," he began, "is—"

"Clara!"

At the sound of Lady Anna's curt tone, Clara straightened and Lucien quickly stood. Equally embarrassed at having been caught in such an intimate embrace, they turned to face the study's open doorway. The sight of Lady Anna standing there, liberally covered with dirt, her blond hair falling free of its formerly elegant arrangement, and her gown with one sleeve torn off and its skirt ripped down the side, stunned them.

"Aunt Anna!" Clara cried. "What happened?"

"I'm terribly sorry for the intrusion," the Earl of Manning said as he appeared in an equally shocking condition. "It's my fault, I'm afraid."

"It most certainly is," Lady Anna agreed tightly, clutching the remnants of her reticule with both hands. "Collect your things, Clara. We're returning home at once."

"Robby," Lucien said with open bewilderment, moving to help his uncle brush the leaves and dirt from his coat. "Are you all right?"

"Oh, yes. Quite all right," Robby assured him, adding, when Lady Anna glared at him, "Well, as good as can be expected under the circumstances. We've ruined those lovely rosebushes in your garden, I fear."

"You fell into the rosebushes?" Clara asked with quick concern. "Oh, Auntie, are you sure you're all right? Did you suffer any scratches? And your beautiful dress!"

"Is as ruined as the rosebushes," Lady Anna stated hotly. "And we did *not* fall. Lord Manning pushed me."

"My lady, I realize you're quite upset," the earl said placatingly, "but I didn't actually—"

"You *pushed* me, you wretch!"

"Well, I suppose I did," he conceded politely, "but I certainly didn't mean to, and it was as much your fault as mine, Anna, you must admit that. I did try to catch you before you fell all the way in."

She gave him a cold, level, silent stare, then turned on her heel and walked away. Clara, with a worried glance at Lucien, followed behind.

"Are you sure you're all right, Robby?" Lucien asked, taking his uncle by both shoulders and looking him over. "Your eye . . ." He touched it gingerly, dropping his hand at once when the earl winced with pain.

"It's going to be black by this evening," Robert said with a half-laugh, half-groan. "She's got as much fire now as she did when she was a girl. More, probably. What a facer she planted me! I doubt Gentleman Jackson could have done so well.''

''She *struck* you?''

''Yes,'' Robert admitted, sighing. ''Just as soon as I pulled her out of the rosebushes. That's what sent me in.''

Lucien's expression filled with rage. ''I'll—I swear by heaven that I'll put my hands around that witch's throat and—''

''No, no. Calm yourself, Lucky.'' The earl waved a hand at his furious nephew, then pressed his palm against his aching forehead. ''I deserved what she gave me, and more. God help me,'' he said with sudden misery. ''After all these years, I thought I'd gotten over her, but it's as bad as it ever was. I don't know how she makes me so crazed.'' He dropped his hand from his lowered face. ''I insulted Lady Anna in the worst possible manner, Lucky, by forcing myself on her when she clearly didn't wish it. Oh, she participated for a moment or two, which only encouraged me to take greater advantage. Then, when she tried to push me away, she ended up falling into the rosebushes, adding injury to insult, I suppose you might say.'' He shut his eyes tightly. ''Oh, gad.''

The next moment he felt himself enveloped in his nephew's strong embrace, which for any other man might have been an uncomfortable gesture. For Robert, long used to his nephew's strong emotional nature and equally volatile swings in mood, it was simply comforting. Lifting a hand, he patted Lucien's back.

''Don't fret on it, Lucky. It's my trouble to care for.''

''I won't let her hurt you again.''

Robert hugged his nephew tightly, then released him, stepping back. ''I'm not as foolish now as I was then, my boy. Don't spare a moment of worry on my behalf. You're going to be married in a week's time, and will have your good lady wife to worry about and care for. If you would ease my mind, Lucky, then set your mind to those tasks and do everything in your power to make Lady Clara happy.''

''Of course I will,'' Lucien replied, but Robert could already see the curtain falling over his nephew's eyes, could see him retreating into the coldness that kept safe the vulnerable heart hiding within. Whatever tenderness Lucien had shown Clara earlier in the day was gone, vanishing beneath the fierce distrust he felt for all women.

Angry at himself for being the cause, determined to make whatever repairs he might, Robert said, levelly, ''You see, Lucien, I learned something out of all the misery I suffered after I drove Anna away.''

''You didn't drive her away,'' Lucien insisted angrily. ''She *left* you!''

''No,'' Robert told him firmly. ''I drove her away with my pride, with my insufferable need to be in complete control of our relationship. All she required of me was a sincere apology for what I'd done, and an honest promise that I would never fail her in such a way again. Was it so much to ask in the face of giving herself over to my care for a lifetime?'' He held out a hand to silence Lucien when he began to protest. ''If I could go back to her Aunt Eunice's drawing room and live that moment over, I tell you, Lucky, nay, I swear it, I would fall down on my knees and give her whatever she asked of me, and more. That,'' he said, dropping his hand, ''is the wisdom that comes to a man when he's had years to learn it. I can only pray, my very dear nephew, that you'll learn such lessons before you spend as many years regretting your follies as I have.''

Chapter Eight

❦

The Marquess of St. Genevieve's London town house was ablaze with light, beautiful with decorations, and filled with people. In the elegant ballroom, where those attending this celebration for the coming marriage of Viscount Callan and the marquess's only daughter, Lady Clara, had gathered to await the official opening of the ball, Lucien stood with Jack and Wulf, watching the Earl of Kerlain as he made his way toward them. It was a slow progression, as Kerlain was waylaid by several young ladies and their mamas who, with smiles and giggles, stopped him to speak. Kerlain appeared to be a master at such artifice, however, for he stayed only long enough to ensure near swoons and then deftly extracted himself and continued on his course.

"He's not human," Jack muttered irately. "And women are fools."

"We might as well admit the truth," Lucien said. "He's handsome, intelligent, and an utterly amoral rake."

"And penniless, to boot," Jack put in.

"And," Lucien finished as if he'd not been interrupted, "evidently quite irresistible."

Beside them, Wulf crossed his arms about his massive chest and made an unhappy sound. "Bella says he's charming. I don't know how she can think it." He looked across the room to where his bespectacled fiancée was speaking with Lady Clara. "I don't even know why she'd care about it. She never wants that from me."

Lucien and Jack exchanged amused glances.

"I'm sure that's only because your own charm is so great that she doesn't need to speak of the matter," Jack assured him. "You know what women are. Featherbrained, the lot of them. Can't remember the day of the week, let alone what they want in a man."

Wulf frowned. "Bella's not featherbrained. She can copy equations better than Hemstead's apprentices can. And she don't need help working them, either. I often use her as an assistant in the lab."

"Wulf, you romantic scoundrel," Lucien said dryly. "I'm sure Bella finds that terribly enthralling."

Wulf gave him a puzzled look. "She don't complain," he said. "Lady Clara's not featherbrained, either. At Vauxhall last night we discussed the phlogiston theory at length, and she enjoyed it a great deal."

"You discussed it," Lucien told him, "and Clara employed her good manners and tact to make you think she was listening. She knows how to be a pleasant companion."

"Why, Lucky," said Jack, "that almost sounds like a compliment for your charming bride-to-be."

Lucien shrugged. "It's a simple fact. I don't see why I should deny Clara's abilities. Any lady of good breeding would possess the same skills."

"Perhaps," Jack said, "but Lady Clara has proven to be exceptional. And she's quite popular with the *ton*. Have you noticed that many of the season's come outs have begun to emulate her manner of dress?"

"Clara's elegant," Lucien admitted more softly. "She always has been. Even barefooted and dressed in old clothes, she somehow managed to look . . ." He broke off with a slight shake of his head. "It doesn't matter. Here you are, at last, Kerlain. Thought you'd never make it through your swarm of admirers intact.''

"Callan," the earl greeted with a smile. "Rexley. Severn. Pleasant evening, isn't it? And the ball appears to be a success. Pity Lady Clara's mother couldn't attend. But the marquess is here, is he not?''

Lucien gave a curt nod. "He arrived just this morning. Unfortunately, Lady St. Genevieve has now taken ill, and he plans to leave again tomorrow afternoon."

"Ah, yes," Kerlain said with understanding. "After the wedding. It is a shame, but I understand that he would be anxious to return to the marchioness's side. And how are you holding up, Callan? This will be, as they say, your last night of freedom.''

Lucien gave him a chilly smile. "Hardly."

"Indeed?" Kerlain's expression filled with exaggerated surprise. "But you jest, of course." He turned to gaze at where Lady Clara and Miss Howell were laughing over something one of them had just said. "She's marvelous," he said in a lower, fully appreciative tone. "We'll be fortunate to see much of you at all once you're wed."

"Kerlain," Jack began, warning.

"Jack." Lucien cut him off. "Not tonight."

Kerlain kept his eyes on Lady Clara and Miss Howell. "I hope you won't mind if I dance with your wife—pardon me, future wife—once or twice, Callan. I've enjoyed Lady Clara's company a great deal since she's been in London. She's utterly charming."

Lucien was gazing at Clara, too, taking in her slender, elegant form, which was closely encased in a satiny sheath of royal blue. Her hair was swept up in a simple arrangement that left her unadorned, femininely curved neck exposed. There was something hotly erotic about the sight; it made a man think of what it might be like to press his lips against that smooth, warm skin, to taste and further explore.

"One dance," he said. "Not a waltz."

"Oh, no. Of course not a waltz," Kerlain agreed. "I haven't forgotten the scene you caused the last time I dared such a thing. You'd best be careful, Callan, or I'll begin to think that winning our wager will be far too easy."

At this, Lucien's polite facade crumbled away. He gripped Kerlain by the sleeve and turned him about. "Listen to me well, Kerlain. The wager is between us. You and me. Clara hasn't got anything to do with it. Leave her alone or I guarantee you'll regret it." His eyes glittered dangerously with intent.

The other man regarded him with polite interest. "I understand you perfectly, Callan. Now you listen to me. I consider Lady Clara to be a friend—regardless of our wager—as well as a kind and lovely woman. I'll see her for as long as she'll allow the acquaintance, and will only stop when she wishes it. And now, if you gentlemen will excuse me, I believe I'll make my bow to the lady of honor, and also to Miss Howell, and make certain that I'm able to reserve a dance on their cards."

"Not with Bella," Wulf said, but Kerlain had already walked away. "Damn the man! I don't want him dancing with Bella."

"It can't be helped," Jack said with a sigh. "Not unless you want to ruin the ball, and insult both Lucky and Lady Clara."

"But I don't want him dancing with Bella," Wulf repeated angrily.

"Then you'd best do what I'm about to do," Lucien advised.

"What?"

A hard smile played on Lucien's lips, and he tugged roughly at the edge of his gloves, one after the other, as if he could make their impossibly tight fit even tighter. "Spend the rest of the night by your fiancée's side," he said, and with a bow to his friends, walked away in Clara's direction.

The Marquess of St. Genevieve and his eldest daughter opened the ball with a minuet, after which Lucien claimed his bride-to-be for the first waltz.

"You seem to enjoy Miss Howell's company," he commented shortly after pulling her into the dance. She always felt so light in his arms, so small and delicate. He wondered if he would ever cease to experience the momentary amazement that holding her gave him.

She smiled in her open manner, innocently transforming her features from the ordinary to the exceptional. It was something as instant, Lucien thought, as lighting a flame.

"Indeed, I do. She's so witty and clever. I can't understand why Lord Severn doesn't formalize his union with her at once." She looked to where Viscount Severn and Miss Howell were presently dancing, only a short distance away. "It's clear that he cares for her, and she thinks that the sun rises and sets upon him. They're a charming couple."

Lucien followed Clara's gaze. Bella was a tall, admirably formed female, and yet, whenever she danced with Wulf, she always appeared to be swallowed up by his much greater size.

"They've been betrothed for so long now that I almost can't imagine them being actually wed."

"We were betrothed for much longer," Clara said.

Lucien's gaze settled upon her face once more. "But unlike Wulf, and perhaps unlike yourself, I always knew that you would one day be my wife. I never considered otherwise."

A slight flush infused her cheeks. "Neither did I, my lord."

"It doesn't particularly matter now," he said, despite the

fact that he knew her words were a lie. "Tomorrow you will be my wife, and whatever either of us may once have desired will be of no use. What were you and Kerlain speaking of earlier?"

"Lord Kerlain?" She looked at him curiously. "Nothing out of the ordinary. Merely the latest gossip."

"I have no right to give you commands before tomorrow, but once you're my wife, I want you to stay away from him."

Clara's eyes widened. "But why? I thought Lord Kerlain was one of your closest acquaintances. He's behaved with perfect propriety, Lucien, I assure you."

"You can take lovers after you've given me an heir, Clara," Lucien replied evenly, spinning her about in a smooth, rapid turn, ignoring her gasp. "But not among my friends, although Kerlain only barely qualifies beneath that description. Still, he is, as you have said, one of my closer acquaintances, and I'll not have him bedding my wife. I hope I make myself clear?" He gripped her hand more tightly when she furiously tried to tug free. "Oh, no, my dear. You can't run away now. Only think of how it would look."

"Let me go," she said in a low, seething tone. "Or return me to my aunt."

"Not while you're in such a mood." He continued to move in the dance with perfect ease. "You might do something foolish. Like try to call the wedding off."

"Exactly," she said hotly. "You constantly insult and belittle me, Lucien Bryland, but to speak of my taking lovers—!"

"You would rather that I play the part of the jealous husband?" he asked. "I realize you might find it more entertaining. My mother always did. But I've already warned you that I don't intend to be led about by the nose. Stop struggling, Clara," he said in a fully serious tone. "I won't have Robby humiliated by a scene at our betrothal ball.''

"Robby!"

Clara stared up at him, seemingly more hurt by this than anything he'd said before. Pain tightened her features, and her eyes grew brighter.

"For pity's sake," he muttered. "You're not going to cry, are you? Here, where everyone can see?"

She blinked, and he could see the tears forming at the edges of her eyes. "No," she whispered. "Please return me to my aunt."

He cursed under his breath and circled her closer to the open French doors. It would be impossible to take her out into the gardens without every eye at the ball watching them go, but he had no choice. At least it would be assumed that they'd gone outside to be private with each other. Lucien could almost hear all the other women in the room sighing at the romance of it.

"Come," he said, stopping near the closest door and taking her by the elbow to lead her out onto the terrace. She didn't resist, even as he guided her down the stairs to the garden below.

He took her to the darkest part of the walled courtyard, to a bench hidden within an alcove of bushes. Nearby, a splashing fountain mixed with the now dim music of the ballroom.

"I don't believe we should continue this pretense," he said, attempting to seat her on the bench. She jerked free of his touch, instead, and gave him her back. "It's utter nonsense." He raked a hand through his hair in exasperation. "I know you don't love me, Clara, and that you don't particularly wish to marry me. There's no need for you to behave as if you care for either my good opinion or my devotion."

"I wish to be set free," she said unsteadily, her voice

thick with tears. "I thought I could bear it, but I'm beginning to think it's impossible. We're not even wed and you already accuse me of adultery!" She sniffled loudly and lifted a hand to wipe her face.

He touched her arm and she moved away, saying, angrily, "You're ill, Lucien. Ill in your mind. How could you think that I would ever—" She broke off, weeping.

At the sound of it—the deep pain of it—Lucien felt utterly stricken. Clara was crying. Because of him. Because he had wanted to hurt her, always wanted to hurt her, and tried to do so at every opportunity. The very woman whose love he craved more than life itself—perhaps he *was* mad. But if he was, then she was the one who made him so.

It was impossible to believe in her. She flirted with every man she met, and had done so since he'd known her. Even his own friends found her charming, wonderful, enchanting . . . marvelous. If he trusted her with his heart, she would destroy him. He would be even more of a fool than his father had been to give credence to anything she said.

"Clara," he said, moving to stand in front of her. She tried to turn away, but he stopped her, and when she put her hands over her face and wept, he enfolded her in his arms and held her tightly. He understood her upset for what it was, and the deeper tension behind it. These were her last few hours of freedom. After tomorrow, she would be irrevocably beneath his hand.

"Don't cry," he murmured. "Please. Clara, don't cry." He kissed the top of her head and gently stroked her hair.

"I want to believe you," he said. "But it's hard for me to do. I've never trusted *any* woman. Perhaps it is a . . . sickness with me. Just as you said."

"Wou-would you t-trust me if I vowed"—she sniffled and shuddered—"to be f-faithful?"

"My mother vowed to be faithful to my father." He stroked her back now, letting his fingers trail downward from the bare neck he had earlier admired. "Every woman who's cheated on her husband has made the same promise. It's worthless."

"I don't mean in our wedding ceremony," she said, drawing in a shaking breath. "I mean if I make such a promise here and now. In the garden."

His hand stilled mid-air. "I don't know. Would you do such a thing?"

She nodded against his shoulder. "If you would make a vow, as well."

"For what?"

"To trust me, or at least to make the attempt. To give me a chance to prove that I mean to be a faithful wife in every way. If you would only give me some time, Lucien, before condemning me. Even a few months."

A few months. In six months or less she'd be put away at Pearwood. Alone. Lucien thought of the wager he'd made with a stab of guilt.

"And what will your vow be, Clara?"

She pulled away and looked at him, her face puffy and tear-stained. She had never looked less attractive, and yet his heart contracted with an undefinable ache of longing. She was Clara, to whom he had given his heart, and nothing could change that for him, or change the allure that she alone held.

"That you are the only man I will know in the future," she murmured, "and that I have known no other man in the past."

He took her face in his hands and held her very still, gazing into her eyes.

"Is it true, Clara? Are you a virgin?"

She strove not to gasp, but made a small, shocked, breathy sound despite herself.

"Of course I am!"

He could see the fury starting up in her again, and said,

"If you want plain speaking between us, Clara, then I will admit that I never considered you might be. I've been led down the garden path before, only to find that it had been well tilled before me."

Even in the darkness, he could see her cheeks flaming red. "I see," she said, and swallowed heavily.

She was either the greatest actress the world had ever known, Lucien decided, or as innocent as she claimed. But she must be. She knew that he'd discover the truth on the morrow, and she wasn't such a fool as to lie to him about anything so important.

"Clara," he whispered, afraid for himself for all he felt, afraid for her because he knew how badly he was capable of wounding her. He pushed his fingers into the rich warmth of her hair and tilted her face farther up to his. "If I'm the first to know you, then I'm very glad, but I would have married you anywise and not cared overmuch. You know what I've told you of my mother, you know how Robby suffered after your aunt deserted him for another man."

"She didn't—" Clara began, but Lucien kissed her to make her be silent. By the time he lifted his head, they had both calmed.

"He suffered, Clara. You can't begin to know how much. I traveled half the world seeing him live every moment of his pain. Because of her. Don't ask me to try to understand her side of the matter, because I can't. Robby's all I have in the world, and it isn't in me to give a damn about any one else's feelings."

She set a hand against one of his. Her fingers were cool and feminine, her touch one of gentle sympathy.

"I know that, Lucien."

"For the sake of our marriage—and for both of our sakes—I'm willing to do what you ask. I'll attempt to trust you. Attempt, Clara. Understand that I can promise no more. My experience with women has not been such that trust will come easily for me. But for the next few months, I'll try.''

He meant what he said. If there was any chance that he and Clara might find some measure of happiness together, then he'd gladly concede the wager he'd made and pay Kerlain off. Clara need never even know about it.

''Lucien,'' she whispered, and the next moment she threw her arms about his neck and hugged him. ''Thank you.''

His hands slid over her shoulders, down to the curve of her waist and hips, and he thought of how long he had waited to make her his own, and that soon, in only another day, he would take her to his bed and be one with her.

She lifted her head and gazed at him, her eyes still damp from tears, a pretty smile on her lips. He smiled in turn, slightly, and then lowered his mouth. She was the only woman he'd ever wanted to kiss, and kissing her was nothing short of an epiphany. He and Pamela never touched lips if they could avoid doing so, and he'd never engaged in kissing with the many women he'd taken in past years. It was an intimacy he wasn't willing to share lightly.

But with Clara, it was different. Everything was different. She lay relaxed in his arms, following his lead, clearly enjoying the embrace as fully as he. Her lips were moist and warm, and they parted beneath his tongue's gentle coaxing to allow him entrance beyond. He had kissed her this way before in anger, meaning to punish. Now he stroked and teased, pleasuring her until, with a little moan, she began to return the caresses, tentatively at first, and then with a growing boldness that seduced him almost beyond sense. It was a beautiful dance, and they were perfectly matched. He felt as if he could stand there forever, loving her, joined with her. But his body began to have other, far less noble ideas.

''We'd better stop,'' he said after several long minutes

had passed, pulling away with difficulty. She pressed her face against his neck, nodding, breathing hard against his skin. "Tomorrow," he promised, holding her tightly, knowing that she felt every inch of his arousal through their clothes, "we won't have to stop until we're too tired to do anything but. Tonight, however"—he released her and put the distance of a few inches between them—"we'd best behave. Robby and your father wouldn't like it at all if we anticipated our wedding vows here in the garden."

He smiled, and she smiled, too, and he suddenly began to hope, very much, that the agreement they had made would come to fruition. Her face was still puffy from her tears, and a few strands of hair had escaped her arrangement. Taking her hand, he led her to the fountain and wet his handkerchief before giving it to her.

"I must look a sight," she said, smoothing the cloth over her hot cheeks. "Will anyone be able to tell that I've been crying?"

"I doubt it," he said, tucking the stray strands back into their places. "They'll assume we were out here doing what we were. Kissing. Your lips look exceedingly well kissed."

She laughed. "So do yours."

"Then we'll pass. The night would have been written off as a dead bore if the engaged couple didn't make at least one attempt at being private. But we'd best return to the ball. I wouldn't wish to make your father nervous. Are you feeling better?"

"Oh, yes." She took his hand and held it. "Do you know what I wish for more than anything else, Lucien?"

"What?"

"To go back to the way we were with each other that summer at St. Genevieve."

With a rueful smile, he shook his head. "It's impossible, Clara. The girl you were is gone, and the boy I was has long since been dead."

"But we can still be happy together," she insisted. "Perhaps I'm a hopeless dreamer, but if we're to be man and wife, we can at least try."

"Then we'll try," he murmured. "Only don't forget, Clara. It goes hard with me."

"Oh, Lucien. I have no interest in any other man. I shall be a faithful wife. You've no cause for either distrust or jealousy."

"We shall see," he said. "I told you that I would make the attempt, and I will." He offered her his arm. "Come. We'd best return before Robby starts looking for us. I'm not in the mood for one of his scolds."

His nephew's whereabouts were the farthest thing from the Earl of Manning's mind. He was far more interested in locating Anna Huntington and convincing her to dance with him. He'd attempted the matter earlier in the evening, only to be met with a blunt refusal, but he was confident that he could change her mind. They had used to dance together when they were betrothed. The waltz hadn't yet been fully accepted in England then, but Robert had danced it in France and had taught it to Anna, who had thought it positively wicked. But she was a sensual creature, and had made him dance it with her whenever they could steal a few private moments together.

She had disappeared up the stairs some time earlier, probably to check on Sarah in the nursery. The parlor he'd sauntered into was the perfect place to wait for her return. There were mostly card players in the room, and the two elderly ladies whom he'd engaged in conversation were pleasant companions. He had stationed himself near the door, in a position to keep an eye on the stairs, and found it remarkably easy to do even while discussing the upcoming wedding.

At last he saw her descend, holding the hem of her skirt

up as she moved with the typical grace that he'd always known in her. It amazed him, somewhat, to feel such a breathlessness at every sight of her. On the night when he'd seen her at Almack's, he'd almost thought he was going to faint dead away. It had been so many years since he'd lost her. To walk into a room and suddenly have her there had been the greatest shock of his life.

She didn't glance his way as she reached the final step, but, clearly preoccupied, moved straightway toward the ballroom, where her duties as hostess were pressing. Robert proceeded to politely extricate himself from the two elderly ladies, and moved out into the hall, intent upon following his prey. It was only the merest chance that made him glance up the stairs and catch a glimpse of a small child in a white nightdress. Sarah Huntington jumped into the shadows at once, pressing against the wall in an effort not to be seen.

Robert was arrested by the expression he caught on the girl's face in that fleeting moment. She wanted to see the ball—he remembered the feeling very well from his own childhood, and sneaking downstairs with his brother Edward to peek at the festivities when their parents thought them long asleep. It had seemed so unfair to be left out of such grand events. To be so utterly ignored. Thinking of it, he abandoned his pursuit, turned about and began to ascend the stairs.

"Why, Miss Huntington," he said as he neared the child. "What a pleasant chance. I've been meaning to call upon you to see how Miss Margaret is recuperating from her unfortunate accident."

"Oh, Lord Manning," Sarah said with relief. "It's only you."

"Yes," Robert replied with a slight bow. "Only me. And is this Miss Margaret you've got?"

Sarah held the doll out for inspection. "She's much better. She never complains of the headache anymore."

"I see," said Robert, taking the doll when she was pressed into his hands and looking her over with great interest. "My, she does appear to be much improved. Her color is excellent. You must be taking quite good care of her."

"It's nothing I've done," Sarah said. "Except perhaps to make her eat all her boiled oats, even when she doesn't wish it. You're the one who had her fixed. You received my letter, didn't you? Mama said you wouldn't care for it, but I made her send it, anyhow."

He remembered the letter very well. It had arrived the day after he'd returned the doll to her owner and had been written in an amazingly readable scrawl, filled with effusive thanks. She'd drawn a picture of Margaret and herself, both smiling happily. He'd read the thing through three times in a row and then tucked the missive into a coat pocket. Later, he'd locked it away in his desk, where he kept his most precious papers, putting it with the bundle of letters Anna had sent him so long ago.

"I not only cared for it, I very much appreciated and enjoyed it. It now resides among my most important papers. I shall keep it forever."

Even in the shadows, he could see her young face light up with an eager smile. "Will you?"

"Indeed I shall," he assured her. "The artwork alone makes it invaluable. And now, Miss Huntington, may I ask what you're doing up at this hour, out of your bed? Does your nurse know where you are?"

She frowned. "She's writing letters, and I wanted to see the ball." She moved nearer and took his hand, her expression pleading. "You won't tell Mama, will you?"

She was clearly a master at the art of manipulation, Robert decided. No human possessed of a soul could have done anything but give in.

"It does seem unfair not to be able to attend, does it not? So many grand sights, and you don't get to see but a bit of them."

"Oh," she said, and the pleading expression disappeared, to be replaced by something more genuine. "You understand."

"Perfectly," he said, squeezing her hand. "I only wish I could take you downstairs to see all there is, but I fear your mama would be quite angry with the both of us."

"It looks so lovely," Sarah said, looking longingly toward the lights. "And sounds so lovely." Music drifted up the stairs. "It must be the most wonderful thing. I wish I could dance, just once. I know how to waltz," she declared. "Mama taught me."

Robert could just imagine Anna doing such a thing. He vividly remembered the lessons he'd given her, how much she'd enjoyed them.

"Then perhaps you and I can bring some of the ball to us."

There, in the darkness, he made her his most formal bow.

"Miss Huntington, would you do me the honor of allowing me this dance?"

Almost without a pause she set Margaret upon the floor, then proceeded to lift up the hem of her nightdress and make an elegant curtsey.

"I would be pleased, Lord Manning. But won't we be seen?" She nodded toward the landing below.

"Perhaps," he said thoughtfully, then, after a moment, picked up Margaret and took Sarah's hand. "Up we go," he said, pulling her up to the next landing, where only a single lamp provided light. He set Margaret on a small table against a wall and held out his hands. "Now, Miss Huntington, if you please."

With a grin she set her smaller hand in his and put her other upon the lapel of his dark blue coat.

The music was dimmer now, but Robert hummed along in time and drew his young partner into motion. She'd spoken the truth, he discovered at once. She did know how to waltz, and quite well.

"Miss Hamilton, you're a splendid dancer," he declared, and she giggled.

"Why, thank you, Lord Manning. You're splendid, too."

She was the most beautiful child he'd ever seen, and so much like Anna that he could only guess at how many hearts she would slay when she at last grew into a woman. Her nightdress whirled about her slippered feet, and her long blond hair, tied back with a ribbon, shone like gold silk in the lamplight.

"Mama keeps a portrait of you in her desk," Sarah said conversationally after they had danced a full minute. "A small painting done when you were betrothed to her."

Robert nearly dropped the child's hand, the words were so unexpected and shocking.

"Does she?" he managed in an uneven tone. "I believe I know the portrait you mean."

Sarah nodded. "You gave it to her just after she agreed to marry you. She was having one done of herself to give you, but it was never finished. Of course, she didn't tell me anything about being betrothed to you. I found out on my own."

"Did you?"

"Oh, yes. It was simple. I took the portrait from Mama's desk one day and showed it to her maid, Jilly. Jilly loves to talk. Then I found out what the other servants at St. Genevieve knew. Cook was especially helpful. She remembered you very well, and said that you were always kind to compliment her cooking. She remembered Lord Callan when he was a boy, too. He was a fussy eater, she said."

Robert gazed at the girl with a mixture of distress and amazement. Sarah Huntington was clearly a resourceful child.

"It's true that I was once betrothed to your mama," he said, "but she had the good sense to marry your father, instead. He was a far better choice."

"Of course he was," she stated, as if this was indisputable, "but that doesn't mean you're not a good choice, as well. Far better than any of the other suitors she's got back at St. Genevieve."

Other suitors, Robert thought dismally. Of course Anna would have suitors. The vultures had probably begun plotting the moment Colonel Huntington was laid to rest.

"It's very kind of you to say so, my dear. However, I am not one of her suitors."

"But why shouldn't you be?" Sarah asked. "She's been out of mourning for almost two years, and she's got to marry *somebody*. You wouldn't mind terribly being my papa, would you? I'd be very good, and we'd have so much fun."

Robert smiled. "I'd be honored to be your papa," he said, and was surprised at how true the words were, "but it's not so simple a matter."

"Don't you find Mama beautiful?"

"Yes. Very beautiful." He spun her about in a circle. "But there are other considerations. Your mama's feelings, first and foremost."

"But if she was willing to marry you once, surely she'd be willing again. And if you wanted her for your wife all those years ago, I'm sure you'd be happy to have her now, wouldn't you?"

"I should like it above all things, dear, but I can't force Lady Anna to marry me. Your mama must choose for herself, if she decides to wed again."

Sarah's smile was as bright as day. "Oh, don't worry

about that. I'll take care of everything. As long as you're willing, it will all work out.''

The music came to an end and Robert brought them to a halt.

"Thank you, Miss Huntington." He made another bow. "It was truly a delight being your partner. I would ask if I might return you to your mother, but in this instance, I believe the nursery will have to do."

She leapt forward and threw her arms about his neck, kissing his cheek with a childish vigor that left his skin stinging.

"I shall make my way back, and you must go back downstairs and dance with Mama." She gave him a harder squeeze. "I shall love having you for my papa!" she declared, and gave him another smacking kiss. The next moment she released him, snatched Margaret up from her resting place, and disappeared up the next flight of stairs.

Chapter Nine

❦

"I don't care what's happening in Town," Lucien said as his valet eased him into his tight-fitting coat. "I don't want to be disturbed for any reason. Not for a week, at the very least. That's not too much to ask, is it?"

"Not at all," said Jack, lounging across the dressing room with a glass of ale. "But I suppose you won't blame us for knocking on your door to tell you that your house is on fire, will you?"

Lifting his chin so that his valet might straighten his cravat, Lucien looked at his friend from the corner of his eye. "That would be, most like, the only acceptable excuse. Otherwise, I don't care if Prinny himself wants an audience. Clara and I will be entirely unavailable for the next seven days. Pretend we're out of town, if you must."

"You *should* have taken her out of town," Wulf told him. "Every woman deserves a honeymoon. I'm taking Bella to Italy for a year."

"Yes, so that you can visit your fellow chemists there," Lucien said.

"*If* you ever marry the girl in the first place," Jack put in with a laugh.

Wulf ignored them. "I still say you should take Lady Clara on a honeymoon. It ain't like you can't afford it."

"Marriage," Lucien said, holding his arms out so that his valet could pull his ruffled sleeves out at the wrist, "isn't going to change my life in any remarkable way. I prefer to stay in Town, and so I shall. Aside from that, I promised Pamela that I'd see her in a week or so following the wedding. I shouldn't like to have to hurry back to London on her, or anyone's, account."

"God forbid," Jack said dryly. "It might be inconvenient, after all."

Lucien gave him a steady gaze. "Precisely."

"You're cold as stone, Lucky," Wulf told him. "I can't see why you'd keep on with Lady Halling when you've got such a nice wife in Lady Clara. And you should take her on a honeymoon. Isn't she unhappy to be installed at Barrington so shortly after your wedding?"

A slight smile played on Lucien's lips. "I shall make certain that she is not. Indeed, I shall devote myself to the task."

"Determined to get the heir started and win that bet, are you?" Jack asked.

"Perhaps," Lucien replied as his valet slipped one perfect white glove on his hand. "Perhaps not. Only time will tell. In the meantime, I suggest that neither of you leap to any conclusions regarding my alliance with Lady Halling. I'm considering bringing the relationship to an end."

"Well done," Jack murmured.

"Are you really?" asked Wulf hopefully. "I must say, Lucky, I'd be relieved if you did. She's such an unpleasant woman."

Lucien flexed his glove-encased hands and looked at his reflection in the mirror. With a word he dismissed his valet. When the man had gone, he said, "That's precisely why I don't wish to annoy her any more than I must. If it does, indeed, come to that. Pamela's difficult enough to deal with when she's in a decent mood. When she's vexed, however, she can be intolerable. I shouldn't be amused if Clara were the recipient of her venom."

Jack nodded. "It's well thought of, Lucky. We're all aware of what Lady Halling can do if she wishes to make trouble. Allingham hasn't yet recovered from that poisonous caricature she drew of him last year."

"She nearly got him hanged," Wulf added. "Depicting him as a sodomite when everybody knows the fellow's nothing but shy around females. And after he'd finally got up the courage to ask Miss Finnian to marry him, too. He lost her as well as his reputation, poor fellow."

"It was over the line, I admit," Lucien said, turning to face them at last. "But I took care of it—and of Pamela— did I not?"

"You did," Jack said. "She was meek as a lamb for a full three weeks. But the damage was done. Allingham hasn't shown his face in society since. He's ruined, probably for good. If she ever dared to do something like that to Lady Clara—"

"I'd kill her, and she knows it," Lucien said. "But I'll walk softly where Pam's concerned, nonetheless. Well, my friends." He held up his arms and turned about. "Do I look fit enough to be married?"

"Quite fit," said a voice from the open doorway, and both Jack and Wulf stood as the Earl of Manning entered the room.

"Rexley, Severn," said the earl, and received their greetings in turn. "I should like to have a few moments alone with my nephew before we leave for St. George's, if you'll allow?"

"Certainly, sir," Jack said with a slight bow. "We'll wait downstairs."

"If you've come to give me a speech about being considerate for the delicate sensibilities of my blushing young maiden bride," Lucien said when the door had closed, "then I pray you will remember that everything I know about women, I learned from you."

"Not everything, I hope," Robert said, walking a slow circle about his nephew as he examined him closely. "I've made a great many mistakes in my day, as you very well know. You look perfectly fine, Lucky. Royal blue is quite becoming on you, and the silver vest shows off well. Clara will be more than pleased, I believe."

"You're in fine form, as well," Lucien said, eyeing his uncle's gray satin frock coat and breeches. "Lady Anna should find you irresistible," he teased.

To his amazement, his usually refined uncle blushed.

"I don't know why you should think so."

"You did dance with her last night," Lucien said. "The waltz, too. I remember how the two of you used to sneak off to dance it, when you thought no one was looking."

"Lucky," the earl said with a laugh. "I should have known we'd not be able to keep it from you. Silent as a rock, you were, but so very observant."

"Last night you looked as you used to look. Robby"— Lucien took hold of his arm—"don't let her hurt you. Please. It nearly killed you the first time she deserted you. Don't let her put you through that again."

"You worry overmuch, dear boy," Robert told him affectionately. "But never fear. This time I'm possessed of all my faculties, I promise. I don't want you thinking of anything but Lady Clara and this day. Your wedding day." With both hands he squeezed Lucien's shoulders. "I don't know if I've ever told you before, Lucky, but I'm grateful—very grateful, indeed—to have had the chance to care for you these many years. You've been as my own son." He blinked a few times, rapidly. "I shall miss having you here with me at Manning House. It will seem lonely without you."

"I'm even more grateful, Robby. You're all I have. The only one. What would have become of me if you'd not taken me under your hand? I loved my father, but I'd be a liar if I didn't say I love you just as dearly."

"Well," said Robert, sniffing suspiciously. "Well." He stepped away and continued to blink. "I've brought you something." He fumbled about in an inner coat pocket. "This was your father's, and our father's before him, and his father's before that. I believe it will fit you." He lifted the sapphire-studded ring up into the light, then set it in Lucien's hand.

Lucien held the ring in his open palm, staring. He began blinking, too.

"I remember Papa wearing it," he said softly. "Robby. I remember it."

"It's yours now, and I know that he would want you to have it. Try it on. See if it fits."

Lucien slid it onto his right index finger. It fit perfectly.

"Thank you," he said huskily. "It means . . . a great deal to me . . ."

Robert hugged him once, briefly, and then released him and walked toward the door.

"We'd best be on our way," he said, turning to give him a smile. "Else your bride will think you're not coming at all."

"There. Perfect." Anna Huntington stepped back from her niece and eyed the crown of roses and pearls with satisfaction. "You'll be the most beautiful bride London has ever seen, Clara."

Clara smiled and blushed. "I sincerely doubt that, Auntie. I'm far from being a beauty. I shall be pleased if I look acceptable. And if I don't embarrass Lucien."

"That boy knows what he's getting in you," Anna stated bluntly. "He wouldn't be ashamed if you showed up barefooted and wearing your worst gardening dress. I only wish you could be as certain of him. A fine set of clothes won't change what he is, I'm afraid.''

Clara looked at her pleadingly. "But Auntie, I *told* you—''

"Yes, you did," Anna said, picking up a brush, "and I admit to being impressed that he's willing to at least attempt to give you his trust." With a few delicate strokes, she smoothed Clara's curls back from her face, into a more becoming arrangement. "But what you might consider is that a woman about to be wed to a man shouldn't have to ask such a boon of him."

"With any man but Lucien, perhaps," Clara agreed. "But he's not like other men."

Anna had nothing to say to this, despite the fact that she felt the coming marriage was doomed. Viscount Callan was far too ready to believe the worst of Clara. He might give her his trust for a short while, but the moment Clara made one false step—as any normal human being might do from time to time—he would condemn her without a moment's thought. If she thought it would do any good she would tell Clara one more time that it wasn't too late to bring matters to a halt. But it would be a waste of breath. Clara loved Lucien Bryland, just as fully, and foolishly, as Anna had once loved his uncle. Unlike Anna, nothing was going to stop Clara from her chosen course, and the best that Anna could do was prepare to be of help when the end of the union finally came at hand.

But perhaps she was too pessimistic, Anna thought as she straightened the neckline of Clara's wedding gown. Last night Viscount Callan had treated Clara with a gentle deference and attentiveness that had touched even her. And Clara had been happy, so much so that Anna's heart had ached for her.

"Did you enjoy the ball last night, Auntie?" Clara asked

with a lilting smile. "You danced the waltz with Lord Manning.

"Yes," Anna said evenly. "And so I did."

"It was beautiful to watch. You looked as if you had danced it hundreds of times together. But you must have done so when you were betrothed."

They had, Anna thought wistfully, but never before in public. It had been too sweet to be in his arms again, to feel his body moving so closely to hers, to feel his warmth and strength and heat. It had been a horrible mistake for her to let happen, to allow him to badger her into waltzing. First the kiss in the garden at Barrington, and then the dance . . . if she wasn't careful she would find herself in love with the man all over again, and vulnerable to as much hurt as Clara presently was. Losing him once had nearly killed her. She couldn't live through that kind of loss again.

"We did," she told Clara, "but it was a long time ago. Last night he was merely being polite."

"It didn't look as if he were," Clara countered.

Anna looked at her directly. "It didn't?"

"No." Clara gave a slight shake of her head. "It looked as if you were the only two in the entire room, with eyes only for each other. Neither of you said a word the entire time."

Good heavens, Anna thought. Was that how it had seemed? She would have to be careful in the future, when she was in company with Robert, to keep her feelings more closely contained. But it *had* been very polite, at least compared to the way in which they had used to waltz together. She remembered vividly the lazy, seductive manner in which Robert had used to circle with her about an empty room, so close that her skirts engulfed his legs, around and between them in an intimacy that never failed to both exhilarate and frighten her. The dance, in Robert's command, had been purely erotic. Last night it had been less than a shadow of those remembered moments. But powerful all the same. Because she had known, without a moment's doubt, that while he had danced with aloof civility, he too had been remembering those days of so long ago.

"We didn't have much to say," Anna said. "As I told you. He was merely being polite. You haven't put on your pearls, yet."

"Oh." Clara touched her bare neck. "I meant to put them on at once, but Papa cried so much when he gave them to me that I forgot." She sat very still as Anna fixed on the perfectly matched strand. "I do wish Mama was here. It's so hard on him without her."

"And you shall miss having her with you on this most important of all days," Anna said, gazing at her niece's reflection in the mirror. "But I can assure you, love, that she will miss being here far more. To not see her eldest child wed will be a pain that will never go away. But that's what it is to be a parent to such a large family."

"I do miss her," Clara admitted, setting a hand over one of Anna's, "but I'm so terribly glad that you're here, Auntie."

Anna kissed her cheek. "I wouldn't miss this day for the world, despite my misgivings about the groom. Now, my dear," she added quickly when Clara opened her mouth, "we're *not* going to argue about Viscount Callan, just as we promised. If he can agree to give you his trust for the next few months, the least I can do is attempt the same toward him."

Clara turned in her chair, gazing up at Anna anxiously. "Will you, Aunt Anna? It would be the finest wedding gift you could give me."

"I'll try, love," Anna assured her honestly. "And now, we'd best be on our way. Sarah and your remaining brothers will be tearing the drawing room apart, and your papa will probably have watered all of his handkerchiefs by now. Let's only hope," she said as she pulled Clara to her feet, "that he doesn't flood St. George's with his tears, as well."

Chapter Ten

❈

The wedding breakfast, which was held in the Earl of Manning's home, lasted through most of the afternoon. As soon as it was respectably possible, Lucien collected his bride, made polite farewells to his uncle and new in-laws and, amidst a gauntlet of cheering guests, escorted Clara out to their waiting carriage. Settling beside her, Lucien took her hand in his, closing his eyes wearily against the shouts of good wishes that filled the air as the carriage pulled away.

"Well," he murmured. "It's done then."

"Yes," she agreed softly, and when he glanced at her he saw that the joyful expression she'd held on to all day had at last gone away. She looked as tired, and relieved to be finished with the pretense, as he was.

"We'll be home soon," he told her, and was gifted with a slight smile that warmed him throughout.

He was surprised at his lack of impatience, at the strange calm that had slowly blanketed him during the celebratory meal. He had spent most of his life waiting to possess Clara, both legally and physically, and had expected to be in a welter of frustration at having to spend hours behaving civilly to people he didn't wish to be with. He'd expected that he'd want to have Clara alone, to himself, in their home, in his bed. It was what had possessed him almost entirely during the months leading up to their wedding day, even up to the moment of the actual ceremony. When he'd caught sight of her standing at the front of St. George's, ready to walk down the aisle and join him at the altar, so lovely in her wedding gown that his eyes had stung at the beauty of her, his wanting and frustration had turned into something very like panic. He'd experienced a moment of absolute terror, as if it were all unreal, as if she were going to suddenly disappear. And then she'd come to him on her father's arm, gazing directly into Lucien's eyes, so calm and so certain. She had put her hand into his—he hadn't even realized he'd reached out for her—and his fears had faded away like mist beneath the sun's bright heat.

She was his now, and she had come to him willingly. He had waited too long for that miracle to rush his final possession. It would be a night they would remember for the rest of their lives, when they at last became one, when their bodies were joined, one to the other, for the very first time.

He made no further attempt at conversation while they journeyed toward Barrington; Clara didn't seem to want any, and he contented himself with keeping her gloved hand in his lap, rubbing his thumb gently over the backs of her fingers, and thinking over and again of the way she had looked when they had exchanged their wedding vows. Her voice had been soft and feminine, but unafraid. He had marveled at how readily she had placed herself into his hands. But she must have known how true his word was, that he would honor the promise he had given her. She would not find that faith misplaced, so long as she, in turn, honored the promise she had given him. For the next six months, everything hinged upon her being able to do so.

At Barrington the butler, Hayes, housekeeper, Mrs. MacInnes, and new servants were lined up to greet their lord and lady. Lucien led Clara slowly down the brightly uniformed row, greeting each individual with unhurried care. Afterward, he escorted her upstairs to their respective chambers and left her to remove her wedding clothes and rest before dinner.

And then, without stopping long enough to let himself think of his parents, he went into the suite of rooms that was now his. He hadn't been in them since long before his parents had died, since before he'd gone away to Eton, even. He'd been unable to make himself enter them on the day that Robby had brought him, so long ago, and he'd not returned since his tour of Barrington with Clara had been so furiously interrupted only days before.

He stood still for a few moments after crossing the threshold, taking in the familiar, seeking out the changes. He had used to play here when he was a child, when the rooms between his mother and father had held no locks on them, and had ever been open. They had not seemed to need doors between them, then. He remembered coming upon his parents more than once without notice, finding them together and thinking, in his childish innocence, that they were playing some sort of game. He knew now, of course, that they had been doing far more, but he pushed the memories away. They were bittersweet; perhaps more of one than the other. The love his mother and father once shared hadn't lasted long enough to even think fondly upon. It only hurt now to remember it.

Ghosts.

Barrington held them everywhere. He'd resisted coming home to face them, knowing very well that every room, every passageway, would give him pain. But Robby had been right to insist that he and Clara make their home here. If their marriage was to have any chance at all, then they must find the way in this place where all of the demons that drove him to distrust her lived and breathed. If he wanted her enough, if he wanted the happiness he had dreamed of having with her alone, then he must make his stand at Barrington. And if he failed he would know at last that nothing could make the matter right, and he would send her away. To Pearwood, and to a safety and happiness that she would never be able to know with him. And he, Lucien thought with a sense of futility, would be left with his ghosts and his darkness.

In silence, in his own chamber, he let his valet remove his wedding finery and dress him in evening clothes. When his valet left, Lucien sat down at the small writing desk that had once been his father's and thought of how strange it was that the house was so much the same. It had been years since Barrington had been closed up and left uninhabited. Fourteen years. And yet, despite the changes Clara had made, it was so much the same, as if it had never lain in such a tomblike state.

His father's desk had been polished until it shone like new, just as all of the furniture had been. He turned the key in the top drawer, unlocking and opening it. Empty, as he had expected it to be. Robby's steward had gone through the contents of his father's and mother's various desks shortly after their deaths. The important papers had been appropriately dealt with, and the other various contents had been stored in the attic. He remembered Robby asking him if he wanted them at Manning House, instead, but Lucien had simply shook his head. Even speaking the word ''no'' had been beyond him in those days.

His own personal papers and important items lay in unopened wooden crates nearby. Clara had offered to have a servant tend to the chore of putting them neatly away, but Lucien had declined. He would do it himself, both here and in the study desk that was now to be his. He wanted no one else to see his most private possessions.

The lids on the crates were easily removed, and Lucien settled himself cross-legged on the richly carpeted floor to go through the contents of each one, searching specifically for the gifts that had spent years locked away, waiting only for the coming nights.

"You may go, Bertie."

Clara almost didn't recognize the sound of her own voice.

The young maid made a brief curtsy and then obediently quit the room. She was a new servant, just as the others in the house were, and Clara had felt strangely embarrassed to be in her presence. What must they all think of the lord and lady of the house? And what must they think of the house itself? Clara had spent weeks striving to make Barrington warm and pleasant, but it seemed impossible. The dwelling was more like a sterile museum than a home, and so strangely, uncomfortably silent. Even during dinner, while she and Lucien had striven to make conversation, it had been thus. The emptiness of the house, the loneliness, was like an ever-present shadow hanging over them. Surely the servants felt it as well, and wondered.

How very different from St. Genevieve it was. How different from *any* other home that Clara had known or visited. It would change in time, she thought, when she and Lucien had more of a chance to become settled. And when there were children to fill the house with noise and laughter and gaiety. Lucien seemed not to mind the silence and stillness. In truth, he appeared to be perfectly comfortable with it, as if such a cold, bare environment was just what he expected at Barrington.

Perhaps he did, Clara thought with a measure of distress. Perhaps it was all he'd ever known there, even while his parents had been alive. She had worried constantly about the memories he carried while she had so many changes made, but there was only so much she could do to keep them at bay. He had told her once that she and Robby and a few certain officials were the only people who knew the truth about how his parents had died, but even knowing the truth didn't give her any extraordinary help in managing her new husband. She knew too little about him yet to be able to understand how his mind worked.

Most bewildering of all was the fact that he could want her. She held no false perceptions regarding herself. The mirror before her revealed frankly what she already knew. Unremarkable gray eyes, unremarkable brown hair, unremarkable features. And yet he wanted her. It was such a mystery, especially when a man who was as beautiful as Lucien could have any woman his heart desired.

She hoped he'd be patient and considerate when he made her his wife, as Mama had always said a husband should be. Clara was a bit afraid of Lucien in that regard, for he'd been purposefully cruel before in many of his embraces. But, she reminded herself, he'd never actually hurt her. Even during the afternoon when he'd caught her laughing with the stable hands, when he'd been so furiously angry and bent on teaching her a lesson, he'd not hurt her. Humiliated her, yes, because he'd made her want him so badly with his skilled kisses and touches, made her just as wanton as he'd always accused her of being, but by the time he'd gotten her down on a pile of straw and lain beside her, he had gentled. His caresses had grown loverlike, soft and tender, and she had fallen completely beneath their spell. It was only afterward that he'd regained his anger, mostly because he'd been unable to control his own physical responses, despite the fact that he'd not removed any of his clothes. And so they had both been humiliated, and both learned a lesson that afternoon.

Clara stood and pulled her thin, silk wrapper more tightly about herself as she moved restlessly about the room.

Barrington was one of the older homes in London, built when there was enough land to allow such expansive palaces, and thus was both large and elegant. The grounds on which it had been built had not been sold and divided, and Clara found herself in the enviable position of being able to surround herself with a large, beautiful, parklike garden, even in Town. These chambers, which had always housed the mistress of Barrington, were magnificent. The ones she'd had at St. Genevieve were simple by comparison. She stood in the middle of the bedroom and felt small and very alone, and wished that Lucien would come. She prayed that he would stay with her the entire night, even just for tonight. Tomorrow, she would be braver, she told herself. Tonight, she couldn't bear the thought of sleeping in this cold, massive room by herself.

"Clara?"

She turned about at the sound of his voice, and found Lucien standing at the door that adjoined their common sitting room. He was dressed in a soft-blue robe. Nothing else. The sight of his bare legs peeping out between the folds of cloth as he leaned casually against the door frame made her swallow.

"Yes, my lord?"

"Are you well?"

"Yes."

He pushed away from the door and strolled slowly toward her.

"Are you pleased with your rooms?"

"Yes." She folded her hands together and tried to push away the feeling of nakedness that possessed her. He was her husband, after all. She shouldn't mind that he saw her wearing such a transparent nightdress and robe. Her mother had given her the daring ensemble, assuring Clara that it was just what every man would wish to see on his bride on their wedding night. Now, Clara wasn't so sure. The lacy outfit seemed positively indecent. As Lucien's gaze moved over her, she had the distinct feeling that he could see every inch of her flesh beneath the cream-colored silk.

"My mother loved them," he said softly as he neared her. "She enjoyed having her friends attend her while she dressed for parties and balls, simply to show them off. Barrington compares very favorably even to Carlton House. And she brought all of her lovers here and had them in her bed. She sneaked them in more than once while my father and I were sleeping. I remember the loud commotion on the following morns, when my father inevitably discovered strange men in his wife's bed. Or perhaps not so strange men, as she was in the habit of bedding his friends as well as his enemies. Such a pleasant way to greet the day," he said, stopping before her. "The shouting was horrid. I used to lie in my bed and put my pillow over my ears and pray to God to make it stop. That never worked, of course. I've often wondered," he said even more conversationally, "why she did it, when she knew how unpleasant it would be and afterward always acted so amazed and offended at my father's reaction."

"Perhaps she wanted his attention and that was the only way she could get it," Clara whispered, gazing up at him.

"Perhaps," he agreed. "Or perhaps she wished to torment him, knowing how greatly he loved her. To see her with another man, when he would have given his very life to make her happy, was worse than death."

Clara felt chilled all the way through to her bones, and crossed her hands over her chest to warm herself.

"While I am the occupant of these rooms," she said, looking at him very directly, "no other man but you shall ever enter, unless you are also present or have agreed to allow him here—a physician or servant."

His hand lifted and his fingertips stroked lightly against her throat. "Make certain that you speak the truth, Clara. For if I ever find another man sharing your bed at Barrington, I shall kill him without a moment's pause."

"I gave you my word last night."

"Yes," he said, lifting the same hand higher to touch her unbound hair. His fingers petted her, slowly, carefully, as if she might dissolve at his touch. "So you did. Just as I gave mine. What I meant to let you know, by the little tale I told, is that I cannot bring myself to slumber in this room, or lie in the bed where my mother played whore to half the *ton*. We will observe our conjugal rights in my chambers, or find some other place, of which Barrington has many. You need only let me know which you prefer."

"Oh," she said, feeling irrefutably foolish to have taken such slight at his words. She should have realized how he would feel. She should have known before he'd had to tell her. "Your rooms, please."

"Come, then. I've made all ready."

He stepped back and held out his hand. She placed her own in it and let him lead her out of her chambers, through the sitting room, and into the open door of his bedroom.

"Lucien," she murmured as he released her to close the door. The room was lit by what must have been a hundred candles, the air was scented with wax and sandalwood. To one side she saw a table set with covered trays and baskets of fruit. Next to that stood a silver wine server, filled with ice and two bottles of champagne.

She felt him come up behind her bodily, enveloping her in his warmth. "Are you pleased, Clara?" His hands touched her waist, lightly, with care.

"Oh, yes," she breathed. "Thank you."

He chuckled, and she felt his breath against her ear, which he next kissed. "I've waited forever for this night. All of my life. Clara"—with his hands on her shoulders he turned her to face him—"you said last night that you wished we could be as we once were during the summer we spent at St. Genevieve. We can't go back to that time, but for tonight, perhaps even for the next several days, we can pretend that nothing . . . unpleasant . . . has occurred between us."

"Lucien—"

"It's much to ask, I realize," he said, setting one finger over her mouth. "I've not been especially kind to you in the past many years. You needn't pretend that you love me, or even that you like me. If you could only forget my sins for a short while, that will be enough."

She searched his eyes, striving to see what lay behind his words. His dark gaze gave nothing away, save that he meant what he said.

"And what of you?" she murmured. "Will you pretend that you love me, Lucien?"

"No," he said. "I won't pretend. Do we have a truce, Clara? For tonight? Perhaps for the next few days?"

"No accusation? No threats?"

"No," he whispered, lowering his head. "We don't even have to speak a word."

But he did speak, constantly, between kisses, while he brought her body closer to his own, as his hands smoothed over her back and hips, when he pulled away her silk wrapper and dropped it on the floor, while she shivered as his mouth traveled over the bare skin of her throat and shoulders.

"You're beautiful," he murmured as he picked her up and gently set her on the bed. "I've never wanted another woman as I want you, Clara," he told her as he moved to lie beside her. "Hush, love," he whispered against her mouth as her gown slid down to her waist and she made a sound of protest, "let me touch you. Don't you know how much I need to touch you? Feel you? You're so warm, Clara. So perfect. Don't be afraid. You're my wife. My beautiful, perfect wife."

His voice, dark and gentle, seduced away all her fears, until nothing else mattered save Lucien. He had said they

couldn't go back, but he'd been wrong. This was the fulfill-
ment of all the promises they'd made in that long-ago summer. This was the destination they'd set out to reach, and
everything that had happened to put them off course melted
out of consciousness. He was her own Lucien again, as
vulnerable and open and loving as she had remembered.

She discovered that she held a certain power over him, as
strong as the one he wielded over her. Her touch made him
shiver, her kisses wrought sounds of utter pleasure. When
she stroked her fingertips over him intimately for the very
first time he said her name in a way that sent a tingle shivering down her spine. He lay as if stunned by the press of her
hands on his skin, powerless to do anything but accept all
that she wished to do to him, and greedily devouring all that
she gave.

Perhaps it was the shadows and light flickering from the
candles, or perhaps the unreality of being with Lucien in
such open, confident intimacy, but Clara began to feel as if
they had ascended to some realm beyond the mere physical-
ity of Barrington. There was a rightness, a oneness between
them. Like a beautiful dance, each touch was in measure,
each word, look, smile following in perfect time. When he
at last came into her, closing his eyes against the pleasure
and whispering her name, even the pain of the moment
could not drive away the stunning fact of at last being filled
by him, joined with him. One with him. The rhythm of their
bodies was instinctive, a second knowledge she seemed to
have always known, so perfect that she almost expected the
wonder that was to come from it.

Afterward, after the hot, dizzying pleasure had at last
subsided, they lay in silence, touching with sleepy, gentle
movements, kissing softly. Lucien finally disengaged himself from her body and moved to lie beside her. One of his
arms burrowed beneath her, and she unresistingly let him
pull her against his shoulder.

"You'll sleep here," he said. It was a statement, not a question.

She closed her eyes as his fingers stroked her arm. "Yes," she murmured, relaxing even more fully against him. She didn't think she could have moved to her own chambers on her own strength, anyway. The press of his lips against her forehead was the last thing she knew as she gratefully slid into slumber.

Chapter Eleven

❧

Three days later, Lucien reclined lazily in the middle of his enormous bed, a silk robe his only claim to modesty. He would have preferred to go without clothing at all, but Clara had proven to be enduringly shy, no matter how often he saw her body or how well he used it, and the sight of his own naked person served only to make her stammer and blush. He found the reaction both enchanting and arousing, but as he had undertaken not to distress her in any manner during their truce, he made it a point to cover himself when they were not in the midst of lovemaking.

It was mid-afternoon and Clara was still sleeping from the exertions of the coupling they had earlier shared, also from the long night that had passed before. He hoped he wasn't exhausting her to ill health, had an idea that he probably was, and knew that the best he could do was try to slow his rampant need for her enough to let her rest as often as she required it. After three nights and three days, he didn't yet feel as if he had even made a dent in the desire that had lived with him for so many years. In truth, he was only just beginning to realize how deep, how great his need for her was. The idea was frightening. He'd set out to enslave her, to make her want him as he wanted her, and yet the opposite seemed to be happening. She was an opiate, and he was completely addicted. He was afraid—yes, very afraid, indeed—that nothing he did was going to save him from being as obsessed with her as his father had been with his mother. Even watching her now as she slept seemed slightly lunatical to him. A worthless, useless venture. He should call for his valet, have himself bathed and dressed, and go out to enjoy an evening with his friends at his club. He should be gone when Clara finally awoke and let her wonder at his absence, and he should return no sooner than tomorrow afternoon and then say nothing of where he had been. Just to let her know that he'd not fallen beneath her spell, living only to see her, to hear her voice, to have her smile turned his way.

But he wouldn't go. He'd stay and watch her slumber, waiting for her to open her gray eyes and look at him with the sweet desire that was a beautiful gift. And he would take what was left of this first week of their marriage and be as her slave, knowing himself a fool all the while. When the week drew to a close, when they left this private idyll, as he knew they must, the ending would only be that much more painful. Their lives would drift. She would again be the gay, much-admired toast of the *ton* that she couldn't seem to help being, and he would return to the people and things that made his life bearable.

He forcibly pushed the knowledge away. They were here now. Together. She was as open and generous and passionate a lover as he had always known she'd be, and, despite her shyness and innocence, delightfully eager to learn. But that was what attracted men to her in such swarms. They must recognize, just as he had done, that Clara would be more than willing to please anyone fortunate enough to curry her favors.

Lucien tilted his head and regarded his sleeping wife from a different angle. No, Clara really couldn't be termed pretty. Her features were simple, small and birdlike. Perhaps that was why, in the hot pain that had engulfed him after he'd discovered her preference for her neighbor, Andrew Blakesley, he'd chosen such a coarse nickname for her. The Peahen. He'd used the epithet with almost sick determination for months, trying to convince himself that she meant less than nothing to him—so little, in fact, that he would even dare to insult her in a manner so unforgivable. Foolish, foolish boy. And foolish man.

No, she wasn't pretty, but neither was she ugly. Far from it. There was a certain calm pleasure in gazing at Clara. She was plain and neat, open and clear. He would never grow weary of looking at her, but suspected, instead, that the reverse would be true. Like a fine piece of Sèvres or a painting by Turner, the pleasure of gazing at Clara would only increase with time and understanding.

She was so slender that he could span her waist entirely with both hands, and so dainty that he was amazed he'd not yet crushed every one of her tiny bones with his physical demands. But she'd not complained at all. She'd taken everything he'd given and demanded even more. He'd never known such a fantastic lover before. His mind told him that she was not the least bit of what a desirable woman was supposed to be, while his heart and body registered her as the only woman who was able to make him completely lose himself in the pleasure she gave. Pamela, who knew everything there was about pleasuring a man, had never been able to work the magic that divorced Lucien's mind from what was happening to him physically. Clara, with but her innocent touch, made him lose his mind altogether.

Another fifteen minutes passed as he watched her slumber, looking so small and childlike in the huge bed, burrowed beneath the covers. She was the stillest sleeper he'd ever come across; not that he had many to compare her with. He'd not made a habit of sleeping with the whores and mistresses he'd kept over the years, although he'd passed out in Pamela's bed a number of times from a combination of drink and exhaustion.

Rising from the bed with slow care, he went to his desk and sat down to write a note with his requirements for the coming evening. He wanted a hot bath drawn within the hour, and the bedroom freshened while he and Clara were occupied in the bathing chamber. Clean linens. New robes. A light repast. Wine. A chilled bottle of his finest French champagne—Clara had decided during the past three days that it was her favorite drink—and a vase of fragrant white roses. He had little doubt that his ingenious butler would readily be able to find such flowers at this time of year. The old candles were to be removed and replaced. He wanted the new ones lit by the time he and Clara returned to the room.

Having finished this missive, Lucien took up a small Italian rosewood box from the top of his desk, worked the myriad drawers and levers until a secret compartment was revealed, as well as a key that lay within. He opened a particular desk drawer and, after a moment of consideration, removed a small item wrapped in silk, then locked the drawer and returned the key to its hiding place. The missive was slipped beneath the door that led to his and Clara's shared sitting room, and Lucien tugged at the bell-pull to notify his staff of its presence. The system had worked quite well thus far. The only human being Lucien had actually spoken with since he and Clara had locked themselves away was Clara herself. And that was just as he wanted it to be. These few days were going to be the most selfish, and glorious, of his life, and he would take them and horde them like a greedy miser. In years to come, when Clara had left him—if Clara left him—he would remember this time the way aged men recalled their lost youth. It would be a blanket to warm the chill of loneliness, the only weakness he would allow himself when she had at last closed her heart to him.

He unwrapped the delicate fan and tossed aside the silk

that had covered it. An unbidden smile tugged at the corners of his mouth. He remembered the day when he'd bought it for Clara, in Italy, in the marketplace of a small town outside of Pisa on a day so hot that the seller had been nearly bereft of goods. But this fan had been too expensive and fine to be sold for the mere pursuit of comfort. It was a work of art, to be used only by a very great lady, to be used only for the fine skill of flirting and teasing. Made of the finest ivory and most delicate cream-colored lace, ornamented lightly with flowers painted in gold, it was as beautiful now as it had been on that long-ago day when he'd outbidden every other buyer to claim it for his beloved. Robby had thought him utterly foolish to do so, but, then, Robby had felt the same way about the small porcelain jewelry box Lucien had bought in Copenhagen, and the elaborate silver necklace—made out of hundreds of tiny silver bells—that he'd found in a small village in Peru. Lucien had found something for Clara in every country Robby had dragged him through during the four years they'd spent away from England, and had guarded each treasure carefully, even on their dangerous journey through the Andes, so that he might present them to her as proof of his love and devotion when they at last returned. A wrap made of the softest, purest wool from Ecuador, incense of spice and sandalwood from India, a perfumed oil from Spain in a scent mixed especially for her, a small wood carving of an angel from Germany. All gifts for Clara. All hidden for years, waiting for just this time to be given.

Sitting on the bed, he leaned over his sleeping wife.

"Clara," he whispered, touching the open fan softly to her cheek.

She made no movement at all.

"Clara," he repeated, and brushed the fan's silken lace with a light, feathery touch from her temple to her chin.

He leaned down farther to tickle the rim of her ear with

his lips. "Good lady wife," he murmured, and pressed his mouth more fully against that delicate part of her body.

Clara stirred. Lucien chuckled and slid a hand about her waist, even as she turned into him. "Good day, my sweet, lazy lady."

"Mmmm." She stretched, then settled all about him, hands, arms and legs nestling close and falling still.

"Are you going to sleep again?" he asked, dropping kisses on the face that lay against his shoulder. He pulled the covers aside and used the fan again, on her neck, shoulders, arm, and back, touching lightly as he went, tickling her into awareness. "I've a gift for you."

"Another?" she murmured, lifting her head with obvious effort before letting it fall back. Her hand slid upward, between the opening of his robe, in a sleepy, intimate caress. "You're going to spoil me horribly, Lucien."

He tapped the fan against her hip. "You know me better than to say anything so foolish. I'm not much in the way of giving women pretty trinkets, but these small things are yours, already. You might as well have them."

She made an exaggerated sigh. "You're also not much in the way of giving a woman pretty words, but I'm well used to it."

He was glad she wasn't the sort of woman to fuss at him and try to plead him into being something he was not. If they couldn't be perfectly happy together, perhaps they could at least be comfortable.

"And they're not small trinkets. The necklace is the loveliest work I've ever seen, and the perfume—"

"Is still making me crazed," he told her, dipping his head to the curve of her shoulder to draw in the rich scent more closely.

"It is beautiful, is it not?" she murmured, pressing against him with a sound of contentment. "I shall use it sparingly, to make it last."

"No. Use it as often as you wish." He wondered if it would be gone at the end of their six months. "I'll have something else made for you when it's run out."

He could feel her smiling against his shoulder. "Very well. What is this?" She twisted slightly to see what he was running up and down her forearm. "Oh, Lucien! How beautiful!"

He let her snatch the fan away, and, as he watched her obvious glee with it, told her the tale of how he'd come to buy it for her.

"It's the most beautiful fan I've ever seen, and I shall be the most envied woman of the *ton* to have it. I shall cherish it always, just as I will the necklace and the perfume. Thank you, Lucien."

He lifted a hand to graze the curve of her spine. She seemed only just to realize that she was sitting up in the bed, giving him a perfectly delightful view of her naked person.

"Do you wish to thank me, Clara?" he asked, smiling as she blushed hotly and gathered the sheets up to cover herself.

"Lucien . . ."

"I'm having a hot bath drawn," he said, his traveling fingers causing his wife to shiver. "Perhaps you might bring your vial of perfumed oil and think of a way to express your gratitude."

"It was a beautiful wedding, Lady Anna. Perfectly beautiful. I'm sure I've never seen another couple so well matched as Viscount Callan and the new viscountess." Lady Earlington tapped Anna's arm with her fan and leaned closer to murmur, confidentially, "Clearly a love match, eh? I knew it the moment I saw Lord Callan take Lady Clara's hand from her father's arm. Such a look as he gave her, I declare it nearly made me swoon." At this, Lady

Earlington and the other elderly women surrounding Anna gave way to congenial laughter.

"Thank you," Anna said, forcing a polite smile upon her lips. "I believe that both the Earl of Manning and my brother are pleased with the marriage."

"Well, of course they are," Lady Makevale agreed at once. "Such a handsome couple, after all, and putting aside all that unpleasantness with the viscount's late parents. But I'm sure that the marquess never gave a thought to that old matter."

"Surely not," Miss Violetta Hampson put in. "It would be perfectly unfair for anyone to place the guilt of the parents on the child. I'm certain Viscount Callan is nothing like his father in temperament, may God rest the man's soul. I'm not one to speak ill of the dead, of course, but I'm sure we've all heard the rumors. Well, and who hasn't," she pressed in a tone that made Anna think of a cloyingly sweet syllabub, "thick as talk was following Edward and Letitia Bryland's unfortunate demise? *And* Lord Ganley's?" She looked significantly about at her companions, and was rewarded with nods and murmurs.

Anna grit her teeth against the blatant insinuation. *She* might dislike Viscount Callan enough to hint that he had the heart of a murderer, but it was the outside of enough for anyone else to do so. "Edward Bryland was my brother's dearest friend," she stated tightly. "He was a kind, good, and generous man, and if his son, Lord Callan, is but half the man he was, then he is a fine man, indeed, and my niece may count herself a fortunate woman to have wed him. And now, if you will excuse me—" She began to turn just as a hard, masculine body came up behind her, blocking her exit.

"Lady Anna," the Earl of Manning greeted, taking hold of her elbow to keep her from leaving as he made his bow to the ladies surrounding her. Anna didn't miss the manner in which the elderly dragons simpered to the handsome and charming earl. She had to bite her tongue to keep from telling him how these same hypocritical ladies had only moments before been maligning his long-dead brother.

"My lord," she said instead. "How nice to see you again, so soon."

"Yes," he replied with the smile that had never failed to make her knees feel as if they were made of butter. "The wedding was delightful, was it not? However, I've been meaning to speak with you about that most unfortunate event which occurred just after . . ." Every gray head within hearing inclined toward him. The earl suddenly seemed to remember where he was. "But I'm sure these ladies don't wish to be bored by such trivialities. Perhaps we might discuss the matter more privately? Will you give me the honor of your company in the gardens, my lady? The weather out of doors is delightful."

"Is it?" she remarked tonelessly.

He smiled and offered his arm. "Shall we, then?"

She would have chosen the most remote corner of darkest Africa at the moment rather than be alone with Robert Bryland, but even his company was preferable to that which she was in presently. She set her hand upon his arm.

"Thank you."

"My pleasure. Ladies," he said, gifting those elderly women with a bow and a smile.

"You've not lost your touch, Robert," she said as he led her away toward the French doors that were already opened to the garden beyond. "And you've certainly given those gossips something to talk about, false as it was. Nothing unfortunate happened after the wedding, as you very well know."

"But they so desperately wanted something juicy to rattle on about," he replied innocently. "I merely gave them another bone to chew on in place of the one they were already worrying.''

"And charmed them in the process," she said somewhat tartly. "But I always did say that you could charm any woman of any age, be she a grandmother"—she glanced at him—"or a child."

"Ah," he said as the cooler outdoor air greeted them. "I must take that to mean that you're displeased about my appointment with Sarah on the morrow."

"With my daughter, *Miss Huntington,* yes," Anna replied hotly, glad to be far enough from polite society to speak as she wished.

"Yes, with Miss Huntington," he agreed congenially. "I'm quite looking forward to it, although I've already visited the Tower a number of times. You're invited to come along with us, if you like, Anna. Indeed, I hope that you will. Otherwise we must take that awful nurse, and the woman is, if you'll permit me to speak bluntly, quite depressing. Sarah tells me—"

"Sarah tells you!" Anna pulled her hand from his arm. "Yes, with all the visiting you've done with her since the day of the wedding I can imagine she's told you quite a great deal. But I will remind you, sir, that Sarah is *my* daughter. I'll not have you speaking freely of her. Or with her. Indeed, I would rather not have you knowing her at all!"

"Would you not, Anna?" he asked gently, holding her gaze. "You know very well that my visits to your brother's town house have been purely a matter of form, and very much expected after our families have so recently been united. Sarah said that she wished to see the Tower of London and asked me to take her. Should I have ignored her? Would you have preferred that?"

Damn him! Anna thought, giving him her back. Damn him for being so calm and righteous. For making her feel like a horrid mother, when she knew very well that she was not. And damn him for being so handsome. She was beginning to hate the perfect features that ever made him look like some ideal Greek god. Time had been more than merciful to him. He looked as attractive, and certainly more masculine, than he had eleven years ago.

"Why are you doing this, Robert? Is it to punish me?"

"Punish you?" he repeated faintly, as if she'd utterly shocked him. "Anna, how could you think it? I should never wish to punish you. For any reason. My God. And even if I did, do you hold me in such low esteem that you think I would ever use a child—a child, Anna—for such a base purpose?"

Now she felt even more foolish. Of course she'd never thought any such thing of him. He twisted her words about, just as he had always done.

"Then why do you pursue this acquaintance with my daughter? You must know that I can't wish it."

"I do know it," he admitted. "But she wishes it, and I, because I very much enjoy her company, wish it. You've raised a lovely child, Anna. And because of what we once shared, I had thought to make her time in London more enjoyable. There is no more evil design to it than that, and you, of all people, should know the truth of that. I loved you, and I—"

"You loved me!" she scoffed, feeling the sharp pain his words gave.

He grabbed her arm and roughly turned her about. His blue eyes were filled with fierce emotion.

"I loved you," he said slowly, "more than I believed it possible to love. More than I had ever known of love or dreamed of it. I would have gladly given my life to preserve it."

"Would you have, indeed? It's a very pretty speech, Robert, but you were always quite good at them, as I seem to remember. I fell for them, at any rate. At least in the beginning. But you forget that I know firsthand just how great this 'love' that you claim to have felt for me truly was.'' She looked pointedly at the hand he still held upon her arm. ''You're hurting me.''

He released her and stepped back. She could see him gathering his mask of civility about him, regaining his perfect social composure.

''You still condemn me for my lapse with Diana—''

''Was that her name?''

He gave her a patient look. ''Don't pretend to an ignorance you do not possess, Anna. It doesn't become you. You may think to hurt me more than you already have, but I assure you it's impossible.''

She felt cold, suddenly, and wished she'd never come out to the gardens with him. Rubbing her gloved hands over her bare arms, she said, ''You're right, of course. It's foolish of me to pretend that I could ever forget what happened. More than foolish. I've detested that name for the past eleven years.''

''Strangely enough,'' he said, ''so have I. Are you cold, Anna? Or is it because of me that you shiver? I promise, on my honor, not to repeat the unfortunate event that occurred when we were last alone in a garden together. Not that I regret what happened, mind you, but I could have wished for it to have ended in a far different manner. Do you wish to return indoors?''

She shook her head, turning about and looking out at the gardens, which were enchantingly illuminated with Chinese lanterns.

''No, Robert. Not yet. And I wasn't afraid that you would assault my person again. The black eye from the last time has only just healed, has it not? Take me down one of these pathways, please.''

He seemed to understand her need for silence, but he'd

always done so. In silence, he took her hand and set it upon his arm, and in silence they walked the length of the garden. When they reached the end he led her to a small bench and sat beside her.

"Were you happy with Colonel Huntington?"

"Yes."

She heard him swallow. A long moment passed before he spoke again. "He gave you your daughter. She's a lovely child."

Anna felt the sting of tears in her eyes, and forced herself to look at her hands. "Yes, she is. I love her dearly."

He cleared his throat. "Anna, perhaps you never realized—" he turned toward her slightly. "Perhaps you were never aware of how . . . much I regretted . . . of how very sorry I was—"

The tears found their way down her cheeks. "I knew," she whispered. "I was sorry, too."

He reached over to take her hands with both of his. The gesture was friendly, comforting. "Then perhaps we shouldn't speak of the matter more. I only wanted to make certain that you knew I never took my sin lightly. I've often looked back and regretted the manner in which I behaved on that last day. You had the right of it, Anna. Never doubt that. Here, please don't cry." He fumbled in one of his inner pockets until he withdrew a small, ornately sewn handkerchief, which he pressed into her hands.

She took it and, feeling it, laughed despite her tears. "Oh, Robert, you silly fop. Do you still carry silk handkerchiefs?"

He chuckled, too. "Yes, of course. My last defiant holdout from my parents' more elegant era."

"You should have been born a hundred years ago," she declared, dabbing at her eyes. "I think perhaps I should have my carriage called for."

"Don't leave, Anna. You haven't danced with me yet."

"I shouldn't have come at all," she said, sniffling. "I knew you'd be here. I knew you'd hound me until I danced with you."

"Yes," he admitted. "It's the only reason I came."

"And it's terribly foolish. I can't think why you do it, and I wish you'd stop."

"Can't you? And do you?"

"Yes!" she said insistently. "I mean no. I don't understand why you do it, and yes, I wish you'd stop."

He smiled his maddening smile. "Come and dance with me. A waltz. You'll feel better after, I vow."

She pressed the handkerchief into his hands. "No. Please, Robert. Don't do this to me."

"What, Anna?" The bit of silk disappeared into his coat.

She searched his face, his eyes. How could she make him understand? She'd survived the hellish misery of losing him years ago, but the thought of suffering through that again was beyond her comprehension.

"It would kill me, Robert," she whispered, staring at him. "I swear it would kill me. You can't begin to know——"

His hand covered hers again. "I do know. I promise you, Anna, that I mean you no harm. And that I would never hurt you apurpose. But sometimes, as we have both learned very well, we do hurt those we love dearly, whether we wish it or not. All I ask of you tonight is a dance. Nothing more. And if you can't give it, I'll not press the matter."

She drew in a breath slowly, willing herself to calm.

"A dance," she said.

He nodded. And then smiled. She felt herself falling prey to him all over again.

"Very well, Robert. One dance. And then I'll go."

"Yes, Anna." He stood, drawing her to her feet. "I understand you perfectly."

Chapter Twelve

Lucien sat in his carriage for a full five minutes, gazing at the exterior of Pamela's small town house. A week he'd told her, but it had been over two months since he'd made any effort to see her, even to send her a note. She was bound to be furious, and he wasn't looking forward to the coming interview. Steeling himself, he at last alighted and went to the door.

Sibby was delighted to see him, blushing and curtseying and becoming even more flustered when Lucien captured her hand and gifted her with one of his rare smiles.

"Sibby, my love," he murmured, amazed to find that he was gladder to see the sweet-faced girl than he was at the idea of seeing her mistress. "What a welcome and lovely sight you are." He kissed her hand with a lingering intent that seemed to make the girl stop breathing. He began to say something else in this same flirtatious vein, but a bruise on the girl's cheek suddenly caught his attention. Frowning, he gently touched it, and watched her flinch. "Lady Halling hasn't been taking her temper out on you again, has she, Sibby? You need only tell me if she has, little one, and I shall make certain that she no longer does so."

If it was possible, Sibby turned even redder. "Oh, no, m'lord," she assured him, looking suddenly fearful and nervous. "She's wonderful to me. Always." She covered the bruise with her free hand. "Always, m'lord."

Lucien wished that Clara was with him. She'd know what to say to put the girl at ease, how to make the situation perfectly comfortable. He was seldom good at such things.

Smiling in what he hoped was a reassuring manner, he squeezed her hand before releasing it. "Is your mistress at home?"

Sibby curtseyed again. "Yes, m'lord. She's been in her studio all morning, but gave strict word weeks ago to announce your lordship no matter what she was about, if you should come." At this Sibby glanced about quickly, then leaned forward and lowered her voice to a whisper. "I shouldn't tell it, m'lord, but she's been in such a state, waiting for you to come. She's been that mad."

"Thank you for the warning," he whispered in return.

Sibby straightened. "I'll just announce you, then, if you'll pardon me, m'lord."

"No, don't bother, my dear," he said when she would have raced away. He removed his cloak and gave both it and his hat into her keeping. "I shall announce myself."

"Oh, but, m'lord—"

He gave her chin a light, teasing pinch. "Don't worry, Sibby, love. Lady Halling won't vent her ire on you. I give you my word."

Pamela was so absorbed in her work that she didn't hear him push wide the already open door. Her workroom was the only place in her home that didn't smell of the heavy, distinctive perfume Pamela always wore. Instead, it smelled of canvas and oils and cleaning fluids. Lucien had never been able to understand how Pamela could bear the fumes for more than a few minutes at a time, but she spent most of each early afternoon and evening here, either drawing or painting. Art wasn't the only passion in her life, but it was, certainly, the only one that drove her. To separate Pamela from her work would have been to separate her from the only thing she actually cared about. It was true that she earned an admirable income from her skills, but even if she did not, she'd yet continue to paint and draw and create. And her works were, admittedly, quite superb. Especially her oil paintings, many of which hung in the homes of society's elites. Prinny himself owned and displayed two of Lady Pamela Halling's landscapes at Carlton House.

That being the case, Lucien had never quite understood her need to concentrate so often on scathing, satirical caricatures, especially those involving the same members of the *ton* whom she so much wanted to be in favor with. She was careful, of course, to keep her caricature work anonymous, signing them only as *Le Chat*—The Cat. It was an apt title for the manner in which Pamela carried out her vendettas through her art, especially when she set out to publicly humiliate someone who'd made the unfortunate mistake of drawing down her wrath. The Cat had destroyed more than one reputation in Town, and was generally disliked and feared by society as a whole, despite the rampant curiosity that continued to draw buyers for the liberal publication that put out her work. If her identity as the artist of the infamous caricatures was ever revealed, she'd become not only a complete pariah but also a target for revenge. There were plenty of people who'd like nothing better than to bring a permanent end to The Cat's career.

She was immersed in the study of a still life at the moment, transferring the image of a collection of flowers and fruits strewn on a table onto the canvas before her. He watched as, utterly absorbed, she deftly copied the scene with near perfection, her skilled fingers seeming to move without any dependent direction. Her long blond hair was swept up in an untidy arrangement; stray strands that had fallen loose brushed against her cheek and neck. The plain, unfashionable day dress she wore was protected by a large apron that covered the front of her from neck to toe. All in all, she looked to be perfectly comfortable, and, as always, stunningly beautiful.

"Good evening, Lady Halling," he murmured with slow care, striving not to surprise her too much.

She jerked upright and dropped her brush, just as if he'd shouted at her. When she whirled about he saw open panic on her features, an expression of fear that he'd never expected to see on the face of Pamela Halling. Her glance darted about the room, as if there might be something there that she didn't want him to see, until at last she seemed to come to herself. Drawing in a breath and releasing it, she gave a laugh and set her palette aside.

"Lucien." Her voice was her own, and she was clearly in charge of herself once more. "You surprised me. How long have you been standing . . . ?" She turned to face him again, except this time with narrowed eyes. "Sibby let you come back here alone?" Anger tightened her features. "I've told her time and again—"

"It doesn't matter," Lucien interrupted. "I wouldn't let her accompany me, despite her protests. You'll not punish her, Pamela."

She looked at him with disbelief. "And you, Lucien, will not tell me how to deal with my own maid."

"Yes, I will," he replied, pushing from the door to step into the room. "And you'll do as I say, my dear, or feel my displeasure. Don't mistreat her again, Pamela. I won't have it." He spoke even more softly. "I hope you understand me?"

"Don't threaten me, Lord Callan," she said with equal menace. "You'll find yourself much the worse for it."

"Threats," he said, running one gloved finger beneath her chin in a light caress, "are useless weapons, Pamela. I never deal in them. If you harm Sibby, you *will* feel my displeasure." Drawing back, he sketched her a very slight, mocking bow. "The time is apparently inconvenient for you, Lady Halling. I shall take my leave."

"Lucien!" She gripped his sleeve to keep him from turning. "Don't go. Please. I apologize for my temper. You know how I am when I'm disturbed from my work, and I've been furious at you for staying away so long, anyhow. I promised myself I'd throw a bowl at your head the moment you walked in the door." She smiled up at him. "Instead, I threw a tantrum."

"Indeed."

"Can you wonder at it?" she asked, releasing him and turning to pick up the brush she'd dropped. "When you've left me waiting all this time? Your new bride must be more proficient than I believed, my dear. You did say to expect you a week or so following your marriage, and yet, from what I hear, you've spent the past two months busily escorting Lady Callan hither and yon, just as any faithfully devoted husband might. I can understand that you had to act the besotted fool for her when she was presented at Court, but to do so everywhere else is beyond comprehension. Really, Lucien." She shot him an amused glance as she began to clean her brushes with swift, vigorous swipes of a cloth. "It begins to sound as if you're in competition with Clarence Parkett."

Lucien, who had turned his attention to an unfinished sketch of the social hour in Hyde Park, murmured, disinterestedly, "Dog Parkett?" He and Pamela had been the first to use the descriptive word, finding the man's slavish devotion to his wife absurdly funny. The nickname had, unfortunately, caught on, and soon everyone was using it. Lucien still cringed inwardly whenever he met the man socially.

"Yes," Pamela said with a laugh. "Even so. We shall have to find a new name for you, will we not? 'Hound' comes to mind. 'Hound' Callan. Or Lord 'Hound.' I like that even better. And it suits you so well, my dear."

"Pamela," he said in a warning tone. And yet he found himself almost in agreement with her. He had left her waiting and wondering, and hadn't been able to bring himself to send a note to tell her that he would be delayed in coming. Every day, when he'd thought of it, he'd decided that he would simply visit her in person. Indeed he had known that he must, in order to keep her from growing too angry and perhaps even foolishly so. And every day he'd found some reason, instead, to spend the time with Clara. The theater and the opera, Hyde Park and any number of museums and shops. Places he'd normally disdained to go had suddenly become his daily haunts. It was laughable. And it was just as Pamela said. He'd become helplessly devoted to his small, unremarkable wife. Even now, he could envision Clara in his mind, her expressive face, neatly kept hair, and slender figure. She possessed nothing in the physical sense that could compare to Pamela's alluring beauty, and yet he longed just to be in the same room with her, to see her and know that she was his. And he was becoming ridiculously jealous. The knowledge that Clara was, at this very moment, probably surrounded by her legion of admirers at Lady Versey's ball, charming each and every one of them with effortless ease, made his heart twist with unwanted fury.

"Tell me, are you very much in love with her?" Pamela taunted. "How horrible it must be. Enslaved by a *peahen*." She said the word viciously, and then laughed again. "I'm overcome with amusement every time I think of it. *You* being caught and chained by the very woman you've hated for so long."

There were never half-measures with Pamela. She aimed for the heart and struck well and true. It was one of the things that had first attracted him to her. They'd been evenly matched in their bitterness and humors. So much so that he'd feared losing her, knowing he'd probably never discover another woman who would understand and complement his darker side so well. That he'd been the one to find something better suddenly made him her prey, rather than her compatriot. He could feel what was to come as if it were already upon him.

Pushing aside the pang of self-recrimination, Lucien tried to summon up anger, or even insult, and yet the only emotion he seemed able to find was pity. And perhaps some measure of sorrow. He'd never loved Pamela, but they'd been friends and good companions. She was going to be furious for a time, and had every right to be. He was rather furious at himself, too, for being such a damned fool, as well as a hypocrite. He'd laughed at so many other men for giving in to love, for letting a woman change their lives. Now he deserved every bit of taunting and insult that was flung at him.

She was watching him, waiting for a reaction. This was a game between them, just as most everything was. Whatever move he made would determine their course, at least until Pamela decided what *her* next move would be. There were any number of replies he might give her. He finally decided to give her the one she expected.

"If I hadn't seen it with my own eyes, my dear, I'd never have believed it. Are you truly jealous, Pam? That must be a novel sensation for you."

With one harsh movement she sent the brushes flying, scattering everywhere about the room.

"Bastard!" she shouted, fury seething hotly in her tone. "Don't you speak to me like that, not after you've left me waiting on your pleasure for the past two months! You've humiliated me completely in the eyes of all our friends, and I will *never* forgive you for it."

"Then I'll not waste time making an apology," he replied coolly, regarding her with a steady gaze. "I understand you've not exactly spent the time in complete seclusion.''

An expression of triumph took the place of her fury. ''That's right, my lord. Did you think I'd sit at home and pine for you after that first week passed? You should have known better, Lucien.''

There had been a time, even only a few weeks past, when he would have punished her for such a slight. Everyone in their circle of acquaintances knew that Pamela was his mistress, despite the fact that he'd never kept her financially, and that she was fully off-limits to any other males. Now, that had all changed.

''Ah, well,'' he said, his gaze deliberately leaving her and lazily perusing the clutter on her worktable. ''My loss, I fear. And another man's gain. Or should I say men? I'm sure you at least gave Heswell and Wolston and your other many admirers their money's worth.''

Her indrawn breath was more than enough warning. Lucien turned just in time to capture her upraised fist before it could descend.

''The question, Lady Halling,'' he murmured with a smile, squeezing the delicate bones of her hand with a warning force, ''is whether you received the satisfaction you sought? Tell me, my dear, was it quite terrible? Poor old Heswell must have tried to gum you half to death, unless he put his teeth in. I'm overcome with amusement every time I think of it.''

''Don't.'' She tried unsuccessfully to wrench free of him. ''Don't!''

He drew nearer, forcibly lowering her hand to her side. ''I'll leave you in peace, Pamela, so long as you never again mention my wife within my hearing. I don't want to hear her name on your lips, or her title, or anything about her. You are to leave Clara alone. Completely and entirely.''

''Lucien, you fool!'' She struggled until he at last released her. Stepping back, she rubbed her hand and met his gaze with a wrath that was more fully contained. "You damned fool! Only listen to yourself. She's going to destroy you. You've *always* known it. How could you be taken in so easily? So quickly?"

Lucien stared, watching as Pamela strove to master herself.

"You've always known it," she said again, more calmly. "She nearly destroyed you once already, just as your mother did your father. You swore you'd not follow in his footsteps, but look at you! Two months with your bride— only two!—and you're slavering at her feet. Hound Callan. I *will* call you that, you perfect fool. You deserve it!"

Silence followed the words. Lucien found that he couldn't deny them. He was like a child where Clara was concerned. A hungry, desperate child, willing to do anything to get what he wanted. Even knowing that disaster was surely going to be the end of it couldn't make him stop. The weeks since his marriage had been the sweetest time he'd ever known. So sweet and so perfect . . . his mind told him that what he had now with Clara couldn't last, and yet his heart was terrified at the very thought of losing it. And her. It would be far better to admit defeat now and send Clara to Pearwood and be done with it.

"She's not even pretty, is she?" Pamela put into the silence, speaking, he noted distantly, in the soft, even tone that meant she was being quite deliberate. "But perhaps she possesses something more than mere beauty," she went on, moving about the room to pick up the scattered brushes, taking her time and moving in an easy, relaxed manner. "Perhaps she knows the secret of making a man feel good about himself. It's not so hard, after all. She knows how to smile just so, I'd wager. Not too coquettish, nor sly. Simply feminine and open, to make a man comfortable. And she knows how to direct the conversation and keep a man talking about himself. To make him feel special, and interesting, even if he's an utter ass and a bore, like Sir Thomas Reedley. She could probably charm him out of his very shoes, if she set her mind to it. Or has she, already?''

She had, Lucien admitted silently. Reedley was one of Clara's most devoted admirers. The man had told Lucien to his face that he held Clara in the highest esteem, and that he'd give anything to find such a "fine, nice-minded female" for himself.

Pamela's mouth turned up in a slow, perfectly controlled smile, which Lucien well recognized from the days they'd spent together.

"Just like your mother," she said, dropping the recovered brushes on the table with a dull clattering. "Just as charming, and as admirable."

She left the rest of it unsaid. Just as dangerous. Just as treacherous. Just as faithless.

Poison, Lucien thought. He had to remember that about Pamela. Pure poison. If he let go of that fact when dealing with her, he'd be finished as quickly as the rest of her victims ever had been.

His expression was emotionless when he finally said, "You forgot to mention the obvious, Pam. Despite my wife's failings, she's an unprecedented partner in bed." He let the words sink in before adding, "I've never had a better one. Nothing else would keep me at her side for so long, as you very well know."

She went white. Her hands clenched into fists. "I'm sure it won't be long before the rest of your friends discover the same fact for themselves!"

It was a laughably lame taunt, especially for someone of Pamela's experience. Lucien laughed out loud, knowing he'd succeeded in throwing her off balance. She recognized her mistake almost at once, and reddened as quickly as she'd paled.

"Bastard," she repeated.

He kept laughing.

"Oh, very well!" she cried, smiling despite herself. "You've won. I admit it. You played your hand very well, Lord Callan, and I concede defeat." She moved closer. "Can we put this foolishness away, then?" She stopped in front of him, her hands resting lightly on his chest. "Please, Lucien, let's not fight or play games. Take me out somewhere. I don't want to be angry with you anymore. It's too exhausting, and I've missed you. I have."

He took her hands and kissed them, more to soothe her than make amends. But when he spoke, he spoke in complete honesty.

"I've missed you as well, Pam. In a strange, familiar way, I think. But it's not enough." He let her go when she wanted it, this time. "My dear, I'm very sorry. But it's not enough."

She shook her head slightly, as if she couldn't quite believe him. "Why did you come, then? Lucien—"

"Just to speak to you. To see you."

Her eyes widened. "Lucien," she said again, and then fell silent.

"I meant what I said about my wife. Stay away from her, Pam."

She stared at him.

"And I meant what I told you about Sibby, as well. That's not a game to me. Ever. Understand it."

She began to shake her head. "Lucien," she murmured. "You aren't . . ." A short laugh escaped her unsmiling lips. "You don't mean this. You can't."

He turned and walked away, down the long hall, calling for Sibby as he neared the home's entrance.

"Lucien!"

He ignored her as the young maid helped him into his cape and then handed him his hat.

"Lucien!"

"Don't be afraid, Sibby, love," he told the pale girl, lifting her shaking hand to his lips. "You need only come to me if she causes you any distress. Simply send me word. I give you my promise, on my word of honor, that you shall not suffer for it."

"Lucien!"

He walked out the door and straight into the waiting carriage, turning away from the sight of a visibly shaken Lady Pamela Halling as she stood at her door, calling out his name.

"Are you certain you won't dance, my lady?" Sir Anthony Sayers pressed. "I vow you mean to break my heart."

Clara laughed lightly and gifted the handsome gentleman with a smile. "I'm very sorry, my lord, but if the choice is between breaking your heart or wearing my feet down to naught, I fear I must decide in favor of my feet."

"And if I offered to rub them for you to relieve their distress?" he teased. "I should be more than happy to do so."

Clara feigned a look of shock and rapped the gentleman's arm with the tip of her closed fan. "For shame, sir. Only think of what my husband would say. And your wife." Clara had always enjoyed innocent flirtations, but found it safest to pursue the hobby with a happily married man, with whom one could safely jest and never worry about the matter getting out of hand. The fact that Sir Anthony was madly in love with his beautiful wife made such teasing even more enjoyable.

Sir Anthony grimaced. "I doubt I should be able to think of anything much for some time once your husband had finished with me. Not that I can blame him, of course." He lifted her hand from his arm and kissed her fingertips gallantly. "I do thank you for the refreshing stroll in the garden, my lady. I hope I've not bored you too thoroughly with so much talk of my family?"

"Indeed not," Clara assured him sincerely. "I enjoyed every moment of hearing about your children. Perhaps one day I shall be able to return the favor, and sooner than later, I hope," she said, and they both laughed. "Ah, there's Miss Howell. Take me to her, if you please, my lord, and I shall gladly rest these troublesome feet."

A few minutes later, seated next to Bella in a relatively peaceful corner of the ballroom, Clara relaxed into her chair and said, with a sigh, "I wonder how much longer Aunt Anna will want to stay. Another hour and I think I shall be done for."

Bella adjusted the spectacles on her nose and looked about. "She was dancing with Lord Manning when I last saw her. Is there something brewing there, do you think? They seem to spend quite a good deal of time together, and there's talk all over Town."

"I know," Clara said. "It has distressed Aunt Anna somewhat, having her past relationship with the earl brought back out into the open. She had thought it all behind her."

"But it's so very romantic." Bella glanced at Clara and blushed. "He must be desperately in love with her to pursue her so openly. Even when she gives him such little encouragement." She unconsciously adjusted her glasses again.

"Yes," Clara said thoughtfully. "I suppose it's romantic, although I don't know if Auntie sees it that way. She always seems to be quite furious with him, and yet there are times . . ." She stopped, then smiled at her friend. "It's of no matter. I shouldn't speak of it. Where has Lord Severn gotten to?" She looked about for the large, hard-to-miss viscount. "I saw you dancing earlier."

"Oh," Bella said with obvious discomfort, "Wulf and Papa went into the library for a few moments. Papa had a sudden idea regarding the new mechanical engine they've been working on, and they decided it would be best to discuss the matter at once rather than risk forgetting it later. It's very hard for them to retain an idea unless they've committed it to paper, you know."

Clara knew. This wasn't the first time she'd seen Lord Severn abandon his fiancée in favor of the pursuit of science. The man was always scribbling and pondering and thinking, even in the midst of social company. It didn't seem to matter where he was or whom he was with; if he came upon some fascinating mental revelation, he simply excused himself and walked off to find a piece of paper and a pencil. She didn't know how Bella was able to stand it, although she supposed that the same might be said of her own situation. There were probably any number of women who'd be unwilling to suffer Lucien's dark silences and wildly varying moods, but she loved him, and because of that was willing to suffer almost anything. The weeks following their marriage had only served to show her how worthwhile such a cause was. Perhaps he wasn't a perfect man, but in the past two months he had tried—really and truly tried—to be a good husband and a pleasant companion, and had even made an effort to escort her to places and events which she knew he'd normally avoid. There had been a few lapses, a few small disagreements between them, but otherwise Clara couldn't remember being happier. She hoped and prayed that it was the same for Lucien.

"I'm certain he'll return soon," Bella said in an unconvincing tone.

"Yes," Clara murmured, setting a hand briefly over one of Bella's in a comforting gesture. "I'm sure he will." In truth, she doubted that either Lord Severn or Lord Hemstead would be seen for the remainder of the evening. The worst part was that most of the other men at the ball would be too wary to ask Christabella Howell for a dance. Viscount Severn's physical size and excessive jealousy were exceedingly effective deterrents to even the most platonic overtures. Lucien and Lord Rexley, both of whom were presently absent, were the only two regular partners Bella had, other than Viscount Severn. And, of course, the Earl of Kerlain, but he was another matter altogether.

"I wish I had your skill with handling men," Bella said wistfully. "They all seem to fall in love with you. Even Lord Callan. I've never seen him behave in such a normal manner before now, if you'll pardon me for saying such a thing." She glanced at Clara meekly. "I was always a little afraid of Lord Callan, although he's never been anything but kind to me. It's just his darkness, I suppose, that tends to make one nervous in his presence. And that way he has of staring so directly at one, as if he can read private thoughts. But since he married you, Clara, he's been really quite . . . nice. And it's obvious that he loves you." She adjusted her spectacles again before folding her hands in her lap and letting out a long sigh. "I wish I could work the same magic with Wulf. I'd give anything to make him look at me the way Lord Callan looks at you."

"But I'm certain that Lord Severn loves you dearly, Bella," Clara assured the other girl. "Despite his tendency to wander off, he does seem to be most devoted to you."

"Yes. When he's not in the midst of being devoted to his science, first. Which he ever is. Constantly."

"Oh, Bella, I'm sure that's not so."

"It is," Bella told her. "There are times when he forgets I'm in the same room with him, or that I'm in his company at all. I won't be surprised if he departs the ball tonight without even taking his leave of me. He's done it before. Too many times to count, in fact."

"Good heavens," said Clara, much shocked by the idea

of this and yet unable to argue that Viscount Severn wouldn't do such a thing. The man did tend to be forgetful when he was in the midst of mental calculations. Twice in the past month he'd left Barrington without taking either his hat or his coat. A footman had been obliged to run after him and bring him back. Lucien had been mildly amused at Clara's surprise and distress, and had assured her that with Wulf, such things happened all the time.

"Oh, dear," Bella said suddenly, looking across the room to where a certain man was generating his usual rash of interest. "Oh, no. Is he coming this way? Oh, dear me." She began to fumble with her spectacles.

Clara followed her friend's panicked gaze to where Lord Kerlain was bowing over a young lady's hand. When he stood full height he glanced in their direction and, catching Clara's gaze, smiled and nodded before setting his sight more intently upon Bella.

"I'm afraid he is."

"Oh, dear. What shall I do?" Bella's hands fluttered first over her hair and then the skirt of her ball gown. "I do wish Wulf were here."

Clara continued to watch as Kerlain made his way toward them.

"Do you know, Bella," she said, "I believe he's the handsomest man I've ever seen. I wonder if all the men in the United States are so well favored."

He was a tall, muscular man with thick, feathery hair the color of pale honey. His eyes were the most beautiful green she'd ever seen before, like fine emeralds. And his facial features were absolutely perfect, masculine, well defined, aristocratic. He was just the sort of man young girls procured in their daydreams, the one who played the parts of romantic hero, wicked pirate, practiced rake, and highway robber, all in one.

"Do you really think so?" Bella asked doubtfully. "I've

always thought that Jack—Lord Rexley—was the best-looking man I'd ever seen. You must admit he's terribly handsome.''

''Jack? He's certainly good-looking enough to make women swoon. The Earl of Kerlain, unfortunately, is good-looking enough to make women lose their wits altogether.''

''Yes,'' said Bella. ''It's just what he does to me. Why can't he leave me alone? I'm certain he only means to upset Wulf, but it's so unkind.''

Clara shook her head. ''It's not to upset Wulf, my dear. I'm afraid it's far worse than that.''

Bella looked at her questioningly, but had no time to ask Clara what she meant. The Earl of Kerlain had arrived.

''Lady Clara,'' he murmured smilingly, bending over her hand, which he kissed briefly before releasing. ''How pleasant to see you again. And Miss Howell.'' He took Bella's hand and held it. ''You look perfectly . . . marvelous.'' The word was drawn out with seductive meaning. ''I believe they're about to play a waltz. Would you honor me, my lady?''

He was already pulling Bella out of her chair, not giving her a chance to decline. And Bella, just like any woman falling beneath the Earl of Kerlain's spell, went with him without a murmur.

Definitely trouble, Clara thought as Kerlain slid his hand about Bella's waist, rather low, only barely just skirting the edges of propriety, and pulled his partner close. She'd teased and flirted with more men than she could remember, and had become well honed at divining when a man's interest was feigned or real. The Earl of Kerlain's interest in Miss Christabella Howell was most definitely *real*. Every time he looked at the girl the fact that he had feelings for her was obvious. The question was, what sort of feelings were they? There was desire in the way he held her, bold appreciation whenever he looked at her—but that was understandable. Bella was not only a beautiful young woman, a perfect model of the golden-haired, blue-eyed beauty who was considered to be the ideal, but her body was shaped in a manner that made thinner and less curved females like Clara grit their teeth with jealousy. But there was something else whenever the Earl of Kerlain sought Bella out. Something Clara couldn't quite put her finger on. It was almost as if he were sorry for the girl, as if he commiserated with the manner in which Viscount Severn so often ignored her, as if he wanted to somehow set things right. Clara wasn't at all sure she understood the situation, but it was, most assuredly, trouble.

From the corner of her eye she saw a dark, handsome man enter the far end of the room, and her heart felt as if it might turn over in her chest. Lowering her gaze, she unfolded the fan that Lucien had given her and prepared to put it to good use.

Lucien found his wife in the confusion of the ballroom after a hard minute's search. He'd expected to see her dancing in the arms of one of her many admirers, but instead she was sitting in a far corner, waiting, it seemed, for him to find her.

She was slowly fanning herself, half hiding her face behind the ivory and lace of the familiar gift he'd given her. Her eyes were fully visible, however, and sending him a clear message that set his feet in her direction.

But he knew how to play this game, too, just as he knew how to play Pamela's. This one, however, he found sweet and enticing, so long as he was the only object of Clara's coquetry. She enjoyed flirting almost to distraction; it was something she was either going to have to put an end to, or that he was going to have to come to terms with.

Ah, but she was a master at the seductive art. Seeing him slow his steps, she lowered the fan just enough to let him see her lips purse with sultry disappointment. Then the fan moved up, tapping her chin lightly, beckoning him forward, before fluttering lightly again beneath the level of her eyes. Lucien looked briefly from side to side to see if any other man had mistaken the clear invitation she'd issued, and was glad to note that his acquaintances had realized his presence in the room.

A feeling that was half arousal, half fury tugged at his emotions. If Clara ever dared to be so blatantly flirtatious with other men, he'd kill her. Or himself. One of them, just to somehow be put out of his misery. But she'd been careful in her dealings thus far, as she had promised. He'd not yet felt her turn her interest to another, not in the slightest manner. Indeed, it was only he who received the full benefit of her talents, just as he was doing now. Still looking at him, she winked one eye slowly, and lowered the fan to let him see her smile.

The flirtatious little tease! he thought, amused despite himself. He'd deliver a reply to her invitation. One she'd never forget.

By the time he reached her she had stood, pretending to be surprised at seeing him.

"Why, Lucien!"

"One dance," he told her, taking her hand and setting it on his arm. "And then I'm taking you home."

She went with him more than willingly, openly showing her pleasure at his presence. Beneath her smiling happiness, Lucien felt as if he were the King of England.

"But I came with my aunt, my lord," she said as he swung her into the waltz, moving quickly to find a place in the midst of the twirling couples. "You'd not make me desert her, I hope?" Her tone was light, teasing. He knew the sort of answer she wanted.

"My uncle informed me shortly after I arrived that he intends to escort Lady Anna to her home. You needn't worry about her in the least. You realize, I hope, that if he has his way, you and I will shortly be related through marriage?''

She laughed. ''Just as we thought to be, so many years ago.''

He pulled her a little closer. ''Yes. Just so. I needn't tell you that I disapprove?''

''No,'' she said, still smiling. ''You needn't.'' Her hand slid along his shoulder, toward his neck, and Lucien felt tingles running down his spine. Her body was light in his arms. Dancing with Clara was as effortless and easy as dancing with a feather. ''I thought you were going to your club tonight,'' she said. ''With Jack. Viscount Severn was impatient to get away and join you before he got busy with something else.''

''Wandered off, did he?'' Lucien asked, pulling her about in a turn, liking the way she so suddenly drew in her breath.

''With Lord Hemstead,'' she told him.

''Gad. They'll be gone for the rest of the night. I only hope Versey has all his parlors checked before the servants turn the lights down for the night, or they'll find Wulf and Hemstead still here in the morn.''

''Lucien,'' she said, ''I'm so glad you're here.''

So was he, Lucien thought with some surprise. Knowing that she was happy to see him did strange things to him, all over. It seemed impossible that any other woman on God's earth was capable of making a man so crazed and insensible.

''I only came to drag you off home so that I can have my way with you, Lady Callan. I've a carriage waiting outside.''

If possible, she looked even more breathless. ''Good,'' she murmured, and he felt his body harden with desire.

To keep his mind off that particular fact, at least until

they were out of reach of society's interested gaze, he looked about.

"Where's Bella, if Wulf's gone off?"

He found the answer before Clara could give it, with the result that his amorous mood was instantly dispelled.

"Kerlain's asking to be killed," he muttered, praying that the dance would come to an end before Wulf saw his fiancée in such close embrace with the Earl of Kerlain.

But it was not to be. He caught sight of Wulf standing at the edge of the dancers, and read the look on his friend's face very well.

Bringing Clara to a halt, he took her hand and led her off the dance floor.

"Lucien?"

"I want you to stay here, no matter what." Taking her by the shoulders, he briefly kissed her lips. "Unless the fight comes this direction. If that should occur, then I want you to leave the room at once. I'll find you afterward."

"Fight!" she repeated, trying, and not succeeding, to grab his sleeve as he walked away. "Lucien!"

He had only reached the edge of the dance floor again when Wulf threw the first punch, landing it squarely in the Earl of Kerlain's handsome face.

Chapter Thirteen

※

He took her home and led her upstairs to the bedchamber they had shared every night since their marriage. She was giddy, humming a waltz, dancing around the room as if she were in the arms of an invisible partner. Lucien, leaning against the closed door while he loosened his cravat, was content to watch as she fluttered about on her small, light feet, filling the room with her music. She set her fan with care upon his desk, pulled off her gloves and tossed them aside, then removed her silk wrap with a twirl and a flourish. When she at last came to him and lifted her smiling face for his kiss, he asked her why she was so happy.

"Because you were so wonderful in keeping Lord Kerlain and Lord Severn from fighting and ruining the ball," she told him, setting her arms about his neck. "And because you came to the ball. If you could only know how much I wanted you—"

He didn't let her say anything more for a long while after that. Not until he had undressed her and himself and taken her to their bed and put himself deeply inside of her. Even then she didn't actually speak, but variously murmured and cried out, sometimes saying his name, just as he said hers. He'd felt desperate for her all night long, starting from the moment he'd left Barrington by himself until this very moment. He felt it even yet, thrusting harder and more deeply and forcing aside the feelings of panic and fear until the desperation at last began to recede, fading in the heat and welcome that Clara gave him. She needed him, wanted him. He gloried in the knowledge. She opened to him and received him as if she felt the same desperation, as if she had to hold him even more closely in order to know that they weren't going to somehow be torn asunder.

Could he ever get close enough to her? he wondered, closing his eyes as the feeling of ecstasy began to wash over him. He would have to crawl inside her skin to do so. He almost wished he could. Beneath him, Clara strained upward, trembling, gripping his body with her hands and arms and legs. She cried out his name, though he barely heard her against the shuddering force of his own release. He had the vague idea, afterward, as he lay heavily and wearily on top of her, that he'd shouted out his pleasure twice as loudly as she had, and that every servant in the house had certainly heard him, as well as neighbors all down the street on either side.

She was stroking one hand lightly along the back of his bare buttock and thigh, something she liked to do after their lovemaking had only just ended.

"You always get the most wonderful bumps on your skin when we do this," she murmured sleepily. She'd told him that before, too. The fact that she was able to exact such a shivering change to his flesh seemed to please her no end.

Lucien laughed and lifted up on his forearms, looking down into her flushed, smiling face and feeling an indefinable rush of tenderness. Clara had vanquished his demons, just as she had done since their marriage. It was never a permanent remedy, but Lucien was grateful even for a temporary reprieve. He brushed a few stray strands of hair from her forehead and lowered his mouth to kiss her gently.

"So do you," he said before moving off her and pulling the covers back so that she could climb inside of them.

"It looks as if a hurricane struck," he remarked as, naked, he moved about the room, putting out candles and lamps.

"As usual," Clara said from the middle of the bed, yawning. "Your valet would worry if it didn't."

"And he'd not have half so many interesting tales to tell the rest of the staff." Lucien climbed beneath the covers beside her, stretching an arm out. She snuggled up against his side, resting her head on his shoulder. It was the position they had gotten into the habit of sleeping in.

Habits. He had collected quite a distressing lot of them since becoming a married man. Tonight he had vowed that he would begin to wean himself away from Clara, and yet rather than take Pamela out for a night of gambling and drinking at Mawdrey's, as he'd intended to do, he'd ended up severing his relationship with her and had then landed in the same spot where he'd spent every night for the past two months. In his own bed, with his wife, at an indecently early hour. His friends were beginning to wink at him and snigger behind their hands. Jack and Wulf thought his rapid domestication the most amusing thing they'd ever encountered.

With a sigh, Clara turned into him, finding a more comfortable position and setting an arm about his chest. He lifted a hand and absently ran his fingers from her wrist to her elbow, back and forth, feeling her relax toward slumber. He would let her rest for an hour or so before making love to her again. Perhaps he, too, would sleep for a while.

"Thank you for coming to the ball tonight," she whispered. Her warm breath fell against his skin with each word.

He kissed the top of her head in silent reply. He didn't want to think either too long or too hard about why he'd gone to Lord and Lady Versey's ball. He didn't want to think about the way he'd behaved or the things he'd felt since he'd made Clara his wife. He only wanted to live each moment and take what it offered. If he was a fool in so many other ways, at least he would never look back and believe that he had wasted this precious time.

"Why do you like to flirt so much?"

He hadn't meant to ask the question, and wondered what had possessed him to speak such thoughts aloud. He already knew what the answer would be. He'd learned it from his mother. She loved the attention and adoration of many men, because the attention and adoration of one alone wasn't enough.

"I think," she said quietly after a moment of silence, "it's because I'm so plain. I always knew that I would never be able to attract a man with my beauty, as I didn't, and don't, possess any. My mother told me that it didn't matter that I was so lacking, because what men really want in a woman is a good companion. She advised me to learn how to become a listener—to listen to a man and be interested in him and what he has to say, rather than to speak of myself or my own interests. And strangely enough, she was right."

"Listening isn't the same as flirting."

"No." She moved against him, sighing. "But once I discovered how easily a man could be distracted from my lack of beauty, simply by paying him a little attention, I began to discover that it was equally simple to gain his interest with smiles and teasing and . . . flirting, I suppose. It made me feel as if I were like other girls. I began to enjoy attending parties and balls, knowing that my company would be sought after, just as if I were beautiful. And do you know, Lucien? I discovered something else. I discovered that other people—not just men—need someone to listen to them and to like them for who they are, rather than for what their appearance is. I've met so many wonderful friends that way. Simply by paying attention to them and making them feel . . . well . . ."

"As if you were truly interested in them," Lucien finished. He knew very well that she possessed such a skill. It was what made her a wonderful hostess, and a much-sought-after guest at every event in London. People wanted Viscountess Callan at their ball or dinner or party; she never failed to make the time more pleasant. He couldn't think of one person, young, old, rich, or poor, whom Clara hadn't managed to utterly charm.

"I know you dislike it, Lucien. I've always been careful never to let it get out of hand, or to hurt anyone else. And I've never let any man think I was serious. I've always been most careful about that."

"I don't dislike it," he said. "I hate it. But we've made our bargain, Clara, and will stay with it." He rolled until he leaned over her, and was gazing into her eyes. "As long as you give no other man honest encouragement, I'll not tell you to stop a practice that you enjoy so well. I want to tell you something, and ask that you never forget or disbelieve it."

"What, Lucien?"

"To me, you are the most beautiful woman who ever has existed or who ever will exist. No one else will ever hold for me the attraction that you do. I swear to you, on my honor, that this is the truth."

She drew in a sharp breath and said his name, and the next moment released a sob. When she began to weep, Lucien determinedly kissed her, and set about taking her mind off of everything but him, and them, and the pleasure that they alone could each give the other.

Chapter Fourteen

❧

The Earl of Kerlain didn't make a habit of visiting Maw-drey's. It was exactly the sort of dark, wretched hellhole he most disliked, peopled with fatuous and dim-witted members of the *ton* who had little else to do with their lives but throw their fortunes away and pursue the path to ruin. He preferred to gamble with more likely, intelligent sport, and made it a point to keep all of his gaming strictly above-board. He needed money, and a great deal of it, in order to secure the future he desired, but he wasn't going to gain it by underhanded means, or by fleecing victims too stupid to save themselves.

Despite his obvious distaste for the establishment, he was admitted without pause and treated with the deference usually reserved for regulars. The only hesitation he encountered after having crossed Mawdrey's threshold was when he asked to be escorted to the Earl of Rexley's table. The maître d' returned, having submitted the request to the Earl of Rexley himself, and with much embarrassment and apology suggested that perhaps the gentleman might better enjoy a visit to the faro tables instead.

Not one to be put off any course he was intently pursuing, Kerlain responded to this suggestion with both a smile and displeasure, and the maître d', much against his better judgment, was soon afterward announcing him into the private room where the Earl of Rexley and his companions were enjoying a game of hazard.

"My compliments," Rexley said tartly as Kerlain took a seat at the table. "I've never known anyone who could pull off such a feat as having his own way in this establishment. A skill you brought from your beloved United States, no doubt."

"Yes," Kerlain replied easily. "Strangely enough, I learned it from an Englishman who was visiting my fair country. He had discovered that if he stuck his nose high enough in the air and spoke in imperious tones, he'd always have his way. As you can see, such behavior is apparently effective no matter where one goes. Another valuable invention the British can lay claim to, don't you think?"

The Earl of Rexley gave no answer, but politely turned his attention to the game. It was only an hour later, when the other members of his table had excused themselves, that he spoke to Kerlain again.

"I'm done as well, I believe," he said, pushing the dice aside. "If you wish to continue the use of the room, I gladly give it to you for the remainder of the night."

"I don't wish it," Kerlain told him bluntly. "I only came to this miserable pit to deliver a message. Otherwise I'd never have stepped a foot through the door."

"Came to tell me that Lord Callan isn't able to attend, did you?" Rexley asked, taking up his wineglass and examining it. "I already knew. Talk travels rapidly in London. I was well aware of the little disagreement you and Severn had at the Versey ball before you showed your face here tonight. Lucky needn't have sent you to tell me that he decided to take his wife home rather than meet me here. He did send you, did he not?"

"Yes."

"Well." Rexley paused to sip his wine. "He's slipping then."

"Take comfort in the fact that I wasn't well pleased, either," Kerlain filled his own wineglass to the brim. "He would have sent Severn, save that the buffoon was too occupied in apologizing to his fiancée to be of use to anyone else."

Rexley laughed. "You're going to get yourself killed over Bella if you don't take a care. Not that I give a damn." He lifted his glass in a salutary toast.

Kerlain returned the gesture. "Nor do I," he said. "You're a heartless bastard. Why do you hate Americans so much?"

The Earl of Rexley set his glass down with care.

"My brother died in America, during the war. My younger brother. His name was David. He was twenty-two."

Kerlain stared at him for a silent moment before his voice broke the silence.

"My younger brother died in that war, too. Joshua. He was a little younger. Just twenty. He was killed outside of New Orleans in '14, serving under the command of General Jackson."

Rexley's gaze riveted to him. "God," he murmured. "David died near New Orleans. In November of that year."

Kerlain lowered his head. "Joshua died in December. I was with him. Just before Christmas. I took his body home to Tennessee."

"I met my brother's body at the wharf, four months later," Rexley said. "Just after Easter. Our parents—" He shook his head and made an attempt at laughter.

Another silence followed before Rexley asked, curtly, "Why did you come to England? Despite the fact that you'd inherited your grandfather's title."

Kerlain let out a breath. "At first it was because I thought I should see where my father had come from. Part of me wanted to hate everything I found and throw it back in the face of what remained of his family. I'm the last living male in my father's line. Did you know that?''

Rexley shook his head.

''After me, there are only distant cousins. All of whom would probably do better at serving the title. But once I arrived I began to take a perverse pleasure in the uproar I'd caused. An American falling heir to such a lauded title.'' His lips curled into a sneering smile. ''How fitting, after the years I'd spent—most of my life, in fact—being labeled a bastard. You can't begin to understand what that does to a man, Rexley.''

''I can imagine it, however,'' Rexley said, fingering his glass.

''Imagining isn't the same as knowing,'' Kerlain told him. ''Before I arrived in England, I accepted the title more for the sake of my mother than for myself. She spent her life trying to prove that my father had legally wed her, but it was only after she was dead that my grandfather finally admitted the truth. And that only because he had no other living heir to take his place.''

''And after you arrived in England?'' Rexley asked. ''Why didn't you simply take what was yours and return to your own country?''

''I can hardly answer you that, my lord, for I don't understand it myself. Something holds me here. Even if I told you, you'd not believe it.''

Rexley looked at him sharply. ''But whatever it is, it's caused you to involve a friend of mine in an unlikely scheme. Is that not so?''

''Viscount Callan among others,'' Kerlain admitted freely. ''But I mean him no harm, or Lady Clara. On that I give you my word of honor.''

The Earl of Rexley looked as if he were about to tell the Earl of Kerlain what he thought of an American's honor, but was diverted by the entrance of two of Mawdrey's most loyal patrons, whom he spied through the private room's open door.

Seeing the look on his companion's face, Kerlain followed the path of the other man's gaze.

"Trouble," he said.

"Indeed," concurred Rexley. "An exceedingly appropriate name for her."

"Who's the man she's with?"

"Someone she hates thoroughly. Her publisher. William Rosswell. If Lucky finds out she's been here with him, the outcome will be most unpleasant."

"Rosswell?"

Rexley nodded. "He puts out the monthly rag her drawings are published in." He glanced at Kerlain. "She despises the man, of course, but keeps well within his favor. She's got to, if she wants her work put out. Still, she'd not be in his company unless she had a particular reason for it."

"I'm afraid I don't understand what you mean. Is Lady Halling published in some form? I had understood she's a respected painter, so far as women can be respected in such a field."

"You've heard of *Glad Tidings*?"

Kerlain laughed. "Hasn't everyone? Is that Rosswell's paper? Never tell me Lady Halling dips her hand into that slanderous gossip sheet."

Rexley nodded. "If you're familiar with it, then perhaps you've also seen the work of *Le Chat*?"

Kerlain nearly choked on the mouthful of wine he'd taken. Staring at Rexley from across the table, he said, "Pamela Halling is The Cat? *She's* the one who draws those damnable caricatures?"

"Perhaps Americans aren't quite as slow as I'd assumed," Rexley said dryly. "Yes. She's the one. If you value your skin, you'd best not spread that little fact about.

Not unless you wish to be her next victim in *Glad Tidings*.''

"God forbid,'' Kerlain said with feeling. "I saw what she did to Miss Cooper several months ago, and then stopped wasting my money on buying the thing. Whatever did that poor girl do to incur Lady Halling's wrath?''

"Not a thing. She simply had the misfortune to be a tad overweight and have spots, also to be somewhat ingratiating and desperate. In Pamela's mind that made her a toad, and so she drew her as one. It was one of her more vicious undertakings, but by no means her worst. Lucien put a stop to those over a year ago.''

"I can well imagine,'' Kerlain said. "I seem to remember that you and Lord Callan paid a good deal of attention to Miss Cooper immediately following the drawing's publication. Trying to undo the deed, were you?''

Rexley set his glass upon the table. "We made an attempt, but it was useless. Miss Cooper didn't possess the stamina to pull through the unpleasantness. Her parents were obliged to take her back into the country, where I understand she has decided to stay.''

"Poor girl,'' Kerlain eyed Lady Halling as she and her companion made their way to a private table. "If I were Callan, I do believe I'd put a stop to such disagreeable behavior completely.''

"As would I. Unfortunately, Lucky doesn't disapprove of all of it,'' Rexley said. "Sometimes he even gives her ideas.''

"She hates her publisher, did you say? They look to be perfectly friendly at the moment. If she smiles at him any more brightly he's going to be blinded.''

"Lucky was promised to bring Pamela tonight and meet me here,'' Rexley said. "Yet he's gone home with his wife, and Pamela arrives instead with William Rosswell.''

"You find something suspect in it?''

"Perhaps."

The answer nettled Kerlain's interest. It was well known that the Earl of Rexley had worked as an intelligence officer during the war, and rumored that he yet served the British government in a similar, secretive position. Having once performed the same service for his own native government, Kerlain knew better than to doubt the instincts of another such man.

"Pamela distrusts me," Rexley remarked. "Not, I admit, without reason. If she were planning on doing anything unpleasant, she'd certainly not confide the matter to me." He spoke as if he were bored, almost disinterested, but Kerlain heard the meaning beyond. Rexley lifted his direct gaze and met Kerlain's. "I wonder . . ."

But Kerlain was already getting to his feet. He wasn't about to let the many plans he'd made go awry. Certainly not because of a jealous, petulant, vengeful woman.

"Don't exhaust yourself, Rexley." He ran his fingers over the front of his coat, then slightly straightened the arrangement of his cravat. "If you'll excuse me, I believe I'll go and make my bow to Lady Halling." Heading for the door, he muttered, "Wish me luck in it."

"Luck." Rexley's laughing voice followed after him as he departed the room.

Chapter Fifteen

❦

"Another one of Lady Clara's triumphs," Jack declared, standing beneath the shade of a large oak tree with Lucien and Wulf. "I can't think when I've seen such a well-organized picnic, or enjoyed one better. Your wife is a marvel, Lucky. Have you decided to keep her yet?"

"I'm considering it," Lucien replied noncommittally. "She may not decide to keep me, of course."

Jack laughed. "There's hardly any question of that. The girl's clearly head over ears about you. You're the most pathetically romantic married couple of my acquaintance. And after the scare you gave us before you were wed, with all that nonsense about sending her off to Pearwood." Jack gave him a reproachful look. "We may all be thankful the rumors never went any farther than they did, since the wager will clearly come to naught. You've called it off with Kerlain, haven't you?"

"Not yet," Lucien said, gazing to where his wife was busy organizing games for the younger children who'd come with their parents. It had been an unusual idea, allowing children to attend a formal picnic, but it had worked out very well. Once the meal Clara had so painstakingly planned had been eaten—and delicious it was, every bite of it—the day had rapidly taken on the aspect of a fair, with amusements and games and prizes for all. He'd seen smiles on the lips of people whom he'd long ago suspected didn't even know how to move their facial muscles.

"I don't know how Bella can talk to that man," Wulf said miserably, staring in the opposite direction, where his fiancée was strolling languidly along the bank of a small river in the company of the Earl of Kerlain. "What's he got to say that could be of any interest to her? He don't know the first thing about science, not in any form. I tried to discuss simple physics with him once and he looked at me as if I was talking utter rot. She can't want to be in close acquaintance with a man like that."

"Can't she?" Jack asked with some amazement.

"Well, of course not," Wulf insisted vehemently. "Bella's got a mind, y'know. She's not one of these blank-headed females you'll usually find in society." His hands curled into fists. "I should have killed Kerlain at the Versey ball, when I had my chance."

"You seem to forget, my friend," said Lucien, "that Lord Kerlain had your hands locked behind your back. You could hardly move, let alone kill the man. He obviously knows more about physics than you give him credit for."

Wulf glowered at him. "It was only because Bella distracted me long enough for him to take advantage. He was only lucky that I was trying to get her out of the way before I killed him."

Lucien shook his head. "Don't underestimate him, Wulf. Kerlain is a fellow who learns from his mistakes. Having suffered punishment from your massive hands before, he realized that his only hope of surviving another such bout was to put to use his wits rather than his muscles. And a good thing it was, too, else society might never have forgiven you for shedding blood in so public a place. Has Bella started speaking to you yet?"

Wulf made an unhappy sound, a low and rumbling growl.

"Not for weeks. Every time I try to say more than two words to her she pretends I'm not even there."

"A true feat, that," murmured Lucien.

"She said if I so much as behave disagreeably to Kerlain, she'll never speak to me again."

"Now *that* sounds like a promising premise on which to begin a marriage," Jack stated. "Better marry her quick, Wulf, before she changes her mind." He laughed when Lucien elbowed him. "Oh, very well. I'll behave." To Wulf, he said, "I don't know why you won't just give in and tell the woman you're sorry for embarrassing her and then get down on your knees and beg her forgiveness. It's what she's waiting for."

Wulf looked at him, clearly dumbfounded. "She is? Do you really think so, Jack?"

"Wulf," Jack said with a sigh. "You're a hopeless dunderhead, especially when it comes to women. Of course it's what she's waiting for. Poor Bella. How has she put up with you all these years?"

"I shouldn't tell you this," Lucien put in, "but Clara says that Bella's been miserable about the estrangement between the two of you. It might be worth a try to make an apology."

"And grovel," Jack added. "Make certain you do plenty of that."

Wulf looked back to where Bella and Lord Kerlain were walking so companionably. "Bella's been miserable?"

"That's what Clara says. She's certainly spent enough time with Bella this past month and more."

Without another word, Wulf walked away in the direction of the river.

"This should be interesting," Jack said.

But nothing untoward occurred. Wulf approached his fiancée and Lord Kerlain and made, for Wulf, a polite bow. A few moments later, after what appeared to be light conversation, Wulf said something and nodded toward Bella. Lord Kerlain stepped back and swept his companions a deep bow and then took himself off.

"Well done, Wulf," murmured Lucien, as Wulf offered Bella his arm and began to lead her in the direction from which she had just come with Kerlain, away from the company.

"If he bumbles on in his usual endearing manner," Jack commented, "he'll have Bella eating out of his hands in no time. As ever. Poor girl. Such a life they'll have together."

"You're too cynical, Jack," Lucien said. "The ideas of love and marriage have always seemed awful to you."

Jack gaped at him. "*I'm* cynical? Can this be Lucien Bryland speaking? May I remind you, dear friend, that you've spent most of your drunken hours, of which there have been many, holding forth on what could only be termed a negative discourse on those same topics?"

"You needn't bother. I remember very well."

"And suddenly love and happily ever after are perfectly reasonable concepts to you?"

Lucien smiled at his friend's disbelieving tone. "Perhaps not as concepts, but as ideals worth pursuing. I don't say they're attainable, mind you."

"You don't deny it, either."

"Not for some," Lucien said, watching as Wulf and Bella, in the distance, stopped and turned to each other. Wulf seemed to be speaking to his beloved in an intent manner, such as only Wulf could do, and Bella—dear Bella—appeared to be melting beneath whatever it was that Wulf, in his fumbling, desperate way, said. "Wulf and Bella can attain them, I think. They love each other."

"Is love the only necessity, then? To have a happy marriage?"

"No. But Wulf and Bella have the added help of being well matched. She understands him perfectly, even if he doesn't quite understand her or any other woman. But he loves her despite that. Poor old Wulf. So confused about Bella, and loving her regardless. He couldn't stop if he tried, you know. If she shaved her head bald and went about screaming mad, he'd find some excuse for it. You know just as well as I do that he'll never love another.''

"Yes," said Jack. "If Bella were to die today, God forbid, Wulf would simply live alone with his sciences. There would be no one else for him." After a short silence he asked, "Is it the same with Robby and Lady Anna, then? Are they fated to be, as well? In all the years since their parting, Robby hasn't found another to take her place."

Lucien inwardly shuddered at the thought, but replied, "I can't speak so much for what's between them, because I can't begin to fathom it. Robby nearly died because of Lady Anna. You'd think he'd give the woman a berth so wide they'd never have a chance to meet face-to-face."

"I would have said the same of you and Lady Clara, after all the pain she's given you. Yet you've not been able to set her aside, either, despite all your boasting."

"No," Lucien admitted. "Not yet."

"Perhaps you and Robby are more like Wulf than you'd be glad to admit, then," Jack suggested gently.

"Perhaps," Lucien murmured. "Or perhaps all men can be enslaved by another person, to one degree or another." He glanced at his friend. "Even you, Jack. You're not immune to love."

Jack gave him a level look. "Wulf would tell you that some theories are too ludicrous to pursue, Lucky. He's right. Ah. The children are about to begin their race. Lady Clara's had a course cleared away for them, I see."

Lucien readily allowed the topic of conversation to be diverted. He was the last man who wished to discuss love or any of its attendant vices. Following Jack's gaze, he looked to where half a dozen or more children were lined up, ready for the start to be given. He saw Sarah Huntington standing at one end, leaning down, a look of determination on her lovely little face. She was an interesting child; tiny, delicate, and exquisitely beautiful, she looked as fragile as a delicate porcelain vase. But she clearly possessed a strength of mind and purpose that belied her physical features. Lucien had a feeling that what Sarah Huntington wanted, Sarah Huntington went after heart, body, and soul. Robby was enchanted by the child, although Lucien suspected that was partly due to the fact that her mother was Anna Huntington, and therefore a link to Lady Anna, herself. But his uncle clearly enjoyed the little girl's company for her own sake, and spent a good deal of time in her company, escorting her to every acceptable spot in London, sometimes with her mother in tow, sometimes with another chaperone. Lucien and Clara had accompanied Robby and Miss Huntington to the Royal Academy one afternoon, and Lucien had been rather amused, and touched, as well, to watch as Robby and Miss Huntington walked hand in hand through the art gallery, stopping and remarking at each painting on display with grave consideration. Robby had always been good with children—God alone knew how well he had handled one angry thirteen-year-old orphan in particular—and Lucien had often thought it a shame that he had none of his own body.

Anna Huntington was standing beside Robby, watching her daughter with a slight expression of anxiety. They made as handsome a couple as they had so many years ago. Perhaps, with the additional countenance of maturity, even more so. Lady Anna had ceased to be so volatile in Robby's presence, in fact, she spent quite a bit of time with him, dancing at balls and riding in the park and going on excursions with Robby and her daughter. Robby had never been happier, and Lucien knew that he should strive to be happy for him, too. In time, perhaps, he would be.

"There they go," Jack murmured as Clara gave the signal for the start.

Sarah Huntington went flying forward, and almost immediately tripped and fell. A chorus of "oh's" went up even as the other participants in the race went on their way. Robby bent down and scooped a furious and tearful Sarah Huntington off the ground, cradling the small, tight body against his chest until she at last gave way and put her arms about his neck, pressing her face against Robby's shoulder and weeping miserably. Robby patted her and spoke in what seemed to Lucien, from his distance, a gentle and comforting tone as Anna Huntington checked the child's arms and legs and made certain that she'd suffered no physical harm. They made a charming picture, the three of them. A perfect family with mother, father, and child.

"He nearly died because of her," Lucien murmured, watching as Robby put Sarah Huntington on her feet and took the child's hand. "It was coming from the moment we left England, but finally arrived nearly four years later in the Andes. He got us stranded on the coldest, most barren, godforsaken mountainside on earth and then he bloody well sat there, three full days and nights, staring over the side of a cliff and waiting to die. I couldn't get him to speak to me, let alone hear me. He wouldn't eat. Wouldn't even drink a drop of wine or water. He was so thin you could see the bones in the back of his neck sticking out through the skin. The wind was so cold and raw that his skin was covered with bleeding sores."

"God, Lucky," Jack said with wide-eyed disbelief. "You never told me any of this. I knew your travels with Robby were difficult, but I never realized how much so."

In the distance, Sarah Huntington set her other hand in her mother's, and soon was strolling contentedly between the two adults, the link that connected all three of them. Behind them, the winner of the race was being cheered by his parents and congratulated by Clara. The additional servants Lucien had hired to tend the picnic began to pull an array of desserts out of baskets, as well as to pour a variety of refreshments to quench different late-afternoon thirsts.

"The winds were never-ending," he said. "I used to wonder if I'd go mad at the death sounds they made. Perhaps I did." He looked at Jack. "I knocked him out with a piece of wood, finally, and with the help of our guides tied him up in blankets and rope. It took five days, with Robby cursing us every step of our descent, but we finally got him down the mountain and into a village. I didn't unwrap him until we were at an inn, in a room I took for us." He laughed humorlessly. "I handed him the knife I'd used to cut the bonds away with and told him that if he was going to kill himself over Anna Huntington, then he should do it and get it over with. For my part, I was going home to Clara, whether he was with me or not. Two weeks later we were on a ship heading to Portsmouth. We never spoke of it again, what had happened on that mountain. I thought it had cured him of her at last, forever."

"Evidently not," Jack said softly. "Perhaps, as you say, he's enslaved." He set a firm hand on Lucien's shoulder. "I know you care about him, Lucky, but you've got to let him do as he pleases."

"I don't want him getting hurt again."

"There's nothing you can do to stop it, short of killing him yourself. He's a grown man, and you've got enough to worry about with your own life, and wife. And mistress."

"Yes," Lucien said, turning his gaze back to Clara, who was in the midst of smilingly accepting a glass of punch from the equally smiling Earl of Kerlain. "How very right you are about that, Jack."

* * *

"Here's to a lovely day, my lady," the Earl of Kerlain said, tapping the rim of her wineglass with his own. "And to an even lovelier hostess."

Clara laughed and sipped her wine before saying, "Please, my lord. None of that. I've told you more than once that I depend upon you to be ruthlessly truthful with me at all times."

"How is it," asked the earl, "that so many delightful ladies carry about such low estimations of themselves? It's most vexing."

"Perhaps," she said, setting her hand in the crook of his arm, "it's because we don't have you about to flatter us so nicely. Come and take me away from all this madness, if you please. I'm quite exhausted."

He drew her in the direction of the river. "And so you should be. I haven't seen you take a moment for yourself the entire day, until just now. I suppose every hostess must pay such a price to make her events a success. And this was a success, in case you haven't yet noticed it. Not a grumble in the crowd."

"Thank heavens," Clara declared. "I did so want everyone who usually stays in Town most of the year to enjoy a day such as we often have in the country. My father and mother loved to hold picnics at St. Genevieve and invite everyone in the neighboring villages to attend. Of course that entailed feeding and entertaining several hundred people, a feat I fear I should not have attempted so near to London on my own."

Lifting his glass to her in salute, he said, "You are not only a lovely and gracious lady, but wise, as well, Viscountess Callan."

"My lord," she said in a chiding tone. "Enough. Please."

"I can't seem to help myself," he told her, smiling. "Women are my weakness."

"Especially one in particular, it seems." Clara nodded in the direction of the woods where Wulf and Bella had disappeared. "Miss Howell seems to have captured your attention most fully, although I can't think it wise. Lad," she said, using his first name for the first time, though he had long since given her permission to do so, "can't you leave her be? Surely you don't wish to cause her trouble with Lord Severn."

"Lord Severn causes his own trouble," Kerlain stated, the laughter suddenly gone from his tone. "He treats Miss Howell as if she were made of air, necessary to his comfort but otherwise not particularly worthy of his attention or concern. It's long past time that he began to see her as the beautiful and kind lady that she is, and if my paying her some small measure of attention spurs him on toward that direction, then I shall continue to do so."

Clara stopped and looked at him. "Is that all there is to it, then? Your heart isn't involved in the matter?"

"My heart," he said, patting her hand reassuringly, "is too battered and bruised to do anyone harm. Especially not someone whom I admire as I do Miss Howell. Let us say that I simply feel a certain kinship with Lord Severn's finacée."

"With Bella?" Clara asked. "Do you, Lad?"

"I know what it is to love and not be loved in turn."

"We all do, to one degree or another."

His eyebrows lifted in surprise. "You can't mean your husband, Lady Clara. That man loves you to the point of madness. Perhaps beyond it. I haven't quite decided whether you're even safe with him or not."

Neither had she, Clara thought, but it was far too late for her to worry over the matter now. Aside from that, she loved Lucien with a certain madness, too, even when his dark moods made him a silent, uncomfortable companion. There had been a few such hours since they'd wed, when he'd withdrawn from her completely, but they were far out-weighed by the days and nights of joy he'd given her. Even Aunt Anna had at last admitted that Lucien had been a kind and attentive husband, far better than most husbands tended to be.

"I can't believe he'd ever lift a hand to you, of course," Kerlain went on, "but words can be weapons that are just as harsh as hands. If he ever gives you cause for worry, my lady, I hope you know that I will always be ready to stand at your service. You need only let me know if you require assistance in any way."

"It won't come to that, but I do thank you." She tilted her head and regarded him with a smile. "Do you know, I can never decide whether you and my husband are friends or enemies. There are times when you seem to be quite content with each other's company, and other times when I sense that something is not exactly right between you. It's a mystery to me."

"And bound to remain so, I fear," he said. "Although I can promise you that I am neither his enemy, or yours. Ah, Lord Callan approaches with a look of fury on his face. I'd better kiss your hand to make his wrath worthwhile." He bent and did so in a grand, exaggerated manner.

"My lord," Clara greeted her handsome husband with pleasure. "What do you think of my picnic?"

He took the hand she held out to him and pulled her close. "I think it wonderful. Everything you do is wonderful, Clara." Then, in front of Kerlain and anyone else who cared to watch, he slid an arm about her waist and kissed her, long and possessively, so that when he finally released her she gasped for air.

"Kerlain," Lucien greeted the other man coolly, keeping his arm about Clara. "You're enjoying yourself, I hope?"

"Indeed, I am," Kerlain assured him. "It's impossible to do otherwise when Lady Clara is the hostess."

"Very true," Lucien agreed.

To Clara the men seemed to be on the verge of an argument. Their words were far too stiff to be friendly. Lucien's hand settled just above her hip in a proprietary manner.

A stony silence settled over the three of them as the two men stared at each other, until Clara cleared her throat and said, "I was hoping, my lord, that you might help me convince Lord Kerlain to join our party tonight at Vauxhall. I've assured him that the company will be most congenial."

"Oh, yes," Lucien said dutifully, his tone void of enthusiasm. "Please do join us, Kerlain." He made it sound as if he'd rather have a tooth pulled.

"Thank you," Kerlain replied with an equal lack of delight. "But I fear I'm already engaged for the evening, although I wish, for the sake of enjoying Lady Clara's amiable company, that it were otherwise."

"A pity," Lucien murmured.

"Quite," said Kerlain.

"Ahem." Clara cleared her throat again. "I do believe one of the footmen is trying to get my attention. I'd best go and see what the trouble is."

Lucien released his wife and watched her go. The moment she was out of hearing, he said, "I appreciate your tact in bowing out of the invitation Clara extended."

"It wasn't tact," Kerlain told him. "I am engaged for the night. But I understand and appreciate your concern. I shouldn't wish my wife to be tainted by anything so ignoble as the wager between us, either. Perhaps"—he lifted one hand and began to examine his nails with apparent interest—"you'd like to concede the winning to me?"

"No. Not yet."

"Very well," Kerlain replied easily, lowering his hand and smiling at his companion for the benefit of anyone who might be watching. "I'm a patient man. I'm glad to have a moment alone with you, as it happens. I should like to warn you of something unpleasant that will occur by week's end."

Lucien gazed at him more sharply. "What is it?"

"Pamela Halling," Kerlain said. "She plans to publish one of her more virulent caricatures in the upcoming issue of *Glad Tidings*. It's to be of a curricle with a broken wheel stopped on a dark country lane. There are to be three people depicted—a woman and two men—and one of the men is to be carrying a pistol in each of his hands, with enough shot and powder bulging from his pockets to make a third shot possible. I don't believe I need tell you what the scene is meant to portray."

Lucien drew in a long, slow breath and waited until he knew he could control the tremor in his voice before asking, "Is there to be a caption?"

Kerlain nodded. "The Sins of the Father."

It was more vicious than Lucien had expected, and he blinked twice with disbelief before gathering himself.

"She's an evil woman," Kerlain said with sympathy, his expression softening with masculine understanding.

"Jack told me you'd made a point of befriending her. I suppose I should thank you, despite the fact I find you a complete fool. Pamela isn't a woman to be taken lightly. But you've evidently discovered that for yourself."

"She's certainly given me pause to reconsider the manner in which I view you, my lord," Kerlain told him. "There are few men in this world who could successfully deal with such a woman for any length of time. You're either an idiot, or insane. Or possessed of a nature that I don't even wish to contemplate."

Lucien couldn't help but laugh. "A masochist, perhaps?"

"Even so," Kerlain said with a frown. "It's nothing I

find even remotely humorous. Lady Halling is a foul disease, if you'll pardon me for saying so.''

"Say what you like," Lucien invited. "It won't touch her, or me. Believe me when I say that many months ago she and I would have laughed with unending amusement to know your sentiments. We would have toasted the knowledge with the finest champagne and made a celebration. But that was the manner in which we tended to entertain ourselves. It's strange and unusual," he admitted, "but you wouldn't be able to understand people such as she and I are, no matter how I tried to explain it."

"More than you think," Kerlain said. "Cruelty can be as much an opiate as any drug."

"Yes," Lucien said with a slight nod. "It is one, however, which I've determined to set aside. For my wife's sake."

"I'm glad to know it, my lord."

"I don't give a damn what you're glad of, Kerlain. I am grateful, however, for what you've discovered. I should have expected it, but my mind, of late, has been otherwise occupied. I'll not forget the service you've done me."

"I didn't do it for you."

"I'm aware of that."

"Good," Kerlain murmured. "I'll not worry over the matter. You'll take care of Lady Halling, then?"

"Oh, yes," Lucien promised. "I'll take care of her. Never doubt it."

Chapter Sixteen

❦

"Oh, Lucien, isn't it beautiful? What a perfect night for a party. I'm going to enjoy every single moment."

Lucien smiled at his delighted wife as he led her into the supper box he'd hired for the evening, where footmen were already laying out preparations for the meal to come.

"I insist that you do," he told her. "So long as you also relax. After the day you've had, overseeing the picnic, you well deserve a night of pleasure. I should think you'd be exhausted. I don't know where you get such energy, love."

She turned and smiled up at him, one of her ecstatic, happiest smiles—he'd learned to expect them whenever they arrived at some new social function—and said, "From you, I think. Because you're such a wonderful husband, Lucien, and because I love you so very much."

She loved him. He had believed that she did, perhaps he'd even known it, because it seemed impossible that she should feel any differently about what they shared than he did, but to hear the words spoken aloud, for the first time, stunned him. For a few moments he couldn't even seem to draw in breath. It was only the arrival of their guests, following them into the booth, that brought him directly to his senses.

"I'm glad," he murmured, belatedly thinking to himself that the words were imbecilic and inadequate. He should have told her of his own feelings, though doing so without some amount of privacy seemed wrong, too.

None of the light left Clara's eyes, however, due to his lack of response. She seemed not even to notice that he made no similar declaration, but turned at once, happily, to ask Bella to sit beside her in the box, and to tell Wulf to move his chair about so that he would be perfectly comfortable.

Lucien stood aside to make way for Clara's cousins, Mrs. Ashcroft and her husband, to find their places in the box. Another young lady, a new friend of Clara's, Miss Darbing, whom Jack had initially been supposed to pair with, was instead led into the box by one of Lucien's own relatives. Christian Fineham had only just arrived in Town to sow his oats and been only too gratified to attend his older cousin's outing at a moment's notice.

"I do wish Jack hadn't bowed out at the last moment," Clara said, taking Lucien's hand and drawing him toward the others. She was managing him, he knew, just as she would manage the others for the rest of the night to make certain that the evening was perfect. She was so clever at arranging conversation and seating and everything else. "But it is wonderful to have Christian with us, is it not, my lord?"

"Yes," he said, letting her lead him to the chair she wished him to take. It was to the left side of her own, and she kept hold of his hand even after she had sat down and begun to speak to Bella.

It was sometime after supper and a good deal of conversation had passed that Lucien caught sight of Pamela. He had to admire her skill in avoiding his notice before that; it was clear that she'd taken a good deal of care to do so. Her box was out of view of his own, and she had covered her hair with a black netted shawl until at last, moving directly into his line of view on the arm of a male companion, she removed it. He couldn't have failed to notice her then—he or any other man, when she was without a doubt the most strikingly beautiful woman present in the gardens and dressed in a manner to make certain she drew attention—just as he couldn't have missed the speaking look she gave him, telling him that she wanted his company. Kissing his wife's hand, Lucien bowed himself out of his box on the excuse that he wished to say hello to an old friend he'd spied across the way.

He did go across the way and greet a group of men gathered about one of the boxes, most of whom he was acquainted with, and then discreetly meandered off in the direction of the Dark Walk. Pamela moved off in the other direction with her male escort.

Fifteen minutes passed before he saw her moving down the dark, unlit path where he waited in the shadows.

"I'm here," he said quietly as she neared him.

"Lucien!"

"Come." He took her elbow in his hand. "I don't wish to be seen."

"No, of course not. Your dear little wife might hear of it, otherwise."

Small, open huts with tables dotted Vauxhall's pathways, providing shelter and privacy for those patrons who desired such. Lucien pulled Pamela into one of these and turned to face her.

"She might," Lucien admitted. "But there are other reasons."

She looked at him questioningly, but he merely said, "Did you wish to speak to me Pamela?"

He had seldom seen her looking more beautiful than she did tonight, dressed in a gown of glittering sea-green silk, her long blond hair swept up into an attractive, yet simple style. The effect was not only attractive, but sensual. He thought of Clara, who had dressed, as usual, in the latest stare of fashion, but who never failed to capture both style and a certain respect in her manner of clothes. It occurred to him, perhaps for the very first time, that despite her devotion to the art of flirtation, Clara never dressed in a seductive manner. Indeed, it was just the opposite. She was ever the model of complete propriety.

"Yes, Lucien," Pamela said, taking a step nearer him. She appeared to be open and earnest, but he knew better than to so readily trust her mask of sincerity. "I wanted to see you. I realize you're angry that I've sought you out so publicly, but I didn't know what else to do. You've not answered any of the notes I've written, or accepted any of the messages I've sent through our friends. When Lad told me that you'd be here tonight—"

"Lad?" Lucien asked with a glimmer of amusement. "Lad Walker, do you mean? Kerlain told you I'd be here tonight?"

"Don't be angry," she pleaded. "He knew how much I wished to see you."

"Did he?" Lucien uttered a laugh. "Pamela, you silly fool. Didn't it occur to you that Kerlain has his own reasons for throwing us together? You've played right into his hands."

"It doesn't matter to me," she said fiercely. "I've missed you more than I thought I would ever miss *any* man, and whether you realize it or not, that means something. I know you won't believe that, but it's the truth. If it's an apology you want, or promises of good behavior, then I'll say them. And mean them. Whatever it is that you require, Lucien, even if I must debase myself for your amusement, then you need only tell me, and I shall do it." She laid one gloved hand carefully upon his chest. "I know you're angry. Perhaps you've even come to hate me, but I can't accept that you won't let me make amends."

He set a hand over hers. "I don't want you to debase

yourself, Pamela. You and I have already done enough in our lives that is purely dishonorable. We've enough shame between us to choke a hundred human beings.''

Her lips parted as if she meant to speak, but she said nothing.

''I'm no longer your playmate, Pamela,'' he told her as gently as he could. ''You won't believe it possible, but I've decided not to live in such a manner any longer. I've come to hate it, and myself. I will no longer view respectable people as fools. Indeed, I mean to become exactly like those whom we used to so often revile.''

Her hand fisted upon the cloth of his coat. ''I can leave it behind, too, Lucien. I can.'' She sounded small and child-like, afraid. His heart ached for her, not for the sake of love, but because they had once shared so much together.

''Can you, Pamela?''

''If you'll help me.''

''It can't be done with help, or for the sake of another. You must choose the path on your own, my dear.''

She pulled her hand away and glared at him. ''You have your wife to lend you aid, to make you better. Isn't that so? Will you deny that a mere woman—ugly and plain as she is—is the reason you so suddenly desire to be respectable, Lord Callan?''

''Clara knows nothing of this. Of you and me. I admit that I wish to be better so that I may keep her, but also for myself. I'm weary of this, Pamela. The deceit and games— I want nothing more to do with any of it, or you.''

She shook her head. ''Don't, Lucien,'' she whispered. ''Please. I need you.''

''I've sacrificed three years of my life to be in your company. Perhaps you've done the same to be in mine. We've always seemed equal in our pursuits until now. But no longer.''

''You're a fool!'' she said vehemently. ''She's not worth

the trouble, Lucien. She's going to make you as mad as your mother made your father. You know I'm right!''

"Even so," he said, inclining his head, "I will take the chance."

"She's not even beautiful! She's *nothing*. Oh, Lucien"— she held a pleading hand out to him—"you can't want her when you can have me. You can't want that . . ."

He took her hand, gripped it. "I do want it, Pamela. I want her. Understand that very, very well. For what we've shared, I owe you a certain amount of gratitude, but nothing more. Don't mistake me. If you harm her, you will pay for it dearly."

"Lucien . . ."

"Understand it, Pamela," he insisted. "Leave her be. Don't make me your enemy. You know better than anyone else what that means."

She shook free of him and turned away. "If you've made your decision, then I suppose I must accept it. Still, I think you a fool. Don't forget what I offered you tonight, Lucien Bryland. It's something I've never offered another man."

"I don't take lightly anything that you've said or done this night." She'd not spoken of love, but what she had offered had cost her dearly. That he had turned it aside, he knew, hurt her deeply. Unfortunately, Pamela wasn't a sentimental female. No matter how badly he felt about hurting her, she'd want revenge.

"We can't part friends," she stated. "You know that."

"Yes. We know too much about each other for that."

"You've brought it down on your own head then. Never say it was my doing."

"Such dramatics," he murmured. "It doesn't become you, Pamela."

"We shall see." She turned to him, a slight, unpleasant smile fixed on her lips. "I brought a little present for your bride tonight."

"How thoughtful," he said with polite calm, his insides tightening into knots. This was the beginning, then. The price he was going to pay for all his sins, for associating with someone like Pamela for so long, and so intimately. He only hoped that he'd be able to keep Clara from the consequences of his folly.

"Yes," Pamela said, her smile widening. "A dear friend of hers whom I chanced to make the acquaintance of at Bawd Claxton's." She let the name of the disreputable hell-hole sink in before going on. "Andrew Blakesley. You can imagine my surprise upon meeting such a fine young man in that awful place, but we fast became friends."

Lucien could envision the meeting. Pamela would have planned and carried it out with care, perhaps she'd even made certain of his presence by having a mutual acquaintance arrange it. As much as he disliked Blakesley, he almost felt sorry that the fellow had become ensnared in such a net.

"You never told me what a handsome gentleman he is," Pamela went on. "But, then, your descriptions of his love-sickened behavior for Lady Clara were always somewhat . . . colored. He's quite dashing in his officer's uniform. Captain Blakesley, he is now. A war hero. Your wife is certain to be impressed."

The idea of Clara being reunited with her ardent young lover set a sickening ache twisting through the knots that had formed earlier. The urge to hurry back to his wife's side was nearly overwhelming; Pamela watched closely to see exactly what he'd do.

Lucien folded his hands behind his back, an unhurried gesture. "I have a little present for you, as well, my dear, although I fear I cannot give it to you yet."

Her eyes narrowed slightly. "What is it?"

He smiled. "I believe you'll discover that upon your return home. And now, if you'll be so good as to excuse me?''

She tried to stand in his way. ''What is it, Lucien? What have you done?''

He brushed past her and began walking down the path, toward the lights and orchestra music. She was right behind him.

''Lucien!''

''Madam,'' he said, coming to a stop. ''I realize that we're now operating in separate camps, but I would ask that you abide by this one rule: allow me the common courtesy of pretending not to have made my acquaintance.''

''What have you done?'' she demanded, gripping his sleeve. ''Tell me.''

He looked down at her gloved hand until she removed it.

''Ask your friend Rosswell,'' he advised curtly. ''He'll be able to give you the details.''

She stepped back, her face clearly white even in the darkness.

''And by the by,'' he added. ''It was a carriage that my mother and her lover took, not a curricle. My uncle paid the driver of it well enough to never speak of what happened after my father caught up with them.''

He turned and strode away, assuming that Pamela would at least have the grace to leave him alone in public. It would do neither of them any good to attack the other openly, before witnesses. But her fury was evidently greater than he'd anticipated, for she continued to follow behind him, right up to the edge of the dance floor.

''Lucien!''

He turned and pinned her with a look that expressed his complete displeasure. She met the look with fiery anger.

''You *bastard!* I'll have you on your knees for that! I swear it before God!''

She raised her hand as if she'd strike him, and he caught her wrist in an inflexible grip.

"Remember where you are, madam," he commanded quietly, fully aware of the notice they were drawing. There were few members of the *ton* who didn't already know of the relationship that had stood between him and Pamela for the past three years, although such matters were always discreetly avoided being mentioned save by those few intimates with whom they frequently socialized. To flaunt their acquaintance now, especially before Clara, was beyond the boundaries of the acceptable. Pamela would quickly lose whatever small admittance to society she'd thus far managed to maintain, and Lucien would be excoriated if he allowed his innocent wife to be publicly humiliated by the presence and behavior of his mistress.

"My art," she said furiously. "My *art,* Lucien."

"Yes, your precious art." He pressed her hand forcibly against her side and released it. "If you don't want your identity as *Le Chat* to be known to one and all, you venomous bitch, then I suggest you leave my wife and family aside when you set out to craft your poison."

She was breathing hard, controlling herself with unusual difficulty. When she looked behind him, her eyes lit with triumph.

"She's coming. Your wife. With her lover."

She pushed around Lucien before he could turn about, her expression brightening as she greeted gaily, "Why Captain Blakesley, I was just telling Lord Callan of our acquaintance. Imagine my surprise when he told me that you and Viscountess Callan were childhood friends."

Lucien registered the scene before him with a sense of detachment. He took in Clara's exuberantly smiling face— he'd seen her so utterly happy on a few other occasions, but always because of him—then the fact that she was holding Andrew Blakesley's arm with both hands. Andrew Blakes-

ley was a surprise. He'd grown considerably in both height
and girth since Lucien had seen him seven years before.
Gone was the boy who'd so clumsily stumbled out the news
of his and Clara's secret engagement, and in his place was a
mature, war-hardened man who was clearly at ease with,
and in command of, both himself and his surroundings. He
reached out his free hand to take the one that Pamela offered and briefly bowed over it before turning his attention
to Lucien.

"Lord Callan," he greeted. "It's a pleasure to see you
again, sir."

The voice was deeper, more masculine than Lucien had
remembered. He felt like planting a fist in the man's face
and pulling his wife away from his side.

"Blakesley," he replied with a nod.

"Lucien, isn't it wonderful?" Clara said with ecstatic
pleasure, beaming up at her companion. "Andrew took me
by complete surprise. I was never so glad." Her smiling
gaze politely took in Pamela. A brief silence stretched as
she waited for an introduction.

Lucien exchanged glances with Andrew Blakesley, wondering which of them would do the honors, before finally
saying, "Clara, this is Lady Pamela Halling. She's an acquaintance of mine." He disdained to lie to his own wife,
despite the fleeting idea he had of doing so. It was bad
enough having to introduce her to his former mistress without compounding the sin with falsehoods. "Lady Halling,
may I make my wife, Viscountess Callan, known to you?"

"Lucien's told me so much about you, my dear," Pamela
said, using his first name with such open familiarity that
Clara's eyes momentarily widened. "I'm delighted to make
your acquaintance at last. If I'd known that you were
friends with Andrew I would have made the effort to meet
you much sooner."

"Lady Halling was kind enough to include me in her

party tonight,'' Andrew Blakesley explained. ''If not for her I might never have known you were in London. And married! I still can't get over the shock of it. That will teach me to pay better attention to my mother's letters, in future.'' He seemed suddenly to remember Lucien's presence and added, ''Although, of course, it was foolish of me to be surprised. I was aware of your long-standing betrothal to Viscount Callan.''

''May I congratulate you on your recent marriage, Lady Callan?'' Pamela said brightly. ''And wish you every happiness?''

''Thank you,'' Clara replied, her gaze darting from Pamela to Lucien. He could see dawning bewilderment in her eyes, a sudden confusion. ''Thank you very much.''

''A waltz,'' Andrew Blakesley said as the orchestra began to play. ''Will you dance with me, Clara?'' He glanced at Lucien, who gave his wordless consent.

''A charming couple,'' Pamela said once they'd gone. ''Still, she's even plainer than I'd thought. What does Captain Blakesley see in her, I wonder?''

''Perhaps the same thing that I do,'' Lucien remarked quietly, declining to take the bait Pamela so aptly lured him with. ''A loveliness that has nothing to do with physical beauty, and which will last throughout her life. Ah, Jack's arrived, at last.'' He met his friend's gaze from across the dance floor, where that man had just stepped into Lucien's supper box. Jack made a slight bow in Pamela's direction before pulling something long and slender out of his coat and holding it up for both her and Lucien to see. With an equally fluid movement the rolled-up drawing disappeared again and Jack turned his attention to the other guests in the box.

Beside him, Lucien heard Pamela gurgle an incoherent sound, somewhere between rage and despair. Her art had been the one thing inviolable in her life; as precious and loved as any child of her body might be, perhaps, being as Pamela was, more so.

"I shall accept it as a wedding gift, Lady Halling," Lucien said. "I believe you know better than to expect a note of thanks."

He left her standing alone, as beautiful and still as a statue, and made his way through the swirl of dancers to claim his wife's hand from her present waltzing partner.

An hour later Pamela stood in her studio, shaking with the rage she'd been forced to hold at bay until at last she was within her own door. Her senses returned to her slowly, one by one, along with an awareness that Sibby was crouching in the corner, weeping piteously and covering her head.

What had she done to the girl? she wondered numbly, unable to remember how they had even come to be in the studio. Her every limb was so frozenly cold that her very bones ached with it.

She was shaking, everywhere, even her lips, when she said, "I'm sorry, Sibby." She swallowed, drew in a breath, tried to speak more calmly. "I've had a very trying evening. Forgive me." Her hand, when she lifted it to press it against her throbbing forehead, was trembling. The drawing she'd done for *Glad Tidings* was gone. She'd stopped at William Rosswell's house before coming home and had the news from his own lips. Someone had broken into the printer's shop and stolen the caricature; the plates that had been made for tomorrow's publication had been broken into bits.

Rosswell, the spineless toad, had attempted to put their association to an end. He'd been afraid to publish the caricature in the first place, until she'd sweetly talked him into it. Now he was afraid to have anything more to do with her. Lucien and his friends were too canny, too dangerous. And he certainly didn't wish to bring down the wrath of the Earl of Manning upon his head, not when that gentleman held so many powerful ties in Parliament.

She hadn't let him sever their relationship, however. It appeared that he feared his wife's wrath far more greatly than he did the Earl of Manning's. A few subtle threats in that direction had him unhappily agreeing to the publication of one more caricature.

"For God's sake, Sibby, get up off the floor and stop that noise."

Sibby obediently scrambled up and stood trembling by the wall.

"Bring me my apron," Pamela told her. "And fetch me coffee."

"You're going to work now, m'lady? So late?"

"Yes," Pamela said as Sibby tied the apron over Pamela's elegant evening gown. In her mind's eye she saw again Lucien taking his wife into his arms, away from Andrew Blakesley, and the nervous smile on Lady Clara's face as her husband moved her back into the dance. The foolish chit had clearly been worried about Lucien's reaction to the sight of her former lover, although she need not have been. Lucien had looked back at her in a manner that had stricken Pamela with a pain far worse than even his rejection of her had done. That he should look at that silly, stupid girl with such tenderness and care when he had never even looked at Pamela with kindness—she simply couldn't accept it, wouldn't allow it. She would kill it, somehow. She would destroy everything that Lucien held dear, starting with his beloved little wife.

"Yes," she said again as she sat down to begin her work. "I have a very special caricature to complete, Sibby, even if I must work all night to finish it. I want you to send Mr. Rosswell a message—take it yourself, if you can't find a reliable boy to deliver it. Tell him I'll have the drawing to him by no later than tomorrow afternoon, and want it published as soon as possible. And this time he'd best keep my work well protected, for if anything should happen again, Mrs. Rosswell will get an earful that Mr. Rosswell will much regret.''

Chapter Seventeen

Clara took her breakfast alone the next morning in the sitting room that joined her room to Lucien's. It had been their habit to eat the first meal of the day together, upstairs in the sitting room rather than in the formal breakfast parlor below, just as they had also, on occasion, when there was only the two of them, taken their dinners there. Clara had especially enjoyed the mornings and the pleasure of being lazy and unconstrained with Lucien, lolling about in her dressing gown, nibbling rolls and drinking hot chocolate and talking with her husband about the plans they each had for the day ahead.

This was the first morning since their wedding day that she'd found herself alone. Lucien had risen early and dressed in silence. His valet, who had gotten into the habit of waiting until he was called for before entering his master's room, had answered Clara's query about her husband's whereabouts with a look of bewilderment.

"Shall I send for Hayes, my lady? Perhaps he knows where his lordship is?"

But Clara hadn't wished to bother the butler or Mrs. MacInnes, at least not before she was properly clothed. It seemed to Clara that there was something foolish about a wife being so desperate to find her husband that she'd not even break her fast, first.

But it was a lonely business eating alone, she discovered

as soon as the footmen had delivered their trays of food. She waited a full fifteen minutes, sitting on a low couch and sipping coffee before finally giving up hope that Lucien would suddenly appear.

Not that she could blame him for staying away, of course. Last night had been awful, horrible—if not for him then certainly for her. A vision of the very beautiful Lady Halling kept hounding Clara, no matter how hard she tried to push the image away. That woman, and Lucien . . . how stupid she had been not to have realized at once that they were more than simply acquaintances. Andrew could not have realized the truth at all, for he'd never have knowingly escorted her over to meet Lucien's mistress. She groaned aloud just thinking of it. How furious Lucien must have been. How rightfully furious and humiliated. Surely everyone else knew that Lady Halling was his mistress; how utterly shocking it was for Clara to have approached him while he was speaking with her. She didn't know what horrified her more—the fact that Lucien kept such a beautiful woman or the fact that she'd made such a fool of herself in front of that woman. Lady Halling had managed the situation far better than Clara had.

She supposed she didn't have any right to feel as if she'd been betrayed, or so angry that she'd like to strangle Lucien with her bare hands, or so hurt that she wanted to weep with the knowledge that her husband had another woman. And not just a woman, but a shockingly beautiful and talented one. But Lucien had never promised that he'd not have a mistress. A great many married men did; it was considered quite acceptable so long as the relationship was played out within certain boundaries—boundaries that were to be respected by both husbands and wives. Clara had unwittingly crossed those lines last night, but, then, so had Lucien and Lady Halling. She'd never purposefully humiliated Lucien with her flirting, while he'd done so by openly flaunting his mistress before her in public.

Clara groaned again and set the palm of her hand over her face. Perhaps she was being unfair. No, she *was* being unfair. Lucien hadn't looked any happier to be seen with Lady Halling than Clara had been when she'd finally realized who the woman was. In fact, if she was going to be perfectly honest, she was the one who had forced the matter by making it clear that she desired an introduction, and Andrew had actually been the one who had caused the trouble from the start, insisting that he wished to say hello to Lucien, whom he'd seen in company with the woman who'd invited him to Vauxhall in her party.

No matter how the thing had happened, the outcome had been inevitable. Lucien had behaved kindly enough afterward, taking her out of Andrew's arms during the waltz so that she didn't have to continue the frozen, smiling mask she'd somehow held on to until he tapped Andrew's shoulder and sent him away. He seemed to have understood, by instinct, that she needed to be sheltered, having been faced with the truth so suddenly, with so many eyes upon her. And so he had held her closely and moved her about in the dance with surefooted ease, and had looked into her face and smiled encouragingly. She'd wanted to weep and press her head against his shoulder and beg him to love her despite all her plainness and failings.

Afterward, he'd taken her back to their supper box and, sitting beside her, had taken over the chore of playing host to their guests. She had a vague memory of the smile being back on her face, of laughing and conversing with everyone around her, but it almost seemed as if she'd dreamed it and not really been there at all. It had been Lucien who'd kept her, and the entire evening, from falling apart. Perhaps their guests hadn't realized that she'd been about to shatter. Or perhaps they'd been too well-bred to pretend anything but that all was well.

It had seemed an eternity before Lucien was handing her into their carriage, and another eternity before they arrived back at Barrington, having ridden home in an almost complete silence. Lucien had only spoken as the carriage had pulled away from Vauxhall, as, having already tucked her in a blanket, he set an arm about her, drawing her against his warmth.

"Don't be troubled, Clara," he said gently. "You've had a long and wearying day. Just rest, my dear."

But his kindness had been given in such a polite and impersonal manner that she'd only felt more despairing. At Barrington he had escorted her upstairs—to her own chamber—and had bidden her a good night, saying that he must go out again.

And so he'd left, probably to go to his mistress, while Clara had lain alone in her huge, cold bed for the very first time and felt utterly miserable. She had tried, in the hours that passed, to reconcile herself to the fact that her marriage was simply going to be as most every other marriage among the *ton* was, but it had been impossible. All she'd been able to find, until she'd fallen asleep, was a multitude of tears.

She never would have been able to say what time of night or early morning it was when Lucien lifted her out of her bed to carry her to the one they had always before shared. She was so wearily asleep that she barely remembered the event at all. He'd smelled heavily of liquor and smoke, and seemed aggravated to find her in her own bed, muttering something about having only taken her to her chamber so that her maid might get her undressed. It had made a vague sort of sense; she did dress in her own chamber, although she was usually undressed, by him, in his chamber.

She'd tried to say something about him undressing Lady

Halling, but he'd merely put her on the bed and said, "I'll leave that to Andrew Blakesley. If he can keep his hands off you long enough, of course. I'd advise you not to encourage him overmuch if you want your dear friend to live much longer."

That, unfortunately, she remembered most clearly, as well as the anger that had lain beneath the words. Even in her sleep-ridden state she'd been furious, probably more than she would have allowed herself to be had she been awake and aware. But feeling so utterly defenseless and hurt and abandoned, she'd wanted to strike back, and she had. With fists and feet. Instead of vanquishing Lucien, her clumsy attack only inflamed him. Lying heavily atop her, he'd held her hands over her head and ripped her nightdress off, then made love to her with a violence that left them both breathless and still. He hadn't even removed his clothes, or his boots. His damp, wretched *cloak* had still been on, for pity's sake. She nearly suffocated in the folds of it before he finally lifted himself from her body and tossed the thing aside.

What had come after he'd undressed had been slower, more careful, certainly not as violent, but it had been far from the tender lovemaking she had always known from him before. Lucien had dominated and possessed her, shown her, without doubt, who it was that she belonged to. It was only after he had finished, when she was weeping with shame and anger, that he'd relented and held her and whispered that he was sorry. Long minutes it had taken before she'd finally relaxed into his embrace, and then weariness had quickly pushed her into slumber. She'd been awakened some hours later by Lucien's movements as he dressed himself in the early morning light. Unshaven and rumpled, he left the room, and her, without a word.

Lady Halling. How long, she wondered, had Lucien known the woman? She cast her mind back through the five months of their marriage and wasn't able to come up with a single night that he'd spent away from Barrington. Even on those occasions when he'd gone out with Jack and Wulf, he'd always come home to her. And they had continuously shared the same bed, despite her initial attempt to remove to her own chamber when she suffered her courses. Lucien had insisted that she'd be just as comfortable with him as she would be alone, and had scoffed at the notion that something so natural should keep a man and wife from sleeping together, even if it temporarily put an end to the pursuit of their conjugal activities. She could account for his presence on every single night, and for most of the days, too. If he had been seeing Lady Halling, his visits must have been remarkably brief, unless he'd lied about the nights when he'd gone out with his friends. But she had reason to doubt that; it seemed the outside of practicality for a man to draw his friends into such deceit.

How did one combat a beautiful mistress? Was it possible? Or even wise? Clara set her cup and saucer abruptly aside and stood, crossing the room to the large mirror that hung over the fireplace.

"If only you could do something about your face, Clara," she told herself, gazing with increasing depression at her plainness. She had no color at all; or, perhaps if she did, they were all varying colors of gray and brown. Short of dying her hair and applying brighter shades of face paint, both of which cures Clara had always before disdained, there was nothing she could do to improve her looks.

She had already done everything that she knew to make Lucien's home a more inviting place for him, and he had declared himself well pleased, despite the memories that yet haunted him. He didn't appear to prefer other locales to Barrington; indeed, on evenings when Clara was away at a party or ball, Lucien had gotten into the habit of inviting his particular friends to Barrington for dinner and cards. She'd often return home in the late hours of the night, or early hours of the morning, to find them still happily ensconced in Lucien's study, smoking and drinking and in a jovial mood. Wulf and Jack had both complimented Clara on the changes she'd made at Barrington, and had declared it always a pleasure to be a guest there.

And Lucien had seemed perfectly pleased with her response to him in their bed. Even last night she'd been unable to conceal the deep pleasure he gave to her; she knew, by some inborn instinct, that he received equal pleasure from her. But perhaps it wasn't enough. She knew so little about men in general, and even after five months of marriage, not all that much about Lucien in specific. Perhaps having her two and sometimes three times in the course of a night wasn't sufficient to sate his needs. Still, she couldn't imagine that there was anything that he could do with Lady Halling that he hadn't also done with her. The things he'd taught Clara about how to please him physically had served to give her an education beyond her wildest imaginings. If there was anything else to do or know, it would have to involve a physical flexibility that only circus performers possessed. If Lady Halling was *that* talented, Clara might as well give up without a fight.

A soft scratch fell on the sitting room door, and at Clara's invitation Mrs. MacInnes entered, bearing a silver salver with a card upon it. The disapproving glance she gave to the yet untouched breakfast tray didn't miss Clara's notice.

"A visitor?" Clara asked, taking up the card to see who it was. "So early?"

"It's past noon, my lady," Mrs. MacInnes said in a tone that matched her expression.

"Why it's Andrew!" Clara cried, looking at the card with a mixture of gladness and concern. "Please ask him to wait in the drawing room, Mrs. MacInnes, and have tea sent

in. And send Bertie to me. I shall dress quickly and attend
Captain Blakesley at once.''

"Bawd Claxton's?'' the Earl of Manning repeated.
"Good heavens, child, never tell me so. And to think I was
distressed that you frequented Mawdry's.'' The earl set his
cup of tea on a nearby table and regarded his nephew with
frank interest. "How in the name of all that's holy did a
nice young fellow like Captain Blakesley end up in a filthy
sinkhole like Claxton's? I remember his parents from the
days when I was first courting Anna, and I'm sure they'd be
horrified to know of it. A nice, old family are the Blakes-
leys.''

"Indeed,'' Lucien murmured dryly. "You must bear in
mind, Robby, that Andrew Blakesley is hardly a child to be
worried or fussed over.''

"No, of course not,'' Robert agreed, "but one does hate
to see a young man of quality become involved with such
malignant company. Especially the likes of Pamela Halling.
Perhaps now that she's done her evil deed she'll leave Captain Blakesley in peace, but somehow I doubt it.'' He
picked up the drawing that rested on his lap and looked it
over carefully. "Not a bad rendering, considering that she
only had rumors and innuendo to go on. A few details are
in error, of course, but overall, not too far from the truth as
you and I know it. A nasty turn of the screw to make your
father over in your likeness and to put Clara's face on your
mother. Is this supposed to be Lord Ganley or Captain
Blakesley that she's running away with?''

"Apparently, you're not concerned over the fact that it
was about to be published,'' Lucien remarked.

Robert smiled up at him comfortingly. "Lucky, my dear,
we kept the complete truth at bay for as long as we possibly
could. And the event is so long in the past now that it
doesn't matter. Most of the *ton* has already guessed what

really happened. I didn't want you to suffer for it any more than you had to when you were a boy, but you're perfectly capable of handling such whispers and stares now, and I can't think anyone would hold you responsible for what your father did, despite Lady Halling's unfortunate choice of title for her drawing.''

''You don't think people are waiting to see if history repeats itself?''

''After the ludicrous wager you made with Lord Kerlain, they could hardly keep from doing so, could they?'' Robert replied. ''But you've got only yourself to blame for that, my boy. The sooner you bring that nonsense to a stop, the sooner you shut the mouths of the gossips.''

''True.''

''And if Clara should ever hear of the thing you'll have the devil's own time trying to calm the matter over. It would be far worse than the ruckus this drawing might have caused, had it been published.''

''Yes.'' Lucien's tone was disinterested, noncommittal.

With a sigh, Robert stopped pursuing such a useless topic. ''Tell me,'' he said more conversationally, folding the drawing and setting it aside, ''was Clara very glad to see her old friend? And did you nearly make a complete ass of yourself with a fit of jealousy?''

Lucien gave him a chilly look.

''You always were unjustly malevolent toward that young man,'' Robert stated.

''Not half so much as you were toward Colonel Huntington, however,'' Lucien countered smoothly.

''Ah, a direct hit,'' Robert admitted with a laugh. ''And true enough. Isn't it odd that the women we've both loved have been involved with military men? Perhaps we should have given up our titles and gone into the army, Lucky. We might have had better luck, or I might have, at least. You've landed your lady with great success.''

"Perhaps," he said, tenting his fingers beneath his chin and staring into the flames of the comfortable fire before which both he and his uncle sat.

"Perhaps?" Robert repeated with a hint of incredulousness. "You've had five months of marital bliss with that darling wife of yours—you aren't going to attempt to deny that you've been perfectly content with Clara, I hope?"

"No," Lucien said quietly. "We've been . . . I've been very happy."

"So much so that you've actually behaved like a normal being for most of the time following your wedding. All of London has been in shock. Viscount Callan has proved to be human after all. I'm surprised it hasn't been written up in the papers as a bona fide miracle."

"Robby," Lucien said, sighing. "Might we dispense with your particular brand of sarcasm for today? I'm not up to it."

Robert looked at him more closely. "Oh, Lucien, don't be a fool. Clara loves you so much it seeps out of her very pores every time she so much as looks at you. Don't mar the pleasure your marriage has given you both with something so idiotic as unfounded jealousy. Hasn't she proven to you that she's nothing like your mother was? And God alone knows that you're nothing like your father."

"Andrew Blakesley is in *love* with her."

"Of course he is. God's feet, what man isn't after meeting that delightful and charming creature? You know very well that you're the most envied man in London. Is there any reason why Clara should be made to suffer for it? You can't honestly think she'd ever run off with another man."

"Why did my mother flirt?"

The question threw Robert off stride. "Why did your *mother* flirt?"

"Yes. My mother. Why? Did she enjoy it, or was there some other reason?"

"In all these years," Robert said slowly, "you've never before asked me anything about your mother. And every time I tried to speak of her you froze me into silence. Clara must be doing you more good than I'd realized."

Lucien waited in patient silence.

"So," Robert said, sitting back and taking up his cup of tea again. "Why did your mother flirt? It was partly because she enjoyed doing so, partly because she was terrified of growing older and gaining the sexual attentions of men made her feel young and attractive. But it was mostly, I think, because your father drove her to it."

Lucien's expression darkened. "I fail to see how either my mother's age or my father had anything to do with it. She was hardly in her dotage, and my father loved her to the point of being pathetic."

"That's just the point, though, isn't it? No one truly wants a pathetic, swooning, clinging love, as romantic as such a thing may seem to the young and inexperienced. Your father suffocated your mother with his dogged devotion, always wringing his hands over her affairs and begging with her like some helpless child to end them when it would have served far better if he'd simply taken her over his knee and put a stop to the business himself. Really, if you stop to consider it, there were any of a hundred effective ways that he might have handled the matter rather than to let your mother lead him about as if he had a ring in his nose. But that was what he chose to do. You aren't fated to make the same choice simply because you're his son."

Lucien frowned. "He killed her, though. He might have simply killed Ganley, or himself, and let her live."

"God alone knows what happened to Edward that night to make him so crazed," Robert said gently. "Perhaps he'd gone mad, or perhaps he had finally realized that your mother was truly leaving him—not just threatening to do so. I loved my brother, Lucky, just as you loved him. But he was far from perfect. I know that you've taken his side over the years, but perhaps that was more from understanding than true sympathy. Like your father, you often had to beg for your mother's attention. Isn't that so?''

"It wasn't like that," Lucien murmured. "She was just too busy . . . and when she was home they were always arguing."

"My dear boy," Robert said, leaning forward to touch his nephew's knee in a reassuring gesture, "you must never doubt that your parents loved you. They were both of them terribly proud of their only child. You must have always known it, despite everything."

Lucien shrugged. "What I know of parental love I learned from you, Robby. If God should bless me with children, you may believe that I shall do my utmost to treat them as you treated me, rather than with what I learned from my natural parents."

"Will you, Lucky?" Robert asked, smiling. "I do believe, my dear, that I've never received a finer compliment. However, I feel it only fair to warn you that if you continue on in such a delightful vein, I shall probably begin to weep and embarrass you entirely."

Lucien's smile was rare and affectionate. "You're becoming emotional in your old age, Robby."

"You don't know the half of it," Robert said with an elegant snort. "If you'd only seen me sitting alone in the library on your wedding night, giving vent to the most awfully maudlin sentiments. It's probably just as well I only had you to raise, and not any daughters. I can just envision myself shedding buckets of tears on their wedding days. But we digress. If I truly were a good parent to you, Lucky, then I should utter the hard words that parents are often called upon to speak. You don't want to hear them."

"When has that ever stopped you?" Lucien asked with a laugh.

"More often than you know. When you've children of your own, you'll understand that well. Lucky, I only want you to hear me out, and then consider what it is that I've said. You've hated your mother for so long and set so much blame at her door, and venerated your father and made him an innocent victim. I loved my brother, but he was at least equally to blame for what happened. He didn't have to react to your mother's infidelities as he did. No one *made* him be sickly obsessed with the woman. Certainly no one made him commit the killing of two other human beings. No matter what your mother and Lord Ganley did, they didn't deserve such as that. To be hunted down and shot like animals. I've never told you this before, but I was almost glad that my brother took his own life directly afterward, for if he hadn't I'm not certain that I wouldn't have."

"God, Robby."

"Let me finish. You need to understand this, Lucky, and understand it well. You've spent years being mortally afraid of becoming like your father, of loving a woman so much that you became her slave. But the truth is, you're far more like your mother."

Lucien looked away, shaking his head, and said, firmly, "*No.*"

"You've always known it," Robert went on. "No, listen to me. It isn't any easier for me to say it than it is for you to hear."

"It's not true," Lucien said hoarsely.

"It is. You remind me so much of your mother that I've always been a little afraid of it. Only think of the way in which you've treated Clara. She's to dance to your tune or to no tune at all, isn't that right? If she doesn't love you devotedly, like a dog, you'll send her away."

"That's not what I want!"

"Isn't it?" Robert demanded. "You wagered ten thousand pounds that it's *exactly* what you want. You want

Clara to love you so fully and deeply that she'll never care
for her own happiness. You want her waiting at the door,
just as your father waited, and worrying and wondering and
hoping, just as your father did.''

''No!'' Lucien stood and stalked to the fire, running a
hand through his hair. ''No,'' he said more calmly. ''You're
. . . wrong. You're mad.'' He swallowed heavily, drew in a
breath. ''I am *nothing* like my mother.''

''I see,'' Robert said. ''Faithful to your marriage, are
you? Completely devoted to it?''

Lucien set the palm of one hand to his forehead, rubbing
as if he had an ache. ''Clara flirts . . .''

''Innocently. Probably more so than any other member of
the *ton*. She's never done anything that could even remotely
be termed questionable. It can't be compared to the blatant
invitations your mother issued. Very well.'' Robert stood.
''You're not like your mother. Prove it. Show that your
marriage means something to you. And don't be as your
father was and let outside forces ruin what's between Clara
and you.''

Lucien's palm lowered to his side. He stared into the fire.
''I don't want to be like either of them. Robby''—he drew
in a sharp breath—''I want to be as you are. After all these
years, even after what she did to you, you've forgiven Lady
Anna, and you're so content, suddenly. It's as if she never
hurt you at all. I can't begin to fathom how you could let
her back into your life, but I must admit that you've never
seemed happier.''

''Just as you are with Clara,'' Robert murmured. ''Perhaps we've both learned an important truth, Lucky. The
moment I was able to admit my own folly in losing Anna, I
found that I was also able to forgive her for hers. And I
could see no reason why either she or I should go on deny-
ing the happiness we once knew together, because it was a

deep and rare love we had. I still love her, although, pray
God, I hope I'm wiser with it now than I was so long ago.''

"You nearly died because of her.''

"Yes." Robert set a comforting hand on his nephew's
shoulder. "Try to imagine your own life without Clara and
I believe you'll understand what it was that I felt in those
days. But it was selfish and foolish of me to so willingly let
my body waste away toward death. Just as selfish and foolish as your father letting your mother ruin his life. My life,
and his—every life—has merit on its own account, and you
needed me then, as well.''

"Yes.''

Robert sighed and returned to sit in his chair. "I discovered something else from that experience. Life is too
precious a gift to so easily throw away. We have a poor
tendency, as human beings, to let ourselves be overcome by
our emotions, and then, instead of thinking clearly and behaving in a rational manner, we do stupid things. Your father should have let your mother go and devoted himself to
your care and building a new life for the two of you without
her. Instead, he selfishly killed two innocent people and
took his own life, and did his son a grave disservice. And I
should have let Anna go and never indulged myself in such
destructive melodrama. It was so unfair to you, Lucky, as
well as to myself.''

"And if your pride hadn't gotten the better of you in the
first place," Lucien murmured, "perhaps Lady Anna never
would have left you?''

"Exactly. And if your father had behaved differently
when faced with your mother's behavior—''

"Things might not have turned out so badly for them,''
Lucien finished. "It's all interesting conjecture, Robby, but
we'll never know whether it's true or not, will we? Still, I
understand what it is that you're trying to say. Tell me,'' he

said, turning to face his uncle. "Are you planning on marrying Lady Anna? Or attempting to do so, I should say."

Robert smiled with beatific innocence. "Perhaps. For the time being, I'm content to enjoy her company and to make certain that she enjoys mine. She's as wary of my intentions as you were about Clara's. It takes time for these matters to smooth themselves out."

"If you do decide that it's what you want," Lucien said slowly. "I just want you to know that—despite the way I've felt about Lady Anna in the past—I'll be fully glad for the both of you."

"Lucien," Robert said, clearly moved by this.

"Perhaps I've been late in learning it, but I've discovered something about life, as well. It's far more pleasant to spend one's days upon the earth if one has someone to love. Perhaps that's what my father should have done with my mother—simply love and accept her for what she was. There was a time, I remember, when they were happy together."

"In a rather childish and infatuated way, yes," Robert said. "Such loves tend not to last overlong. They require constant excitement to keep burning."

"I realize that, and can accept the truth of it in my parents' relationship. But even so, it might have become something better in time if my father had reacted differently, just as you said, since my mother seemed incapable of doing so. It just seems to me that any love is better than no love at all, and a truly good love should be embraced at all costs. I want you to be happy, Robby. You deserve it, and if you can find it with Lady Anna, then you'll have my blessing and best wishes."

Chapter Eighteen

❧

It was difficult for Lucien to hold on to his recently stated belief about love and its merits when he walked into the drawing room at Barrington to find his wife and Andrew Blakesley sitting side by side with their heads nearly together, laughing at some jest in an intimate, familiar manner that made his hands curl into fists. In a red haze he saw the entire scene differently, as it had been so many years ago, except that on that occasion the couple on the couch had been much farther along in their tête à tête. His mother and her lover had at first been horrified by his accidental arrival, then embarrassed, and then, while they hastily rearranged their clothes, they had laughed, just as Clara and Captain Blakesley were laughing, as if it were a wonderful joke that they would enjoy for many days to come.

He had to blink to make the image go away, to make himself realize that both Clara and her companion were fully dressed, and that she was doing nothing more unusual than entertaining a close childhood friend in her home. She wasn't cruel, as his mother had been; Clara never would have hurt him in such a manner, even if she'd had good reason to do so. He thought, then, of what Robby had said, and admitted, with a measure of discomfort, that perhaps he had inherited his own cruel streak from his maternal parent. The idea had never occurred to him before, and he found it vastly unpleasant.

"Lucien, you're home!"

Both Clara and Andrew Blakesley stood; Clara looking anxious and perhaps a bit nervous, Blakesley appearing perfectly glad to see him.

Clara moved toward him with an outstretched hand, which Lucien took and held in an automatic movement, feeling how cold her fingers were.

"I'm so glad you came home," she said, and still he could see the worry in her eyes. What on earth was she thinking? he wondered. That he was going to beat her? Shout at her? Or was it Pamela who still haunted her mind? He'd once thought, years ago, that it might be gratifying for Clara to know that he had such a beautiful mistress. Now he only wished she'd never discovered the truth. At least he'd been able to spare her the publication of Pamela's scandalous work of art, small comfort though it was. He doubted he'd ever forget the way she'd looked at Vauxhall when she'd finally realized who Lady Halling was. And later, her anger at him when he'd returned so late, and his own anger and jealousy over Captain Blakesley. He had handled the matter badly. As Robby had said, there were probably a hundred better ways for a man to react to such situations.

Lucien sifted rapidly through his present options, mentally ordering them. To retreat behind a wall of ice had always been his personal favorite, followed by controlled but sarcastic and blade-sharp anger. By pursuing that route he could, within a few minutes, reduce Clara to tears and have Blakesley ready to meet him at dawn over pistols. With jealousy still pounding hotly in his veins, it was what he wanted to do, what he would have done before without thinking a moment of anything otherwise. Instead, he decided to see what would happen if he behaved the way a normal, well-bred husband might.

Lifting Clara's hand, he kissed her fingers and then covered them with his own, warming them. "I apologize for leaving without a word this morning, my dear. I had an appointment to take breakfast with Robby and didn't wish to wake you."

"With Robby?" she repeated faintly, a look of relief easing some of the tightness in her features. "Oh, I'm glad. I hope you had a nice visit. You so seldom get to see each other with any amount of privacy."

She *had* been worried about Pamela, he realized, lowering his gaze to their hands and striving not to let her see how deeply the knowledge affected him. It was a sweet flood of emotion, just to know that she cared enough to even have a spark of jealousy over him.

"We had an enjoyable visit, thank you," he replied with a smile. "Next time we'll go together, if you like. Blakesley, welcome to Barrington." He moved to greet the other man with a handshake, and tried to sound sincere in his pleasure at his guest. Mentally he was wishing the man to the devil. Or out the door, at the very least, so that he might have Clara to himself.

It was easy, and surprisingly pleasant, he discovered in the ensuing half hour, to assume the best, rather than the worst, of people. Clara sat beside him on the couch, opposite the one Blakesley was on, and held his hand and smiled up at him even when he wasn't speaking. She seemed as eager as he to put the unpleasantness of last night behind them, and to be reassured that their marriage would survive. Blakesley himself wasn't a bad fellow, although he was clearly as besotted with Clara as he ever had been. But he appeared to realize that Lucien had an irrefutable claim to her, and behaved appropriately, in a friendly, unexceptional manner. Although there was an undercurrent there as well, which Lucien didn't miss. An undercurrent of steel.

"Clara," Andrew Blakesley said after finishing yet another cup of tea, "do you happen to have that recipe for brown cake pudding your mother used to have made whenever we went on picnics? It tasted of brandy and nutmeg. Do you recall it?''

''Of course! It's one of Mama's favorite dishes. Indeed, I do have it.''

''Would you be so good as to copy it down for me before I go? I'm sorry to put you to the trouble, but I promised it to a friend. And then I really must be on my way.''

Clara said that she'd be back in a few minutes and left the drawing room to hunt down Mrs. MacInnes. Still standing after having risen for her departure, the two men eyed each other in a frank and mutual assessment.

''I hope you don't mind me visiting with Clara in your absence,'' Blakesley said after a moment's silence. ''I arrived early, expecting you to be home as well.''

''I regret not having been,'' Lucien replied. ''If Clara hasn't filled you to overflowing with tea, yet, would you care for something more interesting to drink?'' With a hand he indicated a tray set with crystal glasses and decanters of brandy, sherry, and wine.

''Thank you. Brandy would be welcome.''

Lucien poured them each a glass, handed Captain Blakesley his, then went to stand by the fire and waited. It was clear that the other man had sent Clara away purposefully.

''I suppose there's no good way to say this,'' Blakesley began, moving to stand opposite Lucien. ''I felt that I should apologize to you for the awkward situation that occurred at Vauxhall last night. I didn't realize until it was too late the manner of your acquaintance with Lady Halling. That Clara should have been introduced to your mistress was unforgivable, and I do apologize.''

Lucien smiled blandly and drew a long sip from his brandy.

''Also,'' the captain went on more uncomfortably, though no less firmly, ''I wanted to say that I care very deeply for Clara. She's been my friend for a good many years, and her happiness is important to me. I don't wish to see her hurt.''

At this, Lucien raised his eyebrows questioningly. ''Do you imagine that I would do so? Hurt her?''

''It's possible,'' Blakesley replied evenly. ''I've known Clara far longer than you—''

''No,'' Lucien interrupted bluntly. ''You haven't. She was mine before she was even yet born. No one knows her better than I do.''

''Be that as it may,'' Andrew Blakesley said with patience, ''I believe you'll admit that I do know her well.''

It wasn't a point Lucien cared to concede, but he gave a light, noncommittal shrug.

''Your relationship with Lady Halling could wound Clara a great deal. She's always believed in love and ever after and all that. She doesn't understand anything about mistresses or women of lesser morals. I only ask, as any decent man would do, that you keep your private activities from touching Clara in any way.''

When Lucien spoke, it was with deadly calm. ''Captain Blakesley, are you insinuating that I deliberately arranged for both my wife and Lady Halling to be present at Vauxhall last night?''

''Certainly not. I merely found it questionable and, to be honest, objectionable that you should take such blatant advantage of the situation.''

''Lady Halling is not my mistress,'' Lucien told him. ''And I was not topping her off in some secluded corner at Vauxhall last night. Disreputable as you obviously find me, even I wouldn't do anything quite so bold as to have relations with another woman while my own wife was within shouting distance.''

Blakesley looked at him with some measure of disbelief.

"Lady Halling made it somewhat clear, after we departed the gardens—what I mean to say is that she indicated—"

"I can very well imagine what she indicated," Lucien said with a laugh. "Yes, indeed. I can almost hear her very words. But, please believe me when I say this, you make a grave mistake in giving credence to anything that she either does or says. Not that I owe you anything, but for Clara's sake I'll warn you to keep your distance from Lady Pamela Halling. She's a dangerous woman."

"My lord, I'm afraid you malign a lady who has been nothing but kind to me."

Lucien laughed again and shook his head. "Oh, Blakesley. If only Pamela could hear you now, how she would laugh. Come, now. You're not a fool, or you never would have survived so many battles. A military man such as yourself will recognize a master of deception more readily than another, and despite the fact that Pamela's such a marvelous actress, if you look closely enough you'll see the signs. Didn't it occur to you to wonder about the sort of female you'd meet at a place like Bawd Claxton's?"

"An acquaintance had taken her there against her will," Blakesley told him. "She was horrified to find herself in such an establishment."

Lucien nearly rolled his eyes. "And how did you come to be there? Wait, let me guess. Could it have been that a fellow named Rosswell took you?"

Blakesley's face reddened, but, much to Lucien's admiration, only slightly.

"I met William Rosswell at The Guards'," he admitted. "He's a publisher, or so he told me. Our acquaintance was of short duration before he invited me out for an evening of gaming. I had assumed he meant to the usual places. Bawd Claxton's was rather a surprise."

"Yes, I can imagine."

For the next few minutes, Lucien gave his companion a

brief accounting of the relationship that had existed between himself and Pamela, of the one that currently existed between Pamela and Rosswell, and of why he, Blakesley, had been pulled into Pamela's scheme.

When he finished Blakesley stared at him in silence.

"Swear to me that you speak the truth," he said at last. "Lady Halling used me only in an attempt to lure you back?"

"More to hurt Clara, I think," Lucien said. "But I do swear that I've spoken the truth to you."

Blakesley nodded. "Then I thank you, my lord, and again offer an apology. Understand, however, that I am more determined than before to make certain no harm comes to Clara. My loyalty is completely to her, and if she should require my help in any manner, I will give it to her."

"It's a fair enough warning," Lucien replied. "Now I'll give you one of my own. I love my wife, and I'll not allow you, or any other man, to come between us."

"I love Clara, too," Blakesley stated baldly. "If I see her hurt because of you or Lady Halling or anyone else in your demented crowd, I'll do whatever I must to remove her from the situation."

"So long as we understand each other, then," Lucien said, turning away as Clara opened the door and entered, a smile on her face and a sheet of paper in one hand. The fact that she went straight to his side instead of to Blakesley's made his heart feel as if it might drown in pride and love. And she stayed by his side while they bid their guest goodbye, moving away only once to kiss Blakesley on the cheek before that man made his bow and took his leave.

When the door to the drawing room had closed, leaving them alone together, Lucien set his arm about Clara, drawing her to him and kissing her briefly and lightly. She was stiff in his arms, taut, and seemed even more fragile and delicate than usual.

"Are you feeling unwell, Clara?" he asked, gazing into her pale face. He wasn't sure whether it was the lacy cap she was wearing over her hair or the plain day dress she wore that made her look so colorless, or if it had been his treatment of her the night before. The latter certainly made sense; he hadn't slept well, either, with all the unpleasantness that had passed between them.

"Perhaps a little tired," she said. Her own gaze fixed on the buttons of his coat. "I did enjoy the visit with Andrew, though. It's been so long since I've seen him. He was only here for half an hour before you came home. There was a footman in the room until just before you came. I sent him out to fetch more tea." Her hands came up and smoothed over the wrinkles in his cravat. "I can see that you dressed yourself this morning," she added with mocking disapproval. "Did you shave yourself, too?"

"Yes." He caught one of her hands and drew it up to rub lightly against his cheek, where stubble was already making headway against the poor job he'd done. "With cold water. I even cut myself on the neck. Don't worry, the cravat hides it." He took hold of her other hand to stop her from pulling his neck cloth off and fussing over the small wound. "Clara," he said, gently pressing his lips by turn to each of her palms. "I know that you weren't doing anything with Andrew Blakesley but talking and drinking tea. What I said to you last night was wrong—wrong of me to say and wrong in content. I've long had a tendency to be unreasonably jealous over you and the men who admire you so greatly. It isn't easy for me to put that aside, but I am trying, and will continue to try. I deeply regret the accusations I made last night, also for my behavior, which followed. Please forgive me."

Her eyes had begun to fill with tears almost as soon as he began speaking; by the time he'd finished they had overflown. She sniffled and blinked, sending two more tears spilling down her cheeks.

"Lucien," she whispered. Still she wouldn't look at him. "I'm sorry, too."

He slid his arms about her and pulled her close. She pressed her face against his coat and wept, and he pulled the lace cap from her head and stroked her silky hair.

"Do you have any appointments for today?"

"B-Bella," she said tearfully. "We were to go shopping."

"I'll send her a note with your regrets, then," he said, rocking her back and forth in a comforting movement. "And I'll let the Landlers know we'll not be attending their party tonight. Clara"—he took her cheeks in the palms of his hands and lifted her face to his—"I'm going to take you upstairs to our bed in a moment and make love to you. If you wish it, that is. But first I'm going to tell you something. Regardless of what it may have looked like last night, Lady Halling is not my mistress. I'll not be accountable to you for the things I did before you were my wife, but I swear before God that since our marriage, I have bedded no other woman but you. I have no mistress, and do not intend to have one. You are the only woman I desire." He smiled. "And if you'll only think, my dear, of how often you and I exercise our conjugal rights, you'll realize that I couldn't possibly have enough energy to even contemplate bedding another woman, even if I did wish it, which, as I've said, I don't."

She turned a charming shade of pink. "I did wonder, Lucien."

He lowered his head and kissed her, tenderly, with all the love he felt for her. "You may ask your aunt whether I speak the truth," he murmured afterward. "I'm sure she'll tell you that I'd have to be a nine-day wonder to keep up such a schedule."

Clara gave a tearful chuckle and wiped her wet cheeks. Then she put her arms about Lucien's neck and, resting against him, gave a sigh.

"Take me upstairs and make love to me," she said. "I don't ever wish to think of last night again."

"Neither do I," he murmured, picking her up in his arms. "Let's erase the memories and replace them with new ones, shall we?"

Some hours later Lucien made his way back downstairs to his study. He wished himself back with Clara in their bed, whom he'd left regretfully, warm and deeply asleep, but there were certain chores that couldn't be left waiting.

Settling behind his desk with a glass of brandy by his hand, he began writing missives. First was a note to Bella, apologizing for not letting her know earlier that Clara would be unable to keep their appointment to go shopping and promising that Clara would be in touch with her on the morrow. Next was the missive that should have gone earlier to Lord and Lady Landler, explaining that an unforeseen occurrence would unfortunately keep Clara and him from attending their dinner party. Lucien worded the apology as carefully as he could; it really was inexcusably rude to cancel at such late notice.

Next was a rather longer letter addressed to his steward at Pearwood, informing that gentleman of his intention to retire to the estate with Viscountess Callan before the end of the month for the duration of the year and probably much longer. He wanted everything made ready in order to receive the new viscountess in proper style.

This was followed by several shorter missives; one to his man of business, requesting that several drafts be prepared for varying sums and made payable to varying parties, another to Raggett, the proprietor of White's, requesting that he enter the outcome of a certain wager in the betting books and inform those patrons who had an interest in the matter that settlement would be forthcoming. Two more notes went out to Jack and Wulf, apologizing for the sums they'd wagered on his behalf, promising to make it up by naming two of his children after them, and asking whether they minded being honored with the feminine forms, Jacksonia and Wulfina, just in case those children all proved to be girls. He could envision, as he sealed these particular missives, the laughter this would provoke from his friends. They'd be glad for him, he thought. He was fortunate to have two such friends, both of whom he could trust so implicitly.

After this he penned a short, rather sentimental note to his uncle, informing him of his intention to take Clara to Pearwood for the long foreseeable future to attempt to put into practice everything that he'd learned from Robby about love and goodness; also, he and Clara would be hard at work on making Robby the youngest grandfather London had probably ever seen. He wrote the word "grandfather" quite deliberately, and added that if Robby and Lady Anna ever decided to wed and have children of their own, it was highly unlikely that anyone would ever be able to untangle the confusion of the family relations.

Lastly, he wrote to the Earl of Kerlain.

I owe you a debt of thanks for doing as I requested and giving Lady Halling the information that I would be at Vauxhall last night, also for keeping Rosswell well occupied for the evening. As unpleasant as I know the task was, it did bear fruit. Jack was successful, and all is well. Not only for my sake, but for my wife's, I do thank you. If I can ever repay the debt, you need only ask. I shall be in your service.

There is another debt for which I must pay you, for the wager we made some months ago at White's. I hereby concede the winning to you. Raggett has been notified, and my man of business will be visiting you within the next few days, at your convenience.

Lady Callan and I will be leaving London shortly, to take up residence in our country estate. If by chance I do not see or speak to you before that time, I convey now my thanks and gratitude. Yrs. Callan

When everything was done, signed, folded, and sealed, Lucien put the missives in the hands of his butler with the instruction, ''Have them delivered today, right away. Make certain each one is set into the hand of the responsible servant. Into their hands, do you understand?''

''Yes, my lord.''

''Send one of the grooms with the missive to Mr. Cauffrey at Pearwood.''

''He'll be on his way within the hour, my lord.''

''Very good.''

He stayed in his study for a few minutes more, alone, drinking his brandy, wandering about slowly, looking at the changes Clara had made for his benefit, seeing the things that had remained when the room had been his father's.

He had memories of the room, just as he did of the entire house. But perhaps the ones here were the most powerful. The last time he'd seen his father had been in this room. It had been the final holiday he'd had from Eton, before his parents had died.

''But I'm done with all that, now,'' he murmured aloud, staring at the portrait of his father that hung over the fireplace. ''I'm done with all of it. As of this moment, I'm burying you and Mother and Lord Ganley and every wretched thing that happened in this house. Barrington is mine, now. And Clara's. And I don't give a damn how many ghosts there are.'' He toasted the silent painting and drained his glass. ''Starting today,'' he said, setting his glass down with finality, ''my life is my own. Not yours, not Mother's." He closed his eyes and set his teeth and freely let fourteen years of rage and anger at last find the source of their birth. "*Damn* you both," he said in a voice raw and aching. His father's face stared down at him, placid, unmoving, perfectly serene. "You never even thought of me in all the mess you made for yourselves. I trusted you. I *worshipped* you. And her." Tears stung his eyes. He blinked them away. "God." Lifting a hand, he rubbed the bridge of his nose until he felt control returning.

"But this is where it ends," he stated, more to himself than any other being. "I won't let my children know such as that. And I'm done with tormenting my own wife. Robby was right. I don't have to let it happen to me just because it happened to you." He lifted his head and looked at the portrait again. "I loved you," he told his father, "but I'm not paying for your sins any longer."

He doused the lamps in the room before leaving it, and stopped a footman just outside the study door to tell him that he and Lady Callan wanted their dinner served in his chamber. Then he made his way upstairs to his chamber, to where his wife lay still asleep. Undressing, Lucien joined her, nesting her warm, supine body with his own. She murmured and turned into him, pushing her forehead into the space between his shoulder and his neck and tossing an arm about his chest.

"What time is it?" she muttered in a cranky tone that made him grin.

"Late," he whispered, kissing her forehead. "Time to sleep."

Later on he would wake her, share dinner with her and then a warm bath. For now he was content to share her slumber, and to know that tomorrow everything was going to be new for them both.

Chapter Nineteen

❦

October

The weeks following the incident at Vauxhall were, for Lucien, blissful in a manner that few other people could have understood or appreciated.

He had not been fully aware of just how much bitterness he'd nurtured until he began to let go of it, and the result was an unexpected sense of buoyancy. He felt lighter, even when he walked, as if he'd unburdened a ten-stone weight he'd been carrying about. The world itself seemed lighter, albeit in a different sense. The darkness that had shadowed his view of everything and everyone had receded. He no longer saw intent and complicity in the eyes of strangers and those acquaintances whom he'd purposefully kept at a distance. It was easy to be friendly, he discovered. Easy to like people. Even—this was most amazing of all—easy to assume the best of them.

When he looked at Clara he couldn't understand why he had once distrusted her, or equated her as being like his mother. He was able, suddenly, to look back on the very events that had so damned her in his eyes and see them for what they were—innocent moments of flirtation; nothing more serious than that. *He* had been the one at fault, assuming the worst and acting on those assumptions without any rational basis for doing so. Considering his behavior, it was a miracle Clara had continued speaking to him, let alone become his wife. Although he supposed he'd not given her much choice in the matter. The fact of that should shame him, he supposed, but it only made him glad. If he'd been a fool in other ways, at least he'd had the good sense to make certain of her as his wife.

The time was reminiscent of their honeymoon week. They spent most of their time together, alone, if not making love, then talking. Everything about Clara fascinated him, every detail, every thought, every event that had happened to her, no matter how small or insignificant it might seem to her. He pressed her endlessly. What was her earliest memory? Her happiest? Her saddest? When had she lost her first tooth, and had the experience frightened her as much as it had frightened him? What was it like having so many brothers, and being the eldest among them all? Had she ever wished to be the youngest, or one in the middle? Or perhaps to be an only child, as he had been?

He asked if he'd been the first boy to kiss her, and realized, with real amazement, that if she'd answered no he wouldn't have been devastated or furious. Jealous, yes, but there were some things about him that would never change. But she had answered yes, and that led to a great many other questions. Had she loved him? Had she ever realized how very deeply he had loved her? Had she missed him after he'd gone away, and during the years of his absence?

She answered him readily, if a bit warily, and Lucien made himself be patient. It would take time for her to learn to trust him as she had done so many years ago. Fortunately, time now spread out before them with all its many possibilities. There weren't just six months, or what was left of six months, there was, if God was gracious, a whole lifetime.

She asked questions, too, about his travels, which she never seemed to tire hearing of, and about Pearwood. What was it like? Was it very large, and grand? Would she feel as lost as she sometimes did at Barrington? And would he be content to live there rather than in Town?

"Yes," he replied very simply. "I'll be content. Wherever you are is the place I'll be most content."

They were lying in bed, comfortable against the pillows. Clara had her back pressed against Lucien's bare front; one of his arms was burrowed beneath her head, the other was settled about her waist. They were gazing out the window across the room, where the curtains were drawn back to reveal the gray, rainy sky of the early fall afternoon.

"Does that bother you, Clara?" he murmured lightly. "I've always found such devotion suffocating"—he curled the arm that was around her waist up to stroke the hair from her temple—"but it isn't my intention to hang on to you and about you every moment. I'll not be a clinging husband."

"Of course I don't expect that you will," Clara replied, although what really bothered her was the idea that Lucien *wouldn't* hang about her, or on to her.

The change in him had been bewildering, and so completely unexpected. She didn't know what had brought it on—the situation with Lady Halling, or Andrew's sudden appearance, or some other incident that she knew nothing about. Whatever it was, Clara hadn't been prepared for such a change in her husband. She knew she should be thankful and glad, but she wasn't.

He didn't need her as he had once done, didn't seem to care whether she flirted or not, didn't seem to care, even, if she'd kissed other men or not.

He was easier with everything and everyone now. Balls and parties, which he'd usually foregone if possible and, if not possible, had stayed at for as few minutes as politely permissible, now appeared to be a perfectly welcome manner in which to spend an evening. He'd gone so far as to accept a few invitations for the both of them, at least for the remainder of their time in London, when before he'd encouraged her to attend whatever she wished and not to let his own disinterest stop her. When he had attended a social gathering with her in the past he'd always stayed at her side, keeping an eye on who she danced with, conversing only with those few people whom he held as friends and generally ignoring everyone else. Unless he danced with her or Bella, he didn't dance at all. Now, however, they would arrive at an event and she would hardly see anything of him, except for when he came to claim his dances. Otherwise he was dancing with other partners, speaking in a friendly, if not exactly convivial, manner—but then he hadn't changed *that* much—to any number of acquaintances whom he'd normally avoided.

Instead of being the Lucien she had married, he had somehow turned into the model husband. He had never lived in her pocket, of course, but now he didn't even appear to live in her vicinity. At least not in public. Clara had once thought that she'd give anything to stop Lucien's jealousies; now, she felt lost without them.

It was foolish! she told herself. Almost to the point of being sinful. And yet she couldn't keep from wondering why he'd stopped caring so much about such things. Although perhaps she did know, deep inside, what it was.

She was a plain woman who'd married an extraordinarily handsome man. So long as he'd been unfathomably jealous of her, she'd felt secure knowing that, even if he hadn't loved her, he had at least wanted her. Inexplicably, yes, but he *had* wanted her. More than in a merely physical sense. Lucien had needed her—above every other woman, he had needed *her*. She had reveled in it, knowing that, despite her lack of beauty, there was something she possessed that Lucien wanted and evidently hadn't found anywhere else. It had been her safety, that knowledge. And now it was gone.

He was just as attentive and loving as he'd ever been,

perhaps even more so. And he'd told her that Lady Halling wasn't his mistress, that he didn't have a mistress at all, and had no plans to take one. Plans could change, of course; he'd not promised never to take one. But he *was* taking her to Pearwood, and had said that they would live there and, God willing, begin a family. It meant that he'd come to trust her, and that he believed they could have a normal marriage, or at least make the attempt.

In her heart she had long known that he was content, that he'd been surprised by the feeling and therefore all the more pleased. His words and actions were loverlike and sincere; since the day they'd wed he'd striven to be kind and, despite a few lapses, he'd succeeded. If she could only let herself relax and trust him completely, Clara thought that she would probably be the happiest woman in England.

But she was a plain woman, and just as Lucien had once found it impossible that she should be different from his mother, she found it impossible that a man so well favored as he could truly love and want a woman such as her. Especially now that he seemed not to need her with the same intensity that he once had. And so the same few days that had been so blissful to Lucien were for Clara quite otherwise. She was beset with fear, yet unable to express it whenever Lucien asked her if anything was wrong. He kept saying that everything was going to be fine as soon as they were at Pearwood, but no matter how optimistic or reassuring he tried to be, Clara couldn't push away the vague sense of dread that filmed her every effort to look toward the future and believe that all would be well.

The house in Cavendish Square was small and proper, not at all what Anna had expected.

"Goodness, Robert," she said, nervously walking about the neat, tidy parlor that the butler had led them to before he'd discreetly disappeared. "I had no idea you kept your

ladybirds in such fine style. This almost looks . . . respectable."

Behind her, the Earl of Manning made a sound of amusement. "You were expecting a den of iniquity littered with
red velvet and gilt cherubs, reeking of opium, perhaps?
Would you like tea, my dear? I should be happy to call for
it."

"Oh, no," Anna replied, turning to face him. He was
standing near the door, his hands behind his back, regarding
her with an expression of gentle interest. He seemed completely at ease, the wretch, just as if what was about to
happen between them wasn't going to happen at all.
"Thank you. Is it . . . is that what you normally do first?
Perhaps you'd like some? Oh, dear." She shook her head
and laughed at her pathetic ignorance. "Forgive me. I'm
not used to this, as you can clearly tell."

He smiled and moved nearer, taking her still-gloved
hands in his. "Anna, are you certain you wish to be here?
Wouldn't you rather that I take you home? Perhaps we
could collect Sarah and go out for a picnic? I could prevail
upon Monsieur Dellard to prepare something, even on such
short notice."

"No." She gripped his hands more firmly. "No, Robert.
I know what it is that I want, and that's to be here with you.
I've thought the matter through quite thoroughly."

"Very well," he murmured, lifting her hands and kissing
each. "But perhaps we'll have some tea, anyway, and try to
relax a bit. Shall we?" He moved to the bellpull.

Tea. It was the last thing Anna had expected of Robert in
this moment. When she'd first asked him to make arrangements for them to meet privately, she'd envisioned him
leading her over the threshold of some dark, gaudy love
nest and directly into an equally dark and gaudy bedchamber, where he would proceed to the main purpose of the
visit without delay. Instead, he'd brought her to a perfectly

respectable dwelling located in a perfectly respectable part of town and instead of making love to her, or even attempting to do so, seemed ready to settle down in the parlor and have a cup of tea and conversation.

"Robert—" she began, then stopped, unsure of herself. She'd already been so forward as to ask him to meet her; if she had to beg him to make love to her before her nerve gave way he'd probably think her a complete idiot. Or, worse, pathetically desperate.

The next moment the butler arrived and Robert was giving him his instructions. As soon as the door had closed again, he turned to her and said, "Yes, my dear? Did you wish to say something?"

With a sigh, Anna began to undo her gloves. "No. I suppose not." The tiny buttons suddenly seemed impossible to release.

"Allow me," Robert said, coming to her and, with deft movements, quickly removing the articles. She noticed, with even greater aggravation, that the beastly man's hands didn't even tremble, as her own were doing. Placing the gloves on a nearby low table with her reticule, he began to unlace her bonnet. "There," he said with satisfaction when the hat had joined the other items. "Much better. Anna, my love, are you feeling quite well? You appear to be somewhat distressed."

"I'm fine," she assured him, wishing that she could stop feeling as if every member of the *ton* was going to know on the morrow that she had trysted with the Earl of Manning. And in a respectable home in Cavendish Square, no less. If her brother ever heard of it, the remainder of her life would be flooded with his disapproving looks. "I'm just not used to . . . this."

"This," he repeated. "Yes, I know that, my dear. And I'm still perfectly willing to take you home. Indeed, I think perhaps I should."

She stared at him. "But, Robert, don't you wish to . . . have I totally misunderstood you? All these weeks?" Horror at the idea began to spill through her, following a path to her every nerve. "Oh, my heavens! I *have* misunderstood."

"Not at all," he replied calmly.

"Why didn't you simply tell me?" she demanded. "Or simply said no? What a *fool* I've made of myself. And you! All these weeks, you've let me think that you wanted me. That you wished to—"

His arms came about her and his mouth lowered to hers all in the same moment, cutting off the remainder of her speech. He had kissed her in the past few weeks, just as passionately and unchastely as he'd used to do so many years ago, and Anna had melted just as quickly and thoroughly. Even so, years and experience had added a good deal of expertise to the Earl of Manning's methods, just as her own experience had brushed away the veil of innocence that had held him at bay when she'd not yet been a bride. But as much as his experience and hers had colored the kisses they'd recently shared, none of those embraces had begun to approach what he was doing to her now. His arms and hands were like vises, melding her body so closely to his own that there could be no doubt as to the level of his arousal. Even when he lifted his head, the arms and hands remained. The one on her bottom attempted to draw her even closer.

"I hope," he said, stopping to draw in a shaking breath, "that you believe in my sincere and ardent desire to take you to the nearest bed?"

She had to draw in several breaths of her own before replying, "Yes. It was the tea that made me doubt you."

With a laugh, his grip on her began to lessen. *Now* he was trembling, she realized with a measure of satisfaction. They both were.

"Anna, this isn't my house."

One kiss really *had* addled him.

"No, it isn't, dear. You live at Manning House."

Another laugh, and he kissed her again, chuckling against her mouth as he did so.

"I mean," he said when he could, "that I don't own this house. It belongs to a friend of mine, who let me borrow it for the day."

Straightening and pushing a handsbreadth away from him, Anna said, "A friend of yours?"

"Yes. He's a banker—my banker, as it happens. He lives here with his wife, a very nice young lady from Cheswickshire. They've gone to visit her family, and Parker was good enough to allow me the use of the house in their absence."

She stared at him.

He smiled. "Parker's a very discreet fellow, you see. And as he and his wife don't socialize in *ton* circles, I felt it safe to bring you here."

"Robert," she said. "You brought me to a banker's home to make love to me?" She assumed he kept a house for his mistresses, one that they would use while they carried out the discreet affair she had proposed. But perhaps he hadn't wished to terminate the arrangement he had with his current ladybird in order to begin an affair with her.

"Not exactly," he admitted somewhat ruefully. "Although I may yet prove amenable to the idea, shocking as it seems. But I had to take you somewhere, didn't I? You seemed so intent upon bedding me—"

"Robert Bryland!"

"—and I couldn't dissuade you from the matter. Although I did try, you must admit."

One feminine brow arched upward. "Not very hard, you didn't."

He had the grace to look guilty. "No, I didn't. I rather

enjoy knowing that a beautiful and eminently desirable woman wants me as I want her. Unfortunately," he said gently, smiling, "I'm a terribly conservative fellow." The backs of his fingers stroked down the softness of one of her cheeks. "I found that, despite my desires or yours, I don't wish to have an affair with you. Or with anyone else, for that matter."

With slow, careful movements Anna disentangled herself from his arms and moved back. "I see," she said, embarrassingly unable to keep the hurt from her tone, as she so wished to do. "Why did you bring me here, Robert?"

"To speak with you. To make a counter offer to the very flattering one you made me. Won't you sit down, my dear? The tea will be here shortly."

She began to feel angry as well as hurt and humiliated.

"No, thank you. I do not wish to sit and I do not wish to have tea. If you will please say what you must, I would afterward appreciate being taken home."

"I've done this badly," he said, lifting and dropping one hand in a helpless gesture. "I meant to spare you the embarrassment I believed you would feel if we truly embarked upon an affair. I realize that a great many ladies of the *ton* engage freely in such relationships, but you wouldn't have enjoyed such an arrangement, my dear. I assure you, you would not."

Anna's face grew hot; she could just imagine how red it had become. "Perhaps you're the one who wouldn't have enjoyed it," she said bitterly.

He shook his head. "No, I wouldn't have. The last thing I want you for, Anna, is my mistress."

Well that was certainly plain enough. Anna couldn't even think of anything to answer to it. She turned away from him and blinked at the small fire that was glowing in the hearth, striving not to burst into tears and make a complete idiot of herself.

"And then there's Sarah to consider," he went on. "I've quite fallen in love with her, you know, and shouldn't like to find myself in her black graces. She'd be furious at me if she ever thought I'd done anything less than honorable in regard to yourself."

"Yes," Anna choked out, wiping furiously at the tears that seemed insistent about falling on her cheeks. "I did think of that, as well. I had supposed she'd never find out about it."

"Yes, well, with Sarah that's rather unlikely, isn't it? The child could wring confession out of the Bishop of Canterbury. I'm already living in fear of how she'll wind me about her finger in years to come. And, of course, I'll probably go half mad when she grows older and all her myriad suitors come knocking at the door—I've even spent a few sleepless nights already in thinking of all the questions I'll put to them in order to determine their worthiness. But there's no help for it. I'm quite determined to have Sarah for my daughter."

Anna slowly turned to look at him.

"What?"

He released a breath and looked embarrassed again. "I'm still making a mess of this, am I not? Did I do so poorly the first time I asked you to marry me? I disremember whether I was quite so nervous so many years ago. It seems impossible." He uttered a self-conscious laugh. "I haven't slept for a week, waiting for today to arrive. There were so many things I wanted to say. You already know that I love you. I'm sure I've been clear on that point. Did I tell you yet that I don't have a mistress, and haven't had one since you left me? I won't pretend that there haven't been women from time to time. I'm a normal man, after all, with the usual needs. *And* unmarried." He ran a hand through his hair in a nervous gesture. "But that's neither here nor there," he went on more determinedly, beginning to pace in a distracted manner. "I certainly can't think you would hold it against me. There was never a relationship of any long standing, certainly nothing more than a night or two. And it didn't occur very often." He strode to the fire, turned and strode back again. "The thing that you must understand, Anna, and believe, is that, regardless of what's occurred in the past, I shall be a faithful husband in every way, and always would have been a faithful husband, and that it would be exceedingly unkind and unfair of you to assume otherwise. I made the greatest mistake of my life in not trying to convince you otherwise eleven years ago, and have wished more times than you could ever imagine that I'd made every attempt possible to keep from losing you." He suddenly stopped mid stride and looked at her. "I have already asked you to marry me, have I not, Anna?"

She shook her head faintly. "Not within the past eleven years, or anytime recently."

"Gad," he muttered. "I appear to be in worse condition than I'd thought. My wits have gone utterly begging, but where you're concerned that tends to be usual."

"Yes, I know the feeling." She sniffled as fresh tears began to fill her eyes. "Oh, Robert."

"Here, love." He pushed his silk handkerchief into her hands. "Why is it that I always seem to make you weep? I never mean to do anything but make you happy. Is the idea of being my wife so awful?"

"No," she sobbed.

"Dare I hope that these are tears of happiness?" He gently folded her into his arms and held her.

She shook her head.

"Darling! What is it, then? I know I've done the thing badly, but I've not had much practice in asking women to marry me. I've only done it twice, in fact, and both times to you. Only imagine how I'll murder the deed if I make a third attempt."

A watery chuckle drifted up from the folds of his now damp cravat.

"That's better," he said, dropping a kiss on the top of her head. "Anna, I love you, and always have loved you, and always will love you. I've made a great many mistakes in the past, and will probably make a great many more in the future, but I will never intentionally bring you or Sarah or any other children we may have any harm. I wish I could promise that I'll never make you angry or hurt your feelings, but I can't. I'm only human. If you'll take me, however, I vow that I shall devote the remainder of my life in striving to make you happy."

"Oh, Robert," she said again, lifting her tear-wet face to gaze at him. "Please don't speak in such a way. You have no need to do so—to even feel as if you must make explanations. I was the one who ruined things. You tried to apologize and I wouldn't accept it as being enough. I was hard-hearted and unforgiving, and I've never stopped regretting it. How could you want me for your wife, after that?"

"Easily," he said, taking her face in his hands. "Because I love you and believe that you love me. Because what we share together is very, very special and not to be taken lightly, and mostly because I think we've already spent too many years apart. Anna, let's forgive each other and put the past behind us and embrace the happiness we lost so long ago. Please? Will you marry me and be my wife and my love?"

"Yes," she whispered. "I do love you so very much, Robert."

A few minutes later the butler scratched on the door, but neither occupant in the room heard the sound, with the outcome that the Earl of Manning and Lady Anna shocked the poor man nearly out of his senses. The earl managed to save the tea tray before it slid to the ground; a good thing, as it took two cups of tea to revive Mr. Parker's butler.

It was just as well, the earl told his newly affianced bride-to-be as he handed her into his coach. It really would have been too bad of them to anticipate their marriage vows, especially in the parlor of his own banker's home. They drove off in the direction of Manning House, intent upon collecting a picnic and then fetching Sarah in order to celebrate their news with her.

"Not that she'll be surprised," Anna said as Robert deftly set his horses into motion. "Between the two of you, I've hardly had a chance. Wellington couldn't have put on a more successful campaign as you and my daughter have done."

Robert laughed delightedly. "And only think, my love. You'll have the rest of your life to put up with us."

Chapter Twenty

It was a shocking thing for a lady to visit a man's residence without a suitable companion in tow, a fact of which both the Earl of Manning and Lady Anna were fully aware. He offered to stop by the Marquess of St. Genevieve's town house to collect Sarah first—even the presence of a young child would lend some measure of countenance to the visit—but Anna declined.

"I've waited years for you to ruin me, Robert," she said with a wicked grin. "If you refuse to do so in the usual method, I must content myself with whatever I can get."

But Sarah, as it turned out, was already at Manning House, waiting for them in his lordship's drawing room.

"And looking quite downcast, my lord," Hemmet said with marked censure as he removed his master's hat and coat. "The poor little girl has waited for your return this past hour and more."

"Sarah? Here?" Anna said in a voice tinged with something between bewilderment and concern. "What on earth could have made her come without my permission?" The look she bent on Robert filled with suspicion.

The Earl of Manning innocently held up both hands. "Sarah and I may have plotted together in the past, but I have no idea why she's here. I promise you."

Sarah was staring pensively into a half-full cup of chocolate when Hemmet opened the drawing room door. "Miss

Huntington," he began, but she had already seen her mother, and the earl standing behind her, and had put the cup aside and stood.

"Mama!" she cried, hurrying across the room. "I'm so glad you're here! I tried to find out where you'd gone, but no one seemed to know, except to say that you'd gone riding with Lord Manning, and I didn't know what else to do except come here and try to find out where he'd taken you, but no one here knew that, either. Oh, Mama! The most dreadful thing has happened."

Lady Anna went down on one knee, setting an arm about her daughter's waist. "Darling, whatever is the matter?"

"Here. I've got it over here." She took her mother's hand and pulled her to the couch, where a small purse lay. Opening it, she withdrew a folded piece of paper. "Some of the kitchen maids were laughing over it this morning. I know I'm not supposed to go in there without permission, but Cook was baking and I only meant to see what there was."

"It's all right, sweetheart," Anna told her, sitting on the couch and drawing her daughter down beside her. "What happened?"

"Some of the maids were laughing," Sarah went on, looking at Lord Manning as he sat on her other side and set a comforting arm about her. "They'd gotten a paper—the kind you always call a dirty rag. It's called *Glad Tidings*. I was only curious to see what was so funny to make them laugh. And then when I did I got so angry that I screamed at them and made Cook take it away!"

"Sarah!" Lady Anna said with disbelief.

"And I called them fat cows, too!" Sarah told her defiantly. "I know you'll box my ears, Mama, but I'm *glad* I said it! Because that's just what they are. Stupid, mean, fat cows!" And with that, she burst into tears and buried her face in Lord Manning's coat.

"Sarah, love," the earl murmured, hugging her gently. "This will never do. Whatever the trouble is, we'll put it to rights."

Anna pulled the folded page from her child's fingers and opened it. "Oh, God," she said after a moment of stunned silence. "Robert."

"I told you!" Sarah sobbed. "I told you!"

"Hush, now," the earl soothed as he took the single page in his free hand and looked at it. His expression grim, he gave the drawing a thorough inspection, forcing himself to register every cruel detail.

"Robert," Anna whispered, her voice edged with horror. "What does it mean? Who would do such a thing? And why?"

He released a hard breath and shook his head. "I can't explain it to you. But there is someone who can, and will, do so." Rising from the couch, he gave a weeping Sarah into her mother's arms and then moved to the bellpull. Hemmet responded at once. "Send a footman to Barrington," the earl instructed curtly, "with a message that my nephew is to attend me here *at once*. And if he's not at home, then I want him tracked down and physically escorted to Manning House. Whatever the case may be, Hemmet, I want Lord Callan in this very room within the hour. Do whatever you must to make sure of it."

The title of the caricature was *A Peahen in a Pearwood Tree*. Not exactly original; certainly far from being witty, but for the purpose, perfectly suitable. If Clara ever saw it, she'd be devastated. Her face, or, rather, a heartlessly ugly version of her face, was clearly imposed upon the body of a grotesquely pregnant peahen, nested in a pear tree. On one wing dangled an exact replica of the Italian fan Lucien had given her, just to make certain, Lucien supposed, that no one looking at the caricature would be left in doubt as to who the peahen was meant to represent. Around her neck was the South American necklace of silver bells he'd also given her, which Clara had worn several times with great pride and stunning success—she'd even started something of a rage with the thing. But the necklace's delicate design had been skillfully changed here. The bells had become links, and the links formed a chain, and the chain was attached to a leash that was locked by a huge padlock to the tree.

Standing beneath the tree was Lucien himself, smiling up at the imprisoned bird with smug self-satisfaction. Pamela had perversely depicted him as being far more handsome than Lucien knew himself to be. Still, the contrast between himself and the bird was vivid, and Clara would be that much more wounded. On his wrist, in the picture, was a key ring bearing one large key—the one that evidently belonged to the padlock—which had written on it, very clearly, *The Viscount Wins His Wager.*

Depicted farther in the background, behind the tree and in the distance, was Lucien's estate, Pearwood. Pamela would know what it looked like. He'd taken her there during the winter season for the past three years, along with several of their more reprobate friends. She'd obviously committed the styling of the house to memory, just as she did everything else. She'd been exact in every detail, leaving nothing out. There were even leaves falling from the pear tree, lying scattered about the ground, indicating Autumn, the time when he would have sent Clara to Pearwood if he'd held fast with the wager he'd made.

It was an obscene piece of handiwork. It was also all over London. A certain numbness crept over Lucien, a feeling of helplessness and hopelessness. He deserved what was going to come from the scandal that would ensue. Deserved every moment of it, because he'd been reckless in his care of the person who mattered most to him, and, worse, cruel in the bargain. That he should lose everything he'd tried to grasp, having wanted it for so long, seemed just and right. And perhaps it was better that he should have believed, for a few brief days, that his dreams were truly within his grasp. Because now he would know the truth. He could have had those dreams if he'd not been such a fool. They hadn't been impossible. He might have known what it was to live in peace with Clara, to love her and be loved by her. But it was crumbling now, all of it. Before his very eyes. There wasn't going to be any way to stop the disaster Pamela had set into motion. Now, for Clara's sake, all he could do was try to keep the damage from being too permanent.

His first instinct upon seeing the picture had been to run. To race home to Barrington and order his curricle and toss Clara into it and drive relentlessly until they were safe at Pearwood. A half-maddened idea that he could somehow keep her from ever discovering about the caricature, or about the wager that it alluded to, had seized him. But only briefly. The stinging slap Lady Anna had delivered to the side of his face after he'd had a first few silent moments to gape at the picture had rapidly brought him to his senses. She'd been furious, and rightfully so. If Robby hadn't held her arms at her sides she would have given him a much better beating.

"What do you want us to do, Lucky?" Jack's cool tone pulled Lucien out of his stony contemplation of the drawing in his hand. "The longer we wait, the more damage will be done."

"Yes," Lucien murmured, setting the paper aside. He lifted his gaze to look at the other men in his uncle's drawing room. Lady Anna and her daughter had left an hour earlier, and shortly thereafter Jack, Wulf, and the Earl of Kerlain had responded to the summons Lucien had sent. He'd nearly decided against sending for Kerlain, but at the moment was grateful he had; the two of them stood alone against the obvious wrath of the room's three other occupants, Jack, Wulf, and Robby—none of whom made an attempt at concealing their damning anger.

"You should get Lady Clara out of town right away," Wulf said. "Take her to Pearwood tonight. Slip out in the dark so no one will see."

"No," Robby said from the comfortable chair he'd wearily dropped into as soon as Lady Anna and Sarah had left, and where he'd been nursing a glass of brandy ever since. "That would be the worst thing."

"Look, I agree it's a nasty business," Kerlain put in, "but not so bad that it can't be set to rights. Everyone in London knows that Callan put an end to the wager days ago. Surely no one will take this rubbish seriously."

"But that's not the point, is it?" Jack replied tartly. "Lady Clara's been made to look a laughingstock. Little though you may credit such as that with your quaint American notions of social standing, it happens to mean something in a civilized land."

"Civilized?" Kerlain repeated with a faint laugh. "You certainly have a strange notion of what that word means, but I take your meaning, Rexley. The upper ten thousand doesn't possess enough of a heart amongst the lot of them to let such an episode pass without some unpleasantness, is that right?"

"There's going to be unpleasantness," Lucien said quietly. "Especially for Clara. Since you and I are the ones who caused it, Kerlain, you and I are the ones who'll do whatever we must to lessen the blows. Jack, Wulf, and Robby will help because they care for Clara."

"Bella will be glad to help, too," Wulf told him. "She loves Lady Clara like a sister."

Lucien nodded. "That's good, because we'll need every hand we've got if we're going to pull this off."

"What do you want us to do?" Jack asked once more.

"I want you to set about tracking down Pamela, Jack," Lucien replied. "She'll have made it difficult, mind. Don't look for anything obvious. But I needn't tell you that, I suppose."

"Lady Halling has to be found?" Wulf asked with bewilderment. "Won't she be at home?"

"She's probably left the country," Kerlain said. "At least, if she has any desire to keep breathing, she has. If I ever see that evil bitch again, I'll—"

"No, she's still in London," Lucien said. "I know Pamela well. She wouldn't want to miss a moment of the turmoil she's caused. Not even at the risk of being found and punished. The game's no good to her unless the winner sees it to the end, to the final kill." He ignored Kerlain's expression of pure disgust and returned his attention to Jack. "Pamela first, then Rosswell. Track them both down. I have a particular interest in seeing Rosswell, in person, before the day is out. Wulf?"

Wulf stopped nervously lacing and unlacing his fingers, a clear sign of his obvious distress. "Yes, Lucky?"

"I want you to discreetly put a stop to the circulation of the current issue of *Glad Tidings*. Scour the entire town, if you must, buy up every issue you can lay your hands on. Whatever you've got to do, do it."

Wulf brightened visibly. "With pleasure. Anything for Lady Clara. She's a nice girl, just like Bella."

"Just don't get yourself thrown into jail. I need you and Bella to make up part of a little gathering I intend to host tonight."

Everyone in the room stared at him.

"Nothing too dramatic, of course," he went on calmly. "Dinner at Barrington and then an evening at Covent Gardens. I'll send a note round to make certain that my box is ready."

"Tonight, Lucky?" Wulf asked faintly. "You're taking Lady Clara out in public?"

"Yes. Along with you and Bella and a few other friends. Jack, you'll come, won't you? Robby, you and Lady Anna, as well, although I daresay you'll wish to sit in your own box."

Robby inclined his head. "We'll be there. Kerlain will sit with us."

"Yes," Lucien agreed, ignoring the Earl of Kerlain's questioning look. "Otherwise it might be too obvious."

"Oh, I see," Kerlain said. "We're to go on display, are we? Like animals in a traveling circus? Give them all a good long look at us? Why don't you just hand out pea-shooters while you're at it and tell them to take aim?"

"Americans," Jack said with a dismal shake of his head. "You have no idea how to go on in such matters."

"Certainly we do. We wait for some idiot to open his mouth and make a comment we don't like, then we knock his teeth down his throat. It's a damned more effective method than slinking about and pretending as if nothing had happened."

"Calm yourself, Kerlain," Lucien advised. "You'll have your chance at revenge, if you've a taste for it. At this moment, however, I want you to think of Clara. Nothing else. Aside from that, you'll need to be at your amiable best for the visits you're about to make."

"Visits?"

"Visits. You and Robby. You'll spend the remainder of the day making them. I'll make a list for each of you, shortly. I believe we'll all be pleasantly surprised to discover just how many friends are willing to stand by Clara. Now listen to me well, and we'll have an understanding of exactly what we're going to do."

The next half hour passed in arguments, rebuttals, and

general debate, but in the end Lucien convinced them to approach the matter his way.

"It may be more difficult for Clara initially," he told them, "but the outcome will be far better. I don't want her living under a cloud for the rest of our lives, and I won't have Pamela come away with even a partial victory."

"What are you going to do today, Lucky?" Wulf asked as the men prepared to set about their various tasks.

"I'm going to make a few visits and throw myself at the mercy of certain gentlemen from whom I'll beg favors, and then I'm going home to my wife. I can only pray that she doesn't find out about this before I'm able to tell her first." He took up the offensive drawing once more. "There isn't any way I can keep Clara from being hurt, but perhaps, God willing, I can keep her from suffering too long for my sins."

Chapter Twenty-one

Clara saw the caricature on Bond Street, where she and Bella had gone to spend an afternoon of shopping. They had both noticed the unusual amount of attention they were drawing, side glances from fellow members of the *ton* and outright stares from their servants. The clerks and seamstresses at the various shops they entered seemed unable to look at Clara without flushing hotly and either stammering or giggling.

They finally made their way to Madame Doutrepont's shop, where Clara intended to speak with the talented modiste about the ordering of winter clothes suitable for Pearwood. Leaving her footman sitting outside with their other packages, she and Bella pushed through the shop's front door, and, as the bell overhead jangled, announcing their arrival, received the same response they'd gotten at every other shop they'd visited. The girl who was greeting customers gaped wide-eyed at Clara, then clapped a hand over her mouth and uttered something in a muffled tone. The next moment she dropped her hand, curtseyed and murmured an apology, and disappeared behind the curtain that divided the shop.

There were a few other customers in the shop, inspecting the outfits displayed on different mannequins, all of whom turned to stare at Clara and Bella.

"Mama!" one young lady said with obvious distress, only to be severely hushed by her parent.

"Why, Lady Burgess." Clara moved forward to greet an acquaintance. "How nice to see you. I'm sure you know my good friend, Miss Howell?"

Lady Burgess seemed incapable of looking Clara in the face. She did, however, manage a brief nod at Bella. "Yes, of course. How are you, Miss Howell?"

"Very well, thank you," Bella replied.

"It was so kind of you to invite us to your dinner party last week," Clara told the older woman. "Lord Callan and I enjoyed it very much."

At this, Lady Burgess blushed, but not with delight. It was evident that the woman was quite uncomfortable. She nervously glanced about at the other customers who had been, one after the other, making their way out the door. Still not looking at Clara, she mumbled something appropriate about being pleased and hoping that Lord and Lady Callan would honor her again with their presence in her home. Then she turned about and followed the last of the patrons out onto the street, shutting the door behind her with a loud jangling of the bell and leaving Clara and Bella gazing at each other with complete bewilderment.

Turning, Clara saw Madame Doutrepont standing at the opening of the curtain, a frown upon her handsome face as she looked out the window at her vanishing customers.

"I do apologize, Madame," Clara said, smiling in an effort to lighten the atmosphere, "but Miss Howell and I seem to have run off the rest of your clientele. What on earth is the matter with everyone today?" She marched to the nearest mirror and inspected herself. "Have I sprouted feathers from my ears?"

"No, no, my lady," Madame assured her at once. "If anything is wrong, it is with the others, not with you. And I do not care if they all go, so long as you stay. There is not a one of them who has the taste my lady has in her dress."

"What a kind thing to say," Clara said with pleasure.

"Not kind," Madame said as she moved farther into the room. "True. My lady has given Madame very good business with her eye for clothes. You are my best *annonce, non*? My best advertisement. If my lady wears one of my creations, the others come flocking to Madame to order the same. But if they will behave in such a manner, I do not care to have their business. And that is that."

"But, Madame," Clara protested. "Surely not."

The sound of giggles drew Clara's attention. Three young seamstresses were peering out of the slightly parted curtain, looking directly at her and laughing. Madame whirled about and, in a flood of angry French, banished them to the back room.

"I do beg your pardon, my lady," Madame said in her thick, stoic accent. "They are silly girls, without manners. You may be certain I will punish them appropriately."

"Oh, no." Clara was beginning to feel truly distressed. "Please don't."

"My lady is too kind. Especially today, of all days, when it would be assumed you must stay indoors. But may I say how much I admire your courage, Lady Callan? It is not always seen in this country, but in France, you may be sure, the crowds would gather on the streets to cheer such bravery."

A laugh mixed with amusement and bewilderment crossed Clara's lips. She tried to smile, but found it impossible.

"Madame, what can you mean? I'm afraid that I don't understand you at all."

"But you do not know, my lady?"

Clara shook her head.

Madame Doutrepont proceeded to remark upon this at

length in her native tongue, in a colorful manner that made
Clara grateful she couldn't quite follow what the woman
said. Turning about, Madame barked a command through
the parted curtain, which one of the young seamstresses
responded to by bringing her mistress a folded newspaper.

"I do not wish to be the one to show you this," Madame
told Clara. "But it is better me than another, for I am your
true friend, and you must always remember that, my lady.
Madame Doutrepont is proud to serve Viscountess Callan
as modiste. Now you will sit, if you please. It is a great
wickedness, and if I knew who this devil *Le Chat* is, God
save me, I would shoot him dead!"

Clara didn't understand it, at first. The only fact that leapt
out at her immediately was that her face was imposed upon
a grotesquely caricatured bird, and when the shock of that
subsided the rest of it came to her more slowly. A darkness
settled over her. She became aware that her breathing had
deepened, that her lungs ached. The ramifications suddenly
struck her, all of them, everything, like a hailstorm. The
stares, the laughs, the nervous avoidance of her eyes. Everyone in London had seen it. Her ugly face on an ugly
bird. Lucien smiling up at her. Everyone had seen it. Everyone . . .

She didn't remember how it was that she managed to get
out to her carriage. Bella had helped, she knew, as well as
her footman. Her face was wet with tears she'd not intended to cry. She recalled one brief moment, catching the
woeful look on her footman's face as he handed her up into
the carriage, and a fleeting desire to comfort him. The paper was still clutched in her hand, crushed in her aching
fingers. Bella was sobbing like a child, her face in her
hands, saying over and over, "Oh, Clara. Oh, Clara."

There was something in the tone that told her, Clara supposed, although she wouldn't think of that until much later.
Something that indicated that Bella knew more than Clara

did of the matter. She'd never been a violent person, but there was something of real violence in the way she grabbed the other girl by the arm and shook her, forcing her to tell the truth about the wager between Lucien and the Earl of Kerlain. Bella cried through all of it, and afterward, Clara stared out a window and let her weep in peace. Only when they arrived at Bella's home did Clara speak again, taking Bella's hand before she could depart and saying, "Forgive me." But that only made Bella cry the harder.

The numbness carried Clara through the rest of the drive, until they arrived at Barrington, and then up the stairs and through the door, where Hayes greeted her with the knowledge that Captain Blakesley had arrived and was waiting for her in the drawing room.

Clara went toward the room without thinking of it. Her steps moved by memory, nothing more. A footman opened the door and she walked inside, taking Andrew by surprise. He was sitting near the fire, gazing into it, until she arrived.

"Clara," he said, standing and moving toward her. "Darling, I came the minute I saw it."

His arms were open and she went into them, closing her eyes and pressing her face against the reassuring solidness of his chest.

"Don't even think on it," he murmured, holding her tight. "I'll take care of everything. There's nothing to worry about. I'm not going to let him hurt you anymore."

She wished that he would hold her tighter. So tightly that she'd not be able to breathe. She wished she knew how to faint, and kept hoping that she would. Instead she let the pain find its way to her heart, and, gripping him with hands, fingers, nails, at last gave way to a savaging grief.

That was how Lucien found Clara as he walked into the drawing room. In Andrew Blakesley's arms. Weeping and clinging to another man—a man who was holding her tenderly, kissing the top of her head, murmuring soothing words. They didn't even seem to notice that he'd entered the room, and so Lucien stood and watched, torn between grief that Clara had discovered the truth without learning it from him and a fury so blinding and hot that his head literally swam with it. It was the nightmare he'd envisioned for so many years come true. Clara and another man. Just like his mother and all her men. Clara and Andrew Blakesley, who had openly declared that he loved her. Andrew Blakesley, who never would have hurt her as Lucien had done. It was that fact alone that tempered Lucien's anger.

He'd wanted to tell Clara the truth, to have her shout and rage and rail at him, to fall on his knees and beg her forgiveness and tell her how much he loved her. To hold her in his arms when she wept, just as Andrew Blakesley was doing. The fantasy had carried him home, despite the fear of admitting his sins to the woman he loved. But it had been foolish and, worse, unrealistic. She wasn't going to want his arms about her. Not now. Perhaps never again. All that was left to him was shoring up the damage, a task he must do whether Clara wished it or not.

"Clara." His voice sounded hard, hollow. Familiar. He must have changed more than he'd realized beneath Clara's gentle influence; his old skin was uncomfortable to him. "Come here."

Blakesley raised his head, and his arms tightened about Clara. She made a gasping sound and lifted a fist to cover her mouth, closing her eyes as if she were in terrible pain.

"You bastard," Blakesley said in a low tone.

"Clara."

"I'm taking her away from here," Blakesley told him angrily. "She's going with me now."

"Clara," Lucien said distinctly, slowly, "if you care at all for your friend, you will stand up and away from him. Now."

"Don't listen to him, love," Blakesley said, sneering openly at Lucien. "I can handle him. Easily."

"No," Clara murmured, pushing out of the embrace. "I don't want any fighting. Please don't make him angry, Andrew." With an effort, she stood from the couch, ignoring Andrew's attempt to help her. On weak, trembling legs, she moved to another chair and sat in it, keeping her back to Lucien.

"Leave," Lucien told Blakesley. "You're no longer welcome here. Don't attempt to see my wife again."

Andrew Blakesley ignored him. "I'll take you out of here this very moment, Clara. You need only come. I'll keep you perfectly safe. He can't stop us."

"Yes," Lucien stated calmly. "I can. She won't go with you."

Blakesley leaned toward Clara. "I'll take you to St. Genevieve. Home, to your parents. Your family. They'll take you back without a word, just as everyone in the village will. Once it's known what you've suffered here at his hands, there'll be no unpleasantness. You know I speak the truth."

"She won't go with you," Lucien repeated. "Clara carries my child. She'll not leave Barrington without my permission."

Blakesley closed his eyes briefly; when he opened them the look he gave Lucien was filled with a killing hatred. "So you've won your wager, have you, Callan? You've gotten her pregnant. Very well. But I won't let you make a prisoner of her at your country estate. *I will not.*" He stood. "You'll have to kill me to stop me. Just as your father killed."

"Lucien," Clara murmured, turning to him at last, pleading with him. The pain on her face made Lucien want to weep.

"If you want him in one piece, Clara," he said softly, "then send him away."

"Come with me, Clara," Blakesley said, holding out a hand to her. "We'll be in St. Genevieve two days from now. I'll not let him bring you any harm, I vow."

Clara looked first at him, then at Lucien. "Please go peacefully, Andrew," she said, holding her husband's gaze. "I don't wish to leave Barrington. But I . . . thank you for coming today." The last two words came out as a whisper, and then she turned away again.

Silence filled the room, save for the crackling of the fire. Andrew Blakesley stared at Lucien, his jaw set, his mouth in a grim line. "I stand ready in your service, Clara, at any time of day or night. You need only send me word, and I shall come. I love you," he said, and Clara lowered her head, shaking it slightly, "and I'm not ashamed to tell you or Viscount Callan or the entire world that fact. You shouldn't be here with him. The marriage was a mistake, and when you come to realize it, I shall be here to take you home to St. Genevieve." Then he left the room.

Lucien closed the door behind him before turning to face his wife. She was still sitting away from him, very still and silent. He could only see one side of her face, but on that side the cheek was pale and streaked with tears. Her gaze was fixed on the floor, though he doubted that she saw anything, even the carpet, at the moment.

"I only discovered about the drawing this morning," he said, not certain where to begin but deciding that, in this unfortunate situation, any spot was probably as good, or bad, as another. "It was what Robby summoned me for." They'd only just finished their midday meal when the missive had arrived, bringing an end to the companionable afternoon they'd been enjoying. "It was my intention to come home and tell you at once."

She made no answer, no sound. At last he asked, "Where did you discover it?"

"On Bond Street," she whispered. "In Madame Doutrepont's shop."

"I see." A pause. His voice became gentler. "I'm sorry for what you must have felt. Was it very bad?"

"Bella was with me."

"Yes. I remember that you said she was to go with you today. I'm glad you had her with you."

He moved silently across the room to sit on the couch Andrew Blakesley had vacated. Clara didn't move at all.

"Do you know about the wager?" he asked.

She nodded. "Bella told me."

"Did she tell you who the wager was made with?"

"Kerlain." The word was faint, fraught with pain.

"Clara," he murmured, "it was a mistake. A terrible, wrong, very foolish mistake. I wish—before God—that I hadn't done it. I'm not going to attempt to make excuses. You know better than anyone else what I believed then, before we wed, but even that gives me no ground to stand on. The wager was made in anger, with full understanding. I knew that if you heard of it, it would hurt you badly, and I didn't care. I don't believe Kerlain realized what it would mean, given the fact that he's an American, but perhaps that doesn't serve as an excuse, either. I only ask you to understand, to give me a chance to—"

"A chance!" she cried, and sobbed, covering her mouth with the palm of her hand to stop the sound, struggling for control.

"Please, Clara . . . I shouldn't be asking that of you. I know what I deserve and am willing to accept the consequences when the time comes. Unfortunately, *Le Chat's* caricature makes you pay as well. Even more heavily than I. I'm asking you to give me a chance to remedy the matter as best I can. Afterward, we'll be able to discuss how our marriage should go on.''

She uttered a humorless laugh. ''Will it go on?''

''I can only pray that it will. You have no reason to believe me, but I love you, Clara.''

''Poor Lucien,'' she said in a scoffing tone. ''How terrible this must be for you, to have to think of what to say to soften my heart. All this time, I've been the one to make that effort.'' Then, more bitterly. ''How many people knew of the wager before today? All of London? Have I been a laughingstock since I arrived?''

He let out a slow breath. ''The wager was put into the betting books at White's. A certain portion of society has been aware of it since before you arrived in London. I doubt that all of our acquaintances knew.''

''Our marriage. Everything.'' Fresh tears began to fill her eyes. ''It was nothing more to you than a game to win. The night before we wed, everything you promised me was a lie.''

''No, Clara. By then I regretted the wager deeply. I won't pretend that I believed our marriage would last in any real way, certainly not that night, but I was willing to give it a chance. I meant everything I said to you then, and everything I've said to you since.''

''How you must have hated me,'' she whispered.

''Yes,'' he admitted. ''As much as I loved you, although the love held me more strongly. I hated you because I believed you had scorned what I'd felt for you when we were younger, what I couldn't make myself stop feeling for you. I hated the unbreakable hold you maintained over my heart, regardless of what I did to destroy it. But I hated myself far more, Clara. Far more.''

''I don't care,'' she told him. ''I don't want to hear anything about you or how you feel right now.''

''I know,'' he said gently.

"I only want to go." She swallowed heavily. "To St. Genevieve."

"I can't allow you to do so. I'm sorry."

"I won't go to Pearwood just so you can win your wager."

"I called the wager off several days ago when I realized that there was nothing that could make me abandon you or our marriage. I conceded the winning to Kerlain. You may ask him if I'm speaking the truth. I realize the fact of that does little—or perhaps nothing—to assuage your pain, but at least you may come to believe that my intention to take you to Pearwood and begin our family there was a sincere one. I no longer had any plan to install you there as a prisoner."

"You simply hoped I'd never discover the truth about the wager, then," she said.

"Yes. I had hoped you'd not."

"Who is *Le Chat*?"

"My enemy. And yours."

She finally looked at him, her gaze penetrating and direct. "*Who* is he?"

The fact that she assumed the artist was a man didn't surprise Lucien. Pamela had purposefully hidden behind the French masculine form for "cat," and the public tended to assume that anyone who drew such crass caricatures must be a man.

"*Le Chat*," he answered, "is a dangerous and vindictive person whom I intend to deal with personally. When the time comes, I'll tell you everything, including who *Le Chat* is. For now, I think it safest if you remain in ignorance. There are far worse things than a nasty caricature that could befall you if it was believed you were going to reveal who *Le Chat* is."

"Why did he make the drawing?"

"To destroy our marriage. But that can only happen if we

allow it. I refuse to do so. I love you as no man will ever love you, Clara.''

"Oh, yes, certainly," she said, emotion tightening her voice. "Your peahen. I can just imagine how you love me. How"—the word broke on a sob—"could you have s-said that of me? I know I'm plain, but I t-trusted you." Fresh tears began to trickle down her cheeks.

He had tried not to go on his knees, so afraid that she would disdain the gesture, or worse, turn away from him. But her pain cut beyond fear, and Lucien found himself kneeling before her, taking her face in his hands, holding her with all the love and care that he felt for this most valuable of all people.

"I won't deny my past cruelties, Clara. Perhaps that was the worst of them. More even than the wager. I was a different man then. If, because of my sins, I've lost your love, then it is no less than I deserve. But I do love you. I have never loved another woman, and I will never love another woman. No, listen to me," he insisted when she began to shake her head. "If you won't understand anything else, you must understand this. I love you. I only pray that you'll give me a chance to prove to you how much and that, in time, I'll find the way to take away the pain I've given you.''

"Then let me go home to St. Genevieve," she whispered, pleading. "Just for a little while, until I've had time to think. If you still want me after a few months, if I can get past some of this, then perhaps we'll find a way together.''

"I shall always want you, Clara. Every day of my life, for the remainder of my life. The thought of being separated from you for any amount of time is awful to me.''

"Please." She pressed her hands over his. "I c-can't bear to be here any longer.''

"Oh, love." With gentle sweeps of his thumbs, he wiped her tears away. "I wish I could take you away this very moment. But if we run now, the scandal will follow you forever. Unpleasant as it is, we must stay in London and face down the stares and gossip. Tonight, we'll attend the theater—"

"No!"

"Yes," he countered calmly. "We'll attend the theater and show all of London how brave and wonderful you are. *Le Chat* is hated by the *ton,* while you are well loved. Tonight, seeing that you are unafraid and uncowed, you'll be the most admired woman in all of England."

"Nothing will take away the stain of that picture. Don't ask this of me, Lucien. I beg you, in the face of what you've already done, don't ask this of me."

"I understand the humiliation you're feeling now."

"Do you?" she asked hotly.

"And I feel the measure of my own guilt more deeply than you can know. This is the only way in which I can begin to make things right, Clara. Not for me, but for you."

"I don't care any longer about what society thinks of me." She pushed his hands away. "I don't care for anything at all, save leaving London altogether and returning to St. Genevieve."

"You don't care now, perhaps, but in time it will matter to you a great deal. And there is *Le Chat* to think of, who will come out the victor if you run with your tail tucked between your legs."

"I don't wish to attend the theater," she told him. "I'll not go. It's the least you can allow after what you've done."

He captured her hands in his and brought them to his mouth, kissing them. "My love, I'm not asking this of you. I'm telling you how it will be. We are going to attend the theater tonight, in our best looks, and there we will face down and vanquish every foe. Together."

She snatched her hands away and stood, pushing away

from Lucien and heading for the door. She stopped just as she reached it, and turned to face him.

"In our best looks, my lord? Do you mean to be the peacock parading about his hen? I see that for what it was now, all these months. Never fear. I won't disappoint you."

She slammed the door after her, and Lucien, still kneeling, rested his elbows upon the chair she'd left and set his face in the palms of his hands. He was torn between intense admiration for the excruciatingly sharp set-down she'd so deservedly given him, and anguish at the knowledge that the love she'd once felt for him had been replaced by an equally deserved hatred. She had once lived beneath the scorn and cruelties he'd visited upon her; now he would have the opportunity to understand what it was like. She hated him, but, despite that, he wouldn't be able to let her go. A better man would do so, but Lucien wasn't a better man. She could despise him and make him know every minute of it, but she'd not be able to put a physical distance between them. Because he loved her in a way that no other man could do, and because he alone knew what she required to be happy. And whether she wanted it or not, that was what she was going to get.

Chapter Twenty-two

Covent Garden was crowded, brimming with members of the *ton,* despite Clara's every prayer that it might be otherwise. The staring began the moment Lucien led her through the theater's entryway.

"Head up," Lucien murmured, sounding perfectly relaxed. His arm, beneath her trembling hand, was strong and steady. "And smile."

Head up she could manage. In fact, she was determined not to give anyone the satisfaction of seeing how deeply wounded she was. But smiling was out of the question. An impossibility. And so she said to her husband, without bothering to keep her voice quiet, "No."

"As you please," he replied with beastly ease, and led her toward their private box, past the gaping crowd that parted like the Red Sea at their approach.

Everyone—*everyone*—who was already seated in the theater turned to look at her as Lucien put her in her chair. Clara's own gaze swept the elegant room without a pause. She took them all in at once, and then, feeling hundreds of pairs of eyes burning upon her, she turned her attention to the program in her hand.

Lucien had brought her to put her on display. Very well. She would be on display. But that was all she would be. Nothing else. It would have served him just as well to have brought a statue, for that was exactly what she was going to be. No one, and nothing, was going to have a reaction from her. She didn't have any emotion left to display, except, perhaps, for anger, and she was finished with doing everything in her power to be the perfect wife for a man who not only didn't love her but who also found her to be as unattractive as a peahen.

She'd been tempted—oh, how very tempted—to give Lucien exactly what he'd called her. A peahen. Plain and dull. She'd gone through every dress she possessed in an effort to find the ugliest, most awful one among them, only to be foiled by Lucien himself. He'd casually entered her room an hour before they were to leave for the theater and picked out what he wanted her to wear—a strikingly composed gown of maroon silk that complemented her coloring and made her figure seem more alluring than it actually was. Having given her maid strict instructions as to the arrangement of her hair and jewelry, Lucien at last departed, not having said so much as one word to Clara or asked her about her own wishes. She'd not spoken to him, either, but that was beside the matter. *He* was the one who'd hurt *her,* and he was the one who should do the talking. And begging. And pleading. As far as she was concerned, he'd be fortunate indeed if she ever decided to speak to him in a normal manner again.

Not that he'd likely care. He'd probably hated having anything to do with such a dull peahen all these past months. He'd only tolerated her because of the wager. Tolerated and appeased her, she amended. How awful it must have been to sleep with her every night. To make love to her. But she wasn't going to let herself think of that, because every time she did she began to weaken. It didn't matter that he'd made love to her so tenderly, with such seeming need. And none of the things he'd said to her during those moments could be trusted. Not a one of them. Not when he'd said he found her beautiful, or that he loved her, or that no other woman could ever claim such power over him as she could.

But she *wasn't* going to think of that, Clara told herself again sternly, touching her forehead with the tips of her gloved fingers, pressing the memories away. Tears ached behind her eyes, and she breathed deeply to dispel them as well.

"Clara," Lucien said from where he sat beside her. His own gloved hand touched her arm. "Are you feeling unwell?"

"No." She sat up, lifting her head and dropping her hands to her lap. Below, the staring continued, save that it was now accompanied by a great deal of murmuring. Behind her, she heard the guests who'd accompanied them taking their seats. Wulf and Bella, Jack, and Lucien's cousin, Christian Fineham. Wulf and Jack had found private moments before and after the dinner Lucien had overseen at Barrington to make apologies to her for their knowledge of the wager and the fact that they had sided with Lucien in the betting books. Clara had received the apologies in silence, thinking as she gazed into their sincere, familiar faces that they'd joked with Lucien about her over the years; that they, too, had called her The Peahen. She'd believed they were her friends. She'd spent countless hours in their company, striving to be pleasing to them for Lucien's sake, so that they should never leave off his company because of her. And all the time they'd known that her marriage was nothing better than a laughable sham.

Several boxes to the left of them was the Earl of Manning's private box, and she saw Robby leading Aunt Anna into it. The earl stopped just before seating her aunt and bowed regally toward Clara—an action that no one in the crowd below missed. Aunt Anna's face was fixed with concern, and she met and held Clara's gaze for a long moment before allowing the earl to put her in her chair. Another

figure, tall and handsome, entered the box behind him, but
when the Earl of Kerlain attempted to make his bow to
Clara, as well, she pointedly looked away. And then regretted it when the murmuring below grew louder.

· There was a measure of relief when the performance began, although Clara barely heard any of it, aware as she was
of the continued interest she drew from the rest of the the-
atergoers. She sat so stiffly and so still that her back and
neck began to ache from the strain. Twice more, Lucien
asked if she was feeling unwell, and twice more she replied
"no." Otherwise there was a nearly complete silence in
their box.

About midway through the performance the murmuring
in the theater grew louder, but this time not because of
Clara. The Prince Regent had made a sudden and unexpected arrival, and until he and his party were fully settled
in his box, nearly every eye was turned upon them. It didn't
occur to Clara that perhaps the royal scion had come because of her until the prince's footman delivered a note to
Lucien.

"His Highness wishes us to visit him during the intermission," Lucien murmured quietly, for her ears only, folding the note and tucking it inside his coat. He didn't look at
her, but returned his attention to the stage.

"He wishes to have a private audience with The Peahen,
does he?" Clara replied in an equally quiet tone.

"No," Lucien answered evenly. "The note specifically
requested the attendance of Viscount and Viscountess Callan. There was no mention of anyone else."

Clara's only answer was to snap open the fan that hung at
her wrist and attempt to cool her fury.

When intermission arrived Lucien wasn't in any hurry to
attend to His Highness's wishes. He turned around in his
chair and conversed politely with their guests, making no
attempt to include Clara in the conversation. Which was

wise of him, Clara thought, keeping her frozen gaze straight ahead until he at last touched her arm and asked if she was ready. She rose without a word.

The hall was crowded again as they made their way, except this time Clara was surprised to find herself faced with many of her closest acquaintances. Even more surprising, they all appeared to wish to greet her.

"Lady Clara," Sir Anthony Sayers said warmly as he and his beautiful wife approached them. "How very good to see you again. Lord Callan, how do you do? I believe you both know my wife?"

Clara stared at the man in silent shock. Surely he knew about the caricature? What on earth had possessed him to so publicly acknowledge an acquaintance with her? Didn't he realize how precarious it would make his own reputation, to be seen speaking with her?

"Of course," she murmured at last, forcing her whirling thoughts into some semblance of order. "Of course. How nice to see you again, Lady Sayers."

They conversed for a few moments—Clara could never after remember what any of them said—and then Sir Anthony bowed and his wife curtseyed, and Lucien led Clara on again.

But only a few steps away they were stopped by another acquaintance, Lord and Lady Drogin, and after them by the Duke of Haithman and his wife, Countess Haithman. And so it went until they reached the royal theater box. Every peer of the realm whom Clara had counted among her intimates was miraculously at the theater, and all of them seemed eager to greet and acknowledge her.

She was stunned, and remarkably buoyed. And so grateful at such a public show of support in the face of such damning circumstances that she felt as if she could weep with it.

Last, and perhaps most amazing of all, was the Prince

Regent's gracious receipt of their visit. He took Clara directly to the front of the box where one and all could see them, and there kissed her hand and made her sit beside him while he conversed with her gaily. When it came time for Lucien and her to return to their own box His Highness kissed Clara's hand again and told her what a pleasure it had been to see her again. Not once did Clara observe a hint of anything but sincerity in his eyes.

The rest of the night passed in a blur, and the ride home from the theater was completed in a silence that Lucien seemed to understand Clara needed. Only when they neared Barrington did he speak.

"We've not yet discussed how we shall go on in the matter of our physical relationship," he said quietly. "My own desire is for us to continue to share the bed in my chambers, but if your wishes are otherwise, you need only tell me."

She thought on the matter as the carriage began to slow. It was evident to her that Lucien was responsible for what had happened at the theater, and the fact that he had gone to so much trouble on her behalf did, in some measure, soothe her. But the pain she felt came from far more than the simple idea of social ruin, hard as that was. It was the knowledge that Lucien found her wanting that wounded so deeply.

The carriage door opened and Lucien hopped down, turning to help her. Their eyes met and held when his hand took hold of hers, and she saw, for the briefest moment, a worried uncertainty lurking in the depths of his gaze.

They traversed the stairs in weary silence. In the hall, before his chamber door, she said, "I believe I will sleep in my own chambers, Lucien. If you will allow it." She couldn't bring herself to look up at him.

His hand touched her elbow lightly. "Of course," he said, and with a gentle movement led her in the direction of her own door. "I'll send your maid to attend you." His fingers, still resting on her arm, tightened slightly before releasing her. "Good night then, Clara," he said, his tone polite. "Sleep well." Sketching her a brief bow, he turned and walked away.

Hours later Clara lay in the midst of the huge, strange bed, awake and miserable and wishing that Lucien would come and carry her to their own bed as he had done once before. She'd believed, after that awful night, that she would never find herself sleeping in this cold and cavernous room again, although she supposed what she was doing now could hardly be termed sleeping.

She was wretched, furious at Lucien and lonely for him, too. No matter how she tried, she couldn't push away the tormenting feelings of betrayal and hurt. He'd made a joke of their marriage, and of her, when she had loved and trusted him and striven so hard to make everything right. And yet, he had gone down on his knees before her and told her that he loved her. He had asked her to give him a chance to prove it, and had already begun to try to make things right.

Clara sat up and hugged her knees tight against her body, staring across the room to where a small fire in the hearth attempted to keep the huge chamber warm. How had Lucien's mother abided such a place? She supposed that Lucien's chamber was just as large, but somehow it had always seemed warmer, more inviting, and certainly more comfortable than this room was. She wondered if Lucien was sleeping, or if he missed her presence in his bed at all.

Pressing her forehead against the top of her knees, she tried to clear the many thoughts warring for attention in her mind, but it proved impossible.

What had made Lucien tell Andrew that she carried his child? She hadn't spoken aloud her own suspicions yet, indeed, it was far too early to be certain that she was expecting. But he'd made the statement as if he truly believed it, and perhaps he did. Perhaps he wanted to believe it so that he could send her away to Pearwood. The idea filled her with despair.

"Clara?"

She looked up and wiped at her cheeks, aware for the first time that tears had dampened them. Lucien was standing at the door that adjoined the sitting room. He was still dressed in the shirt and breeches that had made a part of the ensemble he'd worn to the theater.

"Are you all right? I thought perhaps you were troubled."

She didn't stop to question how it was that he'd known she was troubled; relief at seeing him overrode such trivialities.

"I can't stop thinking," she whispered, striving to keep from sounding too wholly pathetic, "about everything."

Closing the door, he walked slowly across the room until he stood by the bed. Sitting beside her, he stretched out a hand and touched her face.

"Will you let me help, love? Let me take your mind off of all that distresses you so?"

His hand was warm, and she felt so very cold. Closing her eyes, she pressed her cheek needily against his palm.

"Clara," he murmured, drawing her into his arms. "I love you. You've got to believe me. Let me prove to you how much I need you."

Rising, he shed his clothes, and came to her beneath the covers, naked and warm, pulling the nightdress from her body and throwing it carelessly on the floor.

"I love you," he said again as he pulled her body beneath his, caressing her with his hands and mouth. "I'll never let you go."

He loved her with a needy desperation that Clara felt in equal measure. It was impossible to be close enough to him, to fill her hands with the touch of him, her mouth with the taste of him. Every moment he whispered to her, telling her of his love, of his need, that she was beautiful to him, the loveliest woman in the world, and that he would cherish her forever.

"I meant to stay away," he said afterward, cradling her in his embrace, his words sleepy and sated. "But it was impossible. I sat in my room and thought of what it would be like to lose you, Clara, but it was unbearable."

"Lucien," she whispered, stroking a palm lightly over his chest.

He turned his face and pressed his cheek against her forehead. "Don't try to leave me, Clara. I can't let you go."

"I only need time," she began, but he wouldn't let her finish.

"You can have as much time as you need. Only don't go away. If you don't wish to go to the country, perhaps we can travel. At least for a few months, until the baby is farther along. I should like for our children to be born at our estate."

She noticed that he kept from saying the word "Pearwood," and perhaps the thoughtfulness of this touched her as deeply as any of his other attempts to make amends.

"I'd like to travel," she said, and yawned, exhaustion descending upon her like a heavy blanket.

He held her more closely. "Whatever you desire, Clara, I'll give you. Wherever you wish to go, I'll take you."

She was nearly asleep when she suddenly realized where they were.

"Lucien," she murmured, lifting her head only slightly before he pushed it back down upon his shoulder. "You don't wish to sleep here." It was a statement of fact, not a question. "It's your mother's room."

"It's your room," he replied, stroking a hand lovingly down the curve of her back. "And I wish to sleep with you, wherever that may be. I don't care about the past anymore, Clara. It's all gone and done with. The only thing that matters to me is you and our child and the future we have together. That's all. Try to sleep now, love," he said, turning his head to lie more comfortably against the top of her own. "Tomorrow will be a busy day."

Chapter Twenty-three

"Definitely an improvement over the drawing of Lady Clara," Jack stated as he handed the paper back to Lucien. "One of Cruishank's better efforts, I believe."

"Yes," Lucien agreed. "I'm in his debt for taking on the task so quickly. Of course, he despises *Le Chat,* and was only too glad to have a hand in bringing Pamela down, once I told him who she was."

He examined the drawing in greater detail, finding no fault with it. It was well done, exactly what he'd requested, not elaborate, but powerful, nonetheless. The title was simply *Le Chat Revealed.* Pamela's face was drawn onto the body of a rather evil-looking cat—of the ragged, mottled variety generally known as "alley." In one paw was an indistinguishable drawing, and in the other was a sharp pen dripping heavily with liquid from a pot marked "Poison." Surrounding her, depicted in a far more flattering and noble style, were many of her more well-known victims, from Lord Allingham to Miss Cooper to Clara, each and every one of them pointing an accusing finger at The Cat. London would be in a rage when the drawing was made public, and Pamela would find herself utterly friendless and, worse, a complete pariah. It would not only be the end of her career in England, but of her aspirations to make a place for herself among the *ton.*

Glad Tidings, with the aid of Mr. Rosswell—who had

become remarkably helpful since the day Wulf had visited him in order to put a halt to any further publication of the caricature of Clara—was to publish the drawing in a special edition. All that Lucien waited for now, before telling the publisher to proceed, was finding Pamela, herself.

"Have you had luck, yet?" he asked, setting the drawing aside.

Jack shook his head. "No," he replied grimly. "One would think a woman that beautiful would be simple to find, but no one in London seems to have set eyes on her. Or if they have, the temptation of money won't pry their lips apart."

"Mmm." Lucien nodded thoughtfully. "There are a great many people who value their privacy more than money. Pamela's got a fairly large number of acquaintances she can blackmail into doing her bidding, and into keeping quiet regardless of the reward offered. Have you looked into Mawdrey's, or Bawd Claxton's?"

"Those were the first places I went," Jack told him. "Along with every bawdy, gaming hell, and whorehouse in London. She clearly anticipated being sought, for she's covered her tracks quite thoroughly. But don't despair yet." Jack patted his friend's shoulder reassuringly. "I've a few leads left to follow, and have my most talented associates presently sniffing them out."

"I'd prefer to have her found and kept under lock and key before the drawing is published," Lucien said, "but by week's end it won't matter quite so much. Once I've got Clara out of London, the picture may be published whether we've found Pamela or not. She'll not be able to deal out revenge so easily once her identity becomes known. You and Wulf know what to do with her after that, if she doesn't leave the country on her own volition."

"Oh, yes," said Jack, a feral gleam in his eye. "I shall

quite enjoy taking care of Lady Halling when the time comes. Will you have a brandy?''

Lucien accepted the glass with thanks, and settled himself in one of the comfortable chairs in the Earl of Rexley's library. Jack did likewise.

"How is Lady Clara?" he asked. "Have things improved between the two of you in the past four days? I couldn't get her to speak a personal word at all yesterday, although our drive in the park was quite enjoyable. Always pleasant company, is your good lady wife.''

"She enjoyed it, as well," Lucien told him. "Although I do wish that you and Wulf would stop trying to apologize to her. She's already forgiven you both, and having to make so many reassurances is starting to vex her somewhat. Wulf's come by with flowers every afternoon since Covent Garden and attempted to get down on his knees to beg her forgiveness. If you could only see Clara trying to keep him on his feet, you'd laugh until you were sick with it. She's so small compared to his hulking size, but she has to grab his shoulders to push him back up every time he starts to bend.''

Jack chuckled. "I'll have a word with him, shall I?"

"Please," Lucien said. "The only thing that saved her yesterday was that he suddenly thought of something he'd left undone in his laboratory, and asked Clara if he might have a piece of paper to write a note and remind himself before he forgot it again.''

"Oh, gad."

"Yes," Lucien said with a laugh. "Once he got the paper and pencil, all else was lost. I let him spend an hour in my drawing room, scribbling away and drinking tea, before I finally suggested that he might like to go home.''

"Poor Wulf," Jack said with a grin. "He keeps getting himself confused with Kerlain, I think. Lady Clara hasn't forgiven him yet, has she?''

Lucien sighed and shook his head. "Kerlain's sins and mine are harder to forgive. He's called twice to see her, but Clara refused to invite him in. I'm not quite certain what became of the flowers he sent. Not that it matters, I suppose. Half of London has sent Clara flowers lately. Barrington is beginning to look like a greenhouse. But it's helped, I think. Clara loves flowers."

Jack regarded him with a steady gaze. "You haven't answered my question yet, Lucky. Have matters improved between you and Clara?"

"Somewhat, I think," Lucien replied, and wondered at the truthfulness of the words. Clara was trying to behave as normally as possible, at least in front of the servants, to smile and talk and pretend that nothing was wrong. And even when she was alone with Lucien she didn't display any of the anger or hurt that had come to life on the day when she'd first seen the caricature of herself. But she spent much of her day alone, not seeking out his company as she had used to do, and there was a deep, abiding sorrow in her countenance that overrode her efforts to appear cheerful. She didn't wish to discuss the drawing, and when Lucien attempted to lure her out of her silence and talk to him, she found an excuse to take her away to another part of the house. At night, however, in their bed, she needed him in a hungry, demanding manner that showed no signs of abating. When he was inside of her, loving her, her features took on a blissful expression of forgetfulness, a look of pleasure such as he'd never seen on any woman's face before. And because he loved her and wanted to please her, he gave her what she wanted, despite the fact that it seemed more like pure sex than the kind of deep and intimate loving they had used to share and that he longed to share with her again.

The situation between them was fragile, and Lucien was eager to get Clara out of London. She had agreed to go to

Pearwood for one month; beyond that she'd not been willing to make a commitment. But Lucien saw in that a softening in her rather than a hardening. She commented that she wasn't certain whether she would wish to travel while being with child, *if* she was with child, of course, and if she found Pearwood pleasant, perhaps . . . It was the "perhaps" that Lucien presently hung all his hopes on.

"My belief is that once we're at Pearwood, we'll begin to settle matters between us. It is certainly my ardent desire that we do so."

"You love her," Jack said. "Do you know, Lucky, I find the change that Clara's made in you the most compelling argument for a man's getting married? You've quite reversed my mind about the thing."

"Indeed?" Lucien looked at him with interest. "I admit that my own reformation has been rather greater than lesser, given the fact that I had such a far distance to traverse in order to improve, but as far as I can tell, Jack, you're nearly perfect, already. Or so I hear from a great many females of our mutual acquaintance."

Jack laughed. "You know me better than that."

A scratch at the door kept Lucien from making the teasing rejoinder that this statement clearly called for.

"Enter," Jack called, and his butler, carrying a silver salver bearing a sealed note, opened the door and crossed the room.

Taking the note with a murmur of thanks, Jack waited until the servant had quit the room before opening it.

"It's from Pamela," he said, sitting forward with a dark frown as he began to read.

"Pamela?" Lucien set his glass aside and stood. "She sent something here to you?"

" 'My lord,' " Jack read, " 'It is my understanding that you seek an audience with me. I am willing to accept a visit from you at five o'clock this afternoon but *only* if Viscount

Callan will also be present. There is something particular which I wish to say to him personally.' '' He scanned the missive. "She gives a location—God's feet—in Staines, and says that we're to arrive promptly, else she'll not be there."

"Staines! That's impossible. She wouldn't have gone that far away."

"Why not?" Jack asked. "It would certainly explain why we've not been able to locate her in London."

"Damn," Lucien muttered. "Staines. I can hardly countenance it. And it will take two hours of hard riding at the very least to be there in time. I can't help but think it's a wild-goose chase, Jack."

"That may be." Jack was on his feet. "But is that a chance you wish to take? I'll have two of my best horses readied, and we can be gone within ten minutes."

Lucien gave a curt nod. "Very well. I should like to send a note to Clara, however."

"Of course." Jack yanked on the bellpull. "I'll have a footman take it at once."

Dearest Clara, I regret that I shall not return to Barrington in time for tea, as I promised you. An urgent matter has called both Jack and me out of Town, but it is my expectation that we will return by early this evening. Wait supper for me, if you will, for I hope to have information to share, which you have beforehand requested. Don't go out until I've returned. It is, regretfully, a command, not a request, and the last of which I hope I shall ever have to give you. I realize that perhaps you're growing weary of hearing this, also that I told you this morning, but just in case you've forgotten or had any doubts, I love you. Lucien

* * *

Clara read the missive through again before lowering it to her lap. What could have possibly been so important that it had so suddenly taken Lucien out of London? He hadn't even returned home to collect a cape. That he had commanded her to stay at Barrington intrigued rather than irritated her. Perhaps, she thought, he was closing in on *Le Chat*. She knew that he and Jack had been searching for the artist, who had evidently and understandably disappeared, but that was as much as Lucien had been willing to say despite Clara's constant demands. She was determined to know who it was had drawn that awful caricature, simply for her own peace of mind. Until then, everyone seemed to be suspect, the servants, acquaintances, and close friends, even members of her own family. And it was no good telling herself that most of these people couldn't draw such a detailed sketch; she couldn't convince herself that perhaps one or the other of them didn't possess the talent and had kept it well hidden. When she thought of it, however, she couldn't help but feel foolish. And perhaps even a bit childish.

Lucien had reminded her that he loved her. She ran her finger lightly over that part of the missive, considering it. He'd said the words so often during the past four days and nights that she was actually beginning to believe it. He had been trying so very hard to please her and to make amends, although he was touchingly clumsy in the attempts, being, by his own admittance, not used to making himself amenable. She'd been all the more stirred. Her gruff, unsmiling, dark-natured Lucien trying to do the pretty by her, behaving as the perfect gentleman in every way. He hated it, she knew—she could tell from the look that she sometimes caught fleetingly on his face, especially when he was striving to make polite conversation. But he was doing it for her, all for her, and the knowledge went a long way toward healing the wound he had given.

There was a scratch at the open door, and then Hayes, saying, "My lady?"

Clara smiled up at him. "Yes?"

"There is a Lady Halling to see you," he said, crossing the room with a silver salver. "She insisted that I send this up."

With a frown, Clara took the note from the tray and broke the seal. The beautiful Lady Halling was the last person she wished to see; the night she'd met the woman at Vauxhall was fresh in her mind. But Lucien had insisted that the woman was not his mistress, and Clara believed him.

"Very well," she murmured, having read the missive through. "If her need to speak with me is so very urgent, you may send her up. Will you have tea brought in, please, Hayes."

Clara had only a few short moments to regret that her appearance was not in a better state before Lady Halling, clad in a regal walking gown of red and gold, covered by a matching cape that was cuffed in mink and finished with a dark red bonnet fitted with ribbons and cherries, made her entrance into the room. In one hand she carried a large, flat envelope.

"My lady," Clara said, rising, calling upon her years of training to behave as the perfect hostess. "How good of you to visit. I regret that Viscount Callan is from home."

"It is you I came to see," Lady Halling replied. "Thank you for allowing me to make the call. I understand you've not been about Town much since the unfortunate publication."

There was a tightness to the woman's voice that set Clara on edge, and it was far outside of polite manners for the woman to have mentioned the caricature, but she said in a pleasant tone, "Won't you be seated? I've called for tea."

"Thank you." Lady Halling seated herself. "I can't stay

long, but a cup of tea would be welcome. Tell me, how do you find married life?''

Clara took a seat also. ''Quite well, thank you.'' She was relieved when the tea arrived and she had an excuse to keep from looking at her guest, who was gazing at Clara with a direct frankness that could only be described as rude.

Lady Halling accepted her tea and sat back in her chair, still looking at Clara.

''I understand that Lucien has adjusted to it happily,'' she said. ''Marriage, that is. You seem to please him.''

Clara flushed hotly. It was unpardonable for the woman to speak of Lucien by his given name.

''I believe we are content,'' she replied evenly.

''Content,'' Lady Halling repeated. ''Yes, for now, I suppose you are. But will it last? That's the question. Lucien's interest has ever been difficult to hold, has it not? Perhaps you know that even better than me.''

Clara set her teacup down with a telling rattle. ''I believe I know him better than anyone, yes. Tell me, how did you find marriage to your late husband, Baron Halling? I'm sure you must miss him greatly.''

Lady Halling smiled. ''I found marriage to him convenient and exactly to my tastes, and the day he died I deeply mourned the loss of his income and the small measure of protection he provided. But I quickly found compensations. Your husband, in particular, proved to be a helpful and consoling friend.''

Enough was enough. Every bit of polite restraint fled Clara. ''You seem to insinuate a relationship beyond mere acquaintance with my husband, Lady Halling, but I must tell you that he has already assured me that such a relationship does not exist.''

Lady Halling didn't appear surprised at this. ''Certainly he wouldn't admit to it, but what wise husband would? Do you know, I was quite amazed when he told me that he was actually going to wed his little peahen? I can't count the number of times we laughed over that name. It was one of his favorite pastimes, talking of you. I had rather come to the impression that he hated no one else so much, and yet here he is, the contented little man. The ideal husband.''

Heat seeped into Clara's face, and her hands curled into fists. ''You will be good enough to leave. Now.''

''In a moment, my dear,'' Lady Halling said. ''I've come to bring you a little wedding gift. It was remiss of Lucien not to invite me to his wedding, but, then, a man is hardly likely to want his mistress at such an event, is he? But I thought you'd like to have something to always remind you of him when you're locked away at Pearwood and while Lucien's here in London with me. A personal momento,'' she said, picking up the envelope and laying it carefully on a table beside her chair, ''which I'm certain you'll treasure.'' Rising, she smiled down at Clara with a look of clear self-satisfaction. ''I don't believe we'll be meeting again, as Lucien informs me that he's to take you to Pearwood soon and keep you there. But you needn't worry over your dear husband while he's away from you. I shall make certain to take good care of him on your behalf. Good day, my lady.''

Clara sat where she was for a full five minutes after the woman had left, trembling violently, before she slowly began to come to herself. Her breath came in gasps, and she drew each one in through an open mouth that seemed still unable to take in enough air. Another five minutes passed, thoughts whirling, as Clara relived every word and moment of the awful visit.

Her legs were weak and shaking as she stood, but she forced them to take her forward to the table where the envelope lay. It took three tries before her icy, trembling fingers managed to open the thing. Inside was a single piece of paper. She drew it out slowly and stared at what was drawn there. Then, for the first time in her life, Clara discovered that she did indeed possess the ability to faint. The floor and darkness rushed up in a spinning madness that engulfed her entirely.

Both Hayes and Mrs. MacInnes were kneeling over her when Clara groggily came to. Several maids and footmen stood in the background, hovering. She pushed away the sharply scented smelling salts that Mrs. MacInnes was waving under her nose and tried to sit.

"Slowly, my lady," Hayes said, helping her. "I've sent for the doctor."

"We must get you up to bed at once," Mrs. MacInnes stated firmly. "Whatever did that horrible woman do to put you in such a state?"

"I never should have accepted her note," Hayes said. "I deeply apologize, my lady. If I'd but known what manner of female she was, I never should have allowed her into Barrington."

Clara's head was spinning. She set a hand against her forehead and tried to make sense of what had happened.

"You're pale as death." Mrs. MacInnes said worriedly. "We must get you upstairs and to bed. One of the footmen shall carry you."

"No," Clara murmured, blinking, striving to clear her vision. "No, I must—where is the envelope?" She tried to look around, but the movement made her dizzy.

"Envelope?" Hayes asked. "Do you mean this, my lady?"

It had fallen on the ground near her. When Hayes picked it up, Clara took it with an unsteady hand. "Yes. Thank heavens," she said when she realized that she'd somehow managed to shove the drawing back inside before she'd fainted. At least the servants hadn't seen that foul depiction of their master.

"I must write a missive," Clara said. "I must write it at once. Help me to stand."

"But, my lady—" Mrs. MacInnes protested.

"Help me to stand," Clara insisted more firmly. "I'm perfectly fine. I only need to get to the couch." She rested heavily on Hayes's arm as he helped her to sit. "Bring me paper. And pen and ink. I'll write it here."

It was a brief note, direct and to the point. She folded it and gave it to Hayes with the instruction, "Have it delivered at once to Captain Blakesley. Into his hands."

Hayes bowed and left the room, and Clara held out a hand to Mrs. MacInnes. "Will you be so good as to help me upstairs, Mrs. MacInnes? And then I will need you to help me to pack."

"To pack, my lady?" Mrs. MacInnes asked faintly.

"Yes," said Clara. "To pack."

It was only by the merest chance that the Earl of Kerlain saw Viscountess Callan being handed into a carriage by Captain Andrew Blakesley. He'd been on his way to Barrington to make one more attempt at tendering his apologies to Lady Clara, and this time had brought ammunition that he was certain would sway her. Catching sight of her ladyship leaving the house on the arm of Captain Blakesley brought Kerlain to a complete stop. Only briefly did he see her face, white as death beneath the blue bonnet she wore. Blakesley, on the other hand, was flushed. The expression on his face showed clearly that he was enraged. He handed Lady Clara into the carriage and then mounted a horse being held in waiting by one of Viscount Callan's footmen.

Kerlain stood where he was, staring after the coach as it went into motion and slowly rattled down the street with Blakesley riding behind. There was luggage, he thought dimly, stunned. Lady Clara's luggage. And no sign of Callan.

Muttering a curse beneath his breath, he turned on his heel and began striding in the direction of his own lodgings.

It was dark by the time Lucien returned to Barrington. With Jack hard on his heel, he pushed into the house, ignoring the footman.

"Hayes!" he shouted. "Clara!"

"Steady, Lucky," Jack advised. "You don't want to start a panic."

"My lord!" Hayes appeared in the entryway. "You're back. Thank goodness."

"Where's the viscountess?" Lucien demanded.

"Gone, my lord," Hayes answered directly. "She left several hours ago with Captain Blakesley."

"Blakesley?" Lucien's tone was dark.

"Yes, my lord. He was to escort her to St. Genevieve."

"When did she leave?"

"Shortly after tea, my lord. There was a visitor—"

"A woman?" Jack asked.

"Lady Halling, my lord."

"God," Lucien said. "Did Clara see her?"

"Yes, and I fear it was most upsetting. I wish I had not taken Lady Halling's note into her, my lord, for after their meeting was over, I found Lady Clara in the drawing room, fainted upon the floor."

"Fainted? And yet she left here?"

"It was a brief spell. She came to nearly at once, and refused to take to her bed or see the doctor I'd sent for. Mrs. MacInnes and I tried to reason with her, my lord, but she was insistent in the matter of leaving. There is—I believe there is a note for you. In your study."

Lucien said no more, but went directly to his study. He found it there, on his desk, a folded note sitting atop a large envelope, which he recognized at once as the kind that Pamela used to transport her drawings.

My lord, I have gone home to St. Genevieve. The draw-
ing in the envelope will provide ample explanation. I
shall request that my father immediately do whatever is
necessary to obtain for me a divorce, and would appreci-
ate it if you would refrain from contacting either me or
our child in future. I do not wish to see you again.

She hadn't even signed it. Numb with shock, Lucien set
the letter aside and took up the envelope, almost afraid to
see what was within. The drawing of himself, lying naked
in Pamela's bed, made him close his eyes.

"God's mercy," he murmured. "God's mercy. Clara."

He forced himself to look at the drawing more closely. It
was vaguely familiar, although he couldn't recall Pamela
drawing it. She knew how much he hated being made one
of her subjects. It was typical of her serious studies of the
human body, both sensual and elegant. Clara wouldn't begin to understand the sexual undertones of such a work. At
the bottom of the page was Pamela's signature, and beneath
that, the words, *Le Chat.*

So now Clara knew all of it, how *Le Chat* had come to
know about the wager and the odious nickname Lucien had
given her, about the position *Le Chat* had served, at least
before Lucien had married Clara. He had told her that he
had no mistress, and that had been true enough, but she'd
think now that he had lied. She'd think everything he'd ever
told her was a lie.

She was gone. She had left him. Just as he'd always
feared she would. He stood perfectly still for a long, silent
minute, staring blindly at the same room where his father
had learned of his mother's betrayal, and let the fact seep
into him. Clara had left him. But she hadn't betrayed him.
If there was any betrayal, then it was his. All his. He'd
wanted to make her love him, but he'd only driven her
away. Just as his father had driven his mother away. What a

strange and ludicrous thought it was, that he should have
brought about the very thing he'd so dreaded.

"Clara," he murmured. "I'm sorry. I wish I knew how
to let you go, but it's impossible."

"Lucky?"

He turned at the sound of Jack's voice.

"Pamela's maid is here. Sibby. Hayes put her in the
drawing room. She's in something of a state. I think you'd
better come."

"In a moment," Lucien replied.

When Jack had gone, Lucien returned his attention to the
documents in his hands. The note from Clara he folded and
put away in his jacket. The drawing he took and carefully
tore into long strips, then into pieces. A small fire glowed in
the fireplace, and Lucien fed the bits into it one at a time,
followed by the envelope.

"Tomorrow, Pamela," he murmured, "you'll be finished. For once and for all. I swear it by all that I hold
dear."

Chapter Twenty-four

❧

It was full dark by the time the Earl of Kerlain finally tracked his prey to The Joyful Maiden Inn. He'd been riding hard for over three hours in an effort to find Lady Clara. A cold, damp fog had settled on the ground during the last hour, and shortly afterward it had begun to rain. By the time the earl made his way into the inn, soaking wet and chilled to the bone, he was in no mood to be put off by The Joyful Maiden's proprietor.

"But, my lord!" the little man cried, standing in front of the door to the private parlor Kerlain intended to enter. "The lady and gentleman have only now just sat down to their meal. Please, won't you let me send a maid in with a message first? We do so dislike exposing our patrons to such disturbances." His expression filled with added dismay as he made a closer appraisal of Kerlain's wet and muddy attire.

"I assure you that I mean to make no disturbance," Kerlain told him. "Especially if you give me no cause to do so. What Captain Blakesley wishes to do is another matter. Perhaps you'd do better to plead with him. Now get out of my way, if you please."

The man only shrank further against the door. "My lord, I beg of you—"

"Oh, damn it all," Kerlain muttered, reaching past him to pound on the door. "Lady Clara!" he shouted. "It's

Kerlain. I wish to speak with you at once. Blakesley?'' He pounded again. "I'm coming in."

"My lord, please, no violence," pleaded the innkeeper.

The door opened and the small man nearly fell into the room. Captain Blakesley took a fistful of his coat and lifted him upright, setting him securely on his feet while keeping his eyes on Kerlain.

"Kerlain," he said coldly. "For whatever reason you've come, I assure you you're not welcome. Lady Clara wishes nothing to do with you. Be so good as to leave us in peace."

Kerlain, in response, neatly pulled a pistol out of the folds of his wet coat and pointed it at Captain Blakesley's chest.

"Heaven help us," the innkeeper moaned. Behind him, Blakesley froze.

"Your manners, my lord, leave much to be desired."

Kerlain grinned wearily. "I don't care much for manners at the moment. You've led me a merry chase and I'll not go until I've spoken with Lady Clara. Alone."

"And you mean to shoot me if I refuse?" Blakesley asked calmly.

"Oh, yes. I'll shoot you. You'll not be the first Englishman to play target for me. But I don't intend to leave the matter to you. Lady Clara!" he shouted. "Tell your dear friend that you'll speak with me, else he'll soon find a bullet in his gut."

The door opened more widely, and Clara's pale face peeked over Blakesley's shoulder.

"Good heavens! My lord, have you taken leave of your senses?"

"Yes," he replied grimly. "Since the day I landed on England's fair shores, I've been little more than a madman."

"He'll not shoot," Blakesley said. "Go back to your dinner, Clara. I'll take care of this."

"No, please." She touched the captain's arm. "Let me speak with him. I don't wish to importune the other customers with such a vulgar display—"

"God bless you, my lady," the innkeeper murmured.

"—and it's clear that Lord Kerlain has ridden a good distance in this cold and rain simply for this purpose. I would at least allow him an audience." To Kerlain she said, "Please put the gun away, my lord."

He did so with a flourish and a bow. "I'm grateful that you at last allow me a private moment, Lady Clara. I had begun to give up hope that you should ever speak to me again."

"And she'll not do so now," Blakesley told him. "I will not allow it." He set his hand on his sword.

"No, Andrew." Clara stopped him. "I wish to speak with the earl. Please give us a few moments alone."

It took some doing, but at last Blakesley went away on the condition that he would stand outside the door in case Clara needed him, and also that the private interview would last no longer than twenty minutes.

"Kind of him," Kerlain muttered, removing his soggy multicaped greatcoat and tossing it on a nearby chair. He looked at his mud-caked boots with regret. "I apologize for my appearance," he told Clara, who was standing on the other side of the room, regarding him somberly. "I didn't expect the rain."

"You're soaked through," she said. "If you'll sit by the fire, I'll pour you some tea."

"Wine, please. Or ale. Or whatever it is that you were having with your meal. I'm sorry to have disturbed you at such an inopportune moment." He collapsed gratefully into the chair she'd indicated. "However, time is of the essence."

"I'm not going back to London," she said, handing him a glass of wine. "If that was your purpose in coming, then I fear you've gone to a good deal of trouble for no cause. How did you know to find us here?"

Taking the glass from her, he smiled. "I was on my way to Barrington to once more attempt making my apologies and saw you leaving with the captain. It was cruel of you to have kept turning me from your door, my lady. I shouldn't speak of such things, I know, but I'm curious to know why you've forgiven everyone else involved in this awful mess save me. I had thought we were friends."

She moved to stand near the fire. "Were we, my lord? I admit that I once believed that to be so. It seems, however, that you merely wished to keep an eye on the object of your wager. These many months when you've encouraged me in my marriage I thought you so good and kind. Now I know what your true purpose was."

"My purpose," he told her, "was simply to make as much money as I could, in any legal manner that I could. I never meant to hurt Lord Callan and I certainly never meant to hurt you. It seemed a perfect plan at the start. Anyone who took the time to listen carefully when Callan spoke of his fiancée knew that he was in love with you, obsessed almost to the point of madness. I couldn't see the harm of taking advantage of such a sure win."

"Perhaps he was once obsessed," Clara admitted softly, taking a chair opposite him. "But it has gone. As to love, he never has and never will love me. I fear you're going to lose the wager regardless, my lord. You shouldn't have come and tried to convince me to give Lucien another chance. I'll not return to him."

"I've already won the wager. Callan ceded the winning to me over two weeks ago. I was bringing you proof of that today when I saw you leaving." She looked at him with clear suspicion, and Kerlain sighed. "My lady, what on

earth made you take flight? I had thought all was well between you and Callan, despite that grotesque drawing published in *Glad Tidings*. You had seemed to be somewhat
reconciled regarding it.''

Her lips pressed into a thin, tight line before she told him
in a succinct manner about the visit she'd received from
Lady Halling. Kerlain groaned aloud when she came to the
part about the drawing her visitor had left as a ''wedding
gift.''

''And so you see, my lord,'' Clara said, gazing at him
very directly, ''I've discovered what a liar my husband is
and can no longer trust in anything that he either says or
does. He vowed to me that he had no mistress, but he's
clearly had Lady Halling in his keeping since long before
we were wed. If he has lied in the one matter then it's safe
to suppose he's lied in everything. I at least have the satisfaction of knowing that neither of you will win the wager
you made. I'm going home to St. Genevieve and intend to
remain there until my father has procured a divorce for
me.''

''Clara, don't compound the sins that your husband and
I've committed by being a fool.'' Kerlain sat forward, cradling the wineglass in his hands. ''I have no idea what Lord
Callan's past relationship with Lady Halling was, exactly,
although, knowing what he was like before he married you,
I can well imagine. The fact that he spent any measure of
time with that . . . female,'' he said for lack of a more
polite word, ''gives some idea of his state of mind. But I do
know that he's had little or nothing to do with her since his
marriage. As far as I can tell he loathes Lady Halling, and
she obviously feels the same about him, else she'd not have
gone to so much trouble in trying to ruin his marriage. And
as for the wager''—he rose from the chair and went to dig
through the pockets of his discarded coat, at last pulling
from one of them a wrinkled, folded missive—''this is

proof that what I say is true. Your husband ceded the winning to me days before Pamela Halling's poison went spewing forth.'' He dropped the missive into Clara's lap.

She frowned at it. ''How can I be certain you haven't forged this?''

''Clara, Clara,'' he chided, as if she were a naughty child, ''Come now. How can you think such a thing? I admit to being a clever fellow, but forgery is an insult to both my intelligence and yours. Read it and see for yourself if the writing isn't in your husband's own hand.''

With careful fingers she took up the missive, unfolded it, and began to read.

''What does he mean that you gave Lady Halling information that he would be at Vauxhall? He *wanted* to meet with her there?''

''There was another drawing done by *Le Chat,* before the others, which you never saw.'' Briefly, he told her about the original caricature that Lady Halling had planned to publish. ''It was Callan's intention to draw Lady Halling from her lair to a spot where he might be certain of her presence, so that Lord Rexley, with his many talents, could discreetly appropriate the drawing. The part I played was in dropping the information that you and Callan would be at Vauxhall that night, a bait Lady Halling could hardly forbear to take. You'll recall that she brought Blakesley with her that night? That was done by calculation, I assure you. She'd made the fellow's acquaintance with the sole purpose of throwing him in your path, hoping to cause discord between you and Callan.''

''But why?'' Clara asked. ''She couldn't have believed I'd go away with Andrew.''

''Well you have, haven't you?'' He gave her a measured look, watching as her cheeks reddened. ''I believe she harbored some hopes at that point that she and Callan might somehow be reconciled, that Blakesley's presence would inflame the fears and jealousies he's ever felt over you and drive him back to her. Clearly, it had the opposite effect. That missive, as you'll note, is dated on the day following your visit to Vauxhall. Lord Callan evidently made a decision and let Lady Halling know of it. Her failure to regain him as a lover, and the fact that Rexley had stolen her artwork, set her on her chosen course of revenge and the creation of that dreadful caricature. I'm not certain whether she had decided that if she couldn't have Callan, you couldn't have him, either, or whether she simply wished to ruin Callan by taking away the one person he holds most dearly. She must have known that he'd care for nothing else in his life if you were gone from it. Whatever her objective may have been, she did a good job of it. For here you are, fleeing from the man who loves you because of Pamela Halling's poisonous lies."

"It's more than that," she said softly, running one finger lightly over the paper in her lap. "Far more than simply what Lady Halling has done. Perhaps she only made me realize how insurmountable the troubles between Lucien and me are. But I'm glad he conceded the wager to you. It does make things—certain things he said to me—better." Her gaze held fast to the words her husband had written, and she asked, in a wondering tone, "Did he really mean for us to go to Pearwood together, then?"

"Did he not tell you that was his intention?"

"Yes." The word was a faint whisper.

"Clara, I don't know Viscount Callan as well as you do. I don't know what happened between the two of you in the late past or even in the recent past, but I do know that a dark and wretched man married a lovely, gentle lady and began to reach for what he must have always believed to be unattainable. The man you wed is not the same one you're married to. You've changed him so entirely he's not recognizable from what he was many months ago. And that's because of love, my girl. Only because of love. You can sit in your parent's home for the rest of your life and say that your marriage was a disaster because he lied and you're not beautiful, or because he was cruel and unfeeling, but at some point you're going to have to admit the truth. Lucien Bryland loves you, and has made every effort a man can in order to show that love. Perhaps he's made more mistakes along the way than another might have done, but I doubt another man would have tried so hard to make things right. Don't throw away all that you have with him, my dear,'' he said with quiet earnest. "There is nothing so sad in all this world as a true love that's spurned and exiled. I pray you, Clara, don't make the mistakes I have. You'll only live with regrets, and I promise you from my heart that it's a miserable and lonely way to live.''

She was silent for a long moment, gazing at the missive, before saying, "I should like to speak with Andrew. Privately.'' She looked up at him. "Would you be so kind as to call him for me, my lord?''

The house was dark and silent. Jack waited patiently, not mindful of the coldness that increasingly crept in about him as the night grew ever older. He was good at waiting; it was an essential skill in any hunt.

Another hour passed before his quarry made her appearance. The rattle of a key in the front door lock first alerted him to her presence, and then the whisper of her voice.

"Sibby?''

A soft scratching signaled the lighting of a candle or lamp.

"Sibby? Where are you?''

Footsteps moved from room to room, coming ever closer.

"Sibby, you wretched girl,'' she said more angrily. "You'd better be here somewhere.''

She pushed into her working studio, coming to a halt at the sight of the empty room with a shocked gasp.

"Sibby!" she cried aloud.

"I'm afraid she's not here," Jack said calmly. With a deft movement he lit a match and set it to a candle near him. "In fact, she's no longer in London or even Middlesex. I've found new, and much improved, employment for her." He smiled benignly. "You'll never see her again."

Pamela Halling stared at him.

"She wouldn't leave me," she whispered with disbelief. "Sibby's too loyal to do such a thing."

"Loyal, yes, but not to you. Lucien was far kinder to the poor girl, and she felt it her duty to inform him of your plans. It's a pity that she feared you too much to come to him earlier, so that he might have put a stop to your visiting Lady Clara. That," he said, leaning with one elbow on the tall table that stood between them, "was unwise, Pamela. Lucien told me very specifically to show you no mercy, just as you've shown none for any of your victims."

She gazed at the empty room with blank-faced horror. Jack had never seen the woman look so openly vulnerable before.

"My art," she murmured, fear heavy in her tone. "What have you done with it?"

"It's safe enough." He gave a negligent shrug. "I'll have it sent on to you once you're on your way."

Relief didn't soften Pamela Halling. Having been reassured of the safety of her artwork, her expression hardened and sharpened, she turned toward him, honing in on Jack as if she were a clever, hungry beast seeking prey.

"What have you come for, Jack? To threaten me? Murder me? I'm surprised Lucien didn't come himself, but I suppose he's run off after his dear little wife. Will he kill her and Blakesley, do you think? Wouldn't it be marvelous if he did? I should love to see the headlines in the papers.'' She laughed. ''Like father, like son, they'd say.''

Jack had long since learned to listen selectively to whatever Pamela Halling had to say. Her venomous words were her most effective weapon, to upset and unsettle others and throw them off balance. Lucien had always been good at countering such talk; Jack had better things to do with his life.

''I've come to tell you what's to become of you,'' he said simply. ''And to deliver you to your fate, myself.''

Her gaze arrested on him for a brief moment before she laughed again, more loudly this time, with far more amusement. ''Have you, my lord? How very kind. But it's perfectly unnecessary, I assure you. I've already made plans of my own. And there's nothing you can do to stop me.''

''We shall see. By the by, the journey to Staines was exceedingly pleasant, as I'm sure you might imagine. And placing a cat in a cage at the spot we were to meet you was a master stroke, if I may say so. I doubt I could have thought of anything more dramatic, myself.''

She threw a wide smile at him as she began to move about the room, observing, in the dim light, the small clutter that had been left behind.

''I thought Lucien would appreciate it,'' she said, fingering a spot in one wall where nails had been removed and left holes. ''I only wish I might have been there to see the look on your faces. Were you very angry?''

''Extremely. Lucien nearly killed his horse getting back to London. I don't suppose I should tell you this, but he was suspicious of the note you sent from the very beginning. He told me it was improbable that you'd actually be in Staines, but I insisted that we make the effort. My fault, I fear, that Lady Clara had to entertain such a viper in her home.''

She made a *tsk*ing sound. ''Really, Jack. Are we to de-

scend into name-calling?'' Setting her hands behind her
back, she moved toward him slowly. ''There are any number of names I should like to call you, you know. I can't
count the times I've wanted to do a drawing of you for *Glad
Tidings,* but Lucien wouldn't allow it. I rather wish I had
done one, now.'' She drew very near to him, lifting one
hand so that her long, feminine fingers could toy with his
cravat. The scent of her perfume filled his nostrils, repelling
him. Her touch disgusted him. But he remained perfectly
still as she gazed up in a seductive, intimate manner. ''I
know a great many things about you, Lord Rexley. Even the
kind of women you prefer, and the kinds of things you like
to do to them. You've gained quite a reputation among the
brothels of London. I've often wondered what it would be
like with you.''

He began to feel as if he might be sick.

''And I've often wondered,'' he murmured, ''how Lucky
ever stomached bedding you.''

Her eyes widened for the briefest of moments before she
stepped back. The only warning he had of the slap to come
was the flurried movement of her hand. She struck sharply,
her nails leaving streaks of pain across his flesh. But he
continued to stand very still, as if he'd felt nothing.

The corners of her mouth tilted up in a thin smile. ''How
would you enjoy it if all of London knew the truth about
your parentage?'' she asked, sneering. ''That you're not the
Earl of Rexley at all, but Lady Rexley's bastard had off of
the Earl of Manning? Now *that* would give London something interesting to talk about, would it not?''

It took every particle of his will to keep from reacting to
the words. She'd struck true and deep, touching the darkest
fears in his soul. He thought, suddenly, that this was why
he'd always hated her so well—because she'd held the
power to destroy all that he was with her poisonous craft.

''There's no proof to that rumor, most likely because it's

false," he managed calmly. "I doubt anyone would believe it."

"My dear, how naive you are!" she told him, chuckling with amusement. "The masses are only too ready to believe what they're given, especially when it's some nasty piece of business. Perhaps I shall have to prove it to you. One last drawing before I leave for France. I could finish it in an hour and have it to Rosswell long before my boat leaves in the morning. Shall I?" The smile on her face was filled with evil intent.

"Mr. Rosswell and his wife are no longer in London," Jack told her. "They departed only this afternoon for an extended trip to the continent." He was pleased to see her smile die away. Clearly this was news to her. "And *Glad Tidings* is, I fear, no longer in business. However, there was one last issue specially put out just today. I'm surprised you've not yet seen it. It contains a drawing that I'm certain you'll find most interesting." He turned to a chair behind him and took up the copy of the paper he'd earlier put there, then set it on the table beneath the candlelight so that the drawing was clearly illuminated.

Pamela made an inarticulate sound and gaped open-mouthed at the sight before her.

"No!" she cried. "No, it can't—you can't . . ." She lifted the paper with shaking hands. "Cruishank! He must have leapt at the chance to do it. I'll *kill* him!"

"That would add murder to the other charges currently being brought against you. Can you think it quite wise to rack up so many?"

"Charges? What do you mean?"

He smiled lazily. "I think you know, Pamela. Only consider some of the drawings you've done. Many of them could easily be termed treasonous. It's a pity you favored Napoleon so much while he was in power. Apart from that, there are a number of individuals whom you've utterly

ruined with your venom. And now that everyone in England
knows who you are, they'll know who's responsible for
what they've suffered. And they'll know where to find you,
won't they?''

''Yes,'' she whispered, horrified. ''But I'm leaving. I'm
going to France. I'll be safe there.''

''No, my dear, I fear you're not. The captain of the vessel
on which you held your passage has been convinced to
change his mind in the taking of you. He's hated *Le Chat*
devoutly for years, ever since you did that rather nasty caricature about His Majesty's Navy, in which he served during
the war. He said that if he had you as a passenger on his
vessel, you would never find your way to France, having
somehow disappeared quietly in the middle of the English
Channel.''

She closed her eyes and lowered her head.

''I doubt anyone in London will wish to have anything to
do with you, unless it's to make you the center of a hanging
party. Or perhaps they'd rather burn you at the stake. Either
way, the end is the same.'' He let that sink in before saying,
more somberly, ''You have no friends to turn to Pamela.
There's only me who can help you now, so I suggest that
you behave and do as you're told.''

''What do you intend?'' she asked softly, without emotion.

''There's a ship waiting for you at this very moment to
take you to Australia.'' He ignored her gasp of dismay.
''It's far enough away that you'll be perfectly safe. No one
will know you there, and you may begin again. I don't think
I need tell you that you're never to return to England, or to
have any further contact with either Viscount Callan or his
wife. I shall have you watched from time to time to make
certain of your location.'' He pulled the paper free of her
still trembling fingers and laid it carefully on the table. ''I
would advise you not to be so foolish as to cause any trou-

ble in the future, Pamela. Whatever I may appear to be to you, I promise that I'd have no difficulty in putting an end to your existence if you ever seek to gain revenge. To be quite blunt, I'm utterly sick of you and your damned games, and I don't have the patience to put up with anything more. I heartily recommend that you don't try me.''

Chapter Twenty-five

The innkeeper of The Joyful Maiden and his wife had never seen such a night. Despite the ordinary appearance of the young lady occupying their best bedchamber abovestairs, she certainly had more than her fair share of handsome young men determined to dance attendance upon her. The one who'd just arrived was the most insistent of all, standing in the inn's entryway, dripping from the rain. The innkeeper, having been roused from his bed by the commotion the man made, had taken one look at that dark, angry face and realized this was trouble. The fellow looked like the very devil. Now he was demanding to be taken to Viscountess Callan.

"My lord, it's well past midnight," said the innkeeper, striving to quieten this unexpected, and clearly irate, guest, "and everyone in their beds. Can it not wait until morn? Come, you're wet and obviously weary from your journey. I've another room available, and should be pleased to see you to it. I'll have the maid bring up hot water, and a tray of bread and cheese, if you like."

The handsome gentleman tapped his riding whip impatiently against his thigh. "What room is she in?"

"Sir, I fear I cannot allow you to go up. Only think of the lady's reputation, I pray. The viscountess is—"

"My wife," the gentleman told him. "She is my wife.

I," he said bitingly, "am Viscount Callan. Now, what room is she in?"

He told him. What other choice did he have? It was either that or have the man knocking on every door at the inn. The viscount had only left the room before one of the lady's other gentlemen, the one who'd arrived second, entered from the taproom where he'd been sleeping, clearly having been awakened by the commotion. His hair was unkempt, his coat was over one arm, his vest was yet unbuttoned, and he was rapidly tying his cravat.

"I believe I shall take my leave," he said, smiling at the innkeeper's bed-capped wife. "Ma'am," he said, making a slight bow. She responded to this with a sound of clear disapproval and turned back into the bedchamber out of which she'd been peering, shutting the door behind her.

"Sir," said the innkeeper, staring at him. "You mean to leave us *now*? It's the dead of night, my lord, and you've only just got dry."

"True," said his lordship, "and I am loath to leave your fine establishment, but as the viscountess's husband has arrived, I believe I'd best leave while I'm still able. Better part of valor, and all that. And you wouldn't want any bloodshed on your clean floors. Not that I believe Callan would actually try to kill me, of course, especially when he has no reason to do anything but thank me, but it's never wise to take chances with a man in love." He began to shrug into his coat. "They're far and away the most temperamental of all God's creatures."

"I've not yet prepared your bill, my lord" the innkeeper told him. "If you'll give me but a moment—"

The gentleman smiled again, most charmingly, and set his hat upon his head. "Don't bother yourself, my friend," he said. "Simply add it to Lord Callan's bill. He'll be more than glad to pay it."

* * *

Clara wasn't asleep when the knock fell on her door. She'd dozed on and off since saying good night to Lord Kerlain, but actual sleep had evaded her. She wondered if Lucien was going to come after her, as Kerlain predicted. It seemed impossible that he would; he'd always striven to be unlike his father. She thought of the caricature Kerlain had told her about, the one she'd not seen, and ached to think of how greatly it must have wounded Lucien.

He'd told her that he would never let her go. The prospect had warmed her at the time. Now, hearing that stark, firm knock on the door, she felt a certain sense of apprehension.

"Clara?" Lucien said, not bothering to be quiet. "Open the door." More knocking. "Clara?"

He'd wake the entire inn, she thought with aggravation as she threw the covers aside and went to unlock the door.

"Hush, Lucien," she whispered as she opened it, peering around to see him standing in the hallway. The sight of him surprised her. He was dripping wet, his face white and set. Seeing her, he appeared to relax, and something of despair entered the look on his face. He looked so suddenly weary that she almost thought he might drop where he was.

"Clara," he began, but she reached out a hand and took hold of his sleeve, pulling him in.

"Lucien, good heavens! You're soaking wet." She took his hat and riding whip and tossed them to the floor. "I'm beginning to think men don't have the sense God gave animals, so many of you seem to want to catch a chill by going out in such horrid weather. Get out of that coat." Moving behind him, she tugged until the garment slid from his muscular shoulders.

"Where's Blakesley?" he asked, his weariness heavy even in his voice.

"Gone," she told him. "Now come and sit down and I'll

help with your boots. I'm sorry I haven't a maid here to take care of your things. I didn't bring anyone with me."

"Blakesley's gone?" he repeated, thumping down in the chair when she pushed him. "He left you here *alone*? Without any protection?"

"Yes, he went on alone to St. Genevieve," she replied, getting down on her knees to tug at one of his wet boots. "But it was perfectly all right because Lord Kerlain is here. There, that's one. Heavens, your feet are as cold as ice." She set the boot by the fire and turned back to Lucien, finding him staring at her.

"Kerlain's here?"

"Sleeping in the taproom." She tackled his other boot, pulling it off with a little more difficulty. "Although I imagine you woke him with your shouts. Along with everyone else within a mile of hearing." The boot joined its twin, and Clara began to rise. Lucien leaned forward suddenly and set his arms about her waist, pulling her near, holding her tightly, pressing his face against her waist.

"You're undressing me," he said, "and lecturing me. It must be a good sign."

Clara didn't resist the embrace. There was a desperation to it, and to Lucien, that touched her deeply. Hurt and angry as she was, the love she'd always felt for him held fast to the place where it had become anchored to her heart.

"I didn't lie to you," he went on, the words muffled against the cotton of her nightdress. "I have no mistress, and have known no other woman save you since our marriage. I swear before God that's the truth. Pamela drew that picture before you and I were wed."

"She was your mistress," Clara stated softly, and felt his arms tighten about her, as if he feared she'd push away.

"Yes." The word was taut, unhappy. "She was my mistress for a number of years. I hadn't planned on giving her up, even after I married you. You might as well know the truth of that. I can't think you'll be surprised, knowing how I was then.''

Yes, she remembered very well how he'd been. Distrusting, jealous, suspicious of everything she said or did. Had he ever been that way with Lady Halling? she wondered.

''She's very beautiful,'' Clara murmured, gazing down at his dark head.

He made a sound somewhere between a groan and a laugh.

''Oh, my love,'' he said. ''My love, if you only knew— she's not beautiful at all.''

The words confused Clara; she found them almost impossible to believe. ''But then why did you have her for your mistress?''

''She made my own ugliness bearable. And less lonely.'' Slowly, he tilted his face upward, rubbing against her body, until their eyes met. ''Clara, if you leave me, it's all that will be left of my life. That ugliness. I know that I should pay for my crimes by the loss of you, but I can't let you go. I can't bear to live in such darkness again.''

''Lucien,'' she murmured, framing his beloved face with both hands. ''Don't.''

''I love you,'' he said with aching despair. ''Don't leave me. I'll find a way to make everything right, to make up for the pain I've given you. I swear it. Only don't leave me, Clara.''

She lightly touched the still-damp curls of his black hair, and said, somberly, ''I sent Andrew away and asked Lord Kerlain to escort me back to London on the morrow.'' He was very still, gazing at her intently. ''I don't know if I was planning on returning to Barrington or perhaps going to Aunt Anna at my father's town house.''

''You were coming back?'' he whispered. ''Were you, Clara?''

She tried to make some semblance of order of his hair, frowning slightly at her efforts.

"Lord Kerlain showed me the note you sent him, conceding the wager. I suppose I thought that if you had been honest in that, then perhaps you had been honest about not having a mistress, and it seemed wrong to leave without at least giving you a chance to explain, despite the dreadful things that woman said. And so I was coming back, but, my lord"—she set a finger against his lips to quiet him when he would have spoken—"I do not know what will become of us. So much has happened . . ."

"I know," he said, pressing his lips softly against the finger in a gentle kiss. "The suffering for my sins has fallen upon you, who is innocent of any and all of my wrongdoings. If you will but give me the chance, Clara, I vow to spend the remainder of my days making reparation. I love you. Do you believe me?"

"Yes," she murmured, "but it's difficult. I'm not beautiful, Lucien."

"Oh, yes," he said reverently, lifting a hand to cup her cheek. "You are, Clara. The most beautiful woman I've ever known. Far too lovely for a man such as I am, but I can't let you go. No other man will love you as I do, or know and cherish you as I do. I love you with a love that was born the day I first set sight upon you, and perhaps even longer than that. I used to fight against it, and resented such an unbreakable chain, but I've come to realize that what I feel for you is the only thing that drew me onward, away from complete despair during all of the years when I believed you'd betrayed me."

"You've changed so much since then," she murmured.

"You changed me. You saved me from the darkness, Clara. Do you know that I hardly thought of my parents at all as I came after you tonight?"

"Lucien," she said wonderingly.

"I've long since stopped comparing you to my mother, or myself to my father. It's because you've freed me of that, and their shadow is no longer hovering about us. The ghosts have been banished, Clara. I offer you my whole heart now, as I offered it once before, so many years ago when we were but children. If you wish to have it, that is."

"If I wish to have it?" she whispered, smiling despite the tears that misted her gaze. She had found him at last in the dark, needy man who held her as if she were his very life. She had found the Lucien she'd fallen in love with so many years ago. "Oh, yes. I do wish it, very much. I love you, Lucien, and have always loved you."

He pulled her onto his lap and kissed her; she tasted an ardent relief and thankfulness on his lips.

"Clara." He buried his face against her neck. "My own sweet, lovely Clara. Thank God. I don't deserve you, but thank God you're mine. I've been such a damned fool, wasted so much time, but I'll take nothing for granted now. Every day I have with you, I shall cherish."

Much later they lay naked and warm beneath the bedcovers, talking slowly, sleepily.

"Aunt Anna's to marry Robby?" Clara asked with surprise. "I can hardly believe it, although it's wonderful, of course. She's been in love with him all these years."

"He never stopped loving her, either," Lucien said with a yawn. "He told me she has to marry him so that he can have Sarah for his daughter. He's looking forward to all the suitors he'll get to interview when she comes of marrying age. Somehow I can almost feel sorry for the poor fellows."

"Robby's a dear," Clara said.

"Robby's a terror, especially when he's got a proper victim to lecture and scare half to death with all his propriety and soft manners. Being eaten alive by a bear would probably be less painful.''

She smiled. ''Sarah adores him. He'll make a wonderful father. I'm so glad they're to wed. Perhaps it will inspire Wulf to at last set a date to marry Bella.''

Lucien uttered a sleepy chuckle. ''We'll both probably be old and gray before that day comes. Poor Bella.'' He stroked one hand gently over her flat belly. ''We'll have a child next spring,'' he murmured. ''Does the idea please you, Clara?''

They hadn't spoken of the child much in the past two weeks. Too many other matters had occupied both their minds.

''Yes,'' she said. ''I've always wanted a large family, with lots of children running about.''

His eyes were closed, but he smiled. ''We'll try to outdo your parents at St. Genevieve, shall we?''

She laughed. ''Perhaps not that many children. Lucien?''

''Hmmm?''

''How did you know I was with child on that day when you told Andrew? You seemed very certain, but I didn't know yet myself whether it was so.''

He turned on his side toward her, sliding an arm beneath her shoulders and drawing her near.

''I don't know. But I felt it with complete surety. Perhaps it's because you're the only woman I could ever love, that I ever have loved. It's frightening, in a way. You wield so much power over me, Clara.''

She traced the line of his jaw with a fingertip. ''Just as you do over me. We shall have to learn to trust each other completely.''

He kissed her softly. ''In time, we will. For now, I'm content with your love and your presence.''

''To think,'' she murmured, resting her head against his

shoulder, "everything nearly came to ruin through a foolish wager. I'm so glad you lost it."

"Oh, no, my love. I came away the winner of that dark wager." She felt him smiling against the top of her head. "Far and away," he said, "the winner."

Turn the page to preview
Mary Spencer's romantic sequel to
Dark Wager,
Jack Sommerton, the Earl of Rexley's, story,
coming in November 1998 from Dell.

Chapter Two

"You seemed to like that quite well, my lord." The young woman giggled and pressed a little closer. "Didn't you, now?"

With a sigh of great contentment, Jack curled an arm about the girl's ample waist and then closed his eyes.

"Wonderful, Georgie. As always." He yawned, feeling blissfully relaxed and comfortable. "Absolutely wonderful."

"I know what you'll like now," she whispered near his ear, and Jack smiled.

"You're going to kill me, sweetheart. I've got to rest a bit."

"Oh, not for what I've got in mind." Her lips and tongue tickled the skin beneath his ear, while one of her clever hands sneaked beneath the blankets, stroking his thigh. "You just lie there and let Georgie take good care of you."

Jack willingly let her have her way, feeling his exhausted body miraculously coming back to life. Georgie was a delightful girl. One of his favorites, although he had many. He couldn't imagine anything more pleasant than lying in her comfortable bed and letting her take advantage of him.

A loud knock suddenly fell on the door, and Georgie abruptly sat up. The blankets slid down to the foot of the bed.

"What's that?" she asked in a frightened tone, staring at the door as if she expected a constable to come barging in.

Another loud knock.

"Go away," Jack shouted. "I've paid for her for the rest of the afternoon."

A matronly voice answered from the other side of the door. "I'm sorry, m'lord," said Mrs. May, the madam of the house, "but there's a gentleman here asking for you. He's quite insistent."

"Damnation," Jack muttered under his breath. He stretched out a hand and patted Georgie's bare knee reassuringly. To Mrs. May he said, "Whoever he is, send him off. I don't wish to be disturbed by anyone. Is that quite clear?" He couldn't imagine any of his particular acquaintances tracking him down here, despite the fact that they knew he frequented the place. Wulf and Lucky certainly wouldn't do so, and Kerlain, to his knowledge, had never been known to frequent *any* such den of iniquity unless there was some form of gambling to be had.

"He claims to be Viscount Severn, m'lord," said Mrs. May, beginning to sound rather desperate. "And truth to tell, I'm afraid he may tear my house apart. My other girls are becoming quite nervous. He's a big brute, m'lord, and very insistent to see you. Please come and calm him, sir. I beg you."

"Gad." Jack sat up and began looking for his clothes. He'd kill Wulf for interrupting him. The lackwit. If he'd frightened a woman as formidable as Mrs. May, the idiot must have worked himself into one of his vaporish states.

Ten minutes later he opened the door to Mrs. May's private parlor and found his friend nervously pacing in a circle before the fire, nibbling on the nails of one hand. Jack could certainly understand why Mrs. May had been concerned for the safety of her home. Wulffrith Lane, Viscount Severn, was more like a massive mountain that had sprouted arms and legs than an ordinary man. Worse, he was composed mostly of solid muscle. If the fellow hadn't been possessed of an equally impressive brain, which nonetheless seemed incapable of thinking logically unless it was involved in the calculation of numbers or chemicals, he might have been England's most notorious fighter. But fighting was one of Wulf's weakest points. Not that he couldn't wreak havoc when he was in a rage, but he was always terribly messy about it. It was rarely necessary for him to put himself to such trouble, however. One look at Wulf was generally enough to frighten off the most trouble-some pests.

"What the devil's the matter with you?" Jack demanded sharply. "Don't you realize I was occupied?"

Wulf started at the sound of his voice, and his face filled with relief.

"Jack, thank God." He wrapped his meaty hands to-gether as if he'd start pleading. "Thank God. I've been looking for you everywhere. I don't know what I would have done if I hadn't found you."

"What trouble are you in now?" Jack asked, well used to clearing up the difficulties Wulf got himself into. Those who were exceedingly brilliant, he'd discovered, were often as helpless as babes when it came to living among more normal persons.

"None, I swear it!" Wulf said earnestly, wringing his hands. "But you've got to help me, Jack. Kerlain's taken ill. He's . . . he's *bedridden.*"

Jack stared at him. "You came to Mrs. May's house and interrupted my afternoon to tell me that Kerlain is *ill*? Wulf," he sighed, and rubbed at an ache that was develop-ing between his eyes. "Kerlain had better be on his death-bed, or I vow I'll have you committed to an asylum."

"But you don't understand," Wulf said miserably. "I would have gone to Lucky if he'd been in Town, but he ain't, and you're the only one who can help. It's Professor Wells. *Professor Wells,* Jack. His ship is arriving today.

This very afternoon. And Kerlain ain't going to be able to meet him.''

"Ah, Professor Wells," Jack said with understanding. Wulf had talked of little else for the past four months, ever since Kerlain had announced that he'd arranged for the famous chemist to travel to London for a visit with the Royal Society. Wulf worshipped Professor Wells almost as much as he did his mentor, Viscount Hemstead. "I see. But what does that have to do with me?"

"Well, I . . . Jack, I need you to meet him with me, and help to get him and his daughter settled over at Pulteney's Hotel, since Kerlain can't do it. There ain't anyone else. Lucky's out at Pearwood, I told you."

Jack knew it wouldn't do any good to suggest that Wulf might attempt to meet Wells and his daughter by himself. With Wulf's typical bumbling, they'd never make it out of the docks. Not that Jack particularly cared. Wells and his daughter were Americans, a breed Jack thoroughly despised. He would have preferred it altogether if they'd never made the journey to England in the first place.

"What about Hemstead?" he suggested. "Surely he'd be the better choice."

Misery creased Wulf's craggy face. His shaggy black hair waved back and forth as he shook his head. "He's right in the middle of a hydrogen experiment. I begged him to come, but he couldn't leave off at just this moment. You know how important sequence and timing are in chemistry."

Jack didn't know, and didn't particularly care. He sighed again. Loudly.

"What about Robby, then? Surely he'd do it. Only think what an impression it would make on Professor Wells and his chit to have the Earl of Manning welcome them to England's fair shores."

Wulf groaned. "He and Lady Manning are out at

Pearwood with Lucky, seeing the new baby. Won't be home for another week."

"By gad, that's right," Jack muttered, surprised that he hadn't remembered. He usually kept good track of the Earl of Manning's whereabouts, and had done so for years— since he was ten—when rumors had caused him to look more closely at his father's dear friend. What he had seen had caused him to keep looking, and to begin his search for the truth.

"Then I suppose it must be me," Jack said, resigned to his fate.

"Thank you," Wulf said with open relief. "Thank you, Jack. You're the best friend a man could ever have."

"Yes," said Jack dryly. "I only hope you remember that next time I require a favor of you. And Kerlain had best be truly ill. If this is one of his games—"

"It's not," Wulf vowed earnestly. "I promise, he's sick as can be. Saw him with my own eyes. Never saw a fellow so poorly before, and it ain't even from drink."

"Kerlain has gulled you before, my friend," Jack told him, casting a longing glance toward the ceiling, above which Georgie waited for his return. "Come along, then. I'd best get you out of here before either your fiancée or your mistress discovers that you were in Mrs. May's house in the middle of the day. Bella would have your head and Yvette would make you a bullock. I don't suppose you thought to bring your carriage? No? Then we'll have to return to Kendrington to fetch mine."

The *Fair Weather* docked in London on the very day it was supposed to, which, given the storm it had weathered mid-Atlantic, was nothing short of miraculous.

"I hope Lad hasn't been waiting long," Gwendolyn remarked as she tied her bonnet more securely beneath her chin. "Although it appears to be a pleasant day, at least. I had rather expected rain, from what we've heard of London.''

''I only hope the boy is here,'' Professor Wells said from where he was carefully tucking away the notes he'd been making on his latest study. ''I shouldn't like to have to traverse London's unfamiliar streets without aid.''

''Never fear, Papa. Your sense of direction may be dismal, but I'll not let any harm come to you. Do you think this outfit suitable? I shouldn't like Lad to be embarrassed if the fashions in the States differ too greatly from those in England.''

''My dear,'' said her father, glancing at her, ''it won't matter in the least. You'll drive every man who sees you straight to insanity regardless, and that is what Lad will find disconcerting. It's been six years or longer since the boy last saw you. I doubt he'll be prepared for the change.''

''Papa, how you exaggerate,'' Gwendolyn told him, suppressing a sigh. He made her sound like Helen of Troy, or, worse, Medusa. She knew very well that her looks were pleasing, but she was far from being a femme fatale. Her mirror showed that very plainly. Reddish-gold hair, blue eyes, and a face that seemed perfectly ordinary. If men found something in all that to make themselves behave as fools, there was little she could do to stop them.

''I only wish I were,'' said the professor. ''Are you ready, dear? The other passengers are already disembarking.''

''In a moment,'' Gwendolyn said. ''I've only this last trunk to finish packing. You go ahead and find Lad, Papa. I'll join you shortly.''

''Very well.'' He picked up the bag that contained his precious notes. ''I'll send one of the men down to collect the trunk. Don't keep us waiting, Gwennie.''

She applied herself dutifully to her task the moment her father left the cabin, stopping only once or twice to make certain she hadn't forgotten anything and, more important, that her father hadn't left behind any of his scribblings. Nothing could prove more upsetting to any scientist, Gwendolyn knew, than losing such seemingly insignificant scraps.

She had just finished going through the drawers of the small desk her father had used during their journey when a brief knock fell on the door.

"Come in," she called out, and Mr. Hanbury's handsome, rugged face appeared around the door.

"Miss Wells, I hope I haven't intruded?"

"No, of course not," she assured him cheerfully, bending to look under the desk. "My trunk is ready now. I'm terribly sorry for the delay. It's one of my greatest failings, I fear. Being late."

"I can't imagine you have any faults at all, Miss Wells," he said, and she thought he sounded rather odd, as if he were sickening.

"Then your imagination has failed you, kind sir," she said. "Papa says I'll drive him to an early grave and then be late attending the funeral." She laughed, finally straightening. "Which is probably true enough, given that I . . ." The words died away as she caught sight of his expression. It was one with which she was quite familiar, and she gave a silent inward groan. "Mr. Hanbury," she began, but he was already moving toward her.

"Miss Wells, please let me speak," he said in an earnest tone that made her heart sink. She wished, fully, that she hadn't sent Papa away. "I've tried to stop the feelings that have been growing for you in my heart . . ."

Oh, dear, she thought. It was worse than she'd imagined. She already felt like laughing.

". . . but it's impossible. I realize I'm merely a first mate on the ship, and that you could have any man you wished for, but if there's any chance at all that you might consider my suit, I should be the happiest man on God's earth.''

She had to bite the inside of her lip harshly before she could speak in an even tone.

''Mr. Hanbury, you're very kind,'' she said as gently as she could, ''and you've been so good to both my father and me during the voyage, but I'm afraid that I can't—''

''Oh, I realize that!'' he said, moving so quickly that she couldn't avoid him before he took hold of her hands. ''I know the difficulties there would be in a match for us. Your father for one, and the difference in our social standings for another. But where there is love, nothing is impossible.'' He kissed her hands fervently.

''Mr. Hanbury! Please don't!''

Her attempts to free herself only succeeded in inflaming him further. The next thing Gwendolyn knew, she was wrapped tightly in the man's arms.

''I love you!'' he declared hotly, crushing the breath out of her. ''If you but say the word, I'll battle any foe to keep you!''

''Mr. Hanbury, the only word I wish to say is no! Please release me at once!''

He didn't seem to hear her.

''No man could ever love you as dearly as I do, Miss Wells,'' he vowed. ''I shall cherish you forever, and even longer.''

''If you don't kill me with mindless drivel first,'' she managed to say as she gasped for air. ''Mr. Hanbury, I beg you. Let me go!''

He appeared disinclined to do so, and began to drop heavy passionate kisses upon the top of her head, sickening her even further. Gwendolyn remained calm, however. She'd been in such unfortunate situations before, and knew of any number of effective methods to handle them. She had just made a small, tight fist and pulled her arm back in order to put one of them to use when she heard someone speak in a distinct, clipped British accent.

"I beg your pardon."

Mr. Hanbury froze and began to turn his head, and the next moment was physically lifted off the floor. Relieved, Gwendolyn stepped back. She briefly saw a tall, muscular, fair-haired gentleman standing behind Mr. Hanbury, gripping him by the shirt and hefting him up as if he were nothing but a child.

"I believe the lady has made herself perfectly clear," the gentleman continued, ignoring Mr. Hanbury's inarticulate struggles. "She wishes to be left alone. You will be so good as to do so."

"This is a . . . private matter!" Mr. Hanbury choked out, swinging an arm in a useless attempt to strike his captor. "Put me down!"

"It's not very pleasant when you're the one held hostage, is it?" the other man said, and lightly tossed Mr. Hanbury across the room, where he landed against a wall. "I would attempt to explain this matter to you more fully, sir, save that I'm loath to waste my time on an ignorant and savage cretin. Leave now, before I lose my temper."

Something in the man's tone must have convinced Mr. Hanbury to obey him, for the first mate promptly stood, dusted himself off, made a swift bow to Gwendolyn, and left.

The blond gentleman waited until the door had closed before turning to face her. He was beautiful, perhaps the most beautiful man Gwendolyn had ever seen. If an artist were ever able to do justice to the archangel Gabriel, this is what the portrait would look like. His hair was so fair it seemed white, a color against which his blue eyes stood out starkly. His face was aristocratic, finely boned, and yet thoroughly, undeniably masculine. His clothing, cut of the most elegant cloth and in the latest stare of fashion, covered a physique that was not only muscular and fit but also perfectly proportioned. He stared down at Gwendolyn from his superior height with a look of disdain, almost as if he were thoroughly displeased by the mere sight of her.

Perhaps it was because she wasn't used to being frowned at by men, or perhaps it was the memory of what had just passed with Mr. Hanbury, but for some odd reason Gwendolyn met that cold, disapproving gaze head-on and began to laugh. She couldn't stop. And the more she laughed, the funnier everything seemed. She doubled over, laughing as if she'd never cease, and at last sat down on the edge of her bed, chortling so hard that it made her stomach ache.

"Oh!" she said at last, giggling, wiping at tears that rolled down her cheeks. "Oh, forgive me. I'm s-sorry." She grinned up at him and found that he was still frowning, more fiercely than ever.

"D-did you hear him?" she asked, chuckling. "The th-things he said!" Another gale of laughter swept over her.

"I'm glad you found it so amusing," the gentleman said dryly.

"I'll b-battle any f-foe to k-keep you!" she managed to get out, laughing all the harder. "I'll cherish you forever, and even—*even l-longer*! Oh!" She fell back on the bed, rolling with mirth. "Oh, my sides hurt!"

The handsome gentleman stood silently, gazing down at Gwendolyn until she at last began to calm. She grinned at him like a drunken idiot.

"Don't you think it the least bit funny?" she asked.

No, Jack thought. He didn't find it amusing. Or her, for that matter. There wasn't anything even remotely humorous about the situation. In fact, quite the opposite. He was not only unamused, he was utterly terrified.

She was the most beautiful woman he'd ever seen. If he'd attempted to conjure up such a female in his dreams, that fictional female still would have fallen short of the reality of this one. She lay before him, her bonnet come loose and her red-blond hair partly fallen out of its arrangement. Her dress was caught beneath her, pulling the fabric tight against her shapely figure, and she was gazing up at him with a smiling mouth that looked exceedingly kissable and sparkling blue eyes that looked fully inviting. It was almost more than any reasonable man could be expected to take. He wanted nothing more than to tear his clothing off and join her on the bed.

Jack had never been enslaved by a woman. He'd had dalliances with the improper sort. And the other sort—the marriageable kind—had attempted for years to capture his heart, or at the very least his attention, and had always failed. Even the most beautiful and charming among them had done little more than garner his mild appreciation. But this woman—she frightened him to his very core. He had a fleeting notion that if she ever laughed at any love words he spoke to her as she was laughing at the fool who'd been here earlier, he'd want to throw himself in the Thames and never surface.

She sat up at last, still grinning like a silly child, and began to straighten her hair and bonnet.

"Dear me, I am sorry," she apologized once more. "How very foolish. But it was amusing." Her smile widened, and Jack felt his heart pound painfully in his chest. "Still, it was unkind to make fun of Mr. Hanbury. He appeared to be in earnest, and I shouldn't wish to hurt his feelings, despite the unpleasantness of his declarations. Thank you for rescuing me," she said, standing and taking a moment to smooth down her skirts before extending one gloved hand. "I'm Gwendolyn Wells."

Jack stared at her hand for a moment before accepting it in his own. She was dainty and feminine, even in the tiny bones of her fingers. He wanted to turn about and flee.

"I'm Rexley," he said, and watched her eyes widen with recognition.

"Rexley?" she repeated, and pulled her hand away. "The Earl of Rexley?"

"Yes." He felt distinctly uneasy. Kerlain must have written of him to his relatives in America, and he could only just imagine what had been said. He and Kerlain were friends, but a wariness yet existed between them. Kerlain disliked the English almost as much as Jack disliked Americans. "I'm sorry to inform you that the Earl of Kerlain has taken ill. I've come in his place to welcome you to England."

Concern filled her lovely features, and Jack felt an unwelcome urge to take hold of her hand again.

"Lad is ill? Is it serious?"

"Not at all. A mild complaint, merely. He'll most likely be well before a week is out. I should be honored to escort you and Professor Wells to your hotel in Kerlain's stead and see that you're settled."

"How very kind," she said with open gratitude, and Jack's heart began to ache again. She was a dangerous woman, this one. He would avoid her like the plague the moment he got her into Pulteney's. "My father went out ahead of me . . ."

"Viscount Severn and I met him earlier. I left them on the dock and came in search of you. We had waited a quarter of an hour and became concerned."

"Was it that long? I do apologize. Of course I'm so glad that you came to look, else I might never have realized. But I'm sure I would have eventually. Realized, I mean."

"Realized?" he asked, bewildered.

"Yes" was all she said. The smile she gave him made his toes curl in his boots.

God almighty, he thought. A dangerous woman in every way. He had a strong urge to cross himself.

"It's such a relief to finally meet you," she said more softly. "After all this time. It seems as if it's been forever. I was beginning to think our paths would never cross."

"Pardon me?" What on earth was the woman talking about? For how long had Kerlain been writing to her about him? He'd only known the fellow for two years.

She sighed lightly. "Shouldn't we be going?"

He made arrangements for her trunk to be carried down to his waiting carriage and escorted Miss Wells to the dock, where her father and Wulf were deeply involved in a discussion of physics. Wulf, when introduced to Miss Wells, didn't appear to be at all affected by the woman's uncommon beauty. But Jack wasn't overly surprised. Wulf wasn't like other men when it came to women. He was deeply in love with his fiancée, Bella, and, except for his mistress, didn't have the least interest in other females. Expressing his delight at the acquaintance, Wulf took Miss Wells's dainty hand in his enormous one and vigorously shook until Jack told him to stop. The next moment he and Professor Wells went back to their discussion.

Jack reluctantly turned his attention to Miss Wells. "You must be weary from your long journey. We shall have you safely at your hotel as soon as possible." With a signal, his footman opened the carriage door, and Jack offered Miss Wells his hand to assist her in climbing in.

Gwendolyn smiled at him and said, "Thank you, my lord. Would you allow me a private word with my father first, please? There's something important I must tell him."

Lord Rexley's hand dropped and he nodded. "If you can take his attention away from science."

She was glad that he understood just how difficult a task that was. His own experiences with Lord Severn had probably taught him well.

She touched her father's sleeve and leaned closer to him.

"Papa," she whispered. "I promised you'd be the first to know. Him."

Even science couldn't hold him in the face of such a pronouncement. Professor Wells straightened and stared at his daughter.

"Him?"

"Yes." She nodded. "Him."

He looked past Lord Severn, who was blissfully still talking about physics, to where the Earl of Rexley was overseeing the loading of Gwendolyn's trunk. "*Him*?" he asked incredulously.

"Yes," Gwendolyn said again, following her father's gaze. "Him."

"But, my dear, you've only just met him. You've only just set foot in England. The man's done nothing but scowl at you."

"Nonetheless," she said. "Him."

Professor Wells knew better than to debate the issue with his daughter when her eyes held that particular gleam. She had clearly set her heart upon the Earl of Rexley, and if he was the man she wanted, she would certainly have him.

"Very well," he said. "If you're quite certain."

"I'm certain," she said, gazing at the man in question as if he were the most magnificent creature on earth. "Quite, quite certain."

"But what if he doesn't want you, my dear?"

Her smile grew feline. "I shall make him."

"Gwennie," he said in a warning tone, "I don't want you doing anything untoward."

She looked at him with surprise. "Me, Papa? How could you think it?"

"Easily."

"I'll behave myself," she promised. "You'll have nothing to worry about. My lord?" she addressed Lord Rexley, who turned and frowned at her. "We're ready now." Holding out her hand, she let him help her into the carriage.